TIME BOMBER

Robert P. Wack

Boissevain Books
New York, New York
www.boissevainbooks.com

Copyright © 2014 by Robert P. Wack.

All rights reserved. No part of this book may be reproduced in any form or by any electronic or mechanical means, including the use of information storage and retrieval systems, without permission in writing from the publisher.

Boissevain Books LLC
New York, NY 10011
www.boissevainbooks.com

ISBN: 0984523286
ISBN 13: 9780984523283

An earlier version of this work was published by Robert P. Wack in 2012 under the title *In Apple Blossom Time*, Copyright © 2012 by Robert P. Wack.

This is a work of fiction based on the life and writings of Dr. Willem Jacob van Stockum. Words and sentiments expressed by Dr. van Stockum and other historical figures in the work are based on the author's interpretation of historical documents but unless otherwise indicated are not the express sentiments or words of such figures. The names of other real life characters have been changed.

Printed in the United States of America

Acknowledgements

I am deeply indebted to the many people who helped me tell Willem van Stockum's story, with my own embellishments. First, thanks to John Tepper Marlin, Willem's nephew, who encouraged me at every step of the way and opened up the family files to allow me a deeply personal look at the life of the mathematician turned bomber pilot.

Thanks to Anne Turkos, University Archivist at the University of Maryland for helping me track down Willem's records of his time at College Park. Likewise to Erica Mosner of the Shelby White and Leon Levy Archives Center at the Institute for Advanced Studies at Princeton University. The staff at the Library of Congress were also very helpful locating Willem's letters in the Oswald Veblen file there.

Finally, heartfelt gratitude to my draft readers, who prodded me to keep polishing and improving. All the credit is theirs, the blame only mine: Michael Roberts, John Wack, Edward Wack, Karen Kohn, Dean Minnich, and Lisa Wack.

Preface

Although Time Bomber is a work of fiction, its central character, Willem Jacob van Stockum, is very much a real person. Dr. van Stockum was born on November 20th, 1910, in the village of Hattem, Holland. He trained as a mathematician and conducted post-doctoral research at the Institute of Advanced Studies at Princeton University, where he worked with Dr. Oswald Veblen and in the company of Einstein, von Neumann, and Bohr. He accepted a faculty position at the University of Maryland in the Mathematics Department under Tobias Dantzig in the fall of 1940. In the summer of 1941, he left Maryland and joined the Canadian Air Force to train as a bomber pilot. He subsequently transferred to the Dutch unit of the British RAF and flew a Handley-Page Halifax bomber. He flew missions in support of the Allied invasion of Normandy. Dr. van Stockum's writings about his World War II service served as the basis for the historical portions of the story told herein.

His doctoral thesis in Mathematics from Edinburgh University is titled "The gravitational field of a distribution of particles rotating around an axis of symmetry", and demonstrates that Einstein's theory of General Relativity allows for the creation of closed time-like curves.

I discovered Dr. van Stockum during reading about time travel, and I know him primarily as he is described in those resources as one of the Fathers of Time Travel. (Those resources include Clegg, Brian. *How to Build a Time Machine: The Real Science of Time Travel.* St. Martin's Press, 2011 and other works listed under "Time Travel and Physics" in the *Further Reading* section of this book.) Everything I've learned about him since, I see through the filter of his career in mathematics, his prodigious intellectual achievements and his legacy in the world of mathematics and physics. If Willem's work is correct, then time travel is possible. *Time Bomber* is a story exploring that possibility by tying it to the actual events of Dr. van Stockum's life. I hope that through this story I'm able to instill in the reader the same sense of awe and wonder I feel from the implications of his work and personal sacrifice.

Robert P. Wack
February 2014

"One of the endlessly alluring aspects of mathematics is that its thorniest paradoxes have a way of blooming into beautiful theories." - Philip J. Davis

"Pure mathematics is, in its way, the poetry of logical ideas." - Albert Einstein

"Life is like a game of cards. The hand you are dealt is determinism; the way you play it is free will." - Jawaharlal Nehru

Prologue

The reticle of the Ziess Zielvier scope centered on the boy's cheek, precisely quartering the fear and fatigue covering his dirty, sweat-streaked face. A gentle squeeze of the trigger would deliver instant peace. Not your time, the soldier thought, looking up at the gray sky and lowering his rifle. Not this bullet.

Above and behind him, the flowering apple tree glowed in the sidelong morning light, creating a pink nimbus against the sooty sky.

He inhaled deeply, savoring the fragrance of the blossoms, at peace despite the impending violence of his mission. This is a place I could stay. Finish my time.

The blooming trees whispered in the soft breeze, blending blossom sweetness and musty, warming earthiness from the farms and fields in the surrounding French countryside. From his concealment beneath the pile of winter prunings, he had a clear view down a lane of fruit trees toward the knot of bedraggled paratroopers huddled against the raised mound of the surrounding hedgerow.

He raised the Kar98k rifle and peered through the scope again, scanning the cluster of young soldiers, searching for his quarry. The paratroopers edged forward along the hedge line, alert for German opposition. The soldier scoped each one, dismissing each in turn. Assured of his target's absence, he lowered the rifle again. The pilot was not with them, and these paratroopers, lost far behind the lines, would find their own way, without his intervention. This time.

Another place, another time: he sat in civilian clothes at a café in Carentan, sipping weak coffee, the best to be obtained during the German occupation. Despite the quiet streets, the air was electric, the news of the invasion sending residents scurrying about, a *frisson* of hope and fear exciting near hysteria. He spied his quarry leaving the shop across the street, also posing as a civilian. He turned to his newspaper as the other passed, oblivious. He would not fail this time. Though the technicians said it was impossible, he knew the pain he felt from their last several encounters was real and fresh, sending him back to try again, and again.

After a few seconds, he finished his coffee, folded the paper, stood up, and started down the street, following the target. The man was half a block ahead, hurrying, head down. The soldier approached from behind, drew his knife, stepped forward and struck cleanly. The target crumpled and the soldier pulled him into a small alley and concealed the body behind a pile of debris. He cleaned the knife and continued on his way, undetected.

Another place, another time: wearing the baggy uniform of an American paratrooper, he picked his way across the Normandy countryside in the company of a small group of paratroopers trying to regroup, find other members of their scattered unit. He suspected his target was in the area, but wasn't sure what approach he would use this time. The soldier preferred the American uniform to the scratchy wool of the German infantry, especially since his own outfit didn't have the same chemical impregnation as the other paratroopers had – which, as he knew, was an unnecessary precaution against the Germans using chemical weapons.

Time Bomber

The paratroopers found the wreckage of a Halifax bomber, and he explored the remains with them, feigning disinterest. Amongst the dead lay the pilot, easily recognized. He made a note of the coordinates, and, at the next available opportunity, separated from the group and returned to his operational locus to prepare for his next deployment. Back to do it again, and again, until he could go home and live a quiet civilian life. Or just go back, really, because there really was no going home. That was still true, even now.

MAP

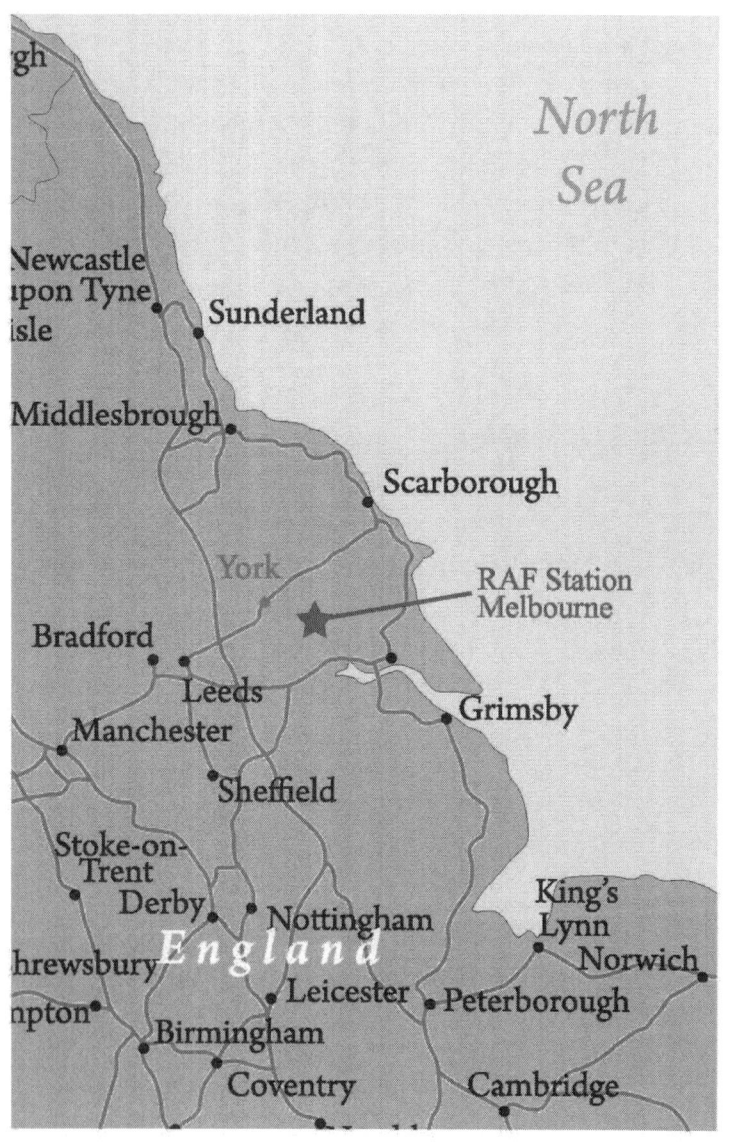

RAF Station Melbourne
Home Base to Squadron 10

MAP

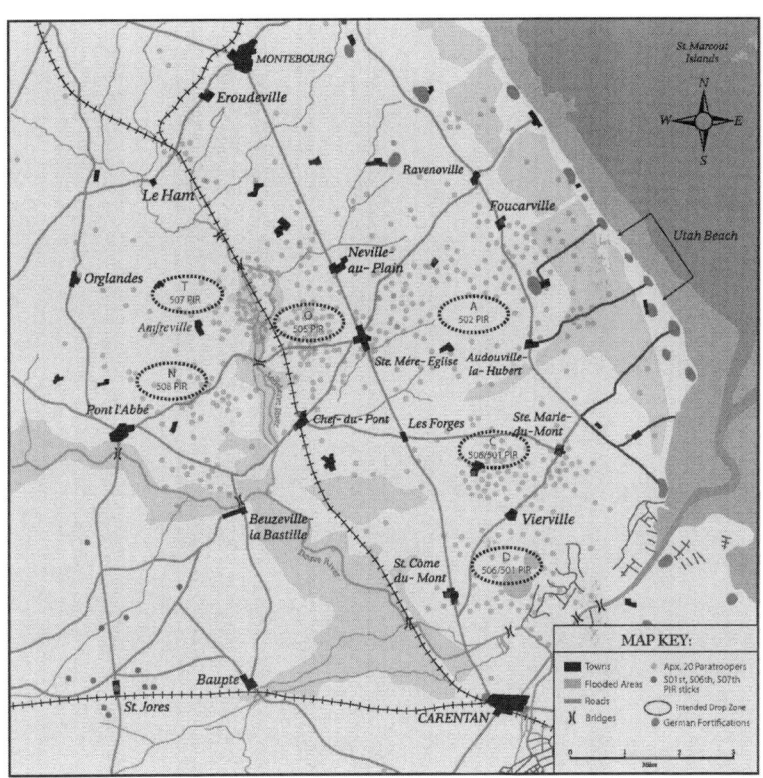

D-Day Invasion Airborne Plan

CHAPTER ONE

0020 June 6th, 1944
Bomber Squadron 10, RAF Station Melbourne
Yorkshire, England

"Go home, van Stockum. The paratroopers have to do their work now."

Flight Officer Willem Jacob van Stockum looked up with a weary smile from the terrain map in front of him, relieved to hear Wing Commander Sheffield's voice. "Good to see you back safely, Sir. How was the new crew?"

"Top notch. Fine group of lads. They just needed a little steadying." Sheffield looked down at the materials arrayed on the table in front of Willem. "What are you into now?"

"Just a little more preparation, Sir."

Sheffield smiled and picked up a small book. "Dickens? Ah, *Dombey*. You certainly have diverse interests. I heard you were reciting Yeats to the men the other day."

Willem blushed. "They're a sharp bunch, with very refined tastes."

Sheffield chuckled and turned the book over in his hands. "I never got to this one. Didn't fancy any of them, really. Too many lucky coincidences."

Willem grinned. "His characters amuse me. There's a little bit of truth in all of them."

"Indeed. Now, Yeats, there's a poet. Any favorites?"

"*The Wanderings of Oisin*," Willem responded without hesitation.

Sheffield nodded, eyes sparkling over a warm smile. "We'll have to discuss it some time. How were your runs today?"

"Excellent. Two against the coastal batteries, and one up to Le Havre. I think we did some real damage."

"Yes, I heard about your little maneuver over Ver sur Mer."

Willem warmed again. "Just making sure Jerry gets his mail."

Sheffield grinned. "Very good. Let's see who's still out."

Who was back? Dennie and his crew, that was certain. Though Willem did not see his friend when he landed, the status board listed his Halifax bomber as back in one piece, just one of the thirty planes of Squadron No.10 out for one more run at the end of their busiest day ever: the final run-up to the long awaited invasion of Fortress Europe.

Sheffield conferred with the prim WAAF clerk, mulling over the five remaining empty squares on the mission tracking board. Willem returned to his papers, picked up the completed letter to his mother and sealed it, then put it to the side. He hoped his cryptic allusions would be vague enough to get through the censors, and that she would note the date and make the connection to this evening's events.

What a long journey it had been. From his childhood in the Netherlands, then Dublin, to America, and now here, to the storied Squadron No.10 in Yorkshire, one of the cradles of the bombing campaign against Germany, the home of the legendary "King Kong" Staton, one of the earliest proponents of a particularly reckless style of flying, devised to ensure that the bombs hit the target and only the target.

Time Bomber

Up on the wall of the officer's mess hung a photo of Staton with his labrador Sam. His towering frame befitted his nickname. Alongside were the mementos and commemorations of the crews from before, a small fraction of those killed and missing.

Willem returned to his maps, the other letter spread out next to it. He stared at the spidery handwriting on the pages received today and shook his head at the contrast between the two. On one piece of paper he planned his future; on the others, how to ensure that as many Nazis as possible had none at all.

He sipped the weak coffee and thought of home. Though a faint imitation of a proper brew, it was still better than tea, which he still wasn't used to after so many years with the Canadians and Brits. He didn't mind tea, but he preferred a good dark coffee like his mother used to make for *koffietijd* – his Irish/Dutch mother, making good Dutch coffee no matter where in the world she might be. He smiled to himself, noting the similarities between her wanderings and his. Did she know she'd end up in Washington D.C. when she left Holland for the Dutch West Indies with Captain Bram van Stockum so many years ago, their baby daughter in her arms? On both sides of his family the adventure gene ran true. In only one generation, his cousins had scattered across four continents. With that familial penchant for boldness, his peripatetic career path made better sense.

At the front of the room, the pretty clerk stole glances at Willem as she neatly printed the results of each of the evening's missions. He studied the board, oblivious to her attempts to catch his eye. Only four out now. How long before they were deleted from the list? He used to feel guilty at the relief he felt when it was none of his friends. But that lessened with each time out – or, at least, he noticed it less.

The second run of the day had been the best. Though he had quickly learned to keep his opinions to himself, the other crews couldn't help but notice his exhilaration at being given the more challenging runs against the coastal batteries, which were sure to be heavily defended. He didn't want any more antagonism about his Crazy Yank ways, but he never ducked an opportunity to defend his tactics. Why drop bombs on targets where you didn't know for sure you were killing Germans? At least where there was anti-aircraft fire you knew two things: there were German soldiers down there, and they didn't want you dropping bombs on that particular spot. That meant raining destruction on it was imperative. Not like the night over Duisberg.

In his first few months with the squadron, he hadn't faced the problem of what he'd do if given an assignment to drop bombs on a German city. The gradual evolution of bombing tactics over the last few years put him in the awkward position of arguing vehemently against the very methods his superiors were now forcefully pursuing: the deliberate destruction of German population centers and the deaths of civilian noncombatants. It was a moral dilemma he hadn't foreseen three years ago at the University of Maryland.

Four weeks before, they'd flown to Duisberg to hit the Messerschmidt airframe assembly plant. Willem's plane was in the third wave, and, as they approached the target, the whole town was ablaze. They released their load, but Willem was transfixed by the hellish spectacle below, fiery blobs and tentacles shrouded in smoke, consuming everything. When Colin Morrison, the tail gunner, screamed into the intercom, Willem was slow to react.

"Corkscrew left! Now!" A German fighter had a bead on them, and as usual, Colin was the first to spot it. They narrowly escaped, but several others didn't.

That night held several lessons for Willem, who still desperately absorbed everything he could from a combat experience while also trying to keep his crew alive. First, light flak over a target meant safe skies for the German fighters too, and they'd likely be there in force. Next, being in the third wave meant that because of the markers and fires you could see the target better; but it also meant the fighters were probably already on station waiting for you. Worst of all, the scruples of only targeting military sites and avoiding civilians were almost meaningless in the darkness, confusion, and terror of a live mission under fire.

"Pack it in, van Stockum. I'll see the rest of them in. You need to be fresh for tomorrow," Sheffield ordered.

Willem pointed at the board. "Isn't that Mickey's plane?"

Sheffield nodded. "He took one of the other new crews out for me, rode second dickey. They were with the bunch headed to Essen. Diversionary raid."

Mickey Mitchell was a perfect choice to send out with a plane full of nervous "sprogs" on their first mission. He was one of the senior Canadian pilots in the Squadron, well respected for his flying skill, and even more so for his capacity for alcohol and his deep baritone. In the pubs, a few rounds of pints usually broke down the silent walls between the crews of various nationalities. Willem really enjoyed the internationalism of Squadron No. 10. French, Norwegian, Dutch and Belgian flyers joined the Australians, Canadians, and Brits to share equally in danger and death. Willem knew Mickey from all the way back to Rockliffe, the training station outside Ottawa they'd both been posted to early on. Meeting up with him again in Yorkshire was an unexpected pleasure.

Willem picked up the day's letters and shuffled the pages again, putting them in order to reread one more time.

"*I share your ambivalence about the use of violence to protect the innocent. Events in our homelands have persuaded me that there are circumstances when we must set aside our qualms and do what is necessary. In a way, I envy your clarity of purpose in that regard. For myself, my disgust for all things military does not diminish my respect for your course of action.*"

All the doubts of the last few years were assuaged by those sentences. Did he do the right thing back in 1941, when he chucked it all to join the Canadian Air Force? Although his teaching position in the Mathematics Department at Maryland was never going to be permanent, staying there had become harder every day through the winter of 1940 with each bulletin from his ravaged homeland. Willem was torn between his mathematics and his desire to do something to aid his family and friends back in Holland, even with Dr. Dantzig's friendly support and Dr. Veblen's encouragement and big plans from Princeton. Ever since the publication of his doctoral thesis on the geometry of spacetime had received attention at the highest level of the mathematics and physics worlds, his career had taken off. One prestigious appointment followed another, and his hard work finally felt vindicated.

As a rising star in the mathematics world, couldn't he have made some important contribution to the war effort by staying with Dr. Dantzig and working on some other war problem? Dantzig's son, George, certainly seemed to have been able to strike that balance. A brilliant mathematician in his own right, George had so impressed his teachers at Berkeley that the government begged him to come and work on statistical problems for the Air Force. But then Willem would criticize himself for just following George. He had to make his own way.

"*Our friend in Chicago was also impressed with your resolve after your visit last winter. I don't share his disappointment with your decision, but then, I think I disappoint him as well. Once I wrote the letters to the President, my interest in the scientific details of that endeavor was quenched. My concern remains the work to be done with a unified theory, which is why I'd like you to return to Princeton as soon as you are able."*

His resolve. Willem laughed to himself, remembering his friend Dennie's reaction to the story of how Willem had threatened to resign his commission when the Canadians sent him to Rockliffe to teach ballistics and aerodynamics.

"Resign? You can't bloody resign. They own you. What did they say when you said that?" Dennie's eyes were wide in disbelief.

Willem laughed. "You know, they never said I couldn't resign. They just kept trying to placate me with reassurances, and then they'd give me another class to teach. I think I just finally wore them down when I asked to be transferred here."

Dennie shook his head. "You requested to be assigned here? You are a panic, as they say in the American films, Will. A bloody fucking panic."

Return as soon as you are able. With the invasion on, some spoke softly of the end of the war. Not in the mission room, where superstition and fatalistic custom forbade any such talk. But Willem sensed a tinge of nervous anticipation creeping into the bomber crews. *Could I be one that survives? Will I have a life when this over?* The lottery of death in the sky over Europe continued, though, with each mission, the Luftwaffe's ability to send them to the ground in flames diminished, and the amount of flak in some areas was noticeably less. The equipment was getting better, too. That was, however, often counterbalanced by the inexperience of the pilots and crews, who were rushed through training to replace the relentless toll of casualties. The death of their newest pilot yesterday on a training run was a reminder and proof of that problem. Willem had watched with several other crews as the new pilot committed the common sprog mistake of banking too soon after take off. The plane slid sidewise in a stall and tumbled to the ground in a flash of burning fuel. The men shook their heads and turned away as the fire trucks and ambulances raced off to the scene to extract the charred and mangled corpses. He'd seen enough of those.

Life after the war. A second chance at Princeton. Seeing his mother and siblings again. A future free of random death and destruction, leaving behind the moral ambiguities of dropping bombs on innocents to protect innocents.

He stared at the mission board, lost in thought. The WAAF clerk looked up from her clipboard again and turned to him, and they finally made eye contact. At first Willem didn't realize she was smiling at him. He caught himself and reciprocated, eliciting a deep blush from her, then she turned away. He returned to the letter.

Could he really be close to heading home? He'd worked so hard to get here, invested so much energy – now could he look forward to getting out? The young enlisted girl's smile beckoned from the other side: the world of peace, and family, and home.

One adapts to the uncertainty of random, sudden death by narrowing the focus, living from hour to hour, doing the next thing very well with maximum attention. He'd arrived at that new equilibrium after that bad spell last winter, when Spike took him away on leave back to Dublin for several weeks of relaxation and new energy. It was at Harrie and Billy's place at Clondarf when he'd had his epiphany and came to terms with the uncertainty of his future. This new idea of life after war shook that balance, in a stimulating, unsettling way.

He looked at the last page one more time before he put the letter away.

"Please finish your work and return home safely. Heartfelt greetings. Yours, A. Einstein."

Even after years of these intermittent letters, he still could not believe they were real. All from one brief encounter over lunch five years ago in the Fine Building at Princeton, and a passing remark about a coffee cup.

At the front of the room, another crew returned, and the pilot spoke in low tones with Sheffield. He nodded, face grim, and Willem caught the words "got the chop."

"Bloody hell," Willem heard Sheffield reply.

The pilot turned away for the debrief room, and Sheffield retreated to his office. Willem watched with a mixture of dread and morbid curiosity as the WAAF clerk picked up the eraser.

His friend Dennie was safe. Sheffield was safe. Tonight, he'd dropped his bombs with a clean conscience. The invasion was on. And Albert Einstein was waiting for him to return, a job for him back at Princeton.

The clerk erased the remaining two flights. 6.6% missing for the evening, Willem calculated automatically. His relentlessly logical and mathematical mind continued compulsively: projected out over the course of a standard tour's required thirty missions – with generous rounding – tour survival probability was down to 13%.

Mickey Mitchell was not coming home.

CHAPTER TWO

0100 June 6th, 1944
Over the English Channel

Staff Sergeant Thomas Sloan looked across at the row of soldiers facing him, ghostly in the faint blue running light: dark faces in a row, glittering black eyes peering from under their helmets. The red glow of cigarettes flared briefly, lighting up the blackened faces, giving the men demonic, red-rimmed eyes. Directly across from him, PFC Hennessy's head lolled in sleep, rolling and bobbing with the movements of Lucky Girl, the C-47 carrying them over the Channel to their drop zone. To his left, Langtry fumbled with his rosary, muttering prayers; to his right, Schwarz squirmed and shifted.

Earlier, when they stood in line to load up at Upottery Field, Schwarz punched his shoulder and gestured at the painted figure of Lucky Girl up on the nose of the plane, one hand holding a royal flush of spades fanned in front of her, the other on her hip, a sultry smile on her face, ample cleavage spilling from a sheer evening gown. For the hundredth time this week, Sloan restrained the urge to punch him back hard in the face. As the mission approached, he'd gotten much better at keeping his impulses in check. Not like at Toccoa, or Breckinridge, or Bragg. Especially Bragg.

Focus on the mission. No trouble, just the mission. He looked at Schwarz.

"Look at that, Top, whaddaya think? Good sign?"

"What?" Sloan replied.

"The spades. She's one of ours." Sloan glanced at the stenciled spade on the side of Schwarz's helmet and grunted, too preoccupied to give it much thought.

Lucky Girl was aptly named. The Douglas C-47 had rolled off the assembly line on the north side of the Long Beach Airport on February 22nd, 1944, serial number 44-02583. She was flown to the Douglas plant in Tulsa, Oklahoma for modification, where she turned into what the Brits called a Dakota. The paratroopers just called them Gooney Birds, after the big winged albatrosses up and down the West Coast, where so many C-47s had flown their first test flights.

During a check flight in Tulsa, number 44-02583 had narrowly averted a crash landing during an unexpected storm, earning her first credits as a charmed craft. That reputation followed her on the convoy east, joining thirty other Gooney Birds from the Oklahoma City plant on the trip to New York, then to Dow Army Airfield in Maine, where she was prepared for the flight to Europe.

On April 7th, 1944, Good Friday, she started across the Atlantic in a convoy to RCAF Station Goose Bay in Labrador, then on to Bluie West 1 in Greenland. They stopped for fuel and a rest, then took off for Meeks Field in Iceland. They were grounded there by weather for two days, then off again for the final leg to Prestwick Airport in Scotland. Once again she had narrowly averted a fatal mishap as they were diverted for weather to RAF Nutts Corner in Northern Ireland. Not expecting their arrival, the runway was occupied, and, dropping out of the low clouds, 44-02583 just missed catastrophe. The crews laid over several days, spending considerable time in the nearby pubs settling their nerves. By the end of April, she'd joined the Troop Carrier Command and begun ferrying training jumps. It was then she was painted and formally christened.

So far, the trip for the members of 2nd platoon, Fox Company, 506th Parachute Infantry Regiment felt like any of the dozens of training flights, except for the excessive amounts of ammo and equipment they carried. Some of the men knelt on the floor, leaning backward to rest on their packs, which were too bulky to fit on the seats along the walls of the transport. Schwarz moved again, wiggling in vain to relieve the pressure on his thigh from the bulky Colt Peacemaker that was strapped to Sloan's thigh. The long barreled revolver, for Sloan, symbolized all the mixed feelings he had about the endeavor: a source of pride and admiration, but also an emblem of the burden of expectations he did not seek or want.

"Just take it," his father told him on his last night home, when he found out about his brother's death in Sicily. His father held the gun out, and Sloan knew the tables were finally turned, that he had the power, and he didn't like it.

"Your mother wanted Frannie to have it, but he laughed said he didn't need it. It'll kill her if you leave without it."

"Dad, I…. What if I lose it?"

"It's come home from three wars. You won't lose it."

His Grandpa Dickerson and his Uncle Mike had both carried and used it, and they both came back. His uncle was still running cattle up in Prescott. It was him who had set up his little sister's husband in the farm equipment business in Mesa.

The next day he headed back to Kentucky, Colt buried in his duffel bag, to get ready for the move from Breckinridge to Ft. Bragg. It was at Bragg when he learned what really happened to his brother and the others in the 504th in the skies over Sicily. He put those thoughts out of his mind, as he did every time they were up in the air with live fire beneath them.

Sloan wondered what Hennessey was dreaming about. He felt no inclination to doze, despite the sedative effect of whatever it was they all took before getting on the plane. His nerves twanged and twitched as he alternately worried about his men and grumbled to himself about being here. His irritation at his C.O., the Army, the Germans, and the whole goddam war was something he kept to himself, nursing it quietly like a small fire, one small twig at a time, occupying his time and giving him motivation when he was tired and depressed. He was going home to resume his life, go to college, get away – and no one, not his dad, not Hitler, not the whole German Army was going to stop him. He tried to stretch his legs to relieve the twitching and cramps, excess adrenaline tormenting confined muscles.

In the distance, faint rumbles and booms intruded over the drone of the twin Pratt and Whitney Wasp engines, and the plane bumped and swerved enough to make the men reach for handholds. He startled at a loud clatter in the passenger space, like a handful of gravel against the metal walls.

The plane lurched sharply, pitching Sloan forward into Hennessey's lap, face pressed into the other man's reserve chute. He felt himself pushed and pulled backward as the men attempted to untangle themselves in the semi-darkness of the plane. He cursed once more the impossible load of gear weighing him down.

It was then that he saw the bright lights outside, the arcs and sprays of anti-aircraft batteries flashing across the small window, spidery fingers of fire with a deadly touch, reaching up from the ground and groping across the sky for the fragile planes full of terrified paratroopers.

The jumbled paratroopers thrashed to reorganize themselves and stand up, but were knocked down again by the pilot's violent evasive maneuvers. While they wrestled, the red light came on and Lieutenant Sowers screamed, "Stand up! Stand up!"

Explosions rocked the plane, but the men managed to pull themselves up the walls, helping each other, holding on to the overhead anchor line. A few attached the metal C-clamp of their static lines and held on to them in advance of the "hook up!" command. Shrapnel rattled and clattered, eliciting grunts and curses as the hot metal found exposed flesh.

Sloan felt a sickening surge in his stomach as the pilot suddenly dropped altitude and accelerated, extracting every one of the 1200 horsepower from the engines.

"Hook up!" Lt. Sowers yelled over the mechanical roar and booming explosions. The rest of the stick reached up and hooked on their static lines, hanging on them for support.

"Sound off!" Sloan felt the man behind him slap his gear. He, in turn, slapped Private Langtry and shouted, "Ten okay!" They all stared at the red light, willing it to turn green as the explosions drew closer and closer and the pilot continued his swerving and diving.

Too low, too fast, Sloan thought. He's gonna kill us.

Another sudden motion knocked several men down. They yelled and cursed, then helped each other back to their feet, and the light turned green. The line surged forward, every man pushing to get out as fast as possible into the slightly safer night air. Sloan shuffled his feet, leaning into Langtry in front, then suddenly bounced backward when Langtry stopped, and the men behind him smashed into him. More screams and cussing ensued, and the men renewed their pushing. Sloan leaned over and looked to the back of the plane. Private Green was stuck in the door, his M1 held across his chest caught on either side of the doorway, the force of the men behind him preventing him from backing up to free himself. Lieutenant Sowers screamed and pushed the line back to free him, then turned and knocked the rifle free and Green went out the door.

    A loud metallic bang knocked them sideways. Something wet hit Sloan's face, and Langtry crumpled to the floor in front of him. Sloan tried lifting him, without success. Everyone in front was out the door, and the men behind Sloan jostled to get past. Lt. Sowers came forward and knelt next to Langtry. He stood up and unhooked him and waved the others to the door, yelling "go, go!" Sloan unhooked and helped Sowers move Langtry to the side as the other men jumped. Sloan's hands were covered with warm wetness as he stood from the injured man and turned to the back of the plane. He looked down at his dying squadmate, then rehooked and stepped to the door. The night sky was filled with an insane fireworks display, multi-colored lines and arcs spraying upward in blue, red and yellow. He reached for the sides of the doorway to pull himself through, but in his haste he slipped in the blood pouring from Langtry's open chest and tumbled forward out the door in a somersault.

    All around, tracers streamed upward, spinning lines and flashing lights surrounding him as he turned through the air. He braced himself for the violence of the opening shock, and the static line went taut, knocking the breath from him and whipping his legs around so hard he thought his knees and ankles would break. His harness squeezed him tight and his twisted risers pressed his helmet forward, forcing his face into his reserve chute on his chest and preventing him from looking up to check his main. He saw the lights on the ground swing and spin, and he could feel he was oscillating and spinning at the same time. He reached up to grab his risers to dampen the swings. Tracers flashed past from below, and he felt more than heard the crack of bullets snapping nearby. He heard the long burp of a German MG 42 below him, circling as he spun. Before he could think what to do next, he slammed sideways into something very soft and pungent.

He rolled to a sitting position and spit manure out of his mouth, then fumbled with the clasps on his harness. They were too tight to unbuckle, so he reached down and pulled out his trench knife and quickly cut himself free. In the faint moonlight he could see his risers trailing behind him over a stone wall, his parachute tangled in the branches of an apple tree in full bloom. Mixed with the stench of manure was the faint perfume of the blossoms in the damp night air. He marveled at the sheer dumb luck that his landing hadn't broken his back across the stone wall not five feet away. Instead, he had dropped on the soft stinking mix of hay and cowshit.

He unsnapped the flap and unholstered the ungainly Colt Peacemaker. He thumbed the hammer back and held it ready, then reached for the risers with his other hand to pull the parachute to him. The movement in the branches prompted another burst of gunfire from the kraut MG, and he dropped back into the manure as bullets ripped through the branches, the parachute twitching and jumping, quickly followed by another characteristic long burp somewhere off in the darkness. A few rounds smacked into the wall, and he dug deeper into the manure pile up against the solid fieldstone wall. Several other guns joined in, pouring a torrent of bullets into the wall and through the branches of the trees next to him. He felt the gossamer touch of apple blossom petals tickle his hands and neck as the rounds shredded the parachute and the surrounding trees.

The machine guns stopped. After several minutes, Sloan lifted his head from concealment and listened. Hearing

Time Bomber

nothing, he uncurled and stood up. He took a step along the wall, then froze at the sound of German voices.

Two soldiers crept on the other side of the wall. Sloan held his breath with the Colt at the ready as they passed by murmuring. He heard rustling as they pulled down his parachute, a few more snatches of conversation, then they hurried away.

Sloan exhaled, carefully lowered the hammer on the Colt, turned the cylinder back to the empty sixth chamber, and reholstered. The last thing he needed was a hole blown through his leg, like that dumbass Harry McPherson at the Arizona State Fair, who had jumped down off the wood fence they sat on watching the fights. They'd snuck off to see one of the backroom boxing matches, and he fancied himself a gunfighter. The doctor at the Grunow clinic said he'd be lucky not to lose his leg, and Harry's dad took the gun away. The promise he'd broken never to carry it loaded was held against him for a long time.

He took a few deep breaths to settle himself, then moved along the wall. Perhaps his father's insistence that he carry this family heirloom for good luck had something to it. From the hills and jungles of Cuba to the fields of eastern France almost thirty years before, the Colt accompanied two prior generations of men from his mother's family into combat and back. The fact that his brother did not take it, and was now buried somewhere in Sicily, was just another piece of the burden.

He knelt down and pulled his M1 out of the canvas Griswold bag slung across his back, assembled it in the dark, loaded a clip, and threw the bag away. Holding the rifle in front, he made his way forward in the patchy moonlight, to search for the rest of his unit.

CHAPTER THREE

0125 June 6th, 1944
Normandy, France

Private Kenneth Green stared at the horizon as he drifted to the ground, hands overhead gripping the risers, knees flexed slightly in preparation for landing. He hoped the cramps would hold off until after he hit and had a chance to find cover. The moon was out, and he could see three other parachutes falling along with him. Before he could brace himself, he hit the ground, rolled, and started gathering in his parachute. Without his M1 he felt naked. Knocked from his hands in the opening shock, he knew it could be half a mile away, lost in the dark fields somewhere. Why had he listened to those guys and not packed it away in the Griswold bag? First it made him get stuck on the way out, and then he dropped it.

After all he'd been through proving to everyone that the skinny kid from upstate New York really could cut it, now this. At every step, from enlistment through boot camp to jump school, they kept trying to kick him out.

"Too small. Too skinny. Too weak." It was only at Toccoa where he'd finally won a permanent place in the 506th. And now this.

He tucked the balled-up silk and lines under his arm and ran in a crouch toward deeper shadows near the closest hedgerow. He stuffed the parachute into the bushes, then listened and watched to get his bearings. In the distance, he heard sporadic gunfire, mostly German, but occasionally the bam-bam of an M1.

After several minutes of silent waiting, his impatience came to outweigh his fear, and he set off back in the direction of where he thought the others might have landed. His squad should do the same, just as they were trained – rolling up the stick despite scattering and darkness. They'd had some screw-ups during training, but never had a transport flown so erratically as tonight. So far, the intestinal distress that had tormented him all day in England was quiet, silenced by the adrenaline. He hurried off into the darkness.

CHAPTER FOUR

In the summer of 1941, Willem van Stockum made a decision. It wasn't abrupt; in fact, he'd been mulling it over since exactly May 7th, just over two months before. He hadn't shared his ruminations with anyone, but his family suspected something was up.

His mother was receiving sporadic letters from Europe, some directly from Dutch relatives trapped in occupied Holland, the rest from those who had escaped the Nazi subjugation of the Continent. Their stories of privation and oppression were made bearable only by the knowledge they were still alive, unlike so many others murdered by the Nazis. When Mother shared the letters, Willem's blood boiled, but he kept his anger and frustration to himself.

Then, standing in front of the classroom, leading eager Maryland students in their mathematics studies, he felt no one seemed to care about the war overseas. Like the rest of the country, the college students were more concerned about their sporting events, their dances, their fraternities and sororities. They were brash and innocent, much more forward and familiar with the faculty than European students ever would be. Especially with the nicknames – it drove Dr. Dantzig crazy.

Dr. Tobias Dantzig, the head of the Mathematics Department and an émigré like Willem, knew the situation in Europe. For him, though, it meant the possibility of landing the next brilliant mathematician on the run from the Nazis. Building a preeminent department was his first priority, and he had big plans for Willem. Through his connection to Dr. Veblen at Princeton, Dantzig kept his eyes open for new recruits. It was Veblen who made the Maryland connection for Willem after his stay at Princeton the year before.

As they walked around campus smoking cigarettes, Dr. Dantzig confided to Willem his frustrations.

"How do I build an elite department while being lead by a football coach? And they call him Curley! To his face!" Dr. Dantzig's frustrations with Dr. Byrd, the university President, and Dr. Talliafiero, Dantzig's predecessor in the Math department – and now the Dean of the Faculty – were frequent topics of his rants.

"Doc Tolley" had been very kind to Willem on his arrival in College Park, having him over for dinner with other new faculty members. He was a genial old man, beloved by the students, but he clearly didn't share Dr. Dantzig's ambition and vision. Dantzig saw in Willem a protégé and an ally in his grand plans for the department. His brilliant son George was now at Berkeley, blazing his own path through the mathematics world. Willem sensed he was filling multiple roles for the department chair. But the politics and maneuvering of academia held less and less interest for him as the letters started arriving.

Then on May 7th, 1941, clarity. He was hurrying across campus to the library after his 1:30 Geometry class. A huge crowd blocked the sidewalks, and white smoke drifted across the quad. The staccato chatter of machine gun fire commanded his attention.

Across the green expanse of grass, gun emplacements pointed toward a hastily erected fort. Groups of infantry in olive drab, topped with vintage helmets from the Great War, raced across with fixed bayonets, while the guns fired endless rounds of blanks and harmless pyrotechnics exploded nearby, simulating artillery. They were National Guard members, supplemented with University students enrolled in the military programs. A large crowd watched and cheered from the sides, some in temporary bleachers erected for the occasion.

Willem stood transfixed. The crowd murmured and roared as if at a football game, and the young men in uniform smiled and joked while waiting their turn to perform. The announcer talked over the public address system about strong national defense, preparations for keeping the country safe. But not a word about Europe or the Nazis. It was all a game, a spectacle, and, at the end, as the crowd dispersed, it was all it took for Willem to stop from shouting at their backs, "Right now! We need to do something right now!"

He confided his frustrations in letters to his mentor in Montreal, Dr. Synge, the man from his Trinity days who had encouraged Willem's mathematics career and connected him to Dr. Veblen at Princeton. It was one particular sentence in Dr. Synge's response that had cemented Willem's resolve: "Some Americans are joining the Canadian forces to get into the action."

Dr. Dantzig took the news better than Willem expected. They walked to the Little Tavern hamburger stand on Route 1 at the edge of campus and Willem treated him to a bag of cheeseburgers. These were Dr. Dantzig's guilty American pleasure. Then they walked to the Dairy and bought milkshakes, Willem's favorite. They finished with cigarettes, walking under the trees on an uncharacteristically mild July afternoon, the blue sky clear and stunning. They walked past Ritchie Coliseum, the site of the dreadful boxing matches so beloved by the students. They stood in front of the giant bronze tortoise, Testudo, the new mascot for the school.

"Look at that. A turtle. Curley's turtle." Dr. Dantzig pointed, shaking his head, unable to avoid connecting anything to his dislike for Dr. Byrd.

Later, Dr. Dantzig sadly gave Willem his blessing – another son lost to the war effort.

A few weeks later, Willem took several long Greyhound bus rides north, arriving tired and hungry at the new recruit depot in Toronto. The bored enlisted clerk looked over Willem's credentials, then up at the grown man standing out amidst the lines of teenagers.

"You want to be a pilot?"

Willem assented, and the clerk beckoned to a man standing nearby with a clipboard. As they conferred in whispers, the clipboard man glanced at Willem and the papers the clerk held, then nodded. He turned away and the clerk made a mark on the papers and gestured toward the next station. Toward the end of the process, Willem was pulled out of line and escorted to an office. He was seated across from an officer behind a desk cluttered with piles of paper.

"Good afternoon, Dr. van Stockum. I understand you want to be a pilot?"

"That's correct."

"You realize you will be significantly older than most of the other trainees, and that it is a difficult and dangerous process?"

Willem nodded. The officer stared at him.

"Are you familiar with the washout statistics? Training accidents? Fatalities?"

Willem nodded again. The officer leaned back and sighed, then put his hands up to his face, rubbing in circles.

"Dr. van Stockum, you are a man of obvious talents, and it's my duty to inform you that you can easily fill other very important positions in the Royal Canadian Air Force that don't involve as much physical risk. You know that, don't you?"

Willem had enough. "I am well aware of what I am getting myself into. I want to get into the action as soon as possible, and this seems to make the most sense for me. I appreciate your concern, but I am determined to proceed."

The officer glanced down at the file in front of him.

"You're American?"

Willem shook his head. "Not yet. My naturalization papers are still being processed. I will be."

"So why not join the American Army? I'm sure they would love to have you."

Willem shook his head again. "And get into the action when? The Americans may never get into this war. I'm Dutch, and my people, my friends and relatives, are suffering now. I need to get over there to help, to be of use as soon as I possibly can. Your army is my best option."

The officer regarded him for a moment, then, with a small shake of his head, scribbled something on the folder, signed it with a flourish, then handed it to Willem.

"I admire your determination, Dr. van Stockum. Good luck with your training. Return to the processing area, and the clerk will direct you to the next station."

"Next table." How many times had he heard that? He received a treatment similar to the officer's interrogation several more times throughout the process. Each time was briefer and less involved as he proved himself unwavering in his commitment.

After finishing his basic training in Toronto, he was off to St. Catharine's, just across the border a bit from Buffalo.

Time Bomber

The other recruits gave him many sidelong glances, wondering what this older man was doing in their midst, Willem conspicuously more senior than the nineteen and twenty year olds around him. Indeed, at thirty-one, he was old enough to be a senior officer, and yet there he was stripped down to his drawers standing amongst kids who just a few months before would have been sitting in front of him in a classroom.

He'd earned his wings, but they didn't make it easy for him. The attrition in his class was horrific, many washing out for the simple problem of uncontrollable airsickness. Willem persisted, until the biting cold clear January day he lifted the Fleet Finch biplane into the crystal blue sky for his solo flight.

His instructor was one of the ball-breakers, intent on pushing every recruit to the breaking point in order to ensure they had the physical and mental toughness to succeed in later phases. His manner wasn't abusive or demeaning, but in a way, it was worse: he would make small remarks, perfectly calculated to nibble away at one's self-confidence, create doubts, prompt second-guessing. Later, Willem would appreciate his method, but at the time it was maddening.

"Why did you do that? You'll kill your crew."

"*When* will you solo? When you are ready. It's not up to me, but you."

"I can't let you solo until you demonstrate better judgment. I won't be responsible for you killing yourself or someone else."

It was infuriating to be treated like a child, but Willem persevered. After the mechanics strapped him in, and he quelled those last minute doubts, he taxied out onto the runway and lifted the plane into the sky, the single prop up front chewing through the thick cold air, the controls now an extension of his own body. He felt every current and eddy rushing across the fabric wings, nudging the directional surfaces; he felt the pockets of varying air pressure. The adrenaline more than compensated for the numbing cold, and his shivering hand guided the plane through take-off, the requisite number of turns and climbs, then downward for a perfect feather-soft landing. The excitement and physical stress was exhausting, but oh-so worth it.

His flight instructor gave him a grudging smile and clinked his glass at the bar in Niagara Falls that night.

"You proved me wrong, Van."

Willem shrugged in response, smiling.

"I bet that's not the first time you've heard that, either."

Willem laughed, and they clinked glasses again.

Later, Willem left the bar and went for a walk and a smoke, savoring the cold night air. He walked down Murray St. toward the river, and then down to the river walk along the Niagara Parkway. In the moonlight the mist from the falls created ghostly halos and rainbows, and the frozen fog coated the surroundings, encasing everything in a glittering shroud. One lamppost had half its coating chipped away, revealing the fluted cast iron entombed in a sarcophagus of frozen water. Willem propped himself on the icy railing and looked out over the jumbled bergs and floes pitched at crazy angles. Below the falls, the river was smooth and still, glowing softly in the moonlight. It would have been an easy walk back to the United States. Off to his right, the falls rumbled their eternal discontent, hurtling over the perfect horseshoe precipice to pound the rocks below. The stillness of the ice and frost was striking in contrast, somehow an ominous portent. In front the tumult of the world in motion, surrounded by frozen silence, stretching away into the infinite distance, the twinkling snow and ice mirroring the fierce brilliance of the stars overhead.

He spent a long time leaning on that railing, thinking about his situation, on a quest far from home in the cold north, and his long journey from Dublin ten years before, a similar self-exile in search of vindication.

It was January, 1942, and the new declaration of war by the U.S. after Pearl Harbor was over a month old. The Germans had brought the war to the East Coast a few weeks ago when a U-boat sank the British steamer Cyclops off the coast of Cape Cod and pushed war hysteria to a new high.

Despite the satisfaction of his achievement earlier that day, his mind kept going back to his Trinity days in Dublin, a similar wintery night when he and Pic spent hours walking around the rugby and cricket pitches, the whole Trinity campus quiet in the blanket of freshly fallen snow, baring their souls to each other, falling madly in love, giddy with plans for a life together. Pic Gwynn, the daughter of the provost and the love of his life, left behind all those years ago. Like the jumbled ice below, a memory now frozen in time, never consummated, the passion gone, leaving only a cold ache.

Willem rubbed his hands and blew on them, leaning on the rail looking down on the frozen Niagara. Just a few weeks before, the Japanese attack completely transformed the American mood, and recruiting stations were swamped with eager young men now determined to get into the fight. Willem had his wings, watching from just up north, set on a different course because of a few months of time.

His meditation was interrupted by the hoots of his fellow flyers, honking the horn ready to head back up the road to St. Catharines, and the next challenge dealing with the military bureaucracy.

CHAPTER FIVE

0545 June 6th, 1944
Near St. Jores, Normandy, France

Sgt. Sloan lifted his head slowly and peered through the hedgerow in front of him. In the soft light of early dawn, gray shapes emerged where once only darkness menaced. He was relieved to see that the groups of large objects weren't German infantry tents or vehicles, but were actually brown and white Norman cattle munching grass with their heads down, oblivious to his presence. Through the small gap he scanned the adjacent field for any evidence of mines, ambushes, or anything else that could exterminate his small group.

The weary band rested along the dirt embankment, including Lieutenant Sowers. There was a bullet through his left arm, but the bleeding had stopped for now. He was pale and sweaty and struggling to keep up, but he was determined to push through and link up with the rest of the company. Three others lay somewhere back in the maze of the *bocage*, unlucky in their several skirmishes the last few hours.

"Any idea where we are?" asked one of the 501st non-coms they'd linked up with a few hours before.

Sloan shook his head. "None of this looks familiar. It sure isn't our drop zone. Judging from the shelling and noise over there, I'd say we're well west and south of where we're supposed to be. Beyond that, who knows."

The other sergeant shook his head. "So, where to?"

Sloan thought for a moment. "I guess we head toward the shooting and figure it out as we go." They listened to the shelling for a few moments. "That's sounds pretty far off. We've got some walking ahead of us. Lieutenant, you doing okay?"

Sowers looked over and nodded unconvincingly, then struggled to stand, and one of the others helped him up.

"The sooner we get moving, the sooner we get there. Let's push on," Sowers said.

Sloan nodded. If he lives, he'll make a good officer, he thought, as he watched Sowers shrug off any further assistance and hobble forward.

They crossed the next field one man at a time, running hunched between the cows toward the next hedgerow. One by one, they threw themselves against the dirt bank. Sloan peered through the hedge at another group of cattle in the next field. One of the men started pushing through, but Sloan grabbed his shoulder and held him back.

"Hold up." He pointed out to the field, where the brown and white cows ambled toward the far corner of the rough rectangle created by intersecting high hedges on raised embankments. Several others stood facing the same spot, fanned in an arc, seeming to point at a common spot in the hedge.

"What are they doing?" Sloan whispered. They watched silently, until one of the men hurriedly tapped Sloan on the shoulder and pointed. Sloan pulled out his field glasses and saw the long barrel of a machine gun poking out from the leaves, the cows arrayed in front. He crawled back along the hedgerow to Lt. Sowers, pale and sweaty, drinking from his canteen.

"We've got a problem, sir. Kraut MG in the corner to our left. I bet there's another one on the right to cover the opening over there. Not sure what else is behind that row. I think we should go a different way."

Sowers shook his head. "We're supposed to engage the enemy wherever we find them, sergeant. Let's figure out a plan and go get 'em."

Sloan hesitated. "Sir, I'm all for killing krauts, but we've got five guys, limited ammo, and no heavy weapons. We also don't know what else is in that hedgerow. We got lucky spotting the one we see."

Sowers grimaced, then shook his head again. "Sgt. Sloan, we're not here to play hide and seek. Let's figure something out and go get 'em."

"Yes, sir."

"Go get 'em," Sowers repeated and wiped sweat from his pale forehead with a shaky forearm.

Sloan turned and cursed under his breath. He quickly made the assignments and split the group. Two men would draw fire from the gap with the lieutenant while he led the rest around to outflank them on the left.

They moved out and, on cue, started shooting. The machine gun immediately returned fire. It was joined by a second – exactly where Sloan thought it would be. The torrent of lead temporarily silenced the M1s behind them.

Sloan's group was halfway to the hidden Germans when they heard a shout ahead of them. Single shots from in front zipped past, and his group hit the ground and attempted to return fire. A moment later, a third machine gun opened up, stitching the earth around them in the open field.

"Pull back! Pull back!" Sloan shouted.

They wriggled in the grass, trying to shoot and move backward while the machine gun fire tracked around, sending geysers of dirt spraying overhead. As the bullets passed by, Sloan marveled at the German gunner's lack of skill. He heard the firing resume from the men behind him, and the Germans paused to redirect their attention. Sloan's group used the opportunity to scramble back to their starting point. As they approached the low ridge of dirt, another machine gun raked the ground around them, and two of his group fell, one right next to him. He reached down and pulled the man forward, while bullets snapped and whined close by. Sloan threw himself over the bank and through the bushes, wrenching his shoulder as he pulled the other man through. He rolled him over, the man's head lolling. Sightless eyes and a slack white face confirmed death. Sloan looked over at the others, staring at their dead comrade, panting and wide-eyed with terror.

They hurried back to the others, still shooting through the bushes, ducking the bursts of return fire.

Sloan bear-crawled up to Lt. Sowers. Even paler now, Sowers peered through the bushes and struggled to stabilize his rifle.

"Sir, we've got to get out of here before they surround us," Sloan suggested.

Sowers turned to him, his face blank. "Okay, which way?"

"The only way we know is clear is back there, but that's the opposite direction of where we want to go. I say we fall back, regroup, and figure out a different way forward."

Sowers considered this, then nodded. "Right." He paused and took a deep breath., "Let's go."

As they pulled together their gear, another German shouted off to their right. Two krauts waved back behind them and pointed. The Americans broke into a run across the field toward the cover of the next hedge. Single shots cracked, none nearby. Sloan was in the lead and made it first. He turned back to see the others following close behind, Lt. Sowers lagging about thirty yards, limping and grimacing. With only one target, the Germans concentrated their fire on the straggler, and several rounds found their mark, spinning him to the ground. Sloan briefly considered going out after him, but several more krauts ran forward, and he waved the other soldiers further to the back. They went on, jogging back the way they came in search of better concealment.

CHAPTER SIX

0615 June 6th, 1944
Near St. Jores, Normandy, France

PFC Green couldn't wait any longer. He eased out of his concealment in the dense shrubbery of the hedgerow and unbuttoned his pants, hurriedly dropping them and squatting down. The waves of cramps were unbearable, and he grunted as his bowels emptied.

While he waited for the next spasm, he mused at the extraordinary bad luck of catching the notorious camp trots just before the big day. He'd been lucky ever since getting to England last fall. Not once did he get it, even when all around him were stricken.

He looked to the east at the brightening sky and wondered where he would go once it got light. Another wave of cramps hit him and he winced.

Head down, he heard before he saw two figures speaking quietly in German, shadows in the patchy morning mist,. But the instant he realized his predicament, they emerged fully into view and leveled their guns at him.

"Halt! Hände hoch! Nicht bewegen!"

From his squatting position, Green slowly raised his hands, staring at the two German soldiers with a pained expression. There was an awkward pause, then an explosion of laughter as the facts of the situation sunk in. The two Germans looked at each other and guffawed, bending over with mirth. Green squatted with his hands up, humiliated.

"*Schade, Freund, hast du ein Problem?*" asked one, still breathless from subsiding laughter. They grinned as the uncomprehending Green stared back. One of the soldiers gestured with his submachine gun slung over his shoulder, pointed at Green.

"*Steh auf! Ziehen sie Ihre Hosen!*" Green deduced his intent from the motions of the gun's muzzle, and he stood slowly, hands still above him. He bent over and grabbed his pants and straightened. As he lifted his head, he saw the two smiling Germans, and, behind them, emerging from the mist, another figure wearing the familiar green baggy pants and tunic of a fellow paratrooper, a demonic wraith gliding silently forward, trench knife in his left hand. He was bareheaded, his head shaved in a Mohawk, his face blackened and streaky with greasepaint. Green put his head down, pretending to focus on his buttons, fumbling nervously, unsure of what to do next.

He heard a grunt and looked up to see the trooper pulling his knife out from the base of the first kraut's neck, releasing a crimson gush, and then turned toward his startled comrade. In a flash, he switched the knife to his right hand as the other soldier tried to bring his gun to bear. The trooper knocked it aside with his left hand and plunged the knife straight ahead into the left side of the German's chest. The German's knees buckled, and with a soft moan he slumped to the ground, the knife still protruding. The paratrooper turned to Green and put a finger to his lips. Green nodded and finished buttoning his pants. The other trooper pulled the knife from the dead

German, wiped it on his pants, then gestured for Green to follow.

Green held up his hand, then bent over the first German and removed his MP40 submachine gun and two extra clips of ammo from his belt. The other trooper scanned the area while Green stripped the weapon, then they hurried to another spot in the hedgerow where the other trooper stashed the rest of his gear. He quickly donned his helmet and slung a Thompson around his shoulder.

"Man, am glad to see you!" Green effused. The other soldier looked at him and nodded, his eyes red-rimmed with fatigue.

"Kenny Green, Fox, 506th." Green stuck out his hand. The other soldier hesitated, then briefly shook it.

"Gardner. Able, 507th. Know where we are?"

Green shook his head. "No idea. Aren't you 82nd guys supposed to be somewhere else?"

"Amfreville. This isn't it."

"Well, our drop was messed up too. I haven't seen anyone from my stick all night."

Gardner shook his head. "FUBAR."

Green grinned. "Yeah, FUBAR. Where to?"

The other soldier looked around, hesitating. He turned back to Green and shrugged. Green reached into his pocket and pulled out a quarter. "Heads east, tails west."

Gardner shrugged again in resignation, but his eyes were a little livelier as he watched. Green flipped, caught it, and uncovered. George Washington stared up at them, and Green nodded toward the blooming dawn. Without another word, Gardner set out, and Green followed, elated to be free, alive, and in the company of a fellow American.

CHAPTER SEVEN

1130 June 6th, 1944
Bomber Squadron 10, RAF Station Melbourne, Yorkshire, England

Mickey was in the dream. Willem lay in bed, listening to Mrs. Wimsby downstairs moving around in the kitchen. It was yet another variation on the same recurring theme. Once again he was on the beach at Sligo, waves off the Irish Sea crashing against the misty emerald-tinged towering cliffs, the slopes of Benbulben strangely near. He rode a horse, but her feet never touched the water, like Oisin's in the story. He gazed up at the cliffs, Benbulben looming above.

It was Hilda's fault, he came eventually to understand. The mountain near Sligo which figured so prominently in Gaelic myth was a frequent fixture of her tales when they were children, the stories that so mesmerized young Willem: Diarmund and Finn McCool, the Fianna Warriors, St. Columba's army and the Faerie Door in the cliffs of Benbulben. The Faerie Door that opened a way between our world and their kingdom was a favorite goal of their childhood explorations, when they would hike along the beach or in the hills.

As in previous dreams, Willem looked up at the cliffs and knew he'd have to ascend. But with the horse how could he?

The mare kept turning toward the ocean, and again Willem noticed her hooves did not touch the waves. Just like Oisin's.

Then he saw Mickey standing in the surf, smiling and waving. He shouted something, but Willem could not hear him over the roar of the waves. Mickey turned and waded deeper through the breakers toward the distant horizon – into the West, Willem thought, to the Danaan lands. His flight suit will get wet.

As always, the mare pulled and turned to the West to follow, but Willem tugged the reins around toward shore to contemplate the slopes he knew he must traverse.

And then it was over. Since last winter in Dublin, the dream, which used to torment him, had become an odd source of comfort. Ascend the cliffs, or ride into the West. It would be one or the other, and he was at peace.

Later, downstairs, Willem scooped up the last shreds of fried egg with a piece of toast, then wiped the plate clean. Mrs. Wimsby clattered about the kitchen. She removed his plate and took it to the sink.

"Off to the airfield, are you?" She looked over her shoulder with a shy smile.

"Yes, ma'am. Another busy day."

"Something big doing, hmm?" she asked without turning from her washing at the sink. Willem pondered his response, but Mrs. Wimsby continued before he could speak.

"Oh, you don't have to tell me, we heard all the planes coming and going. I'm sure we'll be hearing something on the wireless soon enough." She turned from the sink and held a small grey hand towel with both hands, a sad smile on her face.

"You will be careful?"

Willem blushed a little. "Yes, ma'am."

Her gaze lingered, then she turned back to her washing, concealing the tiny sparkle of tears.

"Do y'think you'll be home for tea?" she asked, head bent down to the sink.

Willem lifted his coat off the peg by the door and put on his cap. His eyes rested briefly on the picture of Mrs. Wimsby's son Lawrence, somber in uniform. In early 1942 he had gone missing somewhere in Malaya. Next to it was the picture of her deceased husband from the Great War. The reality of Mickey Mitchell getting the chop last night intruded, and Willem pushed the thought away. He took a deep breath.

"I don't know. It depends on the mission list and the weather. I don't think it's likely. Probably another late night."

"All right." She didn't turn as he opened the door and departed.

He got on his bike and rode down the narrow country lane toward the village and its airfield just to the east. The skies had cleared from the blustery weather of the last few days. Off in the rolling green hills, bells around the necks of sheep tinkled, and a dog barked almost perfunctorily. The sun broke through the patchy clouds and the brilliant emerald hue of the fields dazzled. Though not as green as Dublin, the Yorkshire countryside on a spring afternoon still took his breath away.

He stowed his bike outside the Operations building and went inside. Out by the hangars, mechanics and ground crew busied themselves with the maintenance and repair of their Halifaxes and Lancasters. Carts of bombs were lined up in neat rows, ready for loading. The ever-present smell of kerosene wafted on the light breeze. They'd find out which was their plane for the night and take her up on a test ride. Then back to waiting.

He went into the Officer's Lounge and hung up his jacket and cap, then poured himself a cup of the weak coffee. A group of flyers stood around the radio, one man hunched over the wooden case twiddling knobs, trying to pick up the CBS or NBC stations from the States carrying news of the invasion. The

BBC was mum, but rumors were that the American stations carried fairly current bulletins. At a table nearby sat Dennie Thompson, as usual nursing his tea morosely.

"Hello, Will." Dennie gave him a sad smile, then looked back down at his cup. Will patted his shoulder and sat down.

"You heard about Mickey?" Willem asked.

Dennie nodded. "They've already got a new crew in his bunk." A moment of silence passed while each in his mind consigned their friend to the ranks of the departed lining the walls, though his picture would never appear there. New mementos were banned a while back due to concerns about the effect on morale. Forget and move on. Ignore, really. Forgetting was impossible.

Willem broke the silence. "What's the gen from the Hole?"

Dennie shook his head. "Haven't posted it yet, but word is we're starting with daylight runs and then going well into the night. It will be a busy day." He gave him another sad smile of resignation. "I did hear one amusing quip." Willem raised his eyebrows.

"Butch was driving back to High Wycombe from the Air Ministry late one night recently and a motorcycle constable pulled him over for speeding on the London Road."

Dennie's father worked on the Bomber Command staff at High Wycombe and occasionally shared bits of gossip about Sir Arthur Harris, their Commander-in-Chief.

"The constable said to him, 'You might have killed someone, sir', to which Harris responded, 'Young man, I kill thousands of people every night!" Dennie broke into a wicked grin.

"Oh, my," Willem responded, the darkness of this bit of humor exceeding his current level of cynicism. Dennie was always a step ahead of him in that regard. "Well, that's good news about the daylight missions anyway. We can see what we're bombing."

Dennie shook his head and heaved a sigh. "Yes, that's true. It also works for Jerry, too." He sipped his tea.

Willem leaned over. "We haven't had any significant fighter resistance in weeks. And besides, during the day you can see the flak clouds better."

"But not the tracers."

"Still, I like the odds better during daylight. I can see where I'm going."

Dennie gave his friend a pitying look. "I forget what a sprog you still are."

Willem chuckled at the joke between them. His welcome to the unit alternated on a daily basis between appreciation for the help, confusion about his accent and nationality, admiration of his flying skills, and cold indifference because he was an outsider. He knew he was at least accepted a by his crew after all the long hours of training, and especially since Duisberg. It was "a ropey bit" in the words of Colin Morrison. The tail gunner, and by extension the rest of the crew, absolved Willem over pints the next night when they welcomed their new radio man at Betty's Bar in York with a bit of verbal hazing. Their mission was scrubbed by the Met man due to rain, and, under the guise of indoctrinating him, they explained their lingo and the skinny on the officers of the squadron.

Of all the new experiences since joining his new unit, the new slang was the most reliable source of confusion and entertainment. The new men were "sprogs", the ground crew called "erks", the fuel trucks on the flight line were "bonzers." No detail, no matter how trivial or horrific, was immune from being twisted, mocked, trivialized or transformed by some clever or silly neologism. Far and away his favorite was "gone for a Burton."

"Gone for a Burton? Why, that's right here," Jock Tipton said, lifting his pint. Willem would find out later this would be the most he'd hear from Jock, who was usually very quiet, even when drinking.

"You mean the beer?" Willem asked.

More laughter.

"It's for the WAAFs, really, 'the one's too dim to realize what's going on." This from Nate Hensely, the navigator. He continued in a falsetto: "Oh, where's my Archie? How come he's not back yet? Oh, there now, miss, he's just gone for a Burton."

Colin Morrison chortled deep and throaty. He was a swarthy squat Welshman who had escaped from the coal mines by joining the bomber life. He was the perfect size for the cramped tail position and the most seasoned veteran of the crew, having survived two crashes by quick and nimble egress from the wounded aircraft. Colin returned healthy and uninjured from both wrecks. The first required a long walk south into Vichy France, then across the Pyrenees into Spain. The second one, over Happy Valley, was trickier. Colin jumped at low altitude as soon as he thought they were out of Germany, then the pilot nursed the wounded engines long enough to successfully belly land in a farm field in Belgium. Colin and the pilot met up and were secretly shuttled back to England by partisans and Resistance fighters. The remainder of both crews remained missing. They were assumed to have gotten the chop.

"They serve Burtons in Germany?" Colin chimed in. The crowd broke up again.

"If you say, ahh, he got the chop, they get all weepy," Nate concluded. The little group laughed again and tipped their pints.

"It's from the adverts, for the Burton Ales. A picture of an empty desk, or a missing man in the huddle, and the line says, 'Gone for a Burton,'" Jock explained.

"Okay, then what's a françois?" Willem asked.

"Bloody Waddington is a fucking françois, that's who," muttered Colin. The table exploded in laughter again, then Hensley clarified.

"Someone who only takes the easy flights to France, the milk runs."

"And Waddington...?" Willem asked carefully. Hensley shook his head, the others nodding.

"The worst. You'll see."

The table boisterously christened Willem 'Will', despite his protestations that he'd been called Van in Canada. The new man would be just plain Dec.

"Fuck the canucks! You're Will to us!" roared a now obviously drunk Jock Tipton. Later in the evening, Willem cemented his status first by teaching them how to curse in Dutch, then by successfully completing the challenge of balancing a pint on his head while tiptoeing across the pub to raucous rounds of "Do You Know the Muffin Man?" There were some queasy stomachs the next morning on the test ride.

In the Officer's Lounge some of the other crew arrived and the noise level picked up a bit.

"How many missions have you flown now, Will?" Dennie looked at him over the brim of his teacup.

Willem thought for a moment. "Last night was twelve."

Dennie nodded appreciatively. "Almost half way. That's quite good for just a few months. I have twenty six since last year." Dennie held him with a somber gaze.

Neither courted disaster by violating the superstition about short-timers and the number of tours they had left. If Dennie made it to thirty (when, Willem corrected himself automatically), Willem would miss his companionship. Willem waited for him to continue.

"I joined the unit in August. Guess how many of my group from flight school are still flying?"

"No idea," Willem responded.

"One. Me. Everyone else is either missing, crippled, or flying a desk. In ten months."

The relentless attrition over the past few years was evident all around in the officer's lounge. Pictures, plaques, and remembrances of men from the unit, few more than two or three years old, none of whom were still around. With only a few months of combat, Willem was already well on his way to being an experienced hand.

"Well, it's nothing to worry over. When the time comes, it comes. Until then, duty first." Dennie raised his cup in a toast. Willem clinked it with a smile.

"Oh, before I forget." Dennie reached to his back pocket and pulled out a folded packet of papers. "From Evie. She thought you would enjoy it. Something to divert you from Dickens for a while."

One night over shared pints at Betty's Willem captivated the crowd, including Dennie's girlfriend, with a brazen questioning of their missions and whether they were going about things the right way. The American tactic of daytime missions was a hot issue in the pubs and mess halls around England. The pros and cons were vigorously attacked or defended, depending on the experience, nationality, or plain stubborn pride of whoever was talking. Dennie looked on with a mischievous grin as Willem scandalized some of the other officers with his candid questions about the wisdom of dropping bombs into the darkness, even with the latest electronic navigational and targeting aids. His scientific background inured him to the blind faith that some of his peers had in the technical solutions the RAF military scientists kept adding onto their planes. Willem admired the brilliance and tenacity of the scientists, but it was another thing entirely being up in the night sky trying to figure out whether there were worthwhile targets below.

"That's always been the policy of Bomber Command. Prevent civilian casualties," objected Sir Grant, a genial member of the nobility whose A.C. 16/70 Drophead Coupe was the envy of the unit. Those in his favor were, on Stand Down nights, granted transportation to all manner of illicit entertainments, transported across the countryside in dashing luxury.

Dennie chimed in. "That may have been what was done before, but since Bomber has been in charge, it's all up for grabs. Just drop those bombs!"

"Bomber? You mean Butcher," grumbled another.

Sir Grant huffed. "Well, this isn't the bloody American Army. We salute and follow orders. Can't have everyone dictating policy. It's not proper. Harris is in charge, and the P.M. supports him."

Willem caught Evie's eyes on him as the conversation wound down. It was funny to him how even though he was technically a member of the Dutch unit, his American connection carried so much with the local girls. Dennie was a good enough friend, or too fatalistic, to be bothered by his girlfriend's Yank infatuation.

Willem unfolded the booklet and scanned the title. *Massacre by Bombing*, by Vera Brittain. Willem looked up, eyebrows raised.

Dennie chuckled and shook his head. "Evie is a bit of a radical. She reads all the papers and magazines, and follows the debates closely." Dennie tapped the paper. "Vera doesn't like the military. Lost her fiancé and brother during the Great War. She's been against the war from the beginning. But she's not afraid of a fight. She protested against the BUF in '34, got punched in the nose for her trouble."

Willem smiled and rifled through the pages. Anyone willing to take on the fascists couldn't be all bad.

"I'll read it and we can argue about it at the pub. Tell Evie thanks. She's a good woman, Dennie. You should marry her."

"I wouldn't dream of inflicting my family on such a dear girl. Besides, she deserves better than to be a flyer widow. But what about you? Is that clerk going to be keeping you company now? You Yanks are considered quite a catch."

Willem toyed with his cup and shook his head slowly. "No entanglements for me. I missed my chance."

Dennie leaned back and put his hands behind his head. "Ahh, now who's being unnecessarily fatalistic? Come now, you've got all the chances in the world, the pick of the crop."

Willem smiled and shook his head again. "You don't know the van Stockum curse when it comes to affairs of the heart. Once burned and all that."

Dennie considered this, then leaned forward with elbows on the table. "Some wounds are slow to heal, eh?"

Willem nodded. "It was so unexpected. Things were all set, we made plans, everything was perfect. Then, boom!"

"What happened?"

Willem shook his head. "Families. Mine. Hers. Her father gave me a speech in his office, and I stood there dumbstruck. I didn't say a thing."

"He objected?"

Willem nodded.

"That was it? End of story?"

"No, we kept in touch, but she wouldn't defy her father. I left after that to pursue my post-doctoral studies, and we went our separate ways. I haven't heard from her in years."

Dennie sipped his tea and pondered. "It's strange. No matter how we try, you can't outrun your family. In every situation, they are all there in the back of the room, looking over your shoulder, good or bad."

Willem leaned forward clenching his cup. "My father was a decorated naval officer. He met with the Queen in The Hague. Yes, we had some difficult times, and our move to Dublin was less than auspicious, but everyone has misfortune on occasion. Yet when he attacked my family, I said nothing. It is my biggest regret."

"Will, you can't argue with that kind of small mind. You wouldn't have been able to persuade him."

Willem shook his head. "I don't know. I feel as if I had tried, defended my family, it would have made some difference. That one man not only besmirched my family's name, but also ruined my chance for a family of my own."

"Ah, fathers. So much power over our lives, even from beyond the grave. I have no doubt my father still labors under the yoke placed on him by my grandfather, which makes it easier for me to submit in turn. We do it for our fathers." Dennie raised his cup again, and Willem clinked it with his.

"Does your father ever give you inside information from The Hole?" Willem asked.

Dennie shrugged. "Sometimes, but it's all hush-hush."

"Why don't you get a staff position, get out of here?"

Dennie smiled and shook his head. "No line-jumping. Not proper. I have to finish my tour, official and complete, then on to the next assignment. Besides, I'm not a career man. If I get out alive, it's back to the Square Mile for me."

Dennie looked over Willem's shoulder and covered the booklet with his hand. Behind him, Sheffield's new subordinate, Squadron Leader Sir Charles Waddington entered the lounge. Willem discretely put the booklet under his leg, then folded his hands in front of him.

"Ah, Thompson, van Stockum. Stand ready. Big day, what? Mission list is out. Lots of work. A good mix. Some milk runs, some hot stuff. Lots of support. Word is, the invasion is going well. We've got to keep Jerry on his heels."

"Very good. We're ready," Dennie responded laconically. He made no effort to render any other courtesies, a slight that Willem only recently picked up on. The nuances of British military social interactions still mostly eluded him.

Sir Charles stood with his hands on his hips, twisting back and forth at the waist in his impeccable uniform, alternately fixing each of them with a rigid, overly enthusiastic grin. That grin had earned him the nickname of Smiling Charlie from the crews. Some abbreviated this to just Chuckles, or Chuck. Then there were the more scatological names. An awkward pause lingered.

"Well. Right, then. Oh, and van Stockum. Do try to maintain position in formation, what? I appreciate you have some measure of flying skill, but this left, right, and center bit reflects poorly on the unit. Sloppy, you know. Shows poor discipline, bad example for the new lads. Nice and tight, there's a lad. We go out together, we come home together." Sir Charles bobbed his head, agreeing with himself in order to compensate for the silence from the table. Sir Charles checked his watch.

"First assignments will go up in the operations room at 12:30. Big day!" He turned and strode out.

Dennie's eyes met Willem's and they smiled, Dennie shaking his head.

"*Kloot zak.*" Dennie murmured with a passable Dutch accent. Willem almost spit his tea out with a suppressed laugh. He wiped his chin, smiling.

"Glad to see my lessons are paying off."

Dennie grinned back, and they sipped their cups in silence.

"What do you think of the Mark III's?" Dennie inquired.

Willem shook his head. "Those Bristols aren't as good as the Merlins. I can feel it. Just not as much punch. Handles about the same. I think the crew are still happy with the extra gun."

Dennie nodded. "Well, we'll see which ones are ready to go. Sounds like we'll be up and down quite a bit."

Willem looked toward the operations center. "Why does he always have to say something? I think the first three times were sufficient."

Dennie laughed. "Don't take it personally. He's worried you'll infect us with your American ways. All this fraternization we've been doing. Officially, we shouldn't be drinking with the crews, though all the good ones do it. It offends his sense of military decorum. But that's just it. He'd rather be proper and dead. Or as long as we are, at least. But it doesn't matter. In another few weeks, Sir Charles won't be around. If he's like any of the others, he'll get the chop or transfer out. Just watch."

CHAPTER EIGHT

1730 June 6th, 1944
Near St. Jores, Normandy, France

Sgt. Sloan unscrewed the top of his canteen and drank the last of his water. It had been a long day, and not exactly what they trained for. The two other survivors of the disastrous morning lay next to him in a brush-filled gully, swatting at flies. Lezynski, the other non-com from the 82nd, was proving an able partner. Turturro, from the 501st, was still an open question. So far he had contributed mostly glares and curses.

Sloan rolled prone, pulled out his binoculars, and looked at the farmhouse across the field in front of him. Still nothing. They'd watched for several hours now, with no evidence of activity, no animals, no farmer, no krauts. They were well to the west of the little town they'd spent the day circling. They had been dodging German patrols, getting in and out of minor scrapes, mainly just trying to stay alive and conserve ammunition since the costly attack on the machine guns this morning. Off to the northeast the low rumble and mutter of explosions reminded them of how far away from the action they remained. He rolled back.

"I'm going to check out that barn. You guys cover me. Watch the house. That's the only place I can't make. I'm going around to that side so that it screens me. If you do return fire, don't shoot me. How are you on ammo?"

Lezynski patted his right pocket. "One clip."

Turturro avoided eye contact. "Two."

"How about grenades?"

"Three."

"Four," Turturro mumbled.

Sloan still had two. "Turturro, give me one of yours. If there are krauts in the barn, I'll use these. If you see me running, get ready to shoot anyone coming out of the barn."

Turturro opened his mouth to object. Sloan had his hand out, wiggling his fingers, and Turturro grudgingly obliged.

Sloan put the extra grenade in his pocket and crept toward the barn. He reached the weathered backside and edged around, listening for any activity. He eased around the corner facing the small house and watched its windows. He took a deep breath and approached the doorway. He gently pushed the door open with the barrel of his M1, leaned back and peered into the darkness without exposing himself. He froze at the metallic click of safeties coming off and rounds softly chambered. He reached into his pocket for a grenade.

"Flash!" came a hoarse whisper from inside.

"Thunder!" Sloan replied. He withdrew his hand and pushed the door wider open. As his eyes adjusted to the darkness, he made out the shadowy figures of four troopers with weapons pointed at him. He stepped into the barn and closed the door.

"Are you alone?" said one in the front, his weapon still leveled at Sloan's chest.

"I've got two guys back in the ditch by the treeline. No one else."

"Any krauts out there?"

Sloan shook his head. The rifle slowly dipped toward the ground. Sloan took a deep breath. A voice came from the back of the barn.

"What is it? Who's there?" The four troopers visibly slouched, and one turned away, shaking his head. The trooper who had first spoken turned back toward the darkness in the back of the barn.

"One of ours, sir. A sergeant from the 101st."

A figure emerged from the shadows. He glanced at the white spade on Sloan's helmet.

"506th?"

Sloan nodded. "Fox company, sir."

The Captain swore. "Could this be any more screwed up?" He looked Sloan over. "You're welcome to join our merry little band here, sergeant. We're hunkering down until we can hook up with a larger unit."

The Captain turned away. Sloan caught one of the other NCO's eyes, and he shook his head in disgust. Sloan went to the door, cracked it, and peered through. After a pause, he crept out to the corner of the barn and waved the other two in. He stayed in the crouch with his rifle on his shoulder, covering the approach of each man. He was gratified to see them using good technique, staying low, covering each other, leapfrogging in a brisk and orderly cover/move drill. As the second one rushed through the door, Sloan came back in and pulled it closed.

"What's up, Top?" Lezynski asked.

"We've got ourselves an officer." Sloan gestured back to the Captain, who was now lying down on a pile of hay.

"No smoking," the Captain interrupted, pointing to one of the other enlisted men. The man had a Zippo poised, cigarette dangling from his mouth.

"Sir...."

"No argument. The krauts have noses, you know. And what if you drop that thing in all this hay? I don't want to dodge all these kraut patrols and then burn to death."

He snapped the Zippo closed with a flick of his wrist, then turned away grumbling. "Fuckin' chickenshit...."

The Captain ignored it. Sloan took it all in, then turned to his two men, who were watching expectantly. He jerked his head to the side, indicating they should take a break, then he walked over to the Captain, who was now reclining, helmet off, hands behind his head with his eyes closed. Sloan squatted next to him.

"Sir, what's the plan?"

The Captain opened his eyes. "Plan? Sit tight. Wait for reinforcements." He closed his eyes again.

Sloan looked at the others and they shrugged or scowled.

"But, sir...."

The captain's eyes snapped open and he frowned. "Sergeant, look around you. We've got men from three different regiments here, none anywhere near their intended objectives. For whatever reason, the drops were completely botched. We're almost out of ammunition, we don't know where we are, and there are krauts everywhere. My specific instructions from Colonel Atkinson before we embarked were to lay low until the unit is together. Knives and bayonets only. Don't make noise. Assemble critical mass, then take your objectives. Does any of this look like critical mass to you?" The officer waved a hand at the others.

Sloan thought about the speeches from Col. Sink and Lt. Col. Strayer before they had left about harassing and punishing the enemy wherever they were found: keep them guessing about our intentions, kill as many Germans as possible. This wasn't what this guy was talking about. One of the other troopers chimed in.

"Sir, we're sitting ducks here. We should go find some more guys."

The Captain propped himself up on an elbow. "These guys found us, didn't they? Sit tight, there'll be more. Get some sleep, eat some chow. We're not even thinking of doing anything until morning."

Sloan shifted from one foot to the other. "But sir, if we move out in the dark, we'll have better cover and...."

"Move out where? Do you have any idea where we are?"

"No sir, not exactly, but –"

"So where are we moving out to, sergeant? I have no interest in just wandering around. Best I can make out, we're a good five to ten miles from where we're supposed to be, and there are an awful lot of krauts between here and there. Judging by the noise from the north, we're way south and west of the beaches, and the invasion is on, so we just wait."

An uncomfortable silence settled over the barn.

"Sergeant, reorganize the watch. The rest of you get some sleep. We're not moving."

Sloan hesitated, then turned to Lezynski and Turturro – two men he'd never seen before today, now looking to him for guidance.

"You guys good for chow? I've got some stuff if you need something." Both shook their heads.

"Okay, get some sack. I'll figure something out." Their eyes flicked to the Captain in the hay, then back to Sloan. He gave them no response. After being busted three times, Sloan had finally learned the value of maintaining at least the pretense of respect for a senior officer. Cooped up in a barn far behind enemy lines wasn't the time to challenge the chain of command.

CHAPTER NINE

2230 June 6th, 1944
Near St. Jores, Normandy, France

Green and Gardner followed a low stone wall, watching the far tree line and zig-zagging toward a farm house next to a small barn. The sun finally dipped toward the horizon, and they used the lengthening shadows partially to conceal their approach. With several furtive movements they came to the farmhouse, went in, and progressed stealthily from room to room. The house was empty, looted and filthy, abused by the prior occupants. Bereft of furniture, which must have been either hidden or burned, it had a forlorn air. Trash littered the fireplace, empty shell casings lay scattered on the floor. In one corner, a pile of blackened, dried feces contributed a musty fetor.

They pushed through to the back, then dropped to a crouch at a noise. Gardner raised himself to peer through a window.

A soldier stood by the barn, swaying slightly as he released a long stream of urine.

In the failing light, the baggy pants and bulging pockets revealed the distinctive profile of a fellow paratrooper, but

Gardner wanted to be sure. He pulled out his metal cricket, and crept to the door. Remaining concealed, he click-clacked the folded steel, waiting for the response. After a few seconds, he did it again. Finally he leaned over and looked out the doorway.

"Flash!" he stage whispered. The man did not respond. He continued his unsteady urination. Green could clearly see the American paratrooper uniform.

"Hey! Buddy! Flash!" more loudly this time. The man shook himself, then turned slowly, looking blearily toward the house.

"Flash? Uh, what's it… uh, thunner. Thunder. Who's there?" He patted his pockets as if looking for something. "Where's m' rifle… uh, who goes there?" He took an unsteady step and squinted at the house.

Gardner cursed under his breath and stood slowly.

Green shook his head in disbelief. "He's drunk?" he whispered.

Gardner approached carefully as the other trooper swayed and squinted, hands in his pockets. He broke into a bleary grin.

"Hey! What's cookin' guys? Where ya been?"

Gardner looked around while easing the other man back into the barn. Green followed, walking backward, covering with the MP40.

Gardner pulled the man around in front of him. "Anybody else with you?"

The drunk jerked a thumb over his shoulder. "Jus' me an' Benny, an' 'nother guy from the 82nd, but he's out looking for krauts. Been here since last night. Lotsa apples and cheese and a big barrel a some kinda French plonk. 'S good." They looked over at the other soldier, who was passed out with a pool of sour smelling vomit near his head.

Gardner released the drunk and he staggered over to a bench and sat down heavily. He reached for a canteen, unscrewed the cap and took a swig.

"Want some?" He held the canteen out. Green took the canteen and sniffed, smelled apples and a lot of alcohol. He made a face and handed it to Gardner. He sniffed it and started to hand it back, then pulled it back and took a swallow, grimacing. Gardner gave it back to the first trooper, who took another drink.

"Well?" Green asked.

Gardner shrugged. "Seems quiet enough. We can hole up here for now, see what happens. Not sure what use these guys'll be." The drunk soldier was already dozing, slumped on the bench. The other snored softly.

Green unslung the German machine gun, took off his helmet, and sat down against a post. Gardner walked around the interior of the barn, peering through cracks, checking for other exits, reconnoitering.

"I'll take first watch. You get some shut-eye." Green nodded, then unwrapped some rations. He ate the dry food, washed it down with some water, then laid down and immediately fell asleep. Gardner looked over the sleeping men, then went to the door to stand watch.

Two hours later, Gardner gently nudged Green, who came immediately alert, looking around in the darkness. Gardner leaned close.

"There's someone out there. Can't tell who. Get up." Green scrambled to his feet and put on his helmet, slinging the German machine gun over his shoulder. The other two slept soundly and did not stir. Gardner gestured for him to exit the barn through the back door and take up a covering position on the corner. Green obeyed, kneeling in the dark and peering around the corner. Gardner stayed in the barn door. Together they both had a good angle on the yard in front of the barn as well as the field leading up to the treeline. The moon was out bathing the area in a soft silvery light, with deep shadows.

Time Bomber

Movement on the tree line caught Green's eye. The person moved with considerable stealth, but in the bright moonlight he was easy to pick out. A single soldier moving alone probably wasn't a kraut, and the effort at concealment made it more likely to be an American. But they weren't taking any chances. They tracked his approach and, when he was about thirty yards away, Gardner challenged him, and received an immediate response. The newcomer hurried over.

"Hey, who're you guys?" the new arrival asked.

"Gardner, 507th. He's from the 506th." Gardner nodded to Green, emerging from concealment around the corner.

The newcomer stuck out his hand with a big grin.

"O'Malley, Charlie company, 507th. Pleased to meetcha." They shook hands. O'Malley cocked his head sideways toward the barn.

"What about those other guys? They take off?"

Gardner shook his head. "Passed out."

O'Malley chuckled. "They were jumpy as cats when I first got here, then they calmed down real quick after they found that barrel in the cellar."

Green turned to O'Malley. "What did you see out there? Many krauts? Where are we?"

O'Malley grinned again.

"Lotsa krauts, but they are easy pickins." He reached down to his webbing and lifted up a string with oval shaped objects strung up. Green couldn't make them out in the moonlight, but he saw Gardner grimace and turn away.

"Don't know where we are," O'Malley continued, "but I think it may be off the DZ maps. I haven't been able to place us on the big map. There's a little town over there." O'Malley gestured off toward the trees. "I'll go back out with you and check it out if you want." He turned and went into the barn. Gardner hung back, staring off into the darkness.

"What were those things?" Green asked. Gardner turned to him with a hard look, shook his head, and followed the newcomer into the barn.

CHAPTER TEN

2240 June 6th, 1944
Bomber Squadron 10, RAF Station Melbourne, Yorkshire, England

Willem re-read the letter one more time before sealing it up.

"Lieve Hilda,
Sorry to be so long since my last letter. This airplane flying is really interfering with my correspondence. Spike shared the pictures of the children. Clearly the most beautiful and intelligent nieces and nephews a man could ever dream of. How is little John handling the arrival of his new sister?

I finally was able to obtain a copy of the Benjamin essay about Leskov and give it a read through. Interesting, but I disagree totally. Storytelling is alive and well, and you are proof. And as for information and the transformation of the art, look to cinema. Has he never been to the movies? I think his experiences colored his thinking.

Tell mother I will write again soon. I am lucky if I can scratch a note between missions, eating, and sleeping. Give all the children a big squeeze from Uncle Willem.

A kiss from your loving brother,
Willem"

He folded the letter and posted it outside the Operations Room, now bustling as crews prepared for the coming missions. Willem gathered his jacket and cap, checked his pockets, and went out to the loading area where his crew loitered around the trucks idling by the hangars to carry them out to the dispersal.

They had an easy test flight this morning, everyone cheered by the assignment to their favorite aircraft, Betty Bomb. Betty was a Mark II Handley-Page Halifax bomber, a tried and true work horse, but one of the dwindling number of Mark II's still in service. A little cumbersome in the handling, not too nimble, but reliable and strong. Willem especially liked the Merlin engines on the Mark II's, as opposed to the Bristol Hercules engines on the newer Mark III's. Despite all the talk about the Hercules engines being more powerful, there was a reason the Merlins were being diverted to the Lancaster production lines, and Willem knew he could feel it in the superior performance of Betty compared to the Mark III's.

Betty rolled off the line at the English Electric factory in Samlesbury, in Lancashire north of Manchester, on September 3rd, 1942. She was one of three Halifaxes completed on second shift that day, a record for that factory which stood until the end of the war. She immediately went into service and survived an improbable 64 missions in the following 18 months, only coming out of service three times for maintenance and refurbishment. Willem and his crew first met Betty upon their arrival at RAF Station Melbourne this past March.

After debriefing the erks about the minor problems identified during the test flight, they huddled around the assignment board, scrutinizing the details. The posted fuel allocation seemed large, sparking the daily speculation about the target.

"Too much for Happy Valley. Can't be Paris or the coast. My bet is Munich." Nate Hensley, their navigator, was often correct in his prognostications. Sergeant Johnny Bailey rubbed his neck then shook his head.

"Look at the bomb mix. We're light. That means we're going over the Alps. Extra fuel for weather. Italy, that's my guess."

"What do you think, Skipper?" McGuire asked with his Irish lilt. Willem turned to him with a smile.

"I have no earthly idea. We'll find out tonight." The crew would welcome a run to Italy. The flak over the Italian targets was reliably light, and the German fighters rarely strayed far from the border these days. Although no one in the crew would use the exact words until they were back, a milk run as they called it was a decent prospect.

That afternoon, the men slapped each other on the back and grinned when the assignments were posted. Willem's plane would indeed be flying to Milan. They sat through the mission briefing: a straightforward trip to the rail yards, another effort to slow the movement of German reinforcements northward. With the invasion on, many units were back to missions hitting the heartland of the Reich, or degrading German capabilities in other ways.

The remainder of the afternoon was spent lounging and relaxing, waiting to find out if ops were on for that night. The dicey weather of the last few days seemed to be lifting, and the Met man was increasingly optimistic at each briefing about a window for getting out. Then they received the word to assemble.

They climbed in and Willem looked around the back of the lorry. The men sat hunched on the benches. A few chatted, others smoked quietly. He thanked Providence yet again for the good fortune of lucking into such a group. All good men, and they worked together extremely well: most of them had been a team since training in Scotland last year. Even the new one, young McGuire, the radioman from Limerick, seemed to drop right in like a missing puzzle piece.

The truck swung around next to their aircraft, and the men clambered out into the evening air. The ragged clouds broke, yellow-orange light slanting down across the green Yorkshire countryside. The men sprawled on the grass, several lighting up cigarettes to channel anxious energy. They watched the ground crew finishing up the preflight preparations. Every few minutes, someone would get up and walk to the edge of the pavement and urinate, a nervous habit that would continue until they boarded the airplane. The men told Willem one night at the pub that they used to piss on the undercarriage of the plane for luck, but High Wycombe put an end to that when the landing gear on several aircraft collapsed on landing due to corrosion.

Archie Franklin, the chief of the ground crew, wandered over and exchanged pleasantries with Willem and Johnny Bailey, then returned to supervising the erks. Willem turned to Johnny, then turned back at a nod from Archie, who was drawing his attention to a figure approaching from the maintenance shed. Willem recognized him immediately and called out to the crew.

"Stay sharp, gentlemen."

Wing Commander Sheffield walked up and worked his way through the crew, who were loading gear and preparing to enter the plane.

"Good evening, Hensley, how's the family? Very good." A pat on the back.

"That knee behaving, Bailey? Good luck tonight." Handshake.

"Morrison, you still owe me that pint. I haven't forgotten." The squat gunner grinned and grunted his earthy chuckle. Willem watched with pride as the senior officer of their station worked his way through his crew, greeting each man by name and demonstrating with simple gestures and comments his personal concern for their success and well being. Willem knew this was someone to study and emulate.

"Ah, van Stockum. How's our Yank this evening?"

"Excellent, sir."

"Very good. You know, I would enjoy nothing more than to get some in as second dickey with you and your crew, but I unfortunately have other pressing business. Not that you need it. I hear very good things from Ops. You've made a very good impression in your short time with us."

Willem flushed with pride. "Thank you, Sir. I would enjoy a chance to fly with you."

"Another time then? Very good. Good luck tonight. Oh, I've been brushing up on my Yeats."[1] They clasped hands and Sheffield gave him a warm squeeze. The Wing Commander jumped into the truck and drove over to another plane to see that crew off.

Archie turned to Willem. "The erks are talking about painting an ice cream cone on Betty's nose when you get back." He jerked his head toward the painted cartoon on the fuselage of their plane, Betty Bomb, the cartoon vamp straddling one of their 500 lb. bombs. Just below her were the rows of little painted bombs, each signifying a completed combat mission.

"Ah, Sgt. Franklin, even a trip to Milan has its hazards. But we'll take whatever you give us. We always do."

"No stopping off in Switzerland, now. We've heard about you Yanks." Franklin grinned, meaning no harm by the jibe. It stung a little, but Willem returned the smile, letting it pass. There were stories of American crews landing in Sweden or Switzerland to sit out the rest of the war, fed up with the hazards and uncertainty of the bomber life. Nonetheless he took it as a sign of acceptance that the crews spoke about it openly in front of him. Not that the British crews never bugged out. It was just never mentioned.

Archie gave them the word, and they filed to the hatch to climb into the plane. Willem made his way forward and climbed up to the cockpit. Declan took position directly below him in the radio man's seat, and Toby lay down forward in the bomb aimer's position, the forward gun just above him. Johnny Bailey moved back and forth between the co-pilot's chair and the engineer's desk behind Willem. Nate sat directly in front and below at the navigator's desk, already busy with his calculations for the trip. Jock was up top in the upper turret, and Colin wriggled into the rear turret back in the tail.

Everyone ran through their pre-flight checks, then Willem slid back the window and gave Archie the thumbs up. He pressed the starter button, and, one by one, the four engines belched white flame-shot smoke, coughed, and rumbled to life. The ground crew pulled the battery cart away. Willem checked the oil pressure and throttles, then the revolutions and the magneto drop.

He felt a tap on his shoulder, and he turned to see the Flight Sergeant Fitter with the snag sheet on a clipboard. Willem signed the Form 700 saying he accepted the plane as ready for flight, and without a word the man turned and climbed out of the plane. Willem's headphones crackled with Johnny Bailey's voice.

"Engineer to pilot. Rear hatch closed and secure. OK to taxi."

"Thank you, Sgt. Bailey."

At Willem's signal, the erks unchocked the wheels, and he ran the engines up.

Just below, young McGuire checked the radio set and made a test signal to the airfield Watch Office. Willem couldn't help smiling at the sound of the Gaelic lilt in his voice, which reminded him of his days at Trinity College in Dublin, and the carefree times with Spike and the rest of their gang. And Pic. Willem pushed thoughts of her out of his head. What had Spike said? "*Omnia causa fiunt.*" How they'd argued about that.

Willem eased the plane forward and taxied out of the dispersal onto the perimeter track, moving down the line to the departure point. The sun edged toward the horizon, washing the Yorkshire countryside in a golden glow accented by long dark shadows. The Aldis lamp at the end of the takeoff strip flashed green, and he gave the engines full throttle. The Merlins roared to life as Willem fed them fuel, and the plane rolled down the runway. The crew maintained silence, allowing him to concentrate on the tricky take off, gently nudging thousands of pounds of fuel and explosives into the air.

Willem still enjoyed the unusual challenge of take off. He could visualize the forces at work on the wings, feel the flow of air, the lift created by the differential pressures, all the while thrilling to the physical experience of hurtling down the runway surrounded by flammable liquid and straddling steel-cased TNT. It was a certain and painful death for even the smallest mistake. The unique blend of intellectual stimulation and physical adrenaline was irresistible.

The plane lifted imperceptibly, then gradually climbed over the end of the runway and out into the deepening dusk. Minding his airspeed, he banked gently to the south and joined the rest of the formation headed toward tonight's destination in northern Italy. A milk run, but a long one.

Hensley began taking his bearings from the GEE system. Although Willem appreciated the improvements that the new radar systems made over the dead reckoning used by bomber crews in recent years, he still spent as much time as possible poring over maps and correlating them with terrain features that he could see out his windows, even at night. Moonlight on water, the shadows of hills and valleys, the different shades of gray created by forest and field –he used all of them to build a mental map of the countryside below, always sensitive to the need to drop his loads only on the military targets. Around the base, his scrupulous bomb delivery earned him both respect and derision. But he knew, as long as he brought his crew home safely, they didn't really care where he put the bombs.

"Hello, Skipper."

"Hello, Nate."

"Bearing 182 for now, Skip. Then 180 until we pick up the coast."

"Thanks, Nate. Everything running well, Bailey?"

"Yes, Skip." At every station he checked in, what little formality they might have had before takeoff now dropping away with the ground beneath them. The intimacy of the confined quarters and shared danger fostered more familiarity.

"How about a little weave, Will?" Morrison asked from the tail.

Willem smiled. "We're still in the stream, Col. Let me get clear first." He looked over his shoulder at Bailey. "What do you think, Johnny, high or low tonight?"

Bailey shrugged, ever serious.

Willem chose, one of the many minor, split second decisions he knew would determine their fate, none of which came with sufficient information to provide any certainty, effectively making them random coin tosses. High or low, bank left or right, run with the stream or apart. On any given night, the chance encounter with a stray German fighter or a collision with another bomber could end things quickly in flames.

"Jock, are we clear up above?"

"Yes, Skip, no one above us. Two off to starboard, one behind us to port." Always calm, Jock Tipton, the mid upper gunner, his eyes above and behind them. He rarely joined them on the drinking sessions, but when he did, was a funny and warm man, solidly grounded with his family back in Leeds. It was Jock who introduced the crew to his friend Ferris Newton from 76 Squadron, and had taken them to the pub Ferris owned, The Old Ball just outside Leeds. Ferris' wife Catherine took good care of them that night. The rest of the crew became more tolerant of Jock's quiet spells after that. He would slip away when missions were scrubbed to see his wife and children, returning only after putting the children to bed and spending some time with the wife. Although his odds of not returning to see his family were the same as anyone else, he seemed to Will to be calm, at peace, lacking the haunted, doomed attitude of many of the other flyers with families. The young single men, in contrast, dealt with the constant specter of death by living hard, drinking, and whoring. The human aspects of this existence never ceased to fascinate Willem, even as it took a toll on him as well. His beloved Dickens novels took on a new fascination in comparison.

He gently eased the plane out of the stream, taking up a position another thousand feet above the formation. With the German radar installations knocked out all along the Kammhuber Line through Holland, Belgium and France, they probably didn't need to convoy as much as they used to for punching through and overwhelming the air defenses. Some pilots liked to stay in the middle of the pack, letting the planes on the edge take the first hits in exchange for risking mid-air collision because of someone else's mistake. Others preferred to fly on the edge, or even apart, with more room to take sudden evasive action. Willem mixed it up, keeping himself sharp. Routine was the enemy, with its attendant, boredom – especially on long cold flights like this. One moment of inattention, one mistake, could doom them.

Evasive maneuvers in the cumbersome Halifax were a relative thing. Willem remembered somewhat ruefully his naïve exuberance about how much easier the bigger planes were to fly than the little Fleet Finch he soloed in back in Canada. Flying this thing is a breeze, he used to think. Little did he know how important the maneuverability of a smaller plane would be when someone started shooting at you. In the lumbering bombers, sudden changes in direction or speed were unlikely, and, when taken to extremes, could threaten the structural integrity of the aircraft. The best pilots knew where that fine line was between extracting the maximum performance from the machine and keeping it in one piece. Willem felt very much like he was still learning that aspect of his job.

The destruction of the radar defenses was an example of how much the bombers depended on the other services. It was something Willem admired and accepted, but others resented. Without the daring raids of British commandos, the intelligence services wouldn't have captured one of the Wurzberg radar sets that created the interlocking German air defense. Willem had explained the principles of radar to Spike during a visit to London, coaching him on the scientific principles of reflected electromagnetic radiation so recently perfected by British scientists, which were still secret but discussed in whispers by those in the know. Willem admired and envied the contributions British scientists made on the electronic countermeasures. They continually tweaked and improved the communications, navigation, and defensive electronics in the bombers, for which the pilots were always grateful. Whether they worked or not was another matter. At least someone was trying to improve their odds of success. There was some comfort in that.

Could he have been one of them? Willem watched their contributions to the war effort from a distance, as if watching himself through a glass wall or up on a movie screen, an alternate life that he could have chosen had he stayed in academia and devoted his energies to a different kind of war effort. But now he was in a bomber, heading out over the Channel, a different choice altogether.

Once out over the water, the intercom crackled.

"Permission to give them a squirt, Skip."

"Sounds good, Col. Mind the stream. You too, Jock."

The short, hammering bursts of the quad .303 Browning machine guns in the upper and rear turrets shook the airframe, and the smell of cordite wafted through the cabin. Once assured that the weapons were in good working order, they resumed their silent vigil.

After another few minutes, Willem made the announcement that signaled the real beginning of the danger.

"Enemy coast ahead. Lights out." Sgt. Bailey worked his way around the craft, ensuring that all extraneous lights were extinguished. The interior was now a dark warren illuminated only by the faint glow of instruments. Outside, stars overhead appeared in the indigo sky, the western horizon fading from orange to red.

The rest of the trip out was typically tense but uneventful. Willem edged the plane ever higher, riding every thermal and wind shift, clawing out as much altitude as possible, giving his gunners the widest view possible, hopefully putting them out of reach of any German interceptors they might encounter. He made random course changes, always seeking guidance from Nate and keeping an eye on the rest of the stream.

They made the Alps uneventfully and followed the group over the selected pass. Over the target the flak was light, and the clear night over Italy afforded a perfect view of the rail yard: its steel rails glinted and flashed in the moonlight, leading them to the target. No evasive flying needed tonight. They spotted the load as closely as Willem and Toby could work out.

"Left. Left. Right a bit. Steady." Willem made the adjustments following Toby's corrections while the rest of the crew scanned the skies for fighters. There was a sudden twang, the clattering of bombs tumbling out, and then the plane lifted, free of its load.

"Bombs gone," Toby announced. Willem held course for a few more moments until the photo flash charge went off for their aiming point picture. No picture, no mission credit. They saw the flash and Willem began his turn back to the north and home.

"Good prang, gentlemen."

Banking to the northwest, the high clouds broke, and the full moon flooded the ground with silver light. Just below Lago Maggiore twisted away to the northeast to the base of the mountains. Over the Alps they were treated to a stunning view of the mountains in moonlight. The snowy peaks glowed an ethereal blue white, the stars blazing overhead. The chatter subsided while everyone watched who could.

They passed over the small village of Brig, following the pass. Then came the village of Interlaken, bracketed by the two lakes, the Thunersee and Brienzersee. Willem remembered fondly a childhood trip with his family to Interlaken: the sailing and swimming on the lakes, the hiking in the mountains with his parents and siblings, back in the years before father fell ill and they had to move away. If the American pilots had the same fond memories of vacationing in Switzerland he had, he wouldn't completely blame them for wanting to sit out the war a while. The trips to and around Europe when they were children held so many magical memories: exploring old castles, stunning scenery, the endless pretend games and stories of knights and fairies, battles and rescues, wizards and princesses. His mother's relatives in Ireland and his father's family in Holland both had long traditions and stories, and Willem felt so lucky to be heir to such fine, learned people, many of whom had made important contributions with their accomplishments. On both sides, people of discernment and convictions who made a difference. Vincent van Gogh on his father's side, the Boissevains, MacDonnells, and the Jamesons on his mother's. They were his inspirations and role models. His father, especially.

Some of Willem's fondest childhood memories were of sitting in his father's workshop listening to tales of his daring exploits as a decorated officer in the Dutch Navy. Bram van Stockum was never satisfied with conventional thinking. He was a man of action whose daring tactical innovations were the stuff of legend in naval circles, earning him the admiration of his crews and the resentment of his superiors.

During one exercise, the assigned problem was to attack a coastal installation via a designated route that all but assured victory for the defenders. It was a famously futile drill regarded by the naval crews as rigged to be unwinnable. Bram van Stockum thought otherwise. Under cover of night he carefully maneuvered his ship through shoals next to the mouth of the harbor, sounding carefully with ropes and poles, steering through a gap previously unexplored. He snuck up on the shore battery and captured it at dawn, raising cheers amongst the crews and infuriating his superiors, embarrassed that the impregnable shore defense had been breached.

Later, he was sent by Queen Wilhelmina on a mission to the Dutch Indies, where he further burnished his reputation as a bold and unconventional officer. His exploits probably earned him an early retirement, but he then turned his energies to inventions, creating a series of technical marvels for which he earned only a modest income. His later years weren't as happy. His warm, quiet disposition turned increasingly erratic and explosive, the toll of an undiagnosed nervous illness which eventually resulted in the exile of the rest of the family to Dublin to escape his outbursts. It was the generosity of the Jamesons that allowed the van Stockum family to start over in Dublin, surrounded by his mother's Irish relatives.

"*Omnia causa fiunt*", Spike said last winter in Dublin, challenging his friend on his own area. He argued that if mathematics is the foundation of the sciences, and math meant certainty, then a strict Newtonian determinism should govern the world, with every effect preceded by a known cause, and all events predictable as long as sufficient information is available. Willem countered with a disquisition on quantum mechanics and randomness, playing devil's advocate to the position he and Dr. Einstein would be working to counter when he returned to Princeton. How typical they were discussing affairs of the heart in the language of science and philosophy. Spike, his roommate, debating and drinking partner, confidant, and now his brother-in-law. In one of the many unusual twists of fate that seemed to direct Willem's life, the whirlwind romance between Spike and his sister Hilda had resulted in the permanent inclusion of his friend into the family. Now Spike was in London, working for the U.S. government in some capacity that he could only cryptically allude to, and then only in a hushed voice, the two of them bent so close their foreheads almost touching, the smell of brandy and cigars on their breath. That was another benefit of this posting in England: the unexpected opportunity to see Spike and spend time with him and stay connected to his family.

Willem checked the instruments and verified their location. They were now well across the French border. The tension picked up a bit as the crew sifted the darkness for fighter pursuit. Willem occasionally made random course changes, mixed in with gentle weaving meant to expose the blind spot beneath the plane to the watchful eyes of his gunners. Finished with his bomb aiming duties, Toby McFarlane joined Nate taking turns on the forward guns, extra eyes and firepower to assist with defenses.

Reims slid past uneventfully. They were now on their seventh hour of the trip. Bailey passed the bottle forward so Willem could relieve himself again.

Just as he finished, Colin spoke urgently through the headphones. "Two Jerries far to port and aft, closing fast!"

Willem put the bottle down and leaned forward, craning his head to look back. "Jock, you see them?"

"Nothing yet."

"Colin?"

"Still closing. Not sure who they're tracking." Colin and Jock worked with the understanding that neither would fire until they were sure the enemy was after them and not someone else. At night, the first shot fired immediately revealed their position, and stealth was often more important for survival.

Willem glanced up at the scattered clouds, for the moment concealing the moon. An annoying impediment for good bomb aiming and delivery, cloud cover was a life saver when pursued by fighters. Would it hold?

Since turning home the bomber stream had spread out, scattered across the sky. The two fighters would have to make choices.

"One of them broke off, looks like he's after someone else," Colin reported.

"I've got them now," Jock added.

Willem gently eased the throttle forward, increasing air speed, clearing his mind and steadying his hands. The clouds broke and the moonlight sparkled on the Perspex windscreen. Willem cursed.

They flew in nervous silence, everyone intent on their instruments, waiting for the report from the gunners. Finally it came.

"He's on us! Corkscrew left! Now!" Colin yelled.

Willem heaved the plane over, pulling on the steering column with all his might. Loose materials flew around the cabin. The crew hung on as the plane spiraled and dove, shedding altitude quickly. He pulled out, pushed the engines all the way up and went into a steep climb, then repeated the maneuver again.

"Still on us! Turning aft! Now right, Will, go!" Willem banked and dove again, now accompanied by the sound of Nate retching below him, airsick from the violent maneuvers. The sour smell of his vomit filled the cabin.

Willem pulled out of the dive, leveled off, then dove again, opting for a run along the deck. He was intent on the horizon, scanning for potentially fatal obstacles. In his peripheral vision, he noted the position of the moon and picked what he figured by dead reckoning was a generally accurate course back to the coast toward England. The French countryside blurred beneath them as they flashed through the night to the northwest.

"Pursuit?" he asked the crew.

"Nothing here," Jock replied weakly.

"Clear behind," Colin added.

They flew in silence for a few tense minutes, then Willem checked in with the others.

"Can you give me a bearing, Nate?"

"Yes, one moment please. I have to collect my things. I seem to have ruined my map." Willem suppressed a small smile.

"Dec, how are you doing down there?" Silence. Willem looked back a Johnny Bailey, leaning forward from his seat behind Willem.

"Dec, are you all right?" Willem asked again. He jerked his head toward Sgt. Bailey to check on him. Bailey rose from his seat, revealing a wet stain across the front of his flight suit.

"I'm...here, sir. I'm fine. Just shook up. I'm fine," the radioman finally replied.

"That's good, Dec. We'll need the IFF signals when we hit the Channel."

Willem and Johnny exchanged glances, then Willem returned to the controls. He climbed a bit, then the beach shot past underneath, the water glittering in the moonlight. The usual homeward banter over the intercom was absent. Their nerves were still jangling from the close brush.

The smell of the forbidden post-mission cigarettes wafted up from the rear, refocusing Willem on the approach. He thumbed the intercom.

"Almost home, gentlemen. Mind the oxygen. Looks like I'm buying a round at Betty's."

"That's three, Skip," Hensley chimed in, now recovered.

"Yes, we better get a break soon or I'll be broke next visit."

He was greeted with hoots and jeers from the rear.

CHAPTER ELEVEN

0230 June 7th, 1944
Near St. Jores, Normandy, France

Sgt Sloan woke to darkness in the barn, surrounded by snoring soldiers. Why am I not sleeping, he fretted.

Since landing, the smell of manure and animals had followed him, gently conjuring into consciousness memories of childhood. Three nights he had to sleep in that barn as punishment. The beginning of the end of his childhood, when he looked back on it. It was after that that he swore he'd leave the ranch, leave Mesa, and strike out on his own.

He was fourteen, on the edge of independence and responsibility, enjoying the last days when he could disappear for a few days wandering the mountains, camping out, exploring. That fall, he'd met Wassaja, an Indian boy from over the mountains, about his own age, and together they had ridden all around the McDowell Range and beyond the other side of the reservation to the east.

His father approved of his new friend and allowed him to skirt some chores to spend time with him. Sympathy for the Indians and Mexicans was often discussed at the dinner table, and lessons of compassion and fairness were often demonstrated by his father's quiet support of neighbors in need and local poor families. It was a double life that often put the family in an awkward position. By day he'd sell farming equipment to the landowners and ranchers who would cheat the Indians out of their water rights; his evenings he spent visiting with the friends and family of his old friend Dr. Carlos Montezuma, the recently deceased local advocate for the Indians. Young Tommy Sloan did not understand the why of it all, only that sometimes at school he endured the whispers and taunts of kids whose families were less tolerant of the natives.

He saddled Apple up with a blanket roll, some canned food, and plenty of water. He rode out to meet Wassaja for several days of exploring. They rode all day, stopping to explore caves and rock formations in the hills. Late in the afternoon, they found a secret hollow carved in the massive sandstone towers. It was filled with a deep, frigid pool, and they cooled off in it, swimming and splashing about. They built a fire, and Thomas shared his canned goods, Wassaja his dried beef and beans, supplemented by a desert hare the Indian boy had expertly snared while Thomas watched in awe. Split, skinned and cleaned in a blink, the roasted meat was delicious. They slept under open sky, watching shooting stars mostly in silence. The next day they rode out again, resuming their explorations. Around midday, Wassaja became even more quiet as they approached another cave. They rode up to the mouth and sat there, Thomas unsure of the significance. Then Wassaja told him the tale of the massacre, when hundreds of Indians, men, women, and children hid out here, pursued by white men. They were caught, and the ranchers and farmers sat at the mouth of the cave, shooting in and lobbing sticks of dynamite until almost all the people were killed. Then they left the bodies to rot, which is how it came to be known as Skeleton Cave.

There was no accusation in his voice, but Thomas couldn't help but feel some measure of responsibility that his ancestors, cousins maybe, had been involved in the murder of this other boy's relatives. It bothered him in a way he couldn't articulate.

After that, the adventure went out of the trip, and Tommy wanted to get back home. He bid his friend goodbye, then rode hard to get home. He told himself he couldn't be late, though his father never put any limit on his time with his Indian friend. He pushed Apple hard, harder than he ever had, more than he knew his father would like, but he wasn't going to be late.

He put the horse in the barn and took off the saddle, then ran in the house. His father volunteered to clean Apple up while he ate. Thomas objected, but not too hard. Halfway through his meal, his father appeared at the doorway, face hard, and gestured for him to follow. His mother looked at him and saw the panic on Thomas' face and let out a deep sigh. The wad of chicken and corn bread in his mouth suddenly felt like a lump of dirt, and Thomas struggled to swallow.

Thomas followed his father out to the barn. His dad approached Apple.

"C'mere, boy. What's the matter?" The horse shied, moving his hindquarters away from the senior Sloan. He reached up and stroked the horse's neck, calming him, carefully moving down his flank. He pointed at the right front leg.

"Why is he so swollen? Was he limping?"

"He, uh, just at the end... we did a lot of climbing on loose stones and he stumbled...."

The horse shied again, pushing Thomas up against the wall of the stall. Unheeding of the discomfort and hazard to his son, Mr. Sloan ran his hand over the right hindquarter, feeling the welts in the dim light. He cursed under his breath. He went back to the horse's head and soothed it, stroking the muzzle.

Time Bomber

"Give me your belt." Thomas unhooked it and pulled it off. At the gesture, Apple stepped back and shied, eyes white. His father looked at the horse, then Thomas. He examined the buckle, holding it up to the light, and plucked a few hairs off, scraping a small smear of dried blood with his fingernail. He glared at Thomas, now hanging his head in shame.

"You clean up this horse, and you stay in this barn. You are sleeping out here. No one mistreats an animal in this family. I don't care how much a hurry you were in, or how stubborn he was being. You do not hit an animal."

He lost the horse. It was given to his younger brother, and he spent the night in the hay. Initially the term was a week, but his father relented after the third night, when Thomas came home from school with a black eye.

His mother fussed. "Oh, Tommy, what happened?"

"Nuthin'." She knew not to push.

When his father got home, he only had one question. "Who?"

Tommy shrugged. "McPherson."

His father's silence prodded him on.

"I had some hay on my shirt. They wouldn't stop razzing me. Then someone pushed me." His father nodded then turned away. He never knew whose decision it was to end his exile in the barn, his mother's or father's. He never told either of his parents about the cave, the story he'd heard, or how it affected him. In hindsight, he knew that was part of why he'd ridden so hard, to get away from that place, that burden of history, his people. He did a lot less riding after that. The next year he got his license, and from then on it was the truck. He never saw Wassaja again.

Just like before, the straw in the Normandy barn made him itch, and he shifted position trying to push the thoughts away and focus on the present situation. He lifted his head and saw the sentry by the door peering out and shifting from one foot to another, trying to stay awake.

Then, in the distance, he heard the low droning of airplanes, far off, growing louder every second. The chatter and banging of German antiaircraft fire started up, soon followed by the crump, crump of bombs. He listened, wondering what unlucky bastards were on the receiving end of that barrage.

The sounds increased, and he realized that the streams of bombers were edging closer to their location. As the booms drew closer, he could also discern the whistling of individual bombs. A single bomber roared overhead on a low approach, and the droning heightened as more bombers flew past. The whistling and explosions closed in. An undercurrent of muttered expletives filled the barn.

He rolled over and pulled his helmet tight over his head. He could hear others scrambling for better cover in the darkness.

Outside, the world lit up with the flashes and concussions of detonations in the surrounding fields. Blast waves ripped boards off the side the barn, and dirt and rocks rained down on the roof. The sound of glass tinkling from blown-out windows in the house added a delicate discordant note to the cacophony outside.

The onslaught seemed endless, but eventually the blasts moved farther away. The troopers gradually raised their heads, listening carefully for any further sound of attack.

After a few moments, the Captain called out.

"Anyone hurt?"

There were a few murmured negatives.

"Look around, make sure the barn's not on fire. Check for wounded."

CHAPTER TWELVE

0245 June 7th, 1944
Near St. Jores, Normandy, France

Kenny Green sat by the barn door thinking of home, staring off into the darkness and watching the flash of the far off artillery lighting up the low clouds to the northeast. The two drunks were still out cold.

The rumbles and booms reminded him of a summer thunderstorm rolling across the farms of his home in western New York. He'd be up late listening to far off radio stations: Harry James, Glenn Miller, and Kay Kyser, or his favorite, Tommy Dorsey. He would sing softly to himself, and the bursts of static would herald the approaching storms long before he'd hear or see anything else. He'd go to the window and peer out through the screen, the dead humidity hanging close, everything still. His brother wouldn't stir and the rest of the house was quiet. He would lie in the dark, listening to secret worlds, secret lives of music, glamour and intrigue carried across the airwaves. And, of course, the news from Europe. He'd catch the crackling and hissing BBC broadcasts telling of the Nazi invasions, the Blitz, until he felt the bombs himself. It's why he joined the paratroopers in a way, those late night sessions listening to the troubles of a distant people. Running from his own troubles, he found others in need of help.

The droning of distant airplanes interrupted his reverie. He saw antiaircraft fire arcing up, spiraling and curving as the gunners tried in vain to track the unseen bombers overhead. The sounds were off to the east, and he listened rapt to the rhythmic thumping of bombs landing somewhere in the dark French countryside.

The intensity of the thumping increased, the flashes brighter. Hmmm, that's getting a little close. The explosions were on the far side of the village Gardner and the other guy had gone to explore. Some of the flashes illuminated the small buildings on the horizon, but the village seemed to be safe for now.

After a few minutes, the explosions moved off to the north, and the droning gradually faded. Soon, the only sounds were the distant rumbles from what Green assumed were the beachhead battles. Everything beyond the village was once again quiet.

I hope those guys are okay. He cradled the kraut machine gun and continued his vigil. The other men snored softly behind him in the hay.

CHAPTER THIRTEEN

0500 June 7th, 1944
Bomber Squadron 10, RAF Station Melbourne, Yorkshire, England

The rest of the flight in was uneventful, and Willem landed the bomber without incident. The mood lifted somewhat as the men collected their belongings and exited the plane, joking about the mess the erks would have to clean up. Nate was embarrassed about his vomit splattered all over the front of the cabin. He had been once again unable to reach the airsick bag before the nausea overwhelmed him. He endured gentle needling – that is, until Johnny explained the source of the stain on his suit.

"Flying Officer failed to secure his private belongings," Johnny explained with a sly smile. Willem shook his head, not understanding. Johnny held up the urine canister, lid open, empty.

"Father Will was trying to baptize young Declan and he missed," Jock observed, eliciting guffaws. Johnny tossed the canister back inside the plane as the rest of the crew gathered on the tarmac under Betty's nose.

"Nah, he's just marking his territory so Johnny doesn't get any ideas about grabbing the controls," Nate added. Willem smiled at the teasing, gratified that everyone was ready to put the harrowing flight behind them. The erks shook their heads as they listened to the explanations, ruing the clean-up task ahead of them. Better than blood and guts, another remarked, to general assent.

"I'll catch up," Willem called out as the men walked to the lorry waiting to carry them back. He needed some time to walk off the nerves, collect his thoughts.

He struck out for the Operations building, long strides carrying him across the tarmac. Another near miss. He reviewed events to make sure there was nothing he could have done differently to avoid it. The responsibility for his men's safety weighed heavily on him, and though he knew he couldn't protect them from every hazard, he was merciless with himself in ensuring that no detail was missed. Try as he might, though, he could not focus on the details of the last few hours, and his mind wandered.

He looked up at the stars, and he thought about his mathematics, playing a little game of his own, visualizing the contours of the gravity wells created by the earth, the moon, and the sun, how they folded and twisted around each other in their orbits, the subtle deformations caused by their relative motions. In his little notebook he'd been playing more with the complexities of frame dragging, the relationships between matter and space-time, experimenting with the mathematics necessary to render it comprehensible, building on his thesis work that so interested Dr. Einstein. His hand drifted up to the letter in his pocket, as if to reassure himself it was real, his link to life after the war.

His mind went back to Dublin again, to that winter night he and Pic walked together in the snow, looking up at the stars, planning their future. They laid back in a snow bank together looking at constellations, Pic snuggled inside Willem's wool overcoat.

Willem pointed. "Those three are Orion's belt, and that one there is Polaris, the North Star."

"I know that. You aren't the only one who studies the skies."

He looked at her in mock surprise. "When have you ever put your manuscripts down long enough to look at the sky?"

She playfully slapped his chest and looked back up at the sparkling heavens. "Is it true that this starlight reaching us now first left millions of years ago?"

"Yes, in some cases. Some of these stars are much closer. That bright one there, Sirius, that light left just a few years ago."

"But in that time, it just travels across space, until finally it gets here. What if something bad happened – say, the star exploded – we wouldn't know it until the light arrived, right?"

Willem nodded slowly, bewitched anew by the by the lively mind and beautiful face he gazed down on.

She remained thoughtful.

"....And so?" Willem prodded gently.

"Well, if the star blew up yesterday, we wouldn't know for years. Yet the catastrophe is complete, we just haven't gotten the news yet."

He mulled that, unsure of the direction of her reasoning. "Yes, that is because of the limit on the speed of light. The theory of relativity states –"

She slapped his chest again. "Now, this is boring."

"You said science was romantic!"

"Science is romantic. You going on about it is not."

Willem looked thoughtful for a moment, then bent down and murmured in her ear.

"You stars, across your wandering ruby cars,
Shake loose the reins, you slaves of God.
He rules you with an iron rod,
He holds you with an iron bond,
Each one woven to the other,
Each one woven to his brother
Like bubbles in a frozen pond;
But we in a lonely land abide
Unchainable as the dim tide,
With hearts that know nor law nor rule,
And hands that hold no wearisome tool,
Folded in love that fears no morrow,
Nor the grey wandering osprey Sorrow."

Pic put a hand on his cheek and stared at him, her eyes glistening. Willem pondered the enigmatic play of emotion on her face, too in love and too in awe of her to look any deeper. She pulled him close and they kissed, burrowing further into the warmth of the coat and each other, oblivious to the winter cold around them.

Willem entered the Ops building and looked up at the board. They were the eighth crew back from the seventeen sent out that night. Two more landed while he walked in from the dispersal. The returned crews murmured amongst themselves at who was in, and who was still expected. The WAAF clerk erased and rewrote new information as it arrived from the airfield. She glanced shyly over her shoulder at the men milling around. Willem recognized her from one of their nights out at the pubs. She was a friend of Millie's. The girl turned and smiled.

He went into the debrief room to join his crew.

"We're just getting started. Congratulations, Flying Officer van Stockum. Your men tell me you handled a sticky situation quite well," said the intelligence officer at the front of the room. The men gave a low cheer and Willem smiled.

The intelligence boys from the Air Ministry asked their questions, taking notes about dispersals, defenses, difficulties encountered en route, and other useful bits of information they may have collected along the way. These could be raucous affairs if everyone made it back safely and the boys needed to blow off some excess adrenaline, but somber if losses were high or hit close to home. Tonight, some of his crew laughed about some joke made at the examiner's expense. The intelligence clerk scowled and scribbled furiously in his book, while Toby, Colin, and Nate chuckled. Even the normally taciturn Jock joined the mirth.

Two planes reported missing, both newcomers. Sprog crews accounted for a disproportionate share of the losses. This was the inevitable toll of putting unseasoned fliers in harm's way, often inside the most worn, hard-ridden aircraft spurned by the more experienced crews. It was a rare night everyone came home.

They filed out as the next crew entered, and several took some tea and sat at a table, not ready to turn in quite yet. A group of men were huddled once again around the radio, the familiar reassuring voice of the BBC broadcaster repeating the by now well worn sentence:

"And now for the latest bulletin from Supreme Headquarters, Allied Expeditionary Forces in Europe." This time it was General Eisenhower, a repeat of his earlier broadcast about the invasion. Willem listened, in awe once again of his role in this tremendous undertaking.

He sipped tea with the crew, the fatigue slowly settling in as the adrenaline wore off. He noticed that one of the crews still out was Dennie's. The WAAF edged over, making eye contact to get his attention.

"Millie says hello. She told me to let you know she's free for tea whenever you would like."

"She told you that?" Willem smiled.

The clerk blushed and dropped her eyes.

"Well, not actually. I just think she'd fancy tea with you sometime, that's all."

"Thank you, I'll call her." Willem noticed Declan McGuire watching the exchange with interest. He was fully recovered from his earlier fright.

"Dec, let me introduce you." He turned to the pretty clerk. "This is Declan McGuire, our radioman. Dec, this is…." Will hesitated, unsure of the girl's name. She didn't miss a beat, stepping forward with extended hand.

"Sheila Brown. Pleased to meet you Sergeant McGuire." Willem stepped back, pleased to have played matchmaker. He watched young Declan smile warmly at the clerk, and her blushing response.

Unbidden, another powerful memory of Pic at Trinity intruded. They were walking around campus in the evening, admiring and discussing the architecture of the buildings, debating the merits and deficiencies of the Neoclassical work by Chambers, and the Gothic work of Woodward and Deane, particularly the library. When they found themselves under the Campanile and the bells began to chime, Pic pulled away, in mock fear of the superstition.

"Our exams! We'll fail!"

Willem pulled her close, arms around her slender body, holding tight. "Now, you don't believe that superstition. I thought you were a Rationalist."

She squirmed against him, and he held her closer, devouring her softness, the faint smell of her perfume, their bodies growing warm.

"Willem!" she cried in playful exasperation.

He leaned in and they kissed, reveling in their passion. Willem submitted to the warm pleasure of the happy memory. Why was he thinking of Pic so much?

"Brown!" The clerk turned suddenly with a look of alarm.

"Sir!" Waddington stood in the doorway, clutching a sheaf of updates, pristine in his uniform despite the late hour.

Colin Morrison muttered an earthy insult, just loud enough for the others to hear, eliciting chuckles. The clerk hurried over and took the papers from the scowling Squadron leader, who turned and stalked out. She returned to her duties at the blackboard, updating the lists. Willem saw Dennie's crew was still unaccounted for, in addition to two others he didn't recognize.

One by one, the men drifted off to their bunks, but Willem lingered, sipping his tea, watching the board and the updates. He knew he'd have to leave soon to get some sleep because he'd be back in just a few hours to do it again. Someone tapped him on the shoulder. He turned to see Dennie grinning.

"Oh ho! Welcome back!" Willem put the cup down and gave him a big hug.

Dennie blushed, embarrassed by the open affection. "Well, it was a little diffy there, but we made it. You too, I see?"

"Milk run."

Dennie held him at arms length, sniffing. "Spoilt milk?"

Willem laughed, then noticed the wet stain on his leg. Small flecks of Nate's dinner stuck to the fabric.

Dennie followed his gaze. "Ah, christened by one of your crew?"

"There was quite a bit of christening, as a matter of fact. I thought that smell was following me a little too closely."

"Good show. You were waiting for me?"

Willem smiled. "Just finishing my tea. Off to get some sack."

He looked forward to the relaxing ride home in the dark and the comfort of Mrs. Wimsby's snug home. He no longer cared about the resentment that his billeting provoked amongst some of the other crews. Life in the metal Nissan huts was cold and uncomfortable, but his initial embarrassment at the better accommodations he had was long gone. After a long cold night up in the air, the warm blankets and soft bed were well deserved. Five or six hours of sleep, then back at it again in the morning.

CHAPTER FOURTEEN

0530 June 7th, 1944
Near St. Jores, Normandy, France

A rooster crowed, and Sgt. Sloan looked over at the group of sleeping soldiers sprawled in the hay nearby. The man assigned to sentry duty slumped by the door, snoring softly. He sat up, rubbed his face briskly, and assembled his equipment. Without a word, he nudged Lezynski with his foot and gestured for him to get up. Lezynski woke Turturro, and the three of them quietly buckled webbing and slung their rifles. Soft gray light streamed in through the new gaps in the barn walls.

Sloan turned at a sound from the back of the barn.

"Where do you think you're going?" The captain was watching them.

"Nowhere, sir. Just putting together a patrol. I want to see what's out there."

The captain shook his head. "No dice. I don't want you leading the krauts back to us."

Sloan held his temper and pressed his point. "Sir, we'll stay concealed. It just doesn't make sense to sit here and wait for someone to find us. If we put some feelers out, we may locate other troops sooner. At the very least we need sentries further out, give us a little breathing room with a bigger perimeter."

The captain mulled this over. "Okay, set up a perimeter. Not too far out, and no patrol. We'll rotate men and keep an eye out." He stood up and stretched, then walked over to the wall and relieved himself.

The scene outside the barn left them shaking their heads. The farmhouse across from the barn sustained a hit to the front that neatly lifted off the front of the structure, exposing the rooms within. Bricks and lumber were scattered around the yard. Nearby trees stood naked, stripped of leaves, their bark charred and barren. Small bits of greenery littered the ground like confetti, and all the surfaces were covered with a layer of soot and powdered dirt. In the lower branches of one leafless blackened tree, the recently liberated rooster perched, and crowed again.

Neatly spaced craters led out into the adjacent fields. A couple dozen yards in either direction and the barn would have been obliterated and all of them surely dead. Sloan marveled at their dumb luck.

They scouted out suitable concealment for sentries. Sloan knew they were effectively patrolling, and they widened the circles around the barn, looking for signs of German activity or other Americans. The craters created abundant cover, and Sloan could visualize several arrangements providing excellent interlocking fields of fire.

They made a pass through the adjacent woods, watching the road across the faintly green fields next to the farmhouse. No signs of activity – they turned back to the barn. Before they could move, they saw two more soldiers emerge. Sloan watched them look around, then he stood up and waved. They scuttled forward in a crouch, doing a fair job of concealment. What a waste, he thought, observing the talents of these highly trained paratroopers. His irritation at the lazy captain in the barn would have to be held in check.

The first of the pair approached. Sloan gave him an inquiring look.

"The Captain asked for volunteers to go check on you guys. I think he's afraid you're going over the hill."

Sloan swore, then bit back a sarcastic comment.

"You can say it, Top. He wants to get us killed," the second soldier interjected.

"You guys know this guy?" Sloan asked.

Both shook their heads in response.

"Me an' him are both from the 501st. We don't know him."

"What's your name?"

"Marino. This is Doolan." Marino jerked a thumb at his fresh-faced partner, a surprisingly young kid, almost comical in his paratrooper garb.

Sloan thought for a moment. "Doolan, you go back and tell the Captain we're setting up a perimeter. Make some excuse for why you have to come back out. We'll set up sentry positions – they'll just be very mobile. I want to see what's beyond these woods, and get on the other side of that road."

Doolan ran to the barn and returned, and Sloan organized the men. He and Lezynski scouted while Marino, Turturro and Doolan huddled in a crater. Turturro pulled a Lucky Strike from his pocket and lit it up, then pulled a long drag. Marino eyed the other soldier. "Hey pal, you got any more smokes?"

Turturro turned to him, cigarette dangling from the corner of his mouth. "Nope."

"C'mon, that was your last one? You just carrying around a single butt?"

"Yeah, that's it. No more."

Marino eyed him with a sly grin. "Yeah, right."

Doolan watched the exchange, eyes flicking from one man to the next. A single bead of sweat tracked through the dust on his pink, peach fuzzed cheek.

Marino turned to him. "You see anyone from your unit, kid?"

Doolan shook his head, eyes downcast. "No one alive."

"Bad jump?"

"No, we just came down in the wrong places. Krauts everywhere."

"How'd you get away?" Doolan shrugged.

"I dunno. I guess they didn't see me."

Marino stayed on him, despite the obvious discomfort his questions were causing. "What happened?"

Doolan heaved a big sigh and plunged on. "I saw someone snagged in the trees. I could see he was moving, and I started to go over to help him, but then a bunch of krauts showed up. They took some shots. The guy in the tree was flapping around, trying to get free, get his weapon. The Krauts just kept shooting him, and even after he was dead, they kept shooting for target practice, laughing and pointing. I hid in the bushes until they cleared out. When it was light, I went over, and I saw it was a guy I knew, Pudge. I couldn't even cut him down."

"That's rough, kid. I'm sorry to hear that. Don't beat yourself up about it."

Turturro interrupted. "Hey, why don't you two can it and keep your eyes peeled for krauts?"

Doolan gave him a wounded look and looked back to Marino. "Smokes, what's he so cheesed about?"

Marino shook his head.

Lezynski and Sloan returned and set them up in a string of positions in a curving line leading away from the barn. Sloan sent Lezynski to range farther out. After about forty minutes, he returned and conferred with Sloan.

"Nothing so far, Top. Should we go wider?"

Sloan did want to take the men further afield, but he was loath to openly disobey the Captain. They talked it over more. While in conversation, they heard a motorcycle in the distance. They crawled up to the crest of a ditch and peered over, watching the road. The barn and the damaged farmhouse were behind them to the left at the end of a dirt track leading from the road.

Two German motorcycles approached, then slowed to a stop. Sloan pulled out his field glasses and watched. The two riders conferred briefly, then one turned and roared off back in the direction they came. The other stood his bike, dismounted, and scanned the surrounding fields. Sloan ducked back down and looked at Lezysnki.

"Scouts?"

Sloan nodded.

"Yeah, but for what?"

Sloan thought quickly. "Get back to the others, tell them to sit tight, stay concealed. Tighten up the line so everyone is in visual contact. Get a good line on that road. Let's see if we can set up an ambush."

Lezynski looked at him. "That Captain ain't gonna like that."

"We'll see."

Lezynski smiled, then scrambled backward, keeping low to the ground. Sloan turned back to the road with his field glasses. The lone German scout remained by his motorcycle. Sloan watched the countryside behind the German, following the road back as far as he could. A cloud of dust caught his eye, and he followed its progress. Soon the source came into view: three trucks carrying German infantry, preceded by the first motorcycle.

Sloan's pulse raced. If they could organize before the troops got off the trucks, they could hit them with concentrated fire and have a decent chance of wiping them out. Once they debarked and dispersed, however, the superior numbers and firepower would make a standing fight a losing proposition.

He rolled back over and looked back for Lezynski, who was now returning in a crouched run.

"They're all coming forward."

"Good. Let's set up there and there and here, get good lines of fire on those trucks. Don't shoot until I do. We've got to move quickly."

They hastily deployed while a few of the Germans milled around the trucks. Just as Sloan and his men settled into their positions, the two motorcycles started down the dirt track toward the barn, carrying two other soldiers.

Lezynski tapped Sloan's shoulder. "Uh-oh, Top, you seein' this?"

"Yeah. Don't move."

The Germans stopped short of the barn and dismounted, then spread out, two covering the entrance from a distance, while the other two approached the door.

"Goddam," Sloan muttered under his breath. He knew if they opened fire on the trucks, the Captain and the others were as good as dead. If the Captain opened fire, they at least could hit the trucks and prevent the rest of the krauts from jumping in. It all depended on the men in the barn.

They watched in tense silence. The two Germans approached the door and pushed it open gingerly. After a moment, the one standing next to the door gestured excitedly for the others to come over. Sloan cursed again.

One of the Germans backed out of the barn with his rifle leveled, followed by the Captain and the remaining three Americans with their hands up over their heads. The other three Germans followed, weapons pointed at the Americans. One of the Germans called to the trucks, and immediately they emptied, several squads hustling down the track toward the barn. Sloan made a decision.

"Okay, that settles it. Let's get out of here."

"What about..." Lezynski asked.

"They're history either way. If we open up, the krauts'll kill 'em, and we don't stand a chance now that they're all spread out. We missed it."

They scuttled back through the brush and disappeared into the small stand of trees.

CHAPTER FIFTEEN

1030 June 7th, 1944
Near St. Jores, Normandy, France

Kenny Green swatted at a black fly and peeked through the sliver of daylight from the outside world. He really wanted to get inside the farmhouse and use one of the upper windows for his vantage, but the two other troopers were still passed out from their bender, and the sun was too high in the sky to risk moving around out in the open.

Gardner and the other trooper still weren't back yet. The hairs on the back of Green's neck went up at a scuffling sound along the side of the barn. He raised the German machine gun and stepped toward the door.

"Flash," came a quiet whisper from the other side of the door.

"Thunder," he whispered back, and Gardner stepped into view.

"We've got to get out of here." Gardner's grim face emphasized the circles under his eyes, bigger and darker than before.

"Where's the other guy?"

Gardner shook his head. "I left him. These guys are bad news. We've got to go."

"But, we –"

"Get your stuff. I'm leaving. You should stick with me." Gardner retrieved his musette bag and refilled his pockets with rations and ammo he'd off-loaded for his patrol. Green followed and did likewise, wanting to ask questions but holding back. The two drunks snored softly.

Packed up, weapons slung, they turned to the door to see O'Malley, smiling.

"Hey, where'd you go? I thought you were going to wait for me."

Gardner said nothing in response. Green sensed tension, but O'Malley grinned.

"You guys taking off? C'mon, stick around. This is a pretty sweet spot. Look, I've got some good eats." He held out a sack bulging with pilfered food items. Green looked at the sack, and then his eyes drifted to the objects dangling from the trooper's belt, what he couldn't make out in the dark last night.

Strung on a thin cord like jewelry were a row of blood-smeared severed ears, five or six of them. Green's stomach lurched as he noticed the last two. One was very small, the other a bit larger, with an earring in the dainty red-stained lobe. Green swallowed and felt faint.

Gardner took a step forward, his M1 level.

"We're going to find our unit. Good luck."

"His unit, or yours?" O'Malley made no move from the doorway. Gardner took another step forward. Green followed him, fighting nausea. Without another word, Gardner pushed past, and Green followed. O'Malley stepped aside, still holding the sack out.

"Hey, no sweat. You're missing out."

Green hustled after Gardner, walking briskly away from the barn, heedless of the bright daylight, putting as much distance between them and the barn.

"What happened with him?" Green asked, trotting beside Gardner. He stared straight ahead and made no reply.

CHAPTER SIXTEEN

1330 June 7th, 1944
Bomber Squadron 10, RAF Station Melbourne, Yorkshire, England

Despite the long night Willem woke refreshed from a dreamless sleep, and had a pleasant late breakfast again with Mrs. Wimsby. She shared news from the radio, the Prime Minister's speech from yesterday, the King's speech from last evening, and the optimism that the invasion was going well.

"There's talk of the war being over by the end of the summer. The Americans seem very hopeful. You don't think that's true, do you?" Mrs. Wimsby raised her eyes from her knitting, not daring anything but the most cautious expression. Willem glanced at the pictures. Knowing the years of sacrifice and uncertainty this very tough woman had been through, it was a fine line between keeping hope alive and raising expectations that would only court more heartbreak.

"It does seem to be going well, but one day at a time. We'll see what happens. Mr. Churchill has a keen eye for these things, I'll grant him that."

A brief sad smile flickered across her mouth. She pursed her lips and sighed, turning back to her knitting.

"Yes. Yes, he does. Do be careful today, Mr. van Stockum."

"Thank you, ma'am. I will."

"Home for tea?"

"I don't think so, but I'll telephone if things change."

How far he'd come since last fall. The end of the war? Nine months ago, he couldn't even have contemplated such an idea, much less discuss it.

It was the beginning of his descent into depression, about a month after arriving in Scotland for the final training on the Halifax bomber. The fall of 1943 brought horrendous weather to the Scottish highlands, with driving rain, low clouds, and unpredictable crosswinds. Yet the training schedule was relentless, the instructors unyielding. Up they would go, the insatiable demand for new crews to man the swelling fleets of bombers driving an inexorable training schedule.

It was then that Willem saw clearly the underlying madness, the pitiless brutality of the human endeavor called war, which compelled normally sane, compassionate men to make decisions certain to result in the painful deaths of those entrusted to their care.

The long months he had spent arguing to be posted to a combat unit steeped Willem in the obdurate ignorance of military bureaucracy. But that was just paperwork. These were human lives. During one futile argument with one of the instructors, Willem tried educating him about the toll the training casualties would take on the unit. He sat with a paper and pencil.

"How many casualties did we incur last week?" Willem asked, pencil poised. The instructor eyed him warily.

"Seventeen."

"How many flights?"

"Uh... a little more than eighty?" the instructor replied uncertainly.

"We'll call it eighty five. That's a twenty percent casualty rate."

The instructor raised his eyebrows. "So? Those aren't horrible odds. One in five. It's dangerous work. You've got to be optimistic."

Willem scowled.

"Yes, but for how long? How many flights to complete training? Twenty? Twenty five?"

"A quick study could do it in twenty, sure."

"So eighty percent survival per flight, over twenty flights, is about...." Willem scribbled furiously, rounding and estimating without a slide rule. He circled the answer, then covered it with his hand and put the pencil down, cold inside.

"Care to guess what the chances of surviving those twenty flights, with a twenty percent casualty rate? Or to be optimistic, eighty percent survival?" The instructor shook his head, brow furrowed.

"I don't know. Seventy percent? Sixty?"

Willem uncovered the answer and slid it toward the instructor, whose eyes went wide.

"Two percent? That's impossible!"

Willem pounded the table.

"Surviving this training is impossible if we don't change something! Flying in this weather is a death sentence. You might as well line the men up on the tarmac and shoot them! Get it over with!" They glared at each other, then the instructor raised a finger and pointed at Willem.

"I suggest you adjust your tone, van Stockum. The RAF has been doing this a bit longer than you have. I think they know what they are doing."

"But the figures..." Willem sputtered. The instructor cut him off.

"If you want to teach mathematics, perhaps you should have stayed in Canada." The instructor pushed from the table and stalked off.

The weather broke, and the accident rate dropped markedly, but Willem became obsessed with the probabilities. He knew the combat tour would be thirty missions, making the tour survival function equal to the mission survival rate to the thirtieth power. Using a slide rule on his own time, he constructed the graph describing the relationship, a sweeping hyperbola. As mission survival dropped, tour survival dropped even faster, a gentle slope that turned into a cliff.

Unable to resist further abstracting the mathematical concept, he rotated the hyperbola around the y-axis, creating a funnel shaped surface, very much like Dr. Chandrasekhar's model of what an infinitely massive sphere would do to spacetime: the dimpling deformity, the deepest of gravity wells. Instead of a degenerate super-massive star at the bottom of this one, there was death. Willem's death, and the death of all his friends and crewmates.

Two things changed after that conversation. To avoid thinking about death, Willem refocused on his work, writing to Dr. Veblen with more frequency and renewed energy, spending his free time more often on his equations and ideas. The other was the specter of the well, the pit, the hole that haunted him. On his worst days, the rest of that fall and into the winter, he could sometimes feel like he was physically falling into it, brief moments of vertigo that he concealed from the instructors. Oddly, they never struck while flying, no matter how stressful the situation. Sitting in the cockpit, working with the crew, his surrogate brothers, even in awful conditions and wracked with nerves, he was able to hold it all together, until later when they were on the ground.

Then the dream started, tormenting him until that moment of clarity in Dublin over Christmas.

He rode his bike from Mrs. Wimsby's to the base, the weather overcast and gray. Despite the questionable weather, the check flight in the freshly-scrubbed Betty went well. The plane now smelled of kerosene, grease and hydraulic fluid. The posting showed a relatively small fuel load, lots of bombs. Something in close. Willem was excited for the challenge. The crew teased him about the likely scrubbing of ops that night. Did Willem have enough money to make good on his debts? they asked.

"The Met Man will decide, gentlemen." Willem grinned. He liked nothing more than to spend his money on his men, even though it often meant more borrowing from his family. His lack of financial discipline was a running joke with his loved ones, one of his more endearing and frustrating traits.

With that thought, he scratched out a quick note to his mother.

> *Dear, dear Mother,*
> *I am curious to know whether you took note of the date of my last letter. I cannot tell you how great the satisfaction was to be one of those who dropped the first bombs during the invasion. Officially we did not know it would start on June 5th, but the instructions we got, the mysterious doings, our route and what we could expect while in flight, made us fairly sure that this was The Day. We did our job in difficult circumstances, although there was not a very big opposition. There hasn't been much rest the past few days, but the excitement carries us through. Our kind of job needs hours of preparation, the operation itself takes 6 hours and after that debriefings, etc. Then a meal, to bed, sleep, and again preparations. Of course, we did not know beforehand it would be rather easy, and the nervous strain makes your breathing faster. Soon it will be worse, when the Germans get more information. But I would not want*

to miss this time for anything, and I am very thankful that I resisted the temptation to go to the other station, where Bierens de Haanals is, for then I would be now between two squadrons and perhaps have missed all this. My crew is perfect, calm, matter of fact, and one cannot find any signs of being nervous. I sometimes have the feeling I am the only one who is.... but perhaps they think the same thing of me. I have the feeling there is an enormous energy in everybody and even the B.B. (body building programs) are better and more imaginative. The whole station comes out to see us off when we take off, with their thumbs up and this is a pleasant feeling. I know how you and Hilda enter into my feeling now, and this is an invigorating feeling.

If only you could hear all the fantastic stories people tell, more interesting than the most terrible spy thriller!! Did I write you that I saw in London Aunt Mia quite often? We sympathized with each other about our tastes in literature. We talked about Dostoyevsky and she told me that you had written such a wonderful article about him. How nice there are people who remember this. I would like to see it some time. I long to read it.

Very, very much love from your son,
Willem

Willem sealed the envelope and set it aside, then spread out his clutch of materials. More topographic maps, mixed in with the latest monographs sent to him by Dr. Veblen from Princeton. It was Dr. Veblen who had recruited Willem for his semester at the Institute for Advanced Studies, one of the most stimulating and challenging six months of his career. It was during that semester in the spring of 1939 he first met Dr.

Einstein, as well as other titans of physics and mathematics. Sharing coffee with Dr. von Neumann in Fine Hall. Sitting a few feet from Dr. Bohr as he lectured on new discoveries in nuclear physics, further delving into the mysteries of splitting the atomic nucleus to release incomprehensible energies. Discussing the arcana of meromorphic functions with the nervous and shy Dr. Weyl.

In his letters, Dr. Einstein had posed some questions to Willem about quantum statistics, and Willem in turn had asked Dr. Veblen to send him some background reading. In the last mail came several monographs, the latest work by Dr. Dirac, and some of Dr. von Neumann's writings from the thirties. The tug of war between the physicists and mathematicians about how to articulate the puzzles of quantum mechanics amused and stimulated Willem. He shared Dr. Einstein's intuition that there was something missing, some deeper theory that could make the apparent randomness of quantum paradox more comprehensible. Sitting in the officer's mess Willem smiled to himself, remembering the first time he heard Dr. Einstein almost lisp "shpooky" in his thick accent, and Willem had struggled to maintain his composure.

"Mathematics shows the way. Only then can the data make sense," he remembered from one of the many informal conversations at Fine Hall that spring. Of course, as a mathematician himself, this perspective appealed to his own professional vanity, but there was some truth to it. And how does the math move forward?

"A new metaphor," Dr. Einstein replied with a twinkle in his eye.

Metaphors. It was here that the intersection of Willem's literary interests and mathematics had its most productive use, particularly the images in the poetry of Yeats, read to him and his cousins by their mother when they were children. They would listen to her tales of childhood, spent running through the gray sand and foam on the beaches of Sligo, where her Cochrane cousins summered, and where she first met Sara Harriet Jameson, her good friend –Harrie, she was called.. The children spent long summer days having their own adventures in the moss-covered ruins and barrows, the surf crashing in the mists along the coast, climbing the hill at Knocknarea and scrambling up the stone cairn of Maeve's Tomb, all the while reveling in the tales of Celtic lore: Neave and Oisin, the battles, the hero warriors, tales read to him so many times by his mother, or his sister Hilda, embellishing with her own stories of the door in the side of the mountain Benbulbin, where the Faerie folk pass between the worlds. All these experiences and impressions informed his mathematical ideas.

The one line from Yeats, about the stars being like bubbles in ice, yoked together, particularly stuck with him. It was from part of Oisin's journey to the Western lands following the beautiful goddess Neave on the horse that rode across the waves. He had thought he would be away for only three years, only to find on his return that it really was three hundred. Yeats' intuitive understanding of relativistic time dilation amused and fascinated him, further sparking his imagination and the search for those new, better metaphors. He never tired of that story and Yeats' description of the heroes. So many passages he knew by heart, and shared with anyone given even a little encouragement, as his crew well knew:

> *"Caoilte, and Conan, and Finn were there,*
> *When we followed a deer with our baying hounds.*
> *With Bran, Sceolan, and Lomair,*
> *And passing the Firbolgs' burial-mounds,*
> *Came to the cairn-heaped grassy hill*
> *Where passionate Maeve is stony-still;*

And found on the dove-grey edge of the sea
A pearl-pale, high-born lady, who rode
On a horse with bridle of findrinny;
And like a sunset were her lips,
A stormy sunset on doomed ships;"

And then there was his mathematics. He picked up the thin pages of the top monograph. Dr. Veblen was the perfect resource, forwarding papers published by the Institute and notes from the lectures of many important guests. The packets of technical materials gave the censors fits. This one was from Dirac's stay at the institute during the 1935 academic year, notes from his lectures kept by Podolsky and Rosen. Quantum electrodynamics. Quite a departure from his own expertise in algebraic geometry and general relativity, but, then again, that's why Dr. Einstein gave him the challenge. Inside the cover Dr. Veblen had written a brief note:

"My best wishes for your endeavors, both kinds. Mrs. Veblen sends her warm regards. We received a nice note from your mother after our visit in Washington. She is well and awaiting your safe return, as are we all. Sincerely, Oswald Veblen."

Willem put the thin book down, and picked up the topographic maps of the French coast and Normandy, betting on the prospect of a support mission tonight. Dennie loved to tease him about his reading habits, which jumped back and forth between literature, mathematics, and operations manuals and maps. Willem took the ribbing in stride.

"It's how I stay sharp. I need a little variety to keep me occupied."

"Mail!"

Willem looked up from his maps and watched the postal clerk reaching into his bag. He called names and one by one his colleagues came forward to claim their messages.

"van Stockum!" Willem exchanged the letter to his mother for the newly arrived one. The clerk handed him a thin envelope postmarked from London, and he instantly recognized Spike's handwriting.

After leaving Princeton for the University of Maryland, Willem stayed with Spike and Hilda in Washington, and it was while living with them and commuting to College Park that the decision to join the Air Force was born. Spike was in the Civil Service and would share tales of wartime preparations, while mother read them letters from Holland, smuggled out from friends and family suffering under Nazi oppression. All around him, the government prepared for war, even before the U.S. had been attacked, even despite the isolationism – or, more frustrating, the complacency of most Americans. Sitting around the kitchen of their house in Chevy Chase, the nieces and nephews clamoring and laughing all around, Willem contemplated the horrors endured by their relatives back in Holland. The summer of 1941, he decided to make his own contribution.

He read the letter with relish, always enjoying the news from Spike about the family, the antics of his nephews and nieces, his sister's literary achievements, and the cryptic tidbits about his work. Willem devoured the letter, then caught his breath.

> "You'll be interested to hear that I saw an acquaintance from Trinity in the street on the way to the office, and he gave me news of Pic. She is living in London, but more importantly, her husband has been missing for over three months now. He was thought killed in an air raid, the office where he worked reduced to rubble, but he never turned up (so to speak). Everyone is a bit mystified. Meanwhile, she asks after you. She says she didn't know how to reach you

after you left Princeton and had no new address. She was too embarrassed to write to Hilda or mother, and she didn't want to raise eyebrows by asking anyone from Dublin. But she wants you to write."

The intrusive memories of Pic that had been with him for the last few days surged up again, like a pot boiling over. Pic Gwynn, the love of his life. Willem thought the bittersweet memories of the time in Dublin were contained, under control, but this letter just lifted off the lid, revealing the roiling emotions so long submerged and avoided.

It had all been tucked neatly out of view, locked away and shunned. He preferred to spend time immersed in noise and laughter, surrounded by his nephews and nieces and their warmth and energy, sharing meals in the kitchen with his sister and mother, or all alone with his equations, smoking by the fire and sipping a drink. But here it was, the wound long concealed, open once again, and it was too much to bear. All the regrets and doubts bubbled up with startling ferocity.

Willem reread the letter, trying to puzzle out any hidden meanings between the lines of Spike's prose. He'd been such a good friend when they first broke up, and had gently supported him again when news of Pic's marriage to someone else brought their friendly correspondence to a gradual end.

Was this another chance? First the news from Princeton, and now this. Suddenly the stakes of surviving these bomber missions towered higher. Instead of the depression of the winter, when he gave up all hope of life after the war, now he had two prizes just out of reach.

Emotions churned, reawakened conflicts he thought subdued since Dublin. These were compounded by the stress, fear, and grief of the bomber life, of friends and comrades dying every day.

He put his hands to his face and struggled for control.

He felt a hand on his shoulder, then gentle pressure under his arm.

"Let's get you into the club room, shall we?" came Dennie's voice softly at his ear. Willem stood and walked with his friend, rubbing his eyes and averting his gaze. Spike's letter was clutched in his hand. They left the maps and books on the table.

"Bad news?" Dennie asked.

Willem shook his head. "Not exactly. It's complicated. It just… it reminded me of a lot of things, and it suddenly seemed a bit overwhelming."

Dennie nodded sympathetically. They sat down at a small table in the Officer's Club Room. Dennie waited patiently for Willem to continue.

"Remember that rough patch I had last December?" Dennie nodded. Willem continued.

"Spike saved my life. We spent those weeks together in Dublin, he really cheered me up, and we had a merry time with relatives and friends there. Before that, I had given up. I joined up to do something meaningful, after all the pettiness of my academic pursuits, and when it became clear there was just as much stupidity and frustration in the military, with all the other horrors added on, it was just too much. But after that time with Spike in Dublin, I achieved some measure of peace. I think I became resigned to dying and I would just do my best in the meantime."

"So now what? This letter?"

Willem held it up.

"All the things I thought were behind me, they're back. The letters from Princeton, they were more intellectual stimulation, something to help pass the time and not think about dying. But this. It's different."

Dennie took the letter from Willem's hand, silently asking permission with raised eyebrows. Willem nodded, and Dennie quickly scanned the pages.

"Hmm, another war widow courtesy of Jerry's bombs. Sounds like a perfect opportunity for some relaxation on your next leave," Dennie smirked.

A smile flickered across Willem's face, then he shook his head.

"There's that, yes, but it's so much more. She was my life. Had we married back in '34, I wouldn't be here. So much would be different. If I had, if we…." He shook his head again, struggling for words.

"It is a second chance, Will. This isn't bad news."

Willem looked Dennie in the eye.

"It's not a second chance, it's new. This doesn't undo what happened before. That wound is still there. That bomb can't be undropped. Ten years have gone by. She's older, different. I'm different. What if I go down to London and it doesn't work, again? I'm not sure I could bear it."

CHAPTER SEVENTEEN

1425 June 7th, 1944
Near St. Jores, Normandy, France

Sgt. Sloan peered out from the brush at the lone figure striding across the open field. Lezynski lay next to him, looking through the field glasses.

"He's definitely American, Top. No rifle, but he's got a sidearm. Can't see rank or insignia. He's coming right for us."

"Want me to drop him, Top?" Marino asked from the other side. He rolled over slowly and brought his M1 up and sighted down the barrel.

"Not yet. Cover him. I'll challenge him when he gets closer."

The figure continued his approach, making a beeline for their position, their concealment apparently less adequate than they thought. Sloan nudged Lezynski, and held out his hand for the glasses. He looked across the field at the approaching soldier.

The stranger wore standard OD infantry blouse and pants, a helmet, a sidearm, but nothing else. No pack, no evidence of unit affiliation, and he walked as if he was hurrying to catch a bus – oblivious of hazards, no attempt at concealment or stealth. And he was still coming straight for them.

Sloan studied his face through the glasses. The man stared ahead intently, apparently lost in thought. Fair-haired, craggy features, some kind of scar on the left side of his face. Kind of a good-looking guy. Reminded him of a movie star he couldn't name.

He handed the glasses back to Lezynski and lowered himself into the brush for better concealment.

When the stranger was about 50 yards away he gave the challenge. "Flash!"

The stranger acted as if he hadn't heard and continued straight for them.

"Now?" Marino whispered, placing his finger on the trigger.

"Flash!" Sloan called again, louder. Still no response. Marino's finger tightened. Sloan muttered a curse.

"Top?"

"Flash!" The man was now only fifteen yards away.

"I'm gonna pop...." Marino started.

"Thunder. Keep it down, you're too loud," the stranger admonished as he stepped through the brush directly toward them. Sloan stood quickly and put his M1 to the man's chest.

"Hey, are you trying to get yourself killed? Didn't you hear me?"

The man locked eyes with Sloan. "I heard you Sergeant, but I didn't want to add to the ruckus. I've been watching your group for a while, and I trusted your discipline. You proved me correct."

"Hmm. Tom Sloan, Baker Company, 506th." He held out his hand to the newcomer.

"Tim Anders, Special Operations. Pleased to meet you. I've got some good news for you men. There are some equipment bundles just on the other side of these fields the locals and Germans haven't found yet. This area is pretty clear right now. If we make haste we can rearm and secure provisions as well."

"Hey buddy, how come no insignia? What unit're you with?" Marino eyed him suspiciously, weapon just barely pointed to the side. Anders turned to him.

"Sorry, that's classified." He turned back to Sloan. "Sergeant, ready to move out?" Sloan appraised him with head slightly tilted to one side. He and Lezynski exchanged glances, and Lezynski gave a little shrug.

Sloan gestured with his rifle.

"You lead."

Anders smiled and started back across the field. Sloan looked at Marino and tipped his head at Anders and raised his eyebrows. Marino nodded and took up a flanking position as they moved out, keeping an eye on the new man.

After a brisk hike, they approached a clump of brush and trees. Concealed under dead leaves, they found two of the large canvas supply bags that had been dropped two nights ago. The men dragged them out and opened them up, eagerly pawing through the supplies, jostling for position. Rations and ammunition were distributed around, each paratrooper stuffing his pockets as full as possible. In the bottom of one of the bags were several extra rifles and a Thompson. Marino grabbed the Thompson.

"Dibs." The other men looked at him, two weapons on his back, and went back to divvying up the food and ammo.

"Hey, pal, you weren't just woofing, were you? You're all right," Marino remarked, pointing to Anders. The suspicious glances from before were gone. The men were won over by the delivery of the promised supplies. Sloan knelt off to the side and scanned the surrounding fields, occasionally turning to study Anders.

Several of the men sprawled underneath the short trees, digging into the new food. Anders walked over to Sloan and knelt next to him, checking his watch.

"Sergeant, we can rest here a few more minutes, but then we've got to get moving again."

"We do, do we? What's the rush?" Sloan's sarcasm caught Anders attention.

"No rush, Sergeant, but I can help orient you to the surroundings, and assist you with some easily liquidated targets. That is what we're here for, isn't it?"

Sloan made no reply and turned to the men.

"Start packing it up. We're moving out." He turned back to Anders. "Okay, what have you got?"

CHAPTER EIGHTEEN

1510 June 7th, 1944
Near St. Jores, Normandy, France

Green and Gardner lay in a ditch beside a long straight road, halfway across an open field, scouting the cover of a long hedgerow opposite. Despite the relief of intermittent clouds, they were hot and sweaty, the familiar grit of dirt in every fold and crease. They were also hungry, despite the rations stuffed in their pockets, which were gradually depleting. In front to their left was a minor crossroads. Green waited for Gardner to satisfy himself that it was clear to proceed. The silent guy from the 82nd demonstrated himself an able field operative, and Green followed without comment.

Gardner's caution was rewarded, and soon they heard approaching vehicles. Down the road two long staff cars approached the crossroads. The vehicles slowed to a halt, and three German officers in long coats and hats got out and looked around. A fourth took out a map and spread it on the hood of one of the cars. Two drivers remained in the cars. The men engaged in animated conversation, gesturing around the countryside, pointing down the arms of the intersection, then at the map.

"I think they're lost," Green whispered.

Gardner made no reply, but lifted his M1. He sighted down the barrel, then looked back at Green. "You start from the left, I'll start on the right. If we do it quick, we can get them all."

Green wriggled around and took up a position to Gardner's left. He brought the MP40 up and sighted, tightening his finger on the trigger.

"Go," Gardner exhaled.

Green squeezed off short bursts, while next to him Gardner's M1 hammered with the familiar bam-bam. The figures around the cars spun and dropped to the ground. In just a few seconds, the four outside the car were dead on the ground, and the two paratroopers finished off the drivers by pouring rounds through the windscreens of both cars. The whole thing was done in about twenty seconds.

They peered over the rim of the ditch at the two cars surrounded by sprawled bodies.

"I think they're a bunch of officers," Green speculated.

Gardner grunted. "Let's get out of here." He looked at Green over his shoulder. "Nice shooting, kid."

Green wondered if he saw a fleeting smile.

They put several hours of hard walking behind them, and Green noticed Gardner was limping a little as the day progressed. They finally made their way through several fields to a cluster of trees and brush. The final approach was tense, but at last they could relax. It was a perfect hiding place for the remaining daylight hours.

Private Green unwrapped one of his remaining C-rats and nibbled. He watched Gardner surveying the surrounding fields. Gardner tensed up and reached for his field glasses, scanning the field to the east.

"What is it?" Green whispered. Gardner made no reply. Green waited, holding the uneaten biscuit. Gardner lowered the glasses and stayed in a kneeling position.

"Farmer. By himself. Headed this way." Green put the food down and rolled to his stomach, wriggling through the brush to peer through the branches. Off in the distance, a solitary figure walked alongside a small two-wheeled cart pulled by an old horse. The back of the cart was loaded with a pile of manure, a shovel handle sticking up out of it.

About a hundred yards away, the farmer turned into the field, led the horse forward, then stopped. He climbed up on the pile and began shoveling the manure into the field in wide-swinging arcs. The two paratroopers watched in silence.

"Looks like we're stuck here until dark," Green opined. Gardner watched through the glasses again, then lowered them without reply. He sat back into a squat, lowering himself to a sitting position. That's when Green noticed the difference between his boots.

"What's that?" Green asked, pointing to Gardner's right foot. A green canvas wrap covered the top of his jump boot, extending down the sides of ankle and underneath his foot. Gardner extended his leg and twisted his foot around.

"It's a brace. Broke it back in March on that big jump in the wind."

"Oh, that was a mess. We lost a bunch of guys on that one. Same thing, broken ankles and legs."

"I was at the hospital, then they were going to send me to repple depple because they didn't think I'd be ready to jump with my unit."

"So how'd you get to go?"

"This one medic made this for me, glued some metal strips into some canvas and then made these laces." Gardner rapped the metal with his knuckle. "Works pretty good. I probably don't need it for much longer. Really just for the jump."

Green nodded, even more impressed with Gardner's determination and devotion to the mission.

Gardner sat back and looked out through the brush again. "Why don't you grab some shut eye? I'll keep first watch, then you can relieve me."

"Have you eaten?" Green asked.

Gardner shook his head. "Not hungry."

Green reached into his musette bag and held out his last C-rat. "Still, you should eat this. We can scrounge later, but got to keep the energy up. C'mon, eat it."

Gardner gave him a funny look, and Green smiled back. He hesitated, then took the proffered ration pack without a word.

Green rolled over and munched the crackers, then took a swig from his canteen. He put his musette bag behind his head for a pillow and tried to get comfortable. He was still too wired, and remained sleepless. Finally he gave up, reaching into his side pocket and pulling out a folded up magazine – the most recent copy of *Yank*, which he'd picked up in the recreation tent the day before they left. He opened up the magazine and reread the article on the construction battalions and the work they'd be doing on the captured ports once the invasion began. Funny how, with all the secrecy they'd been subjected to, here they were openly talking about the invasion.

"What are you reading?" Gardner asked him.

"*Yank*. The one from before we left. I read it, but it's all I have. You got anything to trade?" Gardner reached into his pocket and took out two of the small paperback books handed out in the recreation tents back in England, neatly folded inside a magazine.

"Hey, you a big reader?" Green asked.

Gardner shrugged. "I'm a teacher. Old habit."

"Me, too! What do you teach?"

"High school. English and history. Small town near Pittsburgh."

"All right! I teach music. I was between jobs when I joined up. It's been a bit of a switch for me." Green grinned, but Gardner remained impassive.

Gardner looked down at the small GI paperbacks in his hand. "This one is kind of a mystery, about a blue marble. And this is *War of the Worlds.*"

"I have enough war right now, thanks. What's that one like?" Green asked, pointing to the other book.

Gardner shrugged. "It's okay. It's by the lady who wrote *The Fallen Sparrow.*"

"Movie?"

Gardner nodded.

"Didn't see it," Green replied.

Gardner looked down at the book and thumbed the pages.

"Anyway, judging from the back, I thought it would be more of a science fiction kind of book."

"A what?"

"You know, like *Amazing Tales.*" Gardner unfolded the magazine, battered and dog-eared, the March edition of *Astounding Science Fiction.* Green took it and fanned the pages, then handed it back.

"Why'd you think that?" he asked.

Gardner shrugged. "Dunno. The back cover talked about two weird guys chasing after a blue marble that had the secrets of the universe, unlocking the power of the sun, that sort of thing. Sounded kind of interesting. It was mostly about this dame wanting to get back with her ex-husband. Lot of stuff about fashion and celebrities."

Green's eyebrows went up a little, and he put out his hand. "I'll take a look at it. You want the *Yank?*" Gardner made the exchange.

Green eased back and flipped open the book. He got through the first five pages and dropped off to sleep. Gardner watched the farmer spread manure in the afternoon sun.

CHAPTER NINETEEN

1715 June 7th, 1944
Bomber Squadron 10, RAF Station Melbourne, Yorkshire, England

Willem walked into the Operations Room and looked up at the blackboard in the front of the room. Despite the cloudy weather and intermittent rain, ops were still on for tonight.

The assignments were out, and they drew an interdiction mission, close in, hitting the massing German troops behind Carentan. Although most of the other crews were happy about these assignments, Willem was not. Their assignment was to saturate the area - no need for visual identification or precision. At night, it was the most imprecise kind of bombing they did, and with the presence of French civilians almost guaranteed, it was the most troubling for Willem. The quality of the intelligence, the accuracy of the calculations and coordinates, the variability in the skills and attention of the pilots and navigators, all that uncertainty added up to almost a guarantee that bombs would fall on women and children, and it made Willem sick. His mood blackened even further.

Dennie approached and put a concerned hand on Willem's shoulder.

"Are you up for it tonight, Will? You know that the doctor will give you a medical pass, and Waddington isn't a complete ass. The worst thing would be to go up and not be sharp."

Willem shook his head.

"No LMF for me, Dennie. You know he would use it as an excuse to ship me off to Matlock for a rest. I'm not leaving the boys. I'll be fine." It suddenly occurred to Willem to check around to see who was within earshot.

Dennie also looked about, and then he lowered his voice. "It isn't a lack of moral fiber to have doubts. But doubts will get you killed. You know that."

"You know who I'm thinking of. It wouldn't be fair to him, not after what he's been through. Not for the other men either."

They kept an eye out for Johnny Bailey, Willem's Flight Engineer. Johnny had been an officer, then was stripped of rank, ostensibly for brawling in the mess, but rumors dogged him of having refused a mission and being branded LMF. He seemed determined now to redeem himself with his grim dedication to duty.

What really determined Willem to proceed was the example of Wing Commander Sheffield. He was not a man Willem would consider disappointing. His gentle tutoring, unflappable calm, and exhaustive knowledge of the art of combat flying were inspirational, and Willem would do nothing to fall short of his example.

"Know your machine to every detail. Fly every day. Become part of the controls, so that you can focus on the mission and the plane will fly itself. You become the autopilot." Though he looked forward to the experience, Willem was secretly very proud that Sheffield hadn't flown with him as second dickey yet, an obvious endorsement of Willem's competence as a pilot, new as he was.

Time Bomber

On the ride out to the dispersal, Declan MacGuire tapped Willem on the shoulder and held out a thin book.

"You left this in the mess, Sir. I only remembered it just before we left." He handed over the Dirac monograph containing Dr. Veblen's kind note. Willem took the book and stared at it. He opened the flap and reread Dr. Veblen's message. Somehow, it calmed him and cleared his mind. He looked up at Declan.

"Thank you, Dec. This means a lot to me. It would have been sad to lose it." The young Irishman gave him a smile, and they continued the ride out to the planes in silence, bouncing along the track in the back of the transport lorry. Willem tucked the book into his flight suit.

CHAPTER TWENTY

0021, June 8th, 1944
Near St. Jores, Normandy, France

Sgt. Sloan slowly shifted his M1, leaned his cheek against the cool wood stock, and laid his right index finger on the trigger. With his left hand, he flexed the thin wedge of bluish steel between his thumb and forefinger, the one-two click-clack of his metal cricket softly probing the night air. The dark figure in his rifle sight stiffened at the sound, then stirred. Sloan slowly increased the pressure on the trigger.

From this angle, he sighted easily on the silhouette against the glow on the horizon, the low clouds illuminated by artillery flashes and fires from the beachhead. Halfway through the third night since the drop, the fighting on the beaches was still much farther away than they hoped or wanted.

The shrubs ahead were poor concealment for someone on the crest of a small rise. They snuck up easily on the hapless soldier. What he couldn't make out were the exact contours of the rounded helmet moving amongst the leaves.

He blinked and squinted to relieve his burning eyes, and stared intently at the figure. Twenty yards behind him, the rest of the ragtag squad fanned out, waiting for his signal to proceed, urged on by the impatient new member of the group. Even though their bellies were full of rations since the resupply, fatigue was catching up to them. He clicked the cricket again.

Something has to be done about this guy. If we don't get moving soon, half those guys will be asleep. Can't move too fast though. Krauts everywhere, and goddam Turturro makes enough noise to wake up Hitler in Berlin. No way to get to him with a knife, those bushes would give away the approach. Shooting him will make a lot of noise, and where are his buddies? Lone sentry? Guarding what? What's he doing now?

The fate of the young man ahead hinged on the slowly mounting pressure of Sloan's finger on the trigger. It had already happened several times in the previous two nights of fumbling in the darkness of the Normandy hedgerows and fields, chance encounters with both krauts and friendly paratroopers. So far he had a perfect score discriminating friend from foe, and earlier this evening they picked up two new American soldiers for their group, Jones and MacDonald, in addition to a bunch of dead krauts. But there had been some very close calls.

The mysterious new guy, Anders, was working out to be a positive addition, despite the lingering doubts about his origins and intentions. His advice, though in Sloan's opinion too readily offered, had been reliably correct and useful so far. Sloan couldn't shake the feeling that Anders was taking control of their movements, directing them through suggestions and vetoes of alternatives. Although it bothered him, fatigue sapped his will to fight too hard as long as things kept moving smoothly.

He didn't like this particular spot, between two fields along a hedgerow – it was a perfect spot for an ambush. It looked more than vaguely familiar and the possibility that they had circled yet again frustrated and troubled him. This person in the bushes ahead didn't have much time to respond.

He clicked the cricket a third time, impatiently. The shadowy figure moved around, now with an audible rustle and tinkle of equipment, but no sign of a raised weapon. Sloan recognized the sound of an unsecured canteen, and wondered how this soldier had survived this long by himself. Exasperated, Sloan called out in a hoarse whisper.

"Flash!"

The response back was immediate.

"Thunder! Thunder!" The figure rose up, and Sloan kept the sights of the M1 on his chest as he stumbled forward in the darkness.

"Stop right there. What's your unit?" Sloan stage whispered, his rifle lowered only a little.

"Man, am I glad to see you guys! I thought I was the only one left. The krauts are everywhere! Where are we?" The questions came out in a rush, almost hysterical.

"Shhh! What's your name, buddy, and who are you with?"

"Sellars. Able company, 3rd of the 501st. Who are you guys?" At this point several other members of the group crept up to listen.

"Hey, pipe down pal," Lezynski cautioned.

Sloan lowered his rifle and rubbed his eyes and face with slow deep circles.

"Mixed group. Everyone scattered, some guys from 501st and 506th, a couple of guys from the 82nd. I'm in charge. Where's your weapon?" The soldier visibly wilted and he shuffled his feet.

"Lost it in the jump. Lost everything, but I've got my trench knife and some ammo, a couple of grenades. I've been hiding and dodging krauts for the last two days." He lifted his head a little. "You guys got any grub?" Sloan gestured one of the other men forward and pointed to his musette bag, then gestured to the new guy. The soldier unslung his rifle and took off the pack, pulling out a pack of rations. The exchange was interrupted by the breathless arrival of Anders.

"Sergeant, we've got to keep moving. If we're going to intercept those patrols, we've got to pick up the pace."

Sloan looked at him and scowled. "How much farther?"

"Just over that next hill, and then we set up along the road. Let's get to that next rise and I'll show you on the map."

Sloan looked at the rest of the group. "Let's go. We'll hit the patrols and then find some cover to lay up for the rest of the night. Marino, give him one of your weapons."

"Aww, Top...." Sloan glared at him, and Marino unslung his M1 and handed it over, keeping the newly acquired Thompson. The rest of the squad silently fanned out, and they continued their progress forward.

"Hey Marino, maybe your new best friend can get you another one. Maybe he can get you a flame thrower or something."

"Hey Turturro, go fuck yourself, huh?"

"Why don't you get yourself some more chow? Maybe he found a couple a boxes a steaks."

"What're you jealous? I can't help it if you're too slow to get the good stuff."

Turturro took out another Lucky Strike and lit it. Marino caught sight of it.

"Hey, I thought you said you were out of smokes."

Turturro shook his head. "Not for me I'm not."

Doolan crept up to them and whispered. "Top says to shut up. You guys are too loud."

"Okay, kid, thanks. Now go fuck yourself."

Doolan winced at Turturro's insult. He licked his lips and glanced down at Turturro's sloshing canteen. "Hey, can I have a drink of water?" he whispered.

"Go get your own water, kid. Go ask the sergeants." Doolan crept off.

"Fuckin' kid," Turturro muttered.

Sgt. Lezynski approached. "Put the goddam butt out." He glared at Turturro.

"Aww, Sarge....."

"Put it out, you moron. This isn't a boy scout hike."

Turturro glared at Lezynski's back as he stubbed out the smoke, and Marino smirked.

They arrived at the rise, and Anders and Sloan huddled over the map, a rain poncho draped over their heads to conceal the light. Sloan lifted the poncho from over his head and looked off into the darkness of the Normandy countryside. The waning moon broke through the ragged clouds and lit up the rolling warped checkerboard fields, dropping off to the northeast into the woods and swamps of the Douve River. The distant thunder from the beaches continued unabated, punctuated by the drone of bombers overhead dropping their loads behind the lines to disrupt the movement of German reinforcements, doubling the hazard to Sloan's group. Friendless and far from safety, both sides seemed intent on killing them as they ran from hiding place to hiding place, dodging German patrols and hoping for the best when the bombers rained high explosives down near whatever spot they chose to rest and recuperate.

Based on the information from the new addition to their ragged crew, they were well behind German lines, at least ten miles from their planned drop site north of Vierville. Some of the others were even further from their DZ's.

The red glow of the shielded flashlight beckoned from beneath the poncho, and he bent back down to the map to finish conferring with Anders and to make a decision about his crazy plan.

"You're sure about these patrols?" Sloan asked. Anders nodded in response.

"I've been watching them for the last few days as I moved around. They're like clockwork. They relieve these three machine gun nests every six hours. They're the farthest away from this encampment here," he tapped the map, "and they're overextended. The patrols are due at 0100. We can hit both patrols, take out the MGs and still have plenty of time to clear out."

Sloan rubbed his face, trying to massage the fatigue from his eyes and temples. On the one hand, his men were beyond tired, constantly on the run, hungry and stressed, surviving on a few hours of sleep here and there. On the other hand, since joining them, this Anders was batting a thousand. The equipment bags he led them to were invaluable, and they were now fully armed with extra provisions. He also steered them through two separate German positions, enabling their substantial progress to their present location. The previous days of frustration and circling seemed like distant memories now that they were able to move with purpose. Even so, they could really have done with some down time to eat and sleep.

Sloan stood up and turned to the rest of the group and briefed them on the German positions up ahead, pointing to them in sequence.

"Doolan, Lezynski, you, you're with me and Anders and the new guy. Marino, you, you, go with PFC James...."

"It's Jones, sarge."

"Jones. You guys move out to the right just beyond that shoulder. When you hear us start shooting, move toward the MG off to the right. Stay on this side of the road until you're right behind it, then hit it fast. After that, head for the one in front and to the right. Watch out for us, we'll be coming from your left. We'll probably be drawing their fire, so move in fast and we converge on the last position. If we hustle, we can do this."

The moon scudded behind the clouds, plunging the men into darkness as they broke into their groups and crept silently toward the road. Sergeant Lezynski squinted into the dark, struggling not to lose the man in front of him but also not get too close. He squatted down to use the light from the horizon to skylight the men in front and minimize his own silhouette. Every hour since the drop he found himself thankful for some lesson or other from the long weeks and months of training, and also the leadership of Sgt. Sloan. What a break to find him, unlike some of these other guys who were cut off from their units and thrown together with strangers. But they seemed like good guys, and they knew what they were doing. Despite the sometimes heated rivalry between the 82nd and 101st, he respected Sloan's skill and leadership. The 82nd didn't have a monopoly on strong NCOs, or bad officers for that matter.

Lezynski's attention was drawn off to the left by rustling and rapid footfalls in the darkness on his left. He knelt down and shouldered his M1. In an instant, a dark figure brushed past him and dodged another member of the squad then tackled the intelligence guy, Anders. The two of them tumbled to the ground and struggled. In the darkness it was impossible to see who was who, and the group approached the struggle cautiously, a circle of M1s held pointed downward. None of them were interested in diving on and risking their necks for someone they just met less than twelve hours ago.

Three muffled cracks sounded and the struggle stopped. They saw Anders stand slowly, an M1911 Colt in his hand. They edged closer, and someone kicked the helmet off the dead attacker and shined a flashlight on him.

"Kraut. Nice shot." The dead German's face still held a surprised expression, his features unmarred by the gore spilling from the large hole behind his left ear. Lezynski looked at the new guy.

"Why'd he come after you? He blew right past me."

Anders wiped his face with his sleeve then shrugged. "No idea."

The group digested this odd turn of events, then Sloan urged them on.

"Kill the light. Let's go." The group started forward, then froze at a low moan from the brush to the side. Lezynski went to the noise and knelt next to a prostrate figure.

"Top, it's the guy we just picked up, whatshisname. He's hit, looks like he caught one of those rounds."

"Where?" Lezynski ran his hands over the wounded soldier.

"Belly. Doesn't look good." Sloan cursed. Anders spoke up.

"Look, I know this may seem harsh, but we've got to move fast and hit those MGs. We don't have much time." Sloan looked at him with irritation.

"What's the hurry? You wounded this guy." Sloan angrily gestured toward Lezynski and the stricken soldier. Anders stepped toward him and leaned in, voice low.

"We don't have a medic, and he's in bad shape. You know as well as I do he's a dead man. Let's hit the MGs, and if he's still alive when we're finished, we'll take him with us. But we've got to move out." Sloan narrowed his eyes and measured this pushy private. Until now, his amazing knowledge of the terrain and tactical skill had kept his doubts at bay, but this was testing his patience.

"Why? Why the big rush?" The new guy pushed his helmet back, eyes darting.

"Look, these patrols have a schedule. We hit them at the right time, and we can clear out before they figure out what happened. If we just jump them, they converge on our position and we're outnumbered. Hit it and move, you keep saying. Well, we've got to keep moving. We're way behind the lines here, sergeant. The more time we stand around talking, the sooner the Germans find us."

Sloan looked at him, then turned to the group. "Lezynski, give him a syrette of morphine and make him comfortable and conceal him. You go with the second group. You others come with me. Let's get this done."

Just as Anders predicted, the three machine gun nests were relatively unprotected, and the German patrols appeared in the correct places at the appointed times. After twenty minutes of stealthy movement and sudden vicious attacks, a dozen Germans lay dead, with several more scattered into the night.

After searching the dead for useful maps and intelligence, the paratroopers reassembled.

"Let's go, we've got to clear out of here. Lezynski, take two men and run back and check on that guy. Marino and Doolan, get down on that road and watch for movement."

He turned to Private Anders. "What else is around here? Can we head straight for the beaches?"

Anders shook his head.

"That road over there goes to Carentan, and it's crawling with Germans. Over that way goes north, crosses the Douve, and then cuts east to St. Mere Eglise – but, again, loads of Germans. The fewest Germans are that way, toward the marshes and the flooded areas, but no way we're getting through that by morning, and there's Germans on the other side of that."

The other soldiers stood around and shuffled in the moonlit darkness, equipment clinking and rattling while Sgt. Sloan digested this information.

"Let's see what Lezynski says about the kid back there. We've got to find cover before daylight."

Sloan sensed that Anders had no objection to this course, and it irritated him that he even considered factoring the reaction of the stranger into his decision.

Lezynski returned shortly, carrying an extra rifle and a set of dog tags in his fist, out of breath and excited.

"He's dead. But the kraut is gone! I couldn't find him anywhere!"

Everyone turned to Anders, who seemed unfazed by this news and scanned the night sky to the northeast intently, the flashes and booms from the beaches making a steady drumbeat. Lezynski handed Sloan the dogtags he took off Sellars, who just a few minutes ago had been so relieved to find comrades. Marino stepped up and reclaimed his M1.

"Let's get the hell out of here. That kraut couldn't have gotten far, but I don't want to take any chances," Sloan ordered. He glanced at his watch. Five after one. It's going to be a long night.

CHAPTER TWENTY-ONE

0205 June 8th, 1944
Over the English Channel, heading towards Normandy

Flying Officer Willem van Stockum throttled back the engines for the third time. Sgt. Bailey's reminders, though irritating, apparently weren't having their intended effect. They were now well in front of the formation. His flight engineer's obvious concern and calm professionalism had a steadying effect on Willem. He'd rallied out of the black funk of the afternoon, well enough to convince himself he was able to carry off the night's missions. As he hoped, the demands of the mission and the preflight routine had a calming effect on him, distracting him from Spike's letter. And in a lucky twist, their target assignment was switched, and they were now tasked to hit the fuel dump at the airfield near St. Lo, the kind of discrete military target Willem much preferred.

Betty Bomb's powerful Merlin engines thrummed and roared. The older Mark II's like Betty gave him just a little more confidence, and every bit was needed in the lumbering Halifax. Despite all the time in the air over the wheat fields and prairies of Saskatchewan and Manitoba, the training craft weren't like the Halifaxes, and the conditions certainly weren't as they had been. They rarely flew in weather in Canada, and the training relied on the usually excellent visibility so often available in Canadian skies. When they started bomber training in Scotland, the conditions they flew in were preposterous, and the staggering losses from accidents kept everyone very focused. And now, over the Continent, they had the added deadly distractions of flak and German fighters. No wonder many of his colleagues were less meticulous about where their bombs ended up. It was not, however, something he was willing to compromise on.

The intercom crackled and Morrison spoke from the rear gunner position back in the tail.

"Sir, it's pretty hot just behind us. Keep an eye out."

Willem could hear the booming of the explosions below and behind them, but so far the air in front was clear. He glanced at his watch, then thumbed the intercom again.

"Time to target, Nate?"

"Four minutes, Skip," Hensley responded promptly.

"Toby, are you ready?"

"Yes, Will," came McFarlane's nervous reply.

Several explosions detonated in the air off to their left, but the bomber remained steady.

"Final approach. Open the doors." Willem scanned the ground ahead and the horizon looking for the few landmarks he thought might be visible from the maps. Ahead just to the left was the town of St. Lo. Coming up dead ahead would be the airfield and fuel dump. He saw a bare patch in the moonlight, and recognized the lines of the airfield. He made a few adjustments, then spoke.

"Target in sight. Final approach. Prepare to drop. Payload is yours, Toby."

"Yes, sir." MacFarlane's voice was squeaky and ragged with fear, but Willem knew he'd get the job done. They flew a few moments more with only the roar of the engines and Toby's brief corrections. Willem heard the twang and felt the lift as the additional weight dropped to the earth below.

"Bombs gone."

"Bomb bay clear?"

"All clear."

"Close doors." There was a grinding of gears.

"Doors closed." They saw the flash of the aiming point picture.

"Let's go home, gentlemen." He could faintly hear the whistles and cheers from the crew as he banked the plane sharply over the town of St. Lo on the south side, turning back to the north.

Suddenly, three sharp booms in quick succession rocked the plane as the air came alive around them with anti-aircraft fire. The bursts of jagged metal fragments slashed through the thin aluminum skin of the plane, shredding equipment, papers, and Toby MacFarlane's upper torso. Wind whistled through holes in the nose windscreen, blowing his blood deep into the recesses of the machine, mixed with leaking oil and hydraulic fluid. Willem flinched as another piece of shrapnel shattered the Perspex to his right, spraying bits of plastic against his body. Despite the chaos, Johnny moved about, checking equipment and indicators while hanging onto straps and handles, swinging like a monkey as the aircraft pitched and lurched.

"Hold on!" he grunted as he banked hard to move away from the explosions. Willem struggled to maintain altitude while flak bloomed and flashed around them. The plane leveled with a disturbing vibration and he thumbed the intercom.

"Johnny! Status!"

"Two and four are shot sir, and we're losing pressure on three. MacFarlane's dead, sir." Willem fed the remaining engines more fuel and felt the vibrations increase as their altitude gradually dropped. They finally cleared the anti-aircraft fire, allowing him to focus solely on his plane.

"Anyone else hurt?"

"Nate's banged up," Bailey responded. "Col already jumped, and Jock is getting ready." Despite the urgency of the situation, Willem smiled grimly. His crew knew, even before he had decided himself, that they'd have to ditch. Being free of the payload would make things a little easier, but a night landing on strange terrain would be a long shot at best. He nursed the engines as best he could, but a quick calculation of their rate of descent showed that not only could he not make it back to base, but he wouldn't even make the coast before they returned to earth. The decision of a water or dirt landing was taken out of his hands.

He steadied the plane as best he could, fighting the drag created by the dead engines, pushing the remaining engines as hard as they would go, over-compensating on the steering to stay straight. Despite his exertions, they continued to slip earthward.

Off to his right he saw a broad open space in the moonlight and banked toward it, rapidly losing altitude.

"If you are going to jump, now's the time. We're going down. Crash positions." His voice remained calm and steady despite the mounting tension. He banked hard again to what looked like the longest line of the clear space and tried as best he could to ease the plane down. He gunned the remaining engine, thankful again for the extra power in the Merlins. The machinery screamed in protest and the controls bucked under his hands. The underbelly clipped a row of trees, then shortly after they brushed the ground. He did his best to feather and the plane barely rose, but it was enough to soften the blow. The craft settled onto the field screeching and groaning as the metal structure of the fuselage partly collapsed under the strain. They bounced hard then just as quickly came to rest, everything quiet except the clatter of loose items finding their final resting place.

Willem opened his eyes and the cockpit spun. His hand went to his head and felt blood and a rapidly rising mound. He looked around, momentarily disoriented. Straight ahead was grass and dirt, above him twisted metal. A warm moist breeze blew over him from some unseen opening. The airframe ticked and creaked, a dripping noise from some ruptured hydraulic line. He fumbled for the release from the harness and fell sideways. Groping in the dark, he searched for the exit in the tangled wreckage, gasping with pain every time he put weight on his right leg. He felt in the dark for an opening and found himself in the midsection. He could hear movement in the tangled metal of the wreckage.

"Nate? Jock?" he called out.

"It's Johnny, Will. I'm trying to free Jock. He's unconscious and wedged in tight."

"Can I help?"

"How are you?"

"Something with my leg. Head is cut, but I'm moving."

"Get out then, I'll meet you. I've almost got him."

"Let me help."

"There's no room. It's a tight fit. Please, sir, get out before the fuel catches. No sense in everyone burning. Get out."

Willem hesitated, tried to focus, then crawled toward an opening in the side of the fuselage. The metal wall was peeled neatly away, and he crawled through. On the dewy grass he attempted to stand, but stumbled to his hands and knees, gasping with pain from his leg. His head swam and he crawled as far as he could before he had to stop and vomit. He crawled several more yards, then collapsed into the grass, panting. He lifted his head but the world spun again, and he blacked out.

"Jesus, that was close!" Lezynski looked up from where he lay beneath the trees, then sat up and brushed off the shredded leaves and broken branches. About two hundred yards away, the wreckage of the bomber glowed in the wan moonlight where it had come to rest after roaring overhead. Scattered fires twinkled from within the wrecked engines.

One by one, the rest of group scrambled to sitting or stood up. Anders was already staring intently at the wreckage.

Sgt. Sloan followed his gaze. It sounded like a bomber, most likely Allied given recent activities. Could anyone have survived? Maybe. Could they get them out and away before the krauts showed up? Maybe, maybe not, but it's not my chance to take. Mission first, and the men needed a quick decision.

Sgt. Sloan slung his M1. "Okay, let's keep moving. We've got to put some distance behind us pretty quick."

The soldiers settled their loads and formed up. A few heads turned as Anders loped off toward the wreckage.

"Hey! Where are you going?" Sloan yelled after him hoarsely.

"Going to check on survivors. Take two seconds. Wait up."

Sloan cursed and threw his pack down. He glared at Lezynski and gestured toward the wreck. "Well, go with him. Hurry up."

Lezynski sprinted after the new guy, amazed at his speed. He was a tiny figure in the darkness, and as Lezynski approached, he saw him kneeling next to a figure on the dirt. Then he entered the wreck. Lezynski trotted up, out of breath. He started at the sound of a shot, followed quickly by another. Shortly after, the new guy emerged from the larger section of the fuselage, holstering his Colt. He walked past Lezynski to the figure in the dirt.

Lezynski walked to the wreckage and peered into the dark interior. He couldn't see or hear anything inside. He walked back over to the new guy kneeling next to the figure.

"He's out cold. Help me roll him over." Together they gently turned the man over and Anders checked him out. He ran his hands over the supine man's body with brisk efficiency. A large goose egg crowned his forehead.

"I don't like the look of the head, but I don't see anything else serious." Lezynski looked on.

"You a medic?" Lezynski asked. Anders shook his head.

"No. Do you have any medic kit?"

Lezynski grunted a negative.

"Sir, wake up." Anders gently slapped the unconscious man's cheeks, with no response. Lezynski felt his hands. They were warm, with strong pulses.

"Man, he's out. Guess we've got to carry him."

Together they draped his arms around their shoulders, then each grabbed a handful of his flight suit along the inner thigh. Though he was a relatively big man they were able to carry him back to the trees, sharing the load and using the flight suit for handles,

They eased the man down in the brush in front of glaring Sloan.

"So what happened to not being slowed down?" he asked Anders sharply. Anders ignored the needling and turned to the others.

"Didn't one of you pick up a medic bag this afternoon?" Jones stepped forward, and unslung a musette bag from his back and handed it over. Anders flipped it open and rooted through, then pulled out a little packet. He tore it open and cracked a glass vial. He knelt down and waved it under the nose of the unconscious man. From several feet away, Lezynski could smell the sharp odor of ammonia.

The unconscious man groaned and turned and shook his head. Anders leaned into his face.

"What's your name? What's your name?" he shouted at the groggy man. Sgt. Sloan and Lezynski exchanged glances and looked around.

"Hey, keep it down pal," Lezynski admonished.

The man in the flight suit tried to focus his eyes, moving his head around unsteadily.

"van Stockum. van Stockum," he mumbled, barely coherent.

Anders eased him back to the ground, cradling his head gently. He looked up to Sgt. Sloan.

"Sergeant, we've got to get under cover. This man isn't going to be able to travel until his head clears, and we can't be caught in the open at daylight. I don't think we can go much further tonight."

Sloan put his hands on his hips and cocked his head. "Oh, you don't, do you? What do you suggest?" His anger caught the attention of the rest of the group and they shuffled their feet, glancing at each other.

"All I'm saying is we've got to take care of this man, and until he can keep up, he's a liability while we're on the move, so we might as well hunker down. Just a suggestion."

Sloan looked down at him. "That's it, huh?" He turned away and walked off a few paces, staring out into the darkness. Lezynski walked over and stood next to him.

"What do you think's going on there, Top?"

Sloan shook his head. "I don't get it."

"What should we do?"

Sloan shook his head again and continued his meditations. Lezynski looked back at the knot of men, gathered around the figure lying on the ground.

Sloan finally turned back.

"Let's get him up. There's a small town off to the northwest. It's not where we want to go, but there will be cover there. How about it, Magellan? Any krauts there?"

The new guy shook his head. "That'll work."

Sloan stared at him, then turned back. "Somebody help carry him. Let's go."

Behind them, the spilled fuel in the wreckage ignited, illuminating the surroundings with flickering light, setting the shadows dancing in time to the roaring conflagration.

After an hour of silent marching in the dark, they drew up on the outskirts of a small village. Sloan sent three men ahead to scout the area, and the rest waited behind a stone wall on the edge of town. After a long twenty minutes they returned.

"Kraut motorcycles outside one of the buildings a few streets over. A whole bunch of bicycles outside some houses. This is no good." Sloan muttered to himself, glancing at Anders, biting back a sharp remark about this first wrong piece of advice. Only a few more hours until daylight. Anders was pensive, scanning the surroundings. For the first time since his arrival, he showed anything but his usual calm.

The bicycles were a common sight since their arrival: whole squads of German infantry peddling down the roads, weapons on their backs. A cluster outside a building was a reliable indicator of billeted infantry.

The small group hunkered down behind the wall. The scattered clouds broke, and the waning moon shone down on the surrounding fields. Sloan squatted with his back to the village and looked over the gently rolling countryside. In the middle distance he saw an indistinct dark smudge of forest with an unusual white patch next to it, like snow.

"Let's go. We've got to get to those woods." Without a word the group stood up, two new men carrying the unconscious bomber pilot. They set off across the fields toward the trees. Anders made no protest.

Two uneventful hours later, they entered a stand of trees and walked under cover. After twenty yards they hit a dirt track, and, after a turn, a large building loomed in the darkness in a clearing of carefully maintained shrubs and lawn. Some kind of estate. Next to it there was an apple orchard in bloom, which accounted for the bright contrast in the moonlight. There were no lights, no vehicles, no obvious sign of habitation. Sloan's step quickened at this good fortune. He knelt and gestured the men forward, whispering instructions and using hand signs.

"You two go ahead and set up on those two corners. Marino and Lezynski, circle and check out the entrances. If it's clear, try some doors."

After fifteen tense minutes, Lezynski returned.

"Marino's in and he says there's no one on the first floor. Looks empty."

"Okay, let's get this guy in there. Get everyone inside and search the whole house."

A quick search of the upper floors and the spacious cellar revealed an abandoned chateau of modest size. The neatly kept yard was surrounded by dense woods around a hollow in the slightly rising land, which concealed the building from the roads to the east and north. The orchard revealed itself in the dark by the wafting blossom-scent that followed them as they moved around the yard. Behind the house to the south and west were outbuildings and a small barn leading to fields, then more woods as the land continued to rise to low hills. Because of the trees the house was useless for observation, and it was also far enough away from the main road to make it less convenient for housing local forces. Still, the cleanliness gave Sgt.

Sloan the impression that it hadn't been abandoned for very long.

Forty-five minutes later, the sky brightened as they settled in an interior room off the kitchen. One of the first-floor rooms appeared to be set up as a classroom. They pushed desks to the walls and spread out on the floor. Sloan went back out and scouted sentry positions on the border of the woods and worked out communications with two sentries posted upstairs and out by the road. Dawn had broken when he returned to the house.

"Leszynski and Marino will take first shift out by the road, Turturro upstairs. The rest of you get some sleep. We'll rotate every four hours. Stay sharp."

Anders tended to his charge at the back of the room. The bomber pilot was still unconscious, despite groggy mutterings during the jostling of the trip. In just a few moments, the room was filled with the sound of soft snoring. Anders sat in the corner, watching the wounded pilot, eyes alert and bright.

CHAPTER TWENTY-TWO

0930 June 8th, 1944 Outside St. Jores, Normandy

Anders paced the room while the pilot slept against the wall. He turned at the sound of Lezynski entering and waking up MacDonald and Jones. They got up, stretched, and went out to the road to relieve Marino without comment. Lezynski sat against the wall and crunched on a dried biscuit from his rations, watching Anders pace. He finished the biscuit, took a swig from his canteen then stretched out to sleep. He closed his eyes and tried to relax, to no avail. Soon, he was staring at the ceiling, mind running, unable to settle down. The four hours on sentry went by fast. His adrenaline still surged from the last two days, and despite his exhaustion, he felt jittery and tense. It didn't bother him that Marino had slept most of the shift. He wasn't up to handling his questions and chatter. He needed time to think and calm down.

Marino entered and sat down.

"Some chow, that's a good idea." Marino opened his own pack and rooted around.

"You think Top would let us build a fire?" Marino looked up holding a tin of hash. "This stuff tastes much better hot."

Lezynski shrugged from his position on the floor and went back to staring at the ceiling. Marino opened the can and ate it cold, then threw the trash in the corner and pulled out a deck of cards.

Marino shuffled and reshuffled, flipping them back and forth.

"C'mon, Lezynski, let's play a coupla hands. You got money, right?"

Lezynski gave a little smile and shook his head. "No, thanks."

Marino laid out solitaire and started flipping cards. Anders walked to the window and pushed the curtain aside and peered out. Morning light streamed in. Lezynski watched him with concern. He let the curtain fall back, then stepped to the opposite side and looked through again.

"Hey, buddy, stay away from the windows. C'mon, get away from there." Anders ignored him and continued his surveillance. After a few moments he let the curtain drop again and resumed pacing. After a few more circuits he stopped.

"Where are the facilities in this residence?" Lezynski noted something odd about his speech.

"I think there's a wash room over on the other side of that big room." He jerked a thumb over his shoulder toward the back of the chateau. Anders looked down at the pilot asleep on the floor, then back at Lezynski.

"Keep an eye on him. I'll be right back."

Marino looked up from his cards. "I don't think he's goin' anywhere, pal. We'll sit tight, don't worry."

Anders left, and Lezynski watched Marino's game of solitaire.

"That guy seem strange to you?" Lezynski asked tentatively. Marino flipped over three more cards, placed a red jack on the queen of spades.

"What, that guy? Whatever. He's taken pretty good care of us. I thought we'd be eating bugs and bark until he got us those supply bags." Queen of hearts on king of spades.

"Hmmm."

"He's kinda twitchy I guess." Seven of clubs on eight of hearts.

"How come he won't say where he's from?"

"Beats me." Three of diamonds on the four of clubs.

A loud crash and a shout startled them, and Lezynski darted out of the room toward the sound. Marino dropped the cards and scrambled to his feet, whipping his Thompson around. Marino glanced down at the still sleeping bomber pilot, then advanced toward the door. He could hear a struggle, then a shot, followed by another. The disturbance subsided. He advanced carefully into the hall.

As he stepped around the entrance to the large dining hall, he saw Lezynski and Anders standing over a dead German. Lezynski's helmet was pushed back on his head, worry on his face. Anders used his left hand to compress a wound on his upper right arm. Blood stained his uniform. Marino noted again the lack of insignia.

"What the hell...?" Marino asked as he approached. A clatter of footsteps down the stairs heralded the arrival of Sgt. Sloan and Doolan.

"What happened?" Sloan demanded.

Lezynski gestured toward the German soldier on the floor.

"I shot him. Right in the chest."

"Doolan, go back upstairs and tell those guys to stay sharp. Marino, check all the doors and windows again. Find out how he got in here. Don't show yourself. He's probably not alone." Marino and Doolan left to comply. Sloan turned back to Lezynski and Anders.

"Okay, you two, what happened?"

"I went to relieve myself, he jumped out. Sergeant Lezynski saved me," Anders replied. Sloan bent down and rolled the body. The German soldier's face was frozen with a blank expression, a neat hole in his left cheek just below his eye, his helmet overflowing. His head lolled to the left, and Sloan noticed an irregular birthmark on his neck. His right hand clutched a large Jager knife, blood on the blade. Sloan looked up.

"I thought you said you shot him in the chest."

Lezynski nodded. "I did. It didn't do anything." He gestured at Anders. "He rolled him, and I got right up next to them and shot him there." Lezynski pointed with a pale and sweaty hand at the hole in the soldier's left cheek.

Sloan reached down and fingered the bullet hole in the German's uniform. He undid several buttons, and pulled the blouse open. Underneath he wore a thin silvery undergarment, silky soft. He bent down and pulled the jacket open further. Underneath the hole in the outer garment, there was a darkish discoloration on the silver underwear. Sloan ran his hand over it finding no evidence of blood or a wound.

He looked up at Anders. "You're pretty damn unlucky."

Anders made no reply, pulling his hand away from the cut on his arm to check the bleeding. Lezynski stared down at the German's face.

"You know, he looks kind of like that other guy, the one that jumped you last night." Anders ignored him, too. Lezynski pushed the body with his foot, partially rolling it. A luger was strapped in a holster on the dead soldier's right hip.

"I'd say he's lucky this guy didn't use the gun."

Sloan's impatience boiled over. He stood up and advanced on Anders.

"I've had enough. You need to come clean about what's going on here. Who are you? Why do these krauts keep coming after you? Why are you so concerned about him?" Sloan yelled, jerking his thumb over his shoulder toward the injured pilot in the next room.

Anders shook his head.

"Sergeant, I appreciate your frustration, but I can't share any details of my mission with you. You must understand. The pilot is a very important person, and I am to escort him back to London. Nothing else can interfere. I appreciate the cooperation you've given me so far, and I hope you can help me get back to friendly territory."

Sloan stared at him, then shook his head in disgust. He turned toward Lezynski.

"You two drag him in the back. We'll figure out what to do with him later." Marino returned as Lezynski and Anders lifted the dead German's arms.

"The guys on the roof didn't see anything, all the doors and windows are secure. I can't figure how he got in, Top." Marino glanced down at the German. Sloan looked to the side room where the pilot slept.

"We've got to get out of here. There's got to be more krauts." Sloan went to arrange the move. Marino caught Lezynski's eye.

"You gonna take that luger?" They paused and Lezynski looked down and shook his head. Marino looked at Anders, but got no response.

"Hey, thanks." Marino bent down and unbuckled the holster and held the luger up, turning it over and admiring it.

"Hold up a sec." While Lezynski and Ander's held the German's arms, Marino went through his pockets and stripped what few insignia his uniform had.

"Wouldn't ya know. This rube's got nothing." He stood up and eyed the bloody knife on the floor.

"Hey, how about the knife? You want that?" Lezynski shook his head again as they resumed dragging the body.

"It's yours."

Marino beamed.

"Hey, thanks mack. You're alright." He picked up the knife and wiped it on his pants.

Lezynski and Anders dragged the body into the kitchen and laid it next to the back door. Lezynski stood up and looked at the door. Anders turned to go.

"Wait. Give me a hand." Lezynski nodded toward the door and together they dragged the German a little further to block the kitchen door to the yard.

"That'll slow anyone down trying to come in until we can get him buried later."

Anders shrugged. "It won't matter."

Sloan pounded up the stairs and stuck his head into the far corner room.

"Stay sharp. That kraut couldn't have been alone. Watch the tree line especially."

He found Doolan standing at the top of a flight of stairs leading up to an attic.

"No easy way onto the roof, sarge," Doolan observed.

Sloan shook his head. "That's okay. We can see just as well from these windows, and we don't have anything heavy to put up there. There's no cover up there anyway."

He went back down to the living room to check on the pilot.

"Lezynski, go out to the road and make sure Turturro didn't see anything. Stay sharp."

Lezynski left, and Sloan went to the back room where the pilot lay. Marino and MacDonald stood by with Anders.

"We've got to get him up and get ready to get out of here. That kraut must have been a scout. We won't be here when the rest of them show up." He knelt down next to the pilot and gently shook him.

"Sir, wake up. Sir." Sloan gently slapped his face. The pilot's eyes fluttered, then blinked. He lifted his head slowly, wincing, then pushed himself to one elbow and ran his hand over his face and head, groaning. The others stood in a circle, watching. "How are you feeling?"

Willem squinted up at him, slowly getting his bearings. He saw a circle of American paratroopers in their distinctive baggy pants standing around him in a dusty old room.

"Okay. Where am I?"

The soldiers chuckled.

"The Astoria. We're getting ready for dinner," Marino chimed in.

The pilot smiled. "I'll need a few minutes to press my tux. I'll have some champagne, though."

The group chuckled, and the pilot managed a wan smile.

"Sir, we've got to get you up. We need to move out of here, pronto," Sloan advised.

The pilot slowly tried to stand, wincing as he moved his leg. Marino and Sloan took his arms to assist.

"*God verdome!*" Willem gasped and sagged between the two paratroopers on either side. "My leg, there's something wrong." Sloan cursed and they lowered him back to the floor. He knelt down and pushed up the leg of the pilot's flight suit, running his hand gingerly over the extremity.

"I don't know, it may be broken."

Sloan stood up, rubbing his mouth and thinking. Carrying him in the dark was one thing, but broad daylight? He'd slow them too much. These weren't good options.

"Sergeant?" Sloan turned to Anders with a raised eyebrow.

"We don't have to leave yet. I don't think that German soldier was a scout. He was alone."

Sloan fought back the urge to argue. The few hours of sleep he'd just gotten did wonders for his self-control. He turned away from Anders and ignored him for the moment. He looked at the pilot sitting against the wall, who was still holding his injured leg.

"Sergeant, where are the rest of my crew?" Willem asked, looking up at Sloan.

Sloan turned to Anders. "You were there."

Anders looked at Willem. "You were the only one we rescued, Dr. van Stockum."

"But Johnny Bailey ... and Jock ...."

Anders shrugged. "You were the only one."

The paratroopers stood in respectful silence while Willem digested the news. Only Sloan took note of Anders familiarity with the pilot. He looked back at him.

"You're not British," Sloan observed. The pilot shook his head.

"American."

"What's that accent? Where are you from?"

"It's Dutch. I was born in Holland, moved to Ireland, then the U.S. My family lives in Washington, D.C."

"So what's up with the British uniform? How come you joined up with them?"

"Actually, I started out with the Canadians in the summer of 1941. I spent some time as a flight instructor there, got bored, and requested a transfer last year to get closer to the action."

"Just couldn't wait, huh?"

"Actually, no."

"Smart move," Marino muttered. Anders watched the exchange intently but without comment.

"What's your name?" Sloan continued.

"Willem van Stockum. Flying Officer."

Sloan glanced at Anders, who avoided eye contact. Sloan rubbed his chin and looked around the room, then back to the pilot.

"Well, Sir, welcome to our merry little band. Staff Sergeant Tom Sloan." Sloan bent over and they shook hands. "We're trying to figure out where the Germans are, and plan a route back to our lines. Do you know this guy?" Sloan gestured at Anders. Willem shrugged.

"Doesn't look familiar, but I meet a lot of people. How are you?" Willem smiled and nodded at Anders, who remained impassive. Willem's head swam from the movement. Sloan studied the exchange.

"You don't know him?"

Willem shook his head gingerly. Sloan looked at Anders.

"Dr. van Stockum, I'm here to bring you back to London. These men will be helping us."

"Me? Are you with SAS? But you're American," Willem said.

Anders shook his head. "I'm American. You are needed back in the States to continue your work." Willem's eyes widened.

The conversation was interrupted by Lezynski's return from the road.

"Nothing out there, Sergeant Sloan. They didn't see anything." Sloan nodded. The pilot looked at Anders.

"But my term of service...." Willem interjected. Anders shook his head.

"Your work is more important now. We'll talk more about this later."

"His work? And why do you keep calling him doctor?" Sloan asked, eyebrows raised. Willem looked back and forth between the two Americans.

"I'm a mathematician." Anders made no response. Sloan furrowed his brow, digesting the seemingly unrelated facts. He turned to the paratroopers in the room.

"Let's get him fed and fixed up. If he can move, and we can figure out a safe way out of here, we're moving out at dark. Lezynski, go check out the basement, see if we can move him down there." Sloan walked away, with Anders right behind him.

"Sergeant Sloan." Sloan turned back to Anders and raised an eyebrow.

"Are you familiar with British ranks?"

Sloan stared at him, then gave a small nod.

"So are you going to let him take command?"

He didn't respond, and turned to the pilot. "Sir, one more question."

Willem looked up.

"You're the ranking officer here, and I just want to be clear about how this is going to work."

Willem smiled. "Don't worry, sergeant, you're in control. I don't pretend to know anything about your business, and I'm certainly in no shape to try to lead you. I'm grateful for whatever assistance you can give me, and I'll do my best to help out and not be a nuisance. Officers in the RAF are used to letting our NCOs call the shots."

"Can you handle a weapon?"

"I'm eminently trainable."

"Sarge, look what I found."

Sloan turned to the doorway.

Leszynski pulled a bespectacled soldier forward by the sleeve of his uniform. The soldier smiled sheepishly.

"He's got a radio!"

"What the fuck? Where'd he come from?"

"The basement!"

Sgt. Sloan looked the trooper over and studied the radio pack and the insignia on his uniform, but no unit stencil on his helmet. "What's your unit, kid?"

"OSS, sergeant. I'm a Jed. Name's Bill Kellam."

"A what?"

"A Jedburgh. We dropped in last week to help prepare the Resistance for the invasion. My team was wiped out a few days ago. The Resistance stashed me here yesterday morning until they could figure out how to get me out of here."

"Resistance? They know you're here?" Sloan's interest was piqued.

The radioman shrugged. "Yeah, sure. They're supposed to be coming back soon."

Sloan was encouraged by the news. "You were in the basement?"

"Yeah. We heard you, but they wouldn't let me come up until he found me," Kellam concluded, gesturing to Lezynski.

Sloan nodded. "Lezynski, grab that guy Anders. Wait a second, 'we'?"

"Yeah, I was with the ..."

Lezynski interrupted by pulling Anders into the room. Sloan looked at Anders and pointed to Kellam.

"Do you know this guy?"

Anders shook his head.

Sloan turned to the new guy. "He look familiar, Kellam?"

The new guy shook his head.

"Okay, kid, spill it. What are you up to? Who's 'we'?"

"We dropped in ten days ago to make contact with the resistance. Me and two officers, one Brit, one French. We linked up with the maquis, but then we were jumped. The two officers were killed. The maquis brought me here to wait, then they left. The nuns won't let me hook up my radio until they get back."

"The nuns? What nuns?"

Lezynski looked back through the doorway, then grinned at Sloan. "It gets better, sarge."

From the doorway to the basement emerged two small figures clothed in black and white, one short and stocky, the other older and wizened, peering shyly from behind MacDonald's back.

"I think maybe this is a convent, or their school."

The two nuns spoke softly in French.

Sloan looked around in angry disbelief. He threw his helmet across the room.

"Goddammit! I thought you apes said you checked this place out!"

The assembled troopers shuffled their feet and looked anywhere but at Sloan.

"Anyone speak French?" Shaking heads all around – except Kellam, who raised his hand. The nuns gestured insistently, then conferred.

"They don't want you here, Sarge. They say it's too dangerous," Kellam translated.

The older of the two grabbed Sloan by the sleeve and pulled him down the stairs. They descended a few steps, moving slowly in darkness. The basement was now lit by a single fat candle, and she led him to a back room off the central room. A third nun huddled on the floor with about a dozen children of various ages, surrounded by neat piles of clothes and bundled bedding.

"Oh, Jesus." Sloan shook his head.

The nun turned to him and gestured, pointing emphatically away. He walked back upstairs. The younger nun shushed the children, then followed them.

The older nun followed and lectured Sloan in French. "She wants us out of here. It's too risky for the children," Kellam narrated.

"Oui, that is what she said."

Sloan turned around to face the youngest nun, now standing at the front of the group. "You speak English?"

She nodded.

"So we must leave?"

She nodded again.

"She say there are too many of you. We don't have enough food, and if the *boche* come back and find you, they will kill everyone."

"Is this a school? Why are you hiding?"

"They are *sans parents*. How do you say ... *orphelins*?"

"Orphans," the older nun chimed in.

"Oui, orphans." The younger nun nodded her head. The short nun said something in French with a scowl and a shake of her head, and the younger one turned to her and an explosion of heated French back-and-forth followed. The older one shushed them both. The soldiers watched, smirking. The younger one turned back to them.

"She say I should have studied better in school. I say to her maybe if her friends in the Milice had not done their job, these children would have their mothers and fathers. They are Resistance children. Their parents were killed." The short nun scowled while the older one fretted.

Sloan shook his head and turned to the young nun.

"Tell her we're sorry, but we've got to use one of these rooms. We have an injured man, and the upstairs isn't secure enough. We will keep you and the children safe. We have our own food, and it's only until tonight. We will leave, I promise." The young woman's eyes flicked over to van Stockum, who was now standing up between Doolan and Anders. She turned back toward the older woman and spoke softly. A heated discussion ensued, the younger girl seeming to argue the soldier's case.

After a few moments, the older nun threw up her hands and turned away. She turned back, pointed at Sloan, but gave orders to the younger nun, who nodded and turned back to Sloan.

"She say you can use the other room in the basement, but only until tonight. No shooting in the basement. Stay away from the children."

Sloan nodded. "No problem. Tell her we'll be gone tonight. Thank you very much." He turned to the older woman. "*Merci beaucoup.*"

She nodded gravely back to him, then walked back to the room with the children.

"Doolan, help that radio guy set up his antenna upstairs, let's see if we can find out where everyone is."

The young nun spun around and rushed over. "Radio? No, no, no! There can be no radio! They will see the, the wire, the *comment dit-on... antennes*, or they will hear it and find us. They will kill everyone!" She grabbed Sloan's arm, pleading.

He stared at her. "They can locate a transmission? From a radio?"

"Yes, yes! They do it all the time. With trucks. They are always looking. Please, no radio!"

He thought for a moment. "What if we just listen? They can't detect that, right?" He turned to Kellam, now standing in the doorway. "If you set up the radio and just listen, they can't locate us like that, right?"

Kellam shrugged. "I know *we* couldn't do it, but I don't know if they have something new. Maybe they got something more fancy. I don't know."

"Hmmm. Let me think about it. Let's get these people settled."

CHAPTER TWENTY-THREE

1130 June 8th, 1944 Near St. Jores, Normandy

The sun was now high in the sky, and Green started wishing they were still in the small copse at the edge of the fields. Last night was as restful as circumstances had permitted, far from any human habitation or any chance of being discovered. The farmer had finally finished his manure-spreading, and the sun dipped below the horizon as it approached ten p.m. local time. Green slept fitfully, woken at one point by a noise. He lay there, then heard it again: Gardner was talking in his sleep, muttering and moaning. Then he jerked violently and moaned some more. It subsided, then Green fell back asleep. He awoke later to see Gardner in the moonlight, sitting up, looking off through the bushes. He watched him for a while, then slept again.

He woke feeling refreshed and reenergized, but Gardner looked awful. His eyes were darker, more bloodshot. While they prepared to move out, Green saw him take two more of the Benzedrine tablets they were given in their supply kit. Gardner seemed to have an extra stash that he drew on. Looking back, he'd seen him taking them since they met, but he hadn't made the connection.

They trotted across the fields, moving generally north and west toward where they thought the beaches were. As the farm fields fell behind, they saw less evidence of the Germans, but the terrain became less navigable. Water-filled ditches blocked their path more often, and these were always followed by marshy ground. They broke through one cluster of trees and looked out on an expanse of water of unknown depth. Green could see the frustration building in his partner. Swarms of mosquitoes and flies tormented them as they squished through the mud.

As Gardner's pace quickened, Green noticed the limp again, a hitch in his step. Their path blocked to the north, they opted to turn left toward the west. Green decided to withhold the observation that they were now circling back toward where they had come. Except for the roads, the ways east and north seemed blocked by swamps and water. They'd have to backtrack again and try to find another way forward. But back was also where the Germans were.

They crossed another field and came upon bomb craters leading up to the ruins of a small village, pock-marked and shattered. Picking their way through, the air thickened with the sweet stench of decay. Green noticed Gardner looked more drawn and pale. Their pace quickened.

Gardner led the way, and Green occasionally trotted to keep up. At the lip of a crater, Gardner suddenly veered to one side and broke into a run. Green walked up and looked over.

Mixed in the rubble lay the wreckage of a small cart. The bloated, mangled remains of a horse were still tied to the front. The horse's legs spread wide into the air, pushed up by the swollen belly. From underneath the cart a single pale arm protruded.

Green looked at the wreckage, then at the rapidly receding back of his comrade, who was now visibly limping. Why had this spooked him so much?

He turned and ran to catch up, puzzled by the squeamishness of a man who had already proved himself a ready and able killer.

CHAPTER TWENTY-FOUR

1540 June 8th, 1944
Outside St. Jores, Normandy

"Mr. Anders?"

The American turned to Willem. MacDonald and Doolan sprawled along the wall, resting between shifts. Sgt. Sloan was working with Kellam upstairs to get his radio operational.

Willem continued. "Can you tell me more about your mission? You came for me, my crew, or anyone you could rescue? Why is an American rescuing British air crews?"

Anders considered the questions, then shook his head. "Just you, Dr. van Stockum. Your survival is a matter of the highest priority for the war effort."

Doolan pushed himself up on one elbow and addressed Anders. "For the whole war?"

"Victory depends on the success of my mission." Doolan and MacDonald exchanged glances, then MacDonald looked at Anders.

"Is that why you have all those supplies?" MacDonald asked.

Anders hesitated. "Just good information. Those weren't mine, I just knew where they were. But I need all of you to help me with this mission. Sergeant Sloan needs to understand that. I can get more supplies, but I need your cooperation."

"So what's the mission?" Doolan asked.

Anders nodded to Willem. "Get him back to London, alive."

"And we win the war?" MacDonald drawled, eyebrows arched.

Anders nodded gravely.

Willem shook his head. "That is nonsense."

MacDonald cleared his throat. "If this is such a big deal, why only send one guy? Where's your support?"

Anders smiled. "You are my support. The success of these behind-the-lines missions depends on speed and stealth. Big units are too easy to spot. Look at Kellam and his team. Three men, and even they had problems."

MacDonald nodded to Willem. "So how's he going to win the war?"

Anders smiled again. "That's classified."

Willem frowned and shook his head again, but remained silent.

They all turned as Sloan entered and gave new orders. "We've almost got the radio working. Rotate the sentries. MacDonald, go out to the road, send one of them back in. Doolan, go upstairs and send Jones down for a break."

Sloan sat down and took off his helmet, then took a long drink from his canteen.

He smiled at Willem. "Looks like we'll be able to get you out of here tonight, Sir. Once we get the radio going, we'll figure out where our guys are, and head in that direction. We've got to get you fixed up to move, but that shouldn't be too hard."

Anders interrupted. "Sergeant Sloan, leaving tonight might be too soon. We've got to make sure the path is truly clear before venturing out."

Sloan looked at him. "Didn't you say you want to get him back to London?"

Anders nodded.

"Well, I've got to get my men back to their units, and it's in the same direction. I don't like sitting here cooped up. One kraut found us already, I'm not waiting for others."

Anders shook his head. "I have information that this location will remain secure for at least another 48 hours. We should stay until the time is right to move."

"You have information? What information?"

Anders shook his head again. "That's classified, Sergeant. Suffice it to say I am very familiar with the local conditions, and right now is not a good time to be venturing about."

"He is right." From the doorway, the young nun spoke. She moved quietly and no one noticed her arrival.

"How do you know?" Sloan asked.

The young nun shrugged. "We communicate with people in the village and the countryside. They tell us when to hide, when to keep the children inside so they are not seen, when it is safe to be outside. We cannot stay in the basement forever. They need to see the sun, run and play."

"I thought the other sisters want us to leave?" Sloan asked.

She gave a small nod and looked at the floor. "Yes, I know. I am trying to persuade them to let you stay, but I am not having much luck. They are worried about the children, and the attention you might bring to our hiding place."

Sloan looked back and forth between the nun and Anders, then at the pilot. "No offense, sir, but my first priority is my men, and getting us in position to accomplish our objectives, or at least find out what our new objectives are. We'll help you however we can as long as it doesn't take away from that. I'm still planning to leave tonight."

Sloan stared at Anders. They locked eyes and an uncomfortable silence lengthened.

The confrontation ended with the arrival of Jones from upstairs. He unslung his gear and sat down against the stone wall. "Hey, what's this about ending the war? What do we have to do?"

The others looked back and forth, making no response.

Jones rooted through his musette bag for food. "Whatever it is, count me in. I want to go home."

Willem pondered the stranger's words. Finally, his curiosity could not be contained.

"Excuse me, Mr. Anders. You said my work is important to the war effort. I'm confused. What part of my work? Where is it that you want to take me?"

Anders smiled. "I'm sorry, Dr. van Stockum, but I can't share any details with you. London is only a stopping place. They need you back at Princeton, at the Institute. I think you know what awaits you there."

Willem's eyes went wide. "How did you know about that?"

Anders held up his hands, voice soothing. "It's my job to know about your background. It's nothing sinister, I assure you. I just have to get you safely home. My little contribution to the war effort, so that you can make yours."

Jones followed the conversation, and then was joined by Turturro coming in from the road. Turturro unslung his weapon and sat down against the wall. He pulled out a pack of Lucky Strikes and lit one up, blowing out a long stream of smoke.

Jones slapped Turturro's arm and pointed at Anders. "Hey, this guy says the war's going to be over soon." Turturro looked at Anders.

"Yeah, I heard. Sounds good to me." He took a long drag on the cigarette and blew out another cloud of smoke. The smell of the tobacco was too much for Willem.

"Say, you don't have another cigarette?"

Turturro fixed him with a flat look, then slowly reached for his pocket. "Uh, sure, sir, but there ain't exactly an unlimited supply, if you take my meaning." He pulled out a cigarette and lit it off his, then got up and handed it to Willem.

"Thank you very much. Ah, that's nice." Willem took a deep drag and exhaled slowly. Turturro sat back down and avoided making eye contact with Jones or Anders, determined not to offer any other smokes. Willem took another drag and leaned his arm against his left knee, propped up, flicking ash from the cigarette.

"So, Mr. Anders….." he paused. "You aren't with these men?"

Anders shook his head. "Special agent. I work alone."

Jones was nodding his head, smiling. "Hey, that's pretty neat. Save this guy, end the war. You'll be a real hero. What kind of outfit are you with?"

Anders smiled and shook his head again. "That's …"

"Classified." Turturro finished. "Yeah, we get it."

Anders turned to him. "Right."

Willem took another long drag from the cigarette.

"Well, it's nice to hear one is appreciated, but I still don't understand. I haven't done anything substantial in my field in years. This is all very confusing."

"Don't sweat it, sir. Sounds like you've got a ticket home. I'd take it if I were you," Jones opined.

"Yeah, sir, if this means we all go home, do us a favor and don't screw it up," Turturro added.

Sloan gave him a sharp look. "He's an officer, Turturro."

Turturro's eyes flicked back to Willem. "Sorry, sir. No offense."

Willem smiled. "None taken."

McDonald, clattered down the stairs, excited and out of breath. "Top, we got company."

Sloan scrambled upright.

"Old guy with a horse and a cart coming up the drive. No krauts anywhere I can see. He doesn't seem to be in a hurry. He's about half way up the drive. We've got him covered. What should we do?"

Sloan scrambled upright and rushed upstairs. He found the young nun by the front door. "Are you expecting anyone?"

There was a flurry of urgent conversation down the stairs between the nuns and she turned back to Sloan. "He is a farmer. He brings our food. He is a friend."

"He can't come in here. He can't see us."

The nuns conferred again, the older ones arguing angrily. Again, the younger nun seemed to be pleading the soldiers' case. "I will talk with him and tell him the younger children are sick. He will not want to come in. I will have him leave the food on the front and we can bring it in later."

Sloan looked between the three women and nodded. The younger nun opened the front door and slipped out, the others concealing themselves behind corners. She pulled the door closed quickly behind her.

Sloan turned to MacDonald. "You and Doolan cover them from the second floor. If there's any problem, drop the farmer. He can't leave if he knows we're here."

MacDonald nodded and turned to go. He stopped. "Sarge?"

Sloan looked at him. "Yeah?"

"What if she tries to leave with him?"

Sloan stared for a moment. "Kill them both."

MacDonald hesitated, then nodded.

Sloan took up a position at another window and watched the cart approach. With three rifles trained on him, the farmer didn't have a chance of getting out alive if something went wrong. The young nun approached the wagon, and the two conversed. The farmer shrugged and began unloading the wagon. The nun picked up boxes and hefted them to the front door with surprising ease. They quickly emptied the wagon and the farmer climbed back on and gave it a shake of the reins. As Sloan watched him leave, he thought he saw the farmer give a furtive look over his shoulder at the upper windows. He brought his rifle up and sighted on the farmer and tracked him as he moved down the dirt track, without haste. He gradually increased the pressure on the trigger as the cart moved down the path then around the trees and out of sight. Sloan slowly lowered his rifle.

Downstairs, the paratroopers helped the young nun carry boxes down into the basement to the back room where the children stayed. The children milled about. The two older nuns inspected the boxes, chattering in French.

"You see that young sister slinging those crates?" Marino observed from the doorway.

Turturro took a long drag from his cigarette. "So?"

"For a cutie she's pretty strong."

"She's a nun, you pig. Have some respect."

"I'm just sayin'. She's seems like a tough little cookie."

CHAPTER TWENTY-FIVE

1845 June 8th, 1944
Near St. Jores, Normandy

"Hey, wait up. Where are we going?" Green trotted to keep up with Gardner. They'd been walking steadily for several hours, changing directions at any sign of enemy activity, keeping to cover as much as possible, hurrying across open fields. Sometimes they redirected at seemingly random intervals. Green followed without complaint, but he was beginning to wonder if there was a plan other than to go as fast as possible. Gardner had been back to his distant, frozen self since the encounter with the bomb craters earlier in the day. Except for his uncanny ability to steer them clear of trouble, Green was concerned that they were just running away from something instead of toward their comrades, wherever they might be.

They had not stopped to rest or eat since the bombed village. Once Green stopped to pee and almost lost Gardner, who was unrelenting in his mechanical flight.

Gardner made no reply to Green's question, staring straight ahead, his long strides unbroken.

Green continued trotting next to him. "Let's take a break up here in these trees and figure out what we're doing."

Again no reply. As they approached the trees, Green slowed, but Gardner kept walking. Green caught up to him and gently took hold of his sleeve, pulling him toward cover by the side of the road. Gardner initially resisted, but, under Green's firm grasp, gradually yielded. They walked into the brush, Green leading the dazed man.

"Here, sit down." He pulled Gardner down to a sitting position under a small tree. Green noticed he was still panting, disproportionately to their recent exertion. Gardner's eyes darted, his face pale and sweaty.

"Drink." Green put his canteen up to Gardner's lips, forcing him to drink water. He took several gulps, water spilling down his chin. Green opened some C-rats and handed them to Gardner.

"Eat."

Gardner initially held them in his hand, fingers moving without purpose, not eating. Green pushed his hand to his mouth, and he finally took a bite.

After they ate, Green pushed him to a laying position.

"Let's rest until dark, then we'll get going again. Close your eyes and get some shut-eye. I'll stand watch." Gardner laid still and tried to close his eyes, but they kept popping open again, darting. He kept stirring, rolling onto his back, staring up at the leaves, agitated.

"Hey, I've got an idea. Give me one of your books." Gardner fumbled in his pockets and handed Green one of the floppy rectangular paperbacks. Green flipped it open to a random page and began reading in a soft voice.

> *"And before we judge of them too harshly we must remember what ruthless and utter destruction our own*

> *species has wrought, not only upon animals, such as the vanished bison and the dodo, but upon its inferior races. The Tasmanians, in spite of their human likeness, were entirely swept out of existence in a war of extermination waged by European immigrants, in the space of fifty years. Are we such apostles of mercy as to complain if the Martians warred in the same spirit?*

Green stopped and looked up and saw Gardner watching him, less agitated. He went back to the book.

> *"The Martians seem to have calculated their descent with amazing subtlety–their mathematical learning is evidently far in excess of ours–and to have carried out their preparations with a well-nigh perfect unanimity."*

He continued on about how the Martians had prepared, if we'd only looked more closely we could have seen the attack coming, and the ruthless efficiency of the attack. Green looked up and could see Gardner's eyes closed, his breathing more even. Gardner turned his head and opened his eyes. "I've already read that part, go to the middle."

Green riffled the pages toward the middle and continued, in a section describing the flight of refugees to the coast and their evacuation by boat.

> *For after the sailors could no longer come up the Thames, they came on to the Essex coast, to Harwich and Walton and Clacton, and afterwards to Foulness and Shoebury, to bring off the people. They lay in a huge sickle-shaped curve that vanished into mist at last towards the Naze. Close inshore was a multitude of fishing smacks–English, Scotch, French, Dutch, and Swedish; steam launches from*

the Thames, yachts, electric boats; and beyond were ships of large burden, a multitude of filthy colliers, trim merchantmen, cattle ships, passenger boats, petroleum tanks, ocean tramps, an old white transport even, neat white and grey liners from Southampton and Hamburg; and along the blue coast across the Blackwater my brother could make out dimly a dense swarm of boats chaffering with the people on the beach, a swarm which also extended up the Blackwater almost to Maldon."

Gardner opened his eyes again and looked at Green. "Dunkirk."

"Huh?"

"Doesn't that sound like Dunkirk? He wrote that in 1898. Keep going."

Green continued in a low voice, describing the escape from England across the Channel, the attack of the iron-clad warship Thunder Child on the Martian machines, destroying two of them to great cheers. When he finished the chapter, Gardner was snoring softly.

While he slept, Green studied the modification to Gardner's right boot, the brace extending up under his trouser leg. The blousing of his left leg wasn't into his boot top but tied around the top of the brace. It was cleverly constructed and concealed, probably to deceive NCO's or jumpmasters looking to scratch the unfit.

There's an interesting story there, Green thought to himself.

CHAPTER TWENTY-SIX

1930 June 8th, 1944
Near St. Jores, Normandy

Sgt. Sloan finished his tin of K-rat beef. His most recent trip – around the house and out to the road – hadn't helped him make a decision about whether to move tonight. The pilot could not walk, that was clear, even with the crude splint they'd fashioned. MacDonald worked on creating a crutch out of scavenged materials, which might help, but a man on a crutch didn't move a whole lot faster than one being carried. The men buzzed with the news that the pilot was someone special, especially the part about the war ending soon.

"Whaddaya think, Top? We gonna take him along, get him back to London? You think that guy's telling the truth?" The men grilled him with eager eyes, turning to each other to hash out the details of fragmentary information. The rumor was infectious, and it now had a life of its own, inflated and embellished at every retelling. If they sat still any longer, the men would be changing into civilian clothes by tomorrow, convinced by wishful thinking that their work was done.

He rubbed his face. With almost two years of being away from home, he knew why they were so excited. Sitting still made him jumpy. He wanted the men to be moving, attacking, killing Germans. Sitting invited relaxation, and relaxation led to sloppiness, and then mistakes. Mistakes meant more casualties. They had to keep moving.

A shout from downstairs broke his reverie. He rushed down to see Lezynski restraining a German soldier in a chokehold from behind, legs wrapped around his waist. Anders stood over them holding a pistol, preparing to shoot. The angle made it impossible for him to not wound or kill Lezynski in the process. Anders raised the pistol.

Sloan lunged forward and tackled Anders, grabbing for the pistol, knocking it free. Lezynski's choke subdued the German, his face slack and blue. Sloan and Anders fought for the gun.

"Are you fucking crazy? Stop!" Sloan shouted hoarsely. Moving faster than Sloan could believe, Anders knocked him aside and reached for the gun. Sloan lunged again and Anders parried him, momentarily knocking the gun further out of reach. They rolled on the floor, wrestling to reach the pistol on the floor. The other paratroopers watched in confusion. Lezynski loosened his hold on the limp, unconscious German and rolled away, rising to a crouch, ready to spring to Sloan's aid.

Anders reached down and snatched Sloan's Colt from his thigh holster. He brought it up and hit Sloan across the forehead, stunning him. Anders stood up and aimed the gun at Sloan.

"Don't interfere with my mission Sergeant." He turned and pointed the gun at the unconscious German. Lezynski scrambled out of the way. Anders fumbled with the trigger, vainly squeezing it. Sloan pushed himself to one knee and Anders brought the gun around pointing at Sloan's head, still fumbling. Anders finally figured out the mechanism and thumbed the hammer back.

"Drop it buddy!" Marino leveled his Thompson at Anders. Sloan remained kneeling in front of Anders. Lezynski crouched to the side, coiled to spring, waiting for an opening. Safeties clicked off and several other weapons pointed at Anders. He held the Colt steadily to Sloan's forehead.

"Nobody move," Anders ordered.

"No, you don't move," came a voice from behind him. The muzzle of a snub nosed pistol poked the back of his head. His eyes flicked backward. The young nun stepped forward, pushing him, the gun steady in her hand. Anders slowly lowered the Colt, and Sloan stood up and grabbed it from him.

"I've had enough of you." He drove his tightly clenched fist into Anders gut, crumpling him to the floor. "Tie him up."

Doolan and MacDonald quickly complied, hogtying Anders with his hands behind his back, bound to his feet.

"Thanks, sister."

The young nun nodded, keeping the gun trained on Anders gasping on the floor. Sloan rubbed his head and turned to Lezynski and Jones, who were watching wide-eyed.

"Tie the kraut up too until we figure out what the fuck is going on."

They dragged Anders and the German into the front room. Sloan turned to the young nun.

"Okay, what's your story? You're no sister." The young girl smiled and pulled the black fabric coif and white wimple from her head.

"No, I'm not. I'm glad to take this off. My code name is Juliette. I work with the Resistance. I was assigned to watch the radioman, and also to hide here myself. The *boche* are looking for me, too."

"When are the others returning?"

"Maybe tonight. It depends on the German patrols. There are many more troops in this area rushing to the front. We are busy cutting wires and laying ambushes. We must blow up the rail line that passes through St. Jores to Carentan."

Sloan nodded to the German.

"Do you think he is looking for you?"

Juliette shrugged. "Possibly, but that is not usual for how they work. They would send many soldiers, kill everyone. Not one, not alone. This is strange. Your American friend is, how do you say, unreliable?"

Sloan smiled grimly. "He's not my friend, and yes, he is unreliable. This whole thing stinks."

"My unit will be here soon. They can help us decide what to do with them."

"When?"

"Soon. Maybe tonight. You must wait here."

Sloan looked over at the unconscious German on the floor, color returning to his face, his breathing ragged. Marino and Lezynski stepped forward and leaned in, scrutinizing him.

"It's the same damn guy!" Marino remarked.

Lezynski blanched. "Or his twin brother."

Sloan studied the face and the striking resemblance between this man and the one Lezynski killed this morning. He noticed the small birthmark at the base of his neck on the right, very similar to the one on the other soldier.

"Where'd you guys put that other kraut?"

"He's by the back door in the kitchen. We're going to bury him out back once it gets dark."

Sloan stood up and walked back to the kitchen. He looked around, then yelled over his shoulder.

"Lezynski! Get back here!" Lezynski hustled into the room, and his mouth fell open.

"What the ...." He went over to the door and pulled on the handle to no effect, still firmly locked. He spun around and looked frantically around the room.

"He was right here! I swear to God!" He looked down on the floor and pointed to the smeared blood.

"Look! That's where we dragged him!" Sloan noted the stains and studied the rest of the room. There were no other marks, tracks, or smears to indicate the body had been moved any further. They rechecked all the windows and found them to be intact and secure. Sloan scanned the room again.

"Sarge, I swear to God…." Lezynski pleaded.

Sloan waved him quiet and continued studying the room. "Why don't you ask old one-eye Connolly?" Marino observed from the hallway. They returned to the front room and stood between the two bound prisoners on the floor. The German was still unconscious. Lezynski bent over the German and closely examined his face, than ran his hand over the back of his head. It can't be the same guy, he muttered to himself.

"Turturro!" Sloan shouted over his shoulder.

"Yeah, sarge?"

"Go get the pilot."

"Sarge, we just hustled him down those stairs…."

"Go get him! We're going to get to the bottom of this. Marino, get some water or smelling salts or something. Wake up the kraut."

A few moments later, a small crowd assembled in the room. Willem leaned on Turturro and Marino squatted over the German, splashing water on him and slapping his cheeks. The German's eyes fluttered and he gasped, setting off a fit of coughing.

Sloan turned to Anders. "Okay, what is this about? How come these krauts keep showing up? Who are you?"

Anders stared at Sloan. "Sergeant, I told you before, I'm here to escort Dr. van Stockum back to London. That's it. It's an extremely important mission."

"So important you'll shoot us?" Sloan glared.

Anders remained silent.

Sloan turned to van Stockum. "Sir, do you know what this is about?"

Willem shook his head emphatically. "I have no idea, honest. What happened here?" He looked back and forth between the two bound figures.

Marino looked up from beside the German. "This mug shows up from nowhere, tries to jump him again, Lezynski grabs him, then your pal there tries to shoot Lezynski and Top."

Willem absorbed this, face solemn. He caught the German studying him.

Anders spoke again, nodding to the German. "This man is an assassin, sent here to kill Dr. van Stockum. He must be killed immediately. My mission requires it. He must die."

Sloan glared at Anders. "If he's here to kill him, why did he go after you? And this morning, what about that? And what about the guy last night? We didn't even have the pilot then. Seems like they're more interested in you. Only you."

Anders made no reply.

Sloan turned to the group. "That guy Kellam speak German?"

Kellam shouldered through from the back. "Yeah."

Sloan gestured to the bound German on the floor.

Kellam knelt down. *"Wie heissen Sie? Was ist Ihre Einheit?"*

The German's mouth moved, but no sound came out. He grimaced and swallowed, then tried again without effect.

"Looks like Lezynski made him lose his voice," Marino chuckled.

The German nodded his head vigorously.

Sloan looked down. "You understand English?"

The German nodded again.

"What is your business with him?" Sloan gestured to Anders.

The German glanced over and gave Anders a small smile, then back to Sloan, mouthing some words. Sloan watched him intently, then shook his head.

"I can't read lips. Anyone get that?" The group leaned forward studying the German's mouth.

Willem spoke first. "I think he's saying, 'I'm a soldier.'"

The German nodded again.

"He's a liar. Everything he says is a lie. He is an assassin and a murderer," Anders spoke up.

Sloan looked over at him. "You sound like you know him."

Anders opened his mouth, then closed it without reply.

Sloan looked back to the German and hooked a thumb at Anders. "You know him?"

The German glanced at Anders, then back to Sloan, nodding. Sloan gestured toward van Stockum, looking at the German.

"You know him?"

The German nodded again. Willem's eyebrows went up. All heads turned to him.

"You got a lot of admirers, doc," Marino observed.

"So it would seem." Willem shifted his weight, still leaning on Turturro.

Anders spoke again. "Sergeant, you must set me free and let me finish my mission. The entire war effort depends on it. If I can get Dr. van Stockum back to London, the war will be over by September. You are jeopardizing our chances for victory and my failure will cost millions of lives. Think about that."

Sloan's temper boiled over again. "You are not going anywhere, pal, until I say you do, and even then it will be with a rifle stuck in your back. I'm not taking any more chances with you. So just shut the fuck up about your mission."

There was a momentary silence broken only by the shuffling of jump boots and heavy breathing.

"So what are we going to do with these mugs, Top?" Marino asked.

Sloan looked up. "Drag two of those heavy chairs from the dining room into the basement. Tie them to the chairs. Two guys keep a gun on them the whole time. Looks like you've got some roommates, Dr. van Stockum."

"Uh, sergeant, I'd rather not – if that man here is supposed to kill me." Willem nodded to the German. The German shook his head vigorously, looking at Willem.

"Well, we've got to keep a guard on them, and it looks like you are some kind of target, so we've got to keep a guard on you. Better to use one guy for both jobs, which means you stay with them. Sorry, doc. Besides, that basement is the most secure spot in this joint. You'll be fine."

"If you say so." Willem made no attempt to conceal his doubts.

The paratroopers hustled the prisoners upright. As they headed toward the basement, Sloan held up his hand.

"Hold up." He went to the German and lifted his tunic up and the shirt underneath. Underneath was the same silvery undergarment they saw on the dead German this morning. Sloan rubbed the soft slippery fabric between his thumb and forefinger and stared at the German. He let the clothing fall back and waved them forward.

As they walked the prisoners to the basement, Marino called over his shoulder to Lezynski.

"What's the big deal about the kraut's underwear? What's bugging Top?"

"Remember where I shot the kraut this morning?"

"Yeah, in the face."

"No, the first one. Right in the chest. That underwear stopped the slug, point blank. 'Sfucked up."

Marino looked at the German walking in front of him with his head down. "Huh."

CHAPTER TWENTY-SEVEN

2100 June 8th, 1944
Near St. Jores, Normandy

Sloan kept Bill Kellam busy with the radio, desperate for news from the beaches, and possibly some guidance for their bizarre situation. Over the protests of the young nun, he figured out a way to snake the antenna through a gap in the roof near the chimney. The men on watch outside said they could not see it from their locations, so Sloan accepted the risk to be able to listen for a while.

The news garnered from the heavy radio traffic was reassuring. Although they didn't know the call signs and codes for unit designations, they could recognize from the tenor of the conversations a force on the move. Kellam also thought he could detect a difference in signal strength from various conversations, hinting that some of the Americans were closer than others. Kellam confirmed his suspicions.

"So Kellam, tell me about your operation." Sloan sat on the floor, his back against the wall, chewing a fruit bar from his rations. Kellam slowly pulled his equipment apart and repacked it in the canvas bag.

"We're all three-man teams, started dropping in a couple of weeks ago, linking up with maquis units all over France. There are more coming. We set up drop points for weapons and supplies, funnel intelligence back to London, coordinate the Resistance, help with training. Some of these resistance guys are ex-French Army, but many are just kids and old men, on the lam from the Germans, looking for adventure. Some bad apples too. Each team has one French national as a liaison, everybody else has some language skills, either French or German. My team dropped in Brittany, north of Rennes, but the security at the drop zone was horrible. We were ambushed, and we've been on the run since. The maquis down there brought me north, and handed me off to these guys."

"Who do you report to?"

"Our operations group in England. Brits and Americans. OSS and SOE."

"Never heard of them. What are they?"

"Office of Strategic Services and Special Operations Executive. SOE is the Brits. I'm going to have to call them at some point and get new instructions. If you guys are this far inland, my mission is done."

Sloan smiled ruefully. "Well, not quite. We're only here because our jump was screwed up. The lines are actually pretty far away. We're trying to figure out what to do ourselves. How much help are these Resistance guys going to be?"

Kellam shrugged. "The leader who brought me here seems pretty squared away, but it's not a tightly organized group, more like a gang. Factions, cliques. Most around here are loyal to DeGaulle and the FFI. Call themselves Fifi. Then there are the communists in the FTP. I get the impression they didn't used to work together, but now are sort of in a grudging alliance. They go on joint operations, but everyone's still got an eye on each other. Very suspicious of traitors and spies."

"Hmm. Well, we've got to get back to our units, which means pushing toward the lines somehow, and the sooner the better. This hiding-out stuff gives me the willies. I feel like we're sitting ducks."

Kellam laughed. "That's funny. That's all we're supposed to do. Run, hide, run, hide, give the krauts a rash."

Sloan shook his head. "Hey, did you know the girl wasn't a nun?"

Kellam shook his head, smiling. "They didn't tell me anything. She was here when I got here. The maquis just said wait here and they'll be back."

"Any idea when?"

Kellam shook his head and continued packing the radio.

"Why don't you just leave that out? We're going to need to use it again."

Kellam shook his head. "No way. Always be ready to run. It's what saved me down by Rennes and a couple of times since."

Sloan mulled that over as he finished his snack. He went back down and met the girl at the bottom of the stairs.

"I'm sorry, but we've got to put some men out and see what's going on beyond the trees. I don't want to be caught off guard. If we see your friends we'll be careful, but we can't wait anymore."

She shook her head emphatically. "No, that is not good. You must wait. They will be here soon."

Sloan was tired of arguing with the obstinate French girl. He was eager to get out, and the sooner they could figure out a way through the constantly shifting German troop concentrations, the sooner they could get back to their units.

The two prisoners and the pilot sat safely ensconced in the basement, in a storage room opposite where the children slept. The nuns tried to keep them out of the way, but inevitably they snuck out, peering around at the soldiers while they ate and rested. Occasionally one would sneak up the stairs, to be shooed back down by one of the paratroopers or retrieved by a scolding nun.

Sloan didn't know what to make of the situation. The two bound prisoners now presented the impossibility of movement across open terrain, making the problem of the injured pilot almost trivial in comparison. And the connection between the pilot and the prisoners remained to be explained. Despite his protestations of ignorance, both prisoners clearly had some interest in him.

The low grumble of combat from the beaches seemed louder, a reassuring rumor of progress from the landings. At the least it meant that the invasion was still on, that the Allies were still clawing and scrapping their way inland, that they hadn't been wiped out on the first day. Silence would have been ominous.

Sloan climbed back up stairs and conferred with Kellam again, leaning together over a large map of the Cotentin spread on a table.

"Tell me what you know about the area."

"We came in at night, so I didn't see much detail, but I know the major features. The town over there is St. Jores. It's on the road and rail line that goes west out of Carentan. The Resistance is holed up in the woods on the high ground behind us to the southwest. They move out of there to harass the krauts as they move up the roads. Every once in a while the krauts try to clean the woods out, but the Resistance have got so many hiding places they just disperse and reform. They're pretty well equipped ever since we've been making the drops."

"Show me."

"See this road?" Kellam tapped the map.

"Yeah, that's where the 508th is supposed to be, Picauville."

"Crawling with krauts. That road is out. The only other place to cross is Beauzville-la Bastille, right here. Same thing. They've got all the bridges bottled up."

"The Douve doesn't look very big there. Can we swim it, or wade?"

Kellam shook his head. "The French guys told me the krauts dammed up the river. It's all flooded. This map doesn't show it. All this is water." Kellam traced a wide area adjacent to the Douve River. "And you can forget about Carentan. Krauts're concentrating like crazy there. The Resistance guys are working every night to jam up these roads to slow down the reinforcements coming in there."

Sloan mulled this over, then looked up at Kellam.

"Come with me." They walked down the hall and Sloan ducked his head into the dining room where several men sprawled on the floor.

"Marino, Jones, grab your gear and come with me." The men assembled in the hallway, buckling and snapping, adjusting straps.

"We're going out on a patrol to see what's around us. We've got to figure out a way to get moving. I'm sick of sitting around waiting on someone else. Lezynski, you're in charge. Stay with the prisoners and our guest. Keep two guys on the road, one upstairs, one with the prisoners. We'll rotate when we get back. Just a little sneak and peep to see what's going on."

The three paratroopers and the Jedburgh radioman crept through the woods at the edge of the chateau's property.

"I told you she wasn't no sister," Marino whispered to Jones. Jones shook his head.

"You don't talk about a sister like that."

"She ain't no sister! Too ginchy. Minute I saw her, I said to myself, she's a looker, she ain't no sister. And I was right." Jones shook his head again and smiled.

"Yeah, but you don't talk about a sister like that. Ain't respectful."

"You ever see a sister looked like her? I been in Catholic schools with the nuns all my life, and I ain't never seen one like her. No way she's a sister. No way."

"Hey, pipe down!" Sloan whispered over his shoulder.

Marino nudged Jones and winked. Jones shook his head dismissively.

They crossed the road one at a time and huddled in a ditch. Across an adjacent field, a dead cow lay on its side, two legs sticking up in the air forced up by its bloated belly. Marino nudged Jones again and held up two fingers, then pointed to himself. Jones squinted and cocked his head quizzically. Marino leaned close.

"It's a game. First guy to see a dead animal gets the points. One point for the find and one for every leg in the air." Jones couldn't help but smile. He turned away shaking his head.

They set out in a circling patrol, skirting the forest away from the road, following the hedgerows while watching for activity in the fading light. Sloan felt confident he knew the terrain well enough now that he could get them back to the chateau in the dark, especially with the clear skies and the still mostly full moon to help light the way.

They approached the village from the night before and gave it a wide berth, knowing the Germans patrolled nearby. They crossed a wide road leading into the village, one by one, using cover, and made their way around. They came across the rail line running east-west, the one the Resistance girl said led to Carentan, the target for demolition. She said there were tanks coming up from the south and east to reinforce the forces holding back the invasion, and the Maquisards had orders to slow them down or stop them at all costs. The Jedburgh soldier confirmed that they were given orders to hinder any kraut movement toward Normandy.

As they moved away from the railroad tracks and the village, they came across a small cluster of buildings next to a cemetery, surrounded by a smattering of bomb craters. A lone German stood at the edge of a crater. A light burned in one of the buildings, gradually brighter in the fading light.

Sloan conferred with Kellam. The most direct route away from the building and the sentry was across open fields that would give them no cover for a long time, so that they risked the sentry seeing their passing. There was slightly better cover skirting through some of the cratered area toward the cemetery – somewhat closer to the buildings, but less likely to give them away.

They opted to wait for a little more darkness, then make their way through the craters. They hunkered down and watched.

After fifteen minutes, they started out, skirting the rim of the first crater. As they passed the second, Sloan thought to himself they should be clearing each before passing so they wouldn't accidentally walk past a concealed German. As he finished the thought, they froze at the sound of cocking weapons behind and in front of them.

"*Halt! Hande hoche!*" a German commanded from the darkness in front. A bright light blinded them. The group squinted into the glare, slowly raising their hands. Germans hustled up and stripped them of their weapons, pushing them toward the building with the light.

They entered a brightly lit room. Two of the Germans piled the American weapons with a clatter on the floor by the door. A German officer sat at a small wooden table, shirt unbuttoned, drinking from a bottle. Several more soldiers stood nearby, all of them pointing their weapons at the four prisoners. The officer took a slug from the bottle, then turned to them with a big smile. He studied the group, then stood up and walked over to the pile of weapons. He picked up Sloan's Colt Peacemaker.

"Hot damn! It's my lucky day!" the kraut officer said in perfect Midwestern English, studying the huge revolver. Sloan stared at him, befuddled. The kraut switched the gun to his left hand and walked forward with right hand extended.

"Welcome, sergeant. Hans Steinwachs, Evanston, Illinois. Looks like we're going to end this war together." Sloan shook his hand then looked around. The other krauts watched the exchange with interest, some of them clearly just as confused by what transpired. A few muttered in German between themselves.

"Whose is this?" Steinwachs held up the Colt.

"Mine," Sloan answered.

"Pretty swell. You were issued this?"

Sloan shook his head. "My grandfather's. Good luck charm."

"Ahh…" The German officer admired the gun in silence, turning it over in his hands.

"You're American?" Sloan asked uncertainly. The officer nodded.

"Born and bred. My parents and my wife's parents are both big fans of the Fuhrer, Bund stuff, Silver shirts, the whole deal." Steinwachs shrugged. "Seemed like a good idea at the time." Sloan looked around the room. No one seemed particularly hostile.

"Why's it your lucky day?" Sloan asked. Steinwachs gave him a big smile and gestured toward a chair as he re-seated himself, placed the Colt in front of him, and pulled the bottle forward.

"Because you are my ticket home. I'm no dummy, er, what's your name?"

"Sloan."

"I'm not stupid, Sloan. This war's finished. You should see these units I've been commanding. No trucks, no weapons, sending me boys and old men, captured prisoners from Poland and Russia. These two clowns over here?" Steinwachs cocked his head at two scruffy men to his left, their uniforms ill-fitting, holding ancient bolt-action rifles from the First World War.

"They don't speak a lick of German. One's a Pole, the other Ukrainian. These are my troops. You guys are gonna roll this up in a matter of weeks. So you," he gestured at Sloan and the others, "and your buddies are going to negotiate our surrender so that we don't suffer any mishaps at the hands of some overzealous Sad Sack."

"You want to surrender to us?" Sloan was confused.

"No, not yet. For now, you are my prisoners. I don't want my men here to get the wrong idea about me. They'll thank me later. My commander would shoot me himself if he got wind of this. You're my insurance policy. We're going to just sit tight and wait until the lines catch up with us. My German comrades are already talking about falling back. There was talk of a big push to reinforce Carentan, but now they're going to pull back and establish a new line. I'm going to sit that one out, thanks. I'm done."

Marino followed this all with interest, a smile growing on his face. Jones and Kellam remained confused.

"So what do we get out of this?" Marino asked, grinning.

Steinwachs turned to him with a big smile. "How about staying alive for starters? Some of these guys are true believers. To them shooting unarmed prisoners is like taking out the trash. Everybody plays nice, we all make out. You guys just sit tight here. When your buddies get here, we surrender to you. But for now, you are surrendering to us. Got it?"

"Oh, I get it." Marino grinned and sat down. Sloan stood there, and Steinwachs gestured again to a chair.

"No point in turning down our hospitality, Sloan. Relax. Tell you what. This all works out, I'll give this back to you." He patted the revolver and smiled.

CHAPTER TWENTY-EIGHT

2210 June 8th, 1944
Near St. Jores, Normandy

"Sergeant, I'm going to hit the head before I turn in. Don't get up, I can manage." Willem struggled to his feet, fumbling with the makeshift crutches that the soldiers fashioned for him earlier. He paused to let a wave of nausea pass. His head throbbed, but he pushed through the pain and took a few tentative steps, the grinding sensation from his lower leg a painful reminder of his disability. He paused at the doorway.

"You okay, sir?" Lezynski asked.

"Yes, I'm all right."

He steeled himself and hobbled to the makeshift latrine they'd set up in the one of the stone cellar rooms off the main area. Willem relieved himself in the bucket, refastened his pants, and rested against the wall, regaining his equilibrium and mastering the nausea. He looked out on the main room.

Earlier, the nuns had given them a brief history of their new abode. Le Chateau Mont Castré dated from the 15th century, the property of an old Norman family that had changed hands recently (in the last hundred years!) and was now used as a summer retreat by a banking family from Paris. That family disappeared several years ago, and it remained vacant. The nuns moved in during the winter of 1942 and had used it for their clandestine orphanage, disguising it as a religious school. So far, the Germans, who were pillaging and commandeering local residences to billet troops and establish headquarters in, had overlooked it. Now their Resistance friends did the best they could to discourage interest in the location.

The basement was deep, with two levels. A ramp at one end led out to the courtyard behind the house surrounded by outbuildings. In the past it was used to store casks and barrels for wine and other agricultural products. It was where the nuns hid the children when they had to, and now the soldiers as well. The children slept in a large room opposite from where the prisoners were kept. The Americans slept in the main area, as well as upstairs. During the day, the nuns took the children upstairs for lessons, or sent them on the occasional foray into the yard or woods to collect firewood, butcher animals, or, in the case of the older boys, to sneak away and run errands.

Sgt. Lezynski offered Willem the option of sleeping in the main area away from the prisoners, but he declined. He understood Sloan's reasoning, and now felt reassured by the presence of the armed paratrooper. His attention was also gotten by the first man's evident interest in him – this 'Anders' – and now the other one as well, who had revived and been bound to the heavy wooden chair with Anders sitting adjacent against the wall opposite the sole door. Willem caught him staring several times, but, it seemed, without malice. Anders clearly hated the newcomer.

He saw two of the older boys peering out at him. The children took great interest in the visitors, shyly approaching the soldiers when the nuns weren't looking, practicing small phrases of the little English they knew, smiling at the big warm faces of the Americans. Once the chocolate bars came out from the rations, the paratrooper's status became god-like. Then it was all the nuns could do to keep the children under control and away from the soldiers, who pestered them for more sweets or just the opportunity to hang about. The Americans generally loved it, playing with the kids when they weren't on watch or guarding the prisoners. Watching the soldiers with the children Willem saw them almost as children themselves, bumptious older brothers or cousins clowning around with the little ones – but armed to the teeth and trained to kill. The nuns could only watch and fret, the taller one with only gentle reproach, the shorter, heavier one with scowling and seething.

Willem thought of his own nieces and nephews, and his family back in Washington D.C. Of course they'd be worried once his plane was reported missing. He would have to prevail upon the paratroopers to get some word back to the squadron that he had survived the crash, and to let his family know. At the very least Spike could get word to them.

The plane. Where was everyone else? It was all a blur, disconnected fragments. He spoke with Johnny, didn't he? Something about Jock. Yet they said he was the only survivor. Surely some of the others jumped. Colin was always the quickest out, even though the exit from the tail gun position was the hardest to navigate, especially in the dark.

The worry about his family and crew took their toll, and Willem felt the nausea rising as both his head and leg began throbbing worse. He took stumbling step back to the room, and had to put a hand out to brace himself against the wall.

Lezynski looked around the doorway and hurried over. "Hold up, sir, let me give you a hand." He draped Willem's arm over his neck and half carried him back to the room.

"Thank you, Sergeant. I can manage it from here."

Willem sat back down and arranged the rolled blanket he used as a pillow, then laid back and covered himself with the rain poncho one of the troopers gave him. Once supine, the nausea and pain became tolerable. With his head propped on the blanket roll, he could see the whole room.

A lantern spread a circle of light ringed with glowing faces and glittering eyes. Sgt. Lezynski leaned by the door with his M1 over his shoulder, watching the two prisoners. Anders seemed lost in thought, the newcomer staring back and forth between van Stockum and Anders.

The newcomer was non-descript, vaguely ethnic looking, very different from Anders' rugged good looks. Wiry hair cut short, prominent nose, thick lips, skin pocked from some earlier skin condition, now resolved with scarring. He caught Willem studying him. He smiled and cleared his throat with a grimace.

"Good to meet you Dr. van Stockum." Raspy voice, perfect English, no accent. The German grimaced and swallowed again.

"You can talk," Lezynski observed.

The German nodded. "It is quite painful, but yes," he rasped.

Willem raised his eyebrows and gingerly propped himself up on an elbow. "Have we met?" The idea that both strangers knew him raised his interest even more.

"Sort of."

Anders broke from his reverie. "Don't listen to anything he says. He's a liar and a murderer." He gave the newcomer a dire look, eyes glittering with hatred.

The German shook his head. "Hello, Timothy. Trying to figure out a way to untangle this one? Looks like we're off on some interesting new tangents. It will give the analysts years of work, mapping the permutations."

"Shut up."

The newcomer chuckled and turned back to Willem. "Forgive him, Dr. van Stockum. He hates me because I make his job difficult, but I don't hate him."

"Your job? Who are you?"

"Since we rarely ever get this far, I guess an introduction is in order. My name is Barston Stimmel. My job is to stop him." He nodded at Anders.

Anders seethed. "He's lying! His job is to kill you, Dr. van Stockum. I am here to protect you, to escort you back to safety in London. He wants you to die."

Willem looked back and forth between them with a curious blend of fear, fascination, and amusement at the absurdity of the situation.

Lezynski watched the exchange with interest.

Anders turned to him. "Sergeant, you must convince Sloan to help me get Dr. van Stockum to London. The moment for leaving will be soon, and everyone will be home shortly after that."

"How's that work? How soon?"

"A matter of weeks."

Lezynski looked skeptical. "How can you possibly know that?"

Anders paused. "In less than two weeks, Hitler will be dead, and Germany will surrender by the end of this month." His air of certainty silenced the room, except for Stimmel, who was softly chuckling.

Willem's mouth hung open.

Anders continued. "Only if I get Dr. van Stockum to London, and if the rest of my mission is successful."

"That's a lot of ifs, isn't it Timothy?" Stimmel remarked with a smile. Anders ignored him. Lezynski and Willem exchanged glances. An awkward silence followed. Lezynski checked his watch again and looked at the doorway. After a while longer, he got up and stood by the door, watching the stairs, peering up through the floor above and listening. He switched his rifle to his other shoulder and leaned against the doorframe. In the back room, where the children slept with the nuns, soft muffled crying seemed to call from far away. There was a stir, and the cries ceased. Lezynski looked at Willem.

"Sir, why do they keep calling you doctor? Are you a surgeon or something?" he asked from the doorway.

Willem smiled and shook his head. "Mathematics, not medicine. I'm a university professor."

"You're a professor? And you joined up?"

"Yes, back in the summer of '41."

"Before the war started?"

"Maybe before it started for you, but for me it started a long time before Pearl Harbor. I just couldn't stand by anymore. My family is from Holland. When the Nazis invaded, it drove me crazy. The Canadians were taking anybody."

"So how'd you end up flying for the Brits?"

"Once I got my wings, the Canadians stuck me on a training base in Manitoba. I taught aeronautics and ballistics, but I wanted to fly missions, get in the war. Finally, I was able to transfer to the Dutch squadron of the RAF since I was born in Holland, and last year they took me."

"Where'd you teach, sir?" Lezynski asked.

Willem smiled. "Please, call me Willem. I was in the mathematics department at University of Maryland."

"College math? Sounds hard."

"We taught all levels. My specialty is geometry, a special kind of geometry used in other areas of science, like physics."

"Physics? Like Einstein, huh?"

Willem grinned. "Yes, like Einstein."

Lezynski nodded, then leaned out the doorway and called up the stairs.

"Hey, Turturro, is Sloan back yet? The kraut is talking." There was a sound of shuffling feet, and Turturro appeared in the doorway.

"Nope. They went out a while ago. Who knows where they are."

Lezynski checked his watch and muttered an expletive. "We should rotate the guard. Who's out on the road?"

"McDonald."

"Upstairs?"

"Doolan."

"You get any sleep?"

"Nah, I'm good. You want me to go out now?"

"Wait a sec. Have you been upstairs?"

"Yeah, a while ago."

Lezynski looked at the prisoners. "Someone's got to stay here."

Willem spoke up. "Sergeant, if you give me a weapon, I can watch over them."

Lezynski considered this for a moment, started to speak, then reconsidered. He rubbed his chin and looked down.

"Uh, no offense sir, but you're injured, and if, uh, they get to you, then they'll have a weapon. I'd rather not."

Willem studied him, then shrugged and nodded. "Fair enough. Just trying to help. I could stand watch upstairs if you like."

"Uh, let me think about that."

"Excuse me, sergeant?" Lezynski turned to the German, Stimmel. "Where is Private Green?" Stimmel asked.

Lezynski frowned. "Who? Never heard of him. Another friend of yours?"

Stimmel glanced at Anders with a thoughtful look and remained silent. Anders made no comment.

"*Pardon?*" Lezynski turned to see Juliette, now dressed in baggy blouse and brown pants, no longer the young nun. Lezynski raised his eyebrows.

"If you give me a rifle, I will stand guard upstairs so one of the others can sleep."

He considered this. "Hmm, that might work. Turturro, go relieve MacDonald. When he gets back, the girl will go up and relieve Doolan. Whoever wakes up first will relieve me. I'll stay here." He turned to Juliette. "You can handle a rifle?"

She smiled and reached into her pocket, taking out the small pistol. "I can't very well use this, can I? Yes, I have experience with the rifle. I am a soldier also."

Lezynski smiled at her bravado.

Turturro jerked his head toward the door and gestured for him to lean close.

"What about the pilot? Give him a gun?" Turturro whispered.

Lezynski shook his head. "Not until we figure out what's going on. How do these guys know him? Something's fishy."

Turturro left, and Juliette stayed in the basement. The prisoners were silent and Willem tried to sleep, shifting to get into a comfortable position. Lezynski fidgeted, waiting for MacDonald to return so the girl could go relieve Doolan.

The quiet was interrupted by the rapid pounding of footsteps on the stairs. Doolan appeared, out of breath.

"Shots out on the road, sarge. Can't see anything. You want me to go out?"

Lezynski swore profusely, looking around the room. He unholstered his .45, chambered a round, and handed it to Juliette. "You're in charge here. Let's go."

He and Doolan hurried out. Juliette stood by the doorway with the gun, eyeing the prisoners warily.

Willem propped himself up on an elbow. "What's going on?"

She shook her head. "They are going out to see."

After a few tense minutes, there was a bang of the front door and loud voices arguing.

"We shoulda just finished him off. This is crazy."

"Shut up, Turturro."

"Who's gonna take care of him? Who's gonna…."

"Shut the fuck up!" Lezynski's voice was hoarse with anger and tension.

The four paratroopers came down the steps with a fifth person, a young boy in a German uniform, moaning and babbling as Doolan and Lezynski carried him, a large red stain on his uniform. He looked around, eyes wide with fright and pain, face pale. They hustled him into the room and laid him near Willem. Lezynski lifted up the front of the uniform, and there was a neat hole oozing blood just above and to the right of the boy's belly button. Lezynski rolled him over and ran his hand up his back, then withdrew it, covered in blood. He sat back on his heels.

"Went straight through, not a big wound on the back."

"He's a goner. You know that, right?" MacDonald observed with his soft drawl.

"So why are we…" Turturro started.

"Shut up!" Lezynski barked.

MacDonald turned to Turturro. "If you were a better shot, we wouldn't have this problem."

"Me? He was your guy. I dropped my guy."

"No you didn't. He was on the right. I capped the two on the left."

"Stop! Were there any others?" Lezynski stood up.

MacDonald shook his head. "Just the three of them. They were coming up the road toward the house when Turturro came to relieve me. We watched them but they kept coming, so we had to drop them. We hid the other two, but this guy was laying in the road yelling and calling out. We had to get him off the road to shut him up."

"Yeah, shut him up. Coulda done it out there." MacDonald scowled at Turturro's remark.

"You think anyone knows they were here?" Lezysnki pondered.

"Excuse me, sergeant?" Stimmel interrupted.

"Yeah?"

"I speak German. Would you like me to interrogate him?"

The paratroopers exchanged glances.

"Uh, sure."

A conversation between the two prisoners ensued. The young man panted out his answers between grimaces.

Stimmel turned to Lezynski. "He says they were out foraging for food. They snuck away from their camp. No one knows they were away. Looks like you got lucky."

"Wasser, bitte. Durstig. Wasser."

"He wants water. Not a good idea with an abdominal wound, but then again …."

Lezynski hesitated, then picked up a canteen and unscrewed the cap and knelt down next to the soldier. He took a few sips, then pulled away.

"Danke."

"Who's got a first aid kit? Give me your morphine syrettes."

"Sarge, what if…"

"That's it, Turturro, give me yours."

"Fuckin' A, sarge, I'm not going to give this fucking kraut my morphine. He's supposed to be dead. Just because he's slow croaking, now I'm supposed to give him my stuff? No way."

"Give me your goddam first aid kit, or I swear to God…" Their eyes locked for a moment, then Turturro looked away, fumbled in one of his side pockets and threw the first aid kit at Lezynski with a curse. Willem watched the exchange, riveted. The young German watched as well, and his eyes went wild with fear as Lezynski attempted to inject him with the morphine syrette. He tried to push away, too weak to make any meaningful effort.

"*Nein, nein!*"

Stimmel interjected with a stream of German in a soothing voice. The soldier relaxed, looking back and forth between Lezynski and the chair-bound Stimmel. Lezynski gave him the injection and he visibly relaxed.

While the soldier dozed in morphine slumber, Lezynski made a crude attempt at a dressing, sprinkling sulfa powder, laying the young man's hand across the dressing to provide some compression. Willem watched the hand fall away as soon as Lezynski turned. He dragged himself closer, pushing with his good leg, and reached over and gently pressed down on the dressing. He could feel the wet warmth seep through to his fingers.

CHAPTER TWENTY-NINE

0600 June 9th, 1944
Near St. Jores, Normandy

It was a long night on the move, but as dawn approached Green found new energy. Gardner also appeared reinvigorated after the rest in the trees. Neither spoke of yesterday's difficulties. Now they made their way toward yet another farmhouse. They'd moved freely across the open fields in the darkness, but the subtle brightening in the east warned of the coming day, and they needed concealment before it got much brighter. They skirted a small village to the east and settled on this farm.

Whatever bothered Gardner before seemed behind him now. Their pace slowed during the night as they took a few more stops to rest, and Green could see him relaxing again. He marveled at the other man's stamina: almost three straight nights with almost no sleep, although with the help of the pills. He came to trust that the catnaps he was grabbing were safe because of Gardner's insomnia, who would stand guard over Green while he slept briefly.

Green saw Gardner ahead in the soft light, stealthily exploring around the house. This was his favorite part of paratrooper work – attacking a problem – and this also was his favorite time of day: the hour just before dawn, and the moments around sunrise, when the world gradually reveals itself, color seeping imperceptibly, illuminating the gray world with a teal-tinged salmon sky, lifting the curtain from what was once concealed. He felt refreshed and alive, reinvigorated from the short sleep, nerves tingling, almost giddy.

Gardner squatted at one corner and motioned Green forward while he covered, M1 at the ready. Green jogged bent over, softening his footfalls as best he could.

Gardner motioned to the barn, indicating he'd scout it out and that Green should cover. Gardner slipped away like a ghost. Green watched with the German submachine gun held ready.

Gardner reappeared at the opposite side of the barn and motioned Green forward, covering his approach. Green hustled over, and together they entered the barn. The interior was pitch black, and they carefully closed the door, then felt their way forward. A rustling noise farther back froze them, and a loud lowing started up, first one cow, then several others. Green heard Gardner curse, but made no move. Green eased around him, and felt his way to the stalls at the back of the barn, shushing and whispering. The cows stirred in their pens, eager to be fed and milked. Green reached through the slats of the gates and felt around. A huge warm tongue wrapped his hand in a raspy wet embrace. The cows quieted down and Green moved to each one, whispering nonsense and stroking their heads.

"Sssst!" Gardner hissed.

"What?" Green whispered back.

"We've got to get out of here. There's got to be a farmer coming soon to take care of these guys."

"Girls."

"What?"

"Nothing." Green knew he was right, and somewhat reluctantly pulled his hands away. He moved back toward Gardner, and stumbled into him. As they reoriented themselves, the barn door opened, light from a lamp spilling through.

A French farmer stepped in, turned to shut the door, then turned back and froze at the sight of the two paratroopers pointing weapons at him. His eyes went from one to the next. He slowly raised his finger to his mouth to silence them. The paratroopers watched carefully. The farmer raised his free hand over his head and slowly approached. Gardner held out his hand signaling him to stop. The farmer cast a furtive glance over his shoulder back at the house, then leaned forward and whispered urgently in French.

"You speak French?" Gardner asked Green.

"Just some phrases."

"You know what he's saying?"

"Beats me."

"*Les Boches! Ils sont dans la maison! Avec ma famille!*" The farmer repeated this with several variations, increasing urgency each time, gesturing at the house. Understanding gradually dawned on Green.

"I think he's saying there are krauts in his house. *Les Boches?*" Green gestured at the house.

The farmer nodded his head vigorously. "*Oui! Oui! Les Boches! Les Boches!*"

Green signaled that they understood and turned to Gardner. "What do we do?"

Gardner thought for a moment. "What does he want us to do?"

"We could just bug out and get away from here as fast as possible."

"Yeah, but are these krauts going to come looking for us when this guy tells him we were here?" They looked at the farmer, who was watching their conversation intently.

"He hasn't ratted us out yet. I don't think he'd give us up," Green opined hopefully.

"Does he want us to kill the krauts?"

"I don't know."

"Well, ask him."

Green turned back to the farmer. "*Les boches....nous... umm....*" The farmer watched him, nodding along expectantly. Gardner stepped forward and gestured to himself and Green, then the house, then drew his thumb across his throat, watching the farmer. He nodded vigorously with a soft ahh, then looked pensive for a moment. Then he looked back up at them.

"*D'accord. Attendez ici.*" He gestured for them to stay and started backing away.

Green looked at Gardner. "Where do you think he's going?"

"Sit tight. I think he's got a plan." They followed him to the door and watched him walk back to house. It was brighter in the east, faint tinges of color emerging. The farmer went in the house and the paratroopers looked nervously, prepared for sudden violence.

"Cover that front door, blast them if they come out." Gardner instructed.

After a few minutes, the farmer reemerged and both men sighted their weapons, trigger fingers poised. A woman and three children followed, an older boy and two small girls. The paratroopers covered them with their weapons as they hurried to the barn, the woman's face contorted in fear. The farmer hustled them inside, and the children stared at the paratroopers with wide eyes. The farmer carried a large butcher knife. The wife let loose a torrent of angry whispered French, gesturing at the soldiers, then the children. He responded, pointing to the house repeatedly. The mother pulled the two little ones closer to her, and the argument continued back and forth in hoarse whispers. Green and Gardner shuffled their feet, watching the house with half-raised weapons. The farmer pulled the boy close and gave him rapid instructions, holding the boy's face between his hands, the knife dangerously close to his throat. The boy nodded earnestly, repeating, "*Oui, oui.*" Then the farmer said "*Allez!*" The mother grabbed the boy and gave him a smothering hug, stifled a sob, then kissed his face several times. The farmer pulled him away and he disappeared out the door. The farmer turned to the paratroopers and nodded toward the house.

"He wants to help?" Green asked Gardner.

Gardner nodded back. "He knows where they are. Ask him how many."

Green swallowed nervously, then turned to the farmer. "*Combien … uh,,. les Boches?*"

The farmer held up six fingers and gave them a grave look. Gardner nodded.

"*Ils dorment.*" The farmer held his hand to the side of his face and tilted it, closing his eyes.

"*Dormez vous, dormez vous…*" Green sang softly. Gardner gave him a sharp look.

"Sorry."

They crept out of the house. The farmer gestured to them where the Germans slept.

Gardner whispered to Green. "Looks like two in the front room, four in the back. I'll go in first with the knife, you cover from the door. I'll do the first two, then we'll both hit the back room. Anybody comes through a door, blast him."

The three assembled by the front door, then Gardner quietly pushed it open and went through. Green knelt just inside, the farmer crouched behind him. Gardner silently approached the nearest sleeping kraut, sprawled across a small couch near the dining area. The other was laid out on cushions on the other side of the room. Green covered the far German as Gardner raised his knife. In one smooth motion, he clamped down on the soldier's face and plunged the knife into his chest. The kraut gave a kick and struggled briefly as Gardner leaned on top of him. Green stayed focused on the second German. The dying kraut went limp, and Green and Gardner waited, listening for any sound of alarm. Hearing none, Gardner withdrew his knife and turned to the second sleeping German.

He took two steps, then froze.

The German stirred, then lifted his head. "*Karl?*"

Gardner remained statue still, waiting to see what would happen. The German laid back down, as if to go back to sleep, but then bolted upright.

"*Was?*"

Gardner drew his .45, but before he could bring it to bear, Green squeezed off several rounds from the MP40, knocking the kraut backward. A shout came from the back room, and a third kraut stumbled out. Gardner shot him with his .45, then dropped to a crouch and unslung his M1. Keeping an eye on the door to the back room, he gestured to Green to enter the room and take up a covering position to the side. Green moved forward, and the farmer followed him, holding the butcher knife.

Green knelt and sighted the MP40 on the doorway. Gardner fired into the doorway and drew return fire from the room. He scuttled backward behind a cast iron stove while the krauts continued shooting. Two Germans advanced through the doorway and Green hit both with short bursts. The third remained in the room firing through the door. Gardner signaled him to keep firing high, and Green nodded. He pumped short bursts through the doorway while Gardner wriggled along the floor. The German fired wildly in return. As Green shot high, Gardner rolled into the doorway and fired three times, silencing the last kraut.

"You okay?" Gardner asked.

"Yeah." Green suppressed the shaking in his arms. The farmer huddled in a corner, clutching his arm, the bloody knife on the floor at his feet. Green hurried over and looked at the wound. The bullet passed cleanly through the surface of his upper arm, more a graze. There was little bleeding, but it was clearly painful. Green examined the arm and tried to reassure the farmer in his broken French. The farmer's face was pale and sweaty, and his whole body trembled. The wife burst in the door and screamed, looking around, then rushed to the farmer and threw herself on him. The two little girls followed, crying, clutching their mother's back. She turned and gave the older one orders. The girl hurried off.

Gardner shushed them all to be quiet, with no discernible effect.

Distracted by the urgency of caring for the farmer's wound, Green's nerves settled quickly. "What's next? We got a house full of dead krauts and some jumpy civilians."

Gardner scowled. "I think we beat it outta here and let them clean up the mess."

Green looked at the distraught mother, the two little girls and the wounded farmer, then looked back at Gardner.

Gardner shook his head. "Goddammit. Let's go, give me a hand."

Together they dragged the dead Germans one by one out of the house and toward the back wall of the garden behind the house. They looked around for something to conceal them. When they returned, the little girls were already busy scrubbing the blood stains off the floor. The mother had recovered her composure, reorganizing the house, concealing damage, covering up bullet holes. The farmer sat at the kitchen table, still pale, sipping a cup of thin coffee, a bottle of brandy next to him.

Everyone turned to see the young boy enter the front door, out of breath and wide-eyed. The farmer asked him several questions, and a torrent of French went back and forth. Green watched, then saw Gardner turn to the door and reach for his weapon. There was a shout and Gardner froze. Green turned just in time to see a brown rifle butt come crashing into the side of his face, knocking him out.

CHAPTER THIRTY

0900 June 9th, 1944
Near St. Jores, Normandy

"They are prisoners. Some boys saw them captured." Juliette struggled to maintain a brave face.

Lezynski cursed. Now this news about Sloan and the others. It had been a long night. The young German, now dead on the floor in a pool of blood, had spent the night moaning and screaming, calling out for his mother and babbling. The nuns came in and relieved the pilot of his nursing duties, and between the crying of the children, the bustling of the nuns, and the increasingly incoherent ravings of the dying youth, nobody had slept. They had run out of morphine syrettes, and the last hours of his slow death were torment for everyone. Lezynski tried to rub the fatigue out of his face, without success.

"We've got to get that guy out of here," he declared to no one in particular.

"You must wait until dark. You can't be seen taking him out of the house," Juliette advised.

"Maybe if we put him by the back door the elves will get rid of him like the other guy." Lezynski was punchy with fatigue.

Anders and Stimmel exchanged a brief glance, unobserved by the others.

He continued talking to himself. "We gotta get out of here. If those guys don't get back, we gotta leave. We're gonna be trapped here."

Juliette leaned forward, insistent. "Please, wait a little longer. Be patient. If you leave, you will be captured as well. There are Germans everywhere. And your prisoners. What will you do with them?"

Lezynski looked toward the entrance to the basement and shook his head. None of it made sense, and he saw no point in risking their lives for the three men in the basement and their convoluted stories. At least one was a killer, that was sure. And the killer was very interested in the one who said he was American but sounded foreign. A math professor who became a bomber pilot? And the one in the German uniform was the only one that sounded and acted like anyone normal.

But it was only him, Turturro, MacDonald, and Doolan. Even without the prisoners and the pilot, it was a pretty thin crew. And even with the ammo Anders got them, they still didn't have much. No heavy weapons, and no idea which way to go. The Resistance girl wasn't going to help them because she didn't want them to leave.

This wasn't something they'd trained for, that was for sure.

CHAPTER THIRTY-ONE

1300 June 9th, 1944
Near St. Jores, Normandy

The German officer cursed loudly in English, then dismissed the messenger with a curt wave of his hand. Sloan watched the other German soldiers shuffling around, glancing sideways at their leader who stalked around the room, scowling and muttering.

"What's the problem?" Sloan inquired.

He stopped his pacing and looked up. "My commander is ordering an immediate mobilization. I'm to break camp and relocate ten kilometers to the southwest. He's taken the liberty of informing my units separately, so they are already starting to move."

"Perhaps this is the time for the role switch?" Sloan inquired nonchalantly.

Steinwachs grinned and shook his head. "I thought of that. Where would you take me? Your lines are still on the other side of the Douve. We can't get there from here without running into quite a few of my comrades. I'd lose you, and you'd be a lot worse off. No, that won't work."

Sloan looked out the window toward the cemetery. After the sunshine of the morning, the weather was overcast again, threatening rain. A long procession made its way down the dirt track and toward the fenced graveyard. This motley assemblage of local citizens shuffled along behind three coffins pulled by horse-drawn carts. Something about the scene seemed odd to Sloan, but he couldn't quite put his finger on it.

"I've got to figure out a way to stall a little longer…" the German continued.

"Ask for more support," Sloan interjected. "You need more trucks. You've got equipment that's stuck. You need clarification of orders."

Steinwachs nodded.

Sloan turned to watch the funeral again. The three coffins were unloaded onto the ground, screened by the carts. The crowd was milling around. Where's the priest? Sloan wondered to himself.

He turned back to Steinwachs. "You trust any of these guys?"

Steinwachs looked around the room at the handful of his troops in the immediate vicinity. The old Pole was still there, in addition to several fresh-faced enlisted men. Boys, really.

"No, not really. They…." Gunfire cut him off, from both sides of the house. Sloan dove to the floor, Marino and the others right behind him. The Germans shouted and rushed about. Steinwachs drew a luger and hid by the door, peering out. The gunfire outside continued, drawing closer. He saw two of the krauts inside drop to the floor bleeding, one slack faced and glassy eyed from a cavernous head wound. There was more shouting outside, then the door crashed in. Steinwachs raised his hands and ordered the rest of the Germans to put down their weapons.

A crowd of French civilians holding a variety of weapons piled into the room, roughly pushing the Germans to the floor, confiscating weapons and passing them out the door. The Resistance fighters ignored the Americans on the floor. Sloan craned his neck to watch the action.

"Sarge!" He turned to see Kenny Green smiling at him, a large purple lump on the side of his face.

Sloan laughed. "Speedy? What the hell…."

Green came over and gave him a hand up. Another paratrooper entered behind Green, head shaved in a mohawk, an 82nd patch on his shoulder, huge dark circles under red-rimmed eyes. He took in the improbable scene without visible emotion.

Marino, Kellam, and Jones slowly stood up looking around in amazement.

"We ran into these guys this morning, and then we heard they were going to rescue some Americans, so we came along. Small world, huh?" Green effused.

"Man, am I glad to see you!" Sloan slapped Green's shoulder, squeezing his hand in a vise grip.

Green grinned, ignoring the pain. "You see anyone else from the Company?"

Sloan shook his head. "You're the first. I think our stick was scattered all over hell's half acre. I met these guys just walking around." Sloan jerked a thumb over to the others. While they talked, the Resistance fighters lined the uninjured Germans up against the wall, searching them.

Steinwachs stood with his hands on his head, looking over his shoulder. "Hey, Sloan, how about a little help here?"

Green looked at Sloan. "You know that guy?"

Sloan shook his head. "Not really. He's American, joined the krauts to help out the Fatherland. He was going to use us to surrender before you guys got here. Who are these guys?" Sloan gestured around to the Frenchmen.

"Resistance. Two groups, from what I can tell. They don't get along so good, but teamed up to come and get you guys. I don't know how they knew you were here."

One of the resistance fighters was gesturing for them to stand to the side. They shuffled to the door still talking.

"Any of them speak English?"

"Yeah, this one guy...." They stopped talking at the sound of cocking weapons. They looked over at the Germans lined up against the wall. Steinwachs was still craning his head around.

"Hey, Sloan...." He was cut off by a burst of gunfire from three of the resistance fighters, followed by several more. The line of Germans crumpled to the ground. One of the fighters calmly walked to each body and put a pistol to the head, pulling the trigger once, then moving to the next. The Americans looked at each other, aghast.

"Come." A Frenchman by the door gestured.

They filed out.

"Are these your weapons?"

The Americans retrieved their confiscated weapons. Sloan went back inside and recovered the Colt from Steinwachs' leaking corpse.

"We must hurry." They moved away from the building quickly, toward the cemetery. The coffins were loaded back on the carts. At the instruction of the resistance fighters, they got in the carts next to the coffins and were covered with blankets. The carts started off at a brisk pace. The rest of the crowd had already dispersed. No evidence was left of their gathering.

They were jarred and jostled for several hours along country paths, through farms and fields. For a while, Sloan heard the other carts creaking along with them, but at some point they split up, and, for a while, they traveled alone through the Normandy countryside.

Finally, the cart stopped, and their driver dismounted and pulled the blankets off. Sloan sat up, blinking, amazed to see that they were back at the chateau, under the shelter of the trees and away from prying eyes. He and Jones climbed down and stretched. Marino and Kellam emerged from the other wagon, and Marino walked to a nearby tree and relieved himself with a loud sigh. Green and the 82nd paratrooper emerged from inside the coffins. Two other carts made their way up the drive behind them. The leader of the Maquis approached Sloan with his hand outstretched, smiling.

"Hello Sergeant. My name is Laurent. I am glad to meet you."

"The same. Thank you for rescuing us."

He shrugged. "It was nothing. Another chance to kill the *boche*. We are glad you are here."

"Can you help us get back to our lines?"

They walked to the house.

"It is difficult. The *boche* are moving all the time, the roads are dangerous. We are busy setting up ambushes and blocking roads. It is possible if the timing is right, but for now we must wait."

Sloan nodded. "What about boats? Can you help us cross the water?"

Laurent shrugged. "Perhaps. We must see."

They climbed the steps to the front door. The young woman, Juliette, met them, smiling.

"Ah, Dardette." Laurent stepped forward and embraced her, kissing both cheeks. They spoke rapidly in French while Sloan watched.

Laurent turned to Sloan. "She says you have prisoners here?"

Sloan nodded. "Two prisoners, and one wounded RAF pilot. We think one may be a spy. The other is German, but speaks like an American. Both seem interested in the pilot. It's very confusing."

"These prisoners, they are valuable?"

Sloan hesitated, trying to discern the implication of the question. The recent scene by the cemetery suggested an answer. "They... yes, they are ... valuable."

Laurent shrugged. "If you say. Moving with your men is difficult. With prisoners, very difficult."

The girl interrupted in French.

Laurent looked at Sloan. "The pilot is injured? You are sure of his identity?"

Sloan nodded.

Laurent shrugged and gave a big sigh. "*Eh bien*. We cannot do anything tonight."

They entered the house and greetings were made all around. Sloan introduced Green, who in turn introduced Gardner. Sloan took Laurent down into the cellar to see van Stockum and the prisoners. Doolan stood guard. Green and Gardner tagged along, curious. Sloan introduced van Stockum.

"Sir, this is Laurent, from the Resistance. He's going to be helping us get back to our lines. How is your leg?"

Willem smiled. "Good to see you made it back, sergeant. The men were worried about you. My leg is fine, as long as I don't try to walk on it."

Laurent knelt down next to Willem and ran his hand along his leg. Willem winced as he pushed and prodded. The Frenchman held Willem's ankle firmly and moved it back and forth, eliciting a sickening grinding and a gasp. Laurent nodded to himself and stood up.

Willem panted, pale and sweaty, staring wide-eyed at the Resistance leader and shocked by the rough cruelty of his examination.

"It is not so bad. We can make a better splint that will help." He turned to Anders and Stimmel. "And these are your prisoners?"

Stimmel smiled, Anders scowled. Sloan caught both looking at Green and Gardner. Green noticed the attention.

"What do they say?" Laurent asked Sloan.

"Not much. He says he's here to protect him," he pointed from Anders to van Stockum, "and he says he's here to stop him." He pointed from Stimmel to Anders. "That's about it. Oh, and the pilot says he's never seen either guy before."

"Have you... interrogated them?" Laurent asked.

"Uh … not intensively." Sloan glanced at van Stockum, who watched with furrowed brow.

Laurent shrugged again. "We can help, if you like."

They stepped out of the room, and Sloan turned to Green.

"Speedy, I want to sit down with you and get the skinny on what you've seen. You, what's your name…."

"Gardner," Green offered, glancing at his partner.

"Come with us and give me your scoop. You look like you need some rest. Doolan, go get Marino, tell him it's his turn to stand watch here, and send me Lezynski as well. Let's go upstairs."

The Resistance girl watched the exchange with interest, following at a distance. After the initial greeting, Laurent seemed to ignore her.

They climbed up the stairs and assembled in an interior room on the second floor, out of earshot of the rest of the group. Laurent, Sloan, Green, and Gardner sat down on the floor and Laurent offered them cigarettes from a pack of Luckys. Sloan and Gardner accepted, Green declined. "They're American. Very good. From your airplanes." A zippo was produced and they lit up.

Lezynski arrived and stood by the doorway, half watching the hallway.

"So what happened, Speedy? Did you see anyone else from our stick, or the company for that matter?"

Green shook his head. "Not a one. I hid out the first night, met Gardner the next day when he bailed me out of a bad situation, and it's just been me and him since. We ran into some guys from the 501st and an 82nd guy the second night, but then left them. Killed a bunch of krauts a couple of times, then we got jumped by Laurent and his guys, then we sprung you and your guys. That's about it. Did a lot of walking around."

"Where'd you go?"

"Way to the east and north. Lots of swamp and water, no easy way through. Ran into krauts every time we tried to push north or toward the beaches. We kept getting turned back south and west."

Sloan nodded. "Same with us. I bet most of the unit either bought it or got captured. I can't imagine there's too many left walking around after this much time with all these krauts running around."

Laurent nodded, dragging on his cigarette. "That is correct. Most of your comrades in this area are *finis*. There is one very large group to the east in a town called Graignes."

Sloan looked up. "How many?"

Laurent shrugged. "Maybe two hundred? A large group. They have the eagle on their patch."

Sloan nodded and rubbed his chin. "Where is this place?"

"South of Carentan. Maybe twenty kilometers or so from here."

"How the hell did they get there? That isn't near any of the drops. Good God."

Laurent shrugged again.

"Can you get us there?" Sloan asked.

Laurent sighed, then took another long drag from the cigarette, taking a long time to blow out a stream of smoke.

He did not make eye contact, and the Americans waited impatiently for his response.

Finally, he shrugged again. "Perhaps. It would be very dangerous, very difficult. It would be better to wait."

"Here?"

"Why not? It is safe, for now. You have shelter and food. We can help with scouts and watching. We can get more weapons, ammunition, and more food also. When the time is right to reach the lines, we will take you. You must be patient."

Sloan looked at the other two. "What do you guys think? Sit tight, or make a move?"

Lezynski looked in at Green, then back at Sloan. "I dunno, Top, there's an awful lot of krauts out there. I'm all for getting out of here, but when you guys didn't come back, and we saw all the convoys on the roads out there, we thought for sure you were done for. It's driving me crazy, but sitting tight might be best, especially now that we have some help."

Sloan turned to Green. "Well?"

"How many guys do we have?"

"With you and Gardner, now we've got nine. A light squad, except no heavy weapons."

"We will help with the weapons," Laurent interjected.

Green continued. "Seems like a small group to be trying to take on all those krauts. Plus, what're you going to do with the pilot? He'll slow us down. And the two other guys?"

Laurent flicked his hand dismissively. "We can hide the pilot, put him to another safe house, if he is who he says he is. We help many airmen get back to England. The prisoners we can take care of as well." He smiled.

Sloan thought for a moment.

"Uh, Sarge, there's something else…." Lezynski interjected.

Sloan looked up.

"This guy Anders? He says he has information that Hitler is going to be dead soon, and if we get the pilot back to London, the war will be over within weeks."

Sloan shook his head. "I don't believe anything that son of a bitch says."

"What does he say of Hitler?" Laurent asked.

"Only he's going to be dead within the next week or so. Didn't say how."

Laurent looked at Sloan. "We must interrogate these men."

Sloan looked at Green, who shrugged and shook his head.

Sloan heaved a sigh. "Okay, we stay. Green and Gardner, why don't you get some sleep. Lezynski, let's figure how we're going to use these two new guys. Goddam, it's good to see you Speedy." Sloan slapped Green's shoulder, both men grinning. Lezynski's head came around quickly, first to Sloan, then Green.

"Wait a sec, what's your name?"

"Me? Kenny Green. Pleased to meet you."

Lezynski looked back and forth between the two men and shook his head, frowning.

Sloan watched the exchange. "What?" he asked.

Lezynski shook his head again and rubbed his forehead. "Nothing. I need some sleep, too. Listen, Top, about these prisoners...."

Sloan and Laurent waited for him to continue.

"They were talking downstairs with the pilot while you guys were gone. They all act like they know each other."

"I thought the pilot said he didn't know them?"

"Yeah, he did, but they sure know him. And you know what? He says he's a math professor from the University of Maryland. Works on something with physics."

Laurent flicked the ash from his cigarette then gestured with it. "Sergeant, you should be very careful with these men.

The Gestapo and the Milice send spies to us all the time, impersonators and poseurs, pretending to be fliers, soldiers, escaped prisoners, all so they may uncover our networks. This could be a trap. Are you sure of who he is?"

Sloan shook his head. "We saw his bomber crash. He's got a broken leg. How could they...."

"Yeah, but how did that Anders guy know where all the weapons were? And the ambushes? Why was he so hot to get to the pilot?" Lezynski interjected.

Sloan turned to Lezynski. "Think about that. He's a German spy, and he's helping us kill krauts?"

"Sarge, he tried to kill you. That guy is definitely not on our side. And how does he know the kraut, who, by the way, speaks perfect English and seems to be buddies with the pilot? He says they've met before."

Laurent frowned. "Sergeant, we must interrogate these men. I do not like having them here. This is an important hiding place for us. We cannot let it be compromised."

"The pilot must have some I.D., papers, something," Sloan said.

Laurent flicked his cigarette and shook his head. "All can be forged. The Gestapo are very clever. We have been fooled many times. Interrogation is the only way to be sure."

"Holy shit. You know what?" Lezynski swore.

Sloan cocked his head.

"I bet that sonofabitch killed the other guys in that plane. I heard two shots when I was with the pilot. Remember he asked about his crew?" Lezynski's eyes were wide, looking back and forth between Laurent and Sloan.

The Frenchman pulled on his cigarette and watched through a cloud of smoke.

Sloan put his hands on his hips and looked at the floor. "Let me think about it. Don't say anything to the pilot until we can get him alone."

CHAPTER THIRTY-TWO

0700 June 10th, 1944
Near St. Jores, Normandy

"Hey, Top, it's Saturday. We get the day off, right?" Marino stood in front of him, grinning.

Sloan sat up and blinked, emerging from a deep sleep. Morning sun streamed in the windows. He'd slept far longer than he'd planned.

"It was your boy Speedy's idea. He took a double watch after he woke up. He and that other guy. They were out on the road with some Maquis, and the others watched the house. We all got a lot of sleep."

Sloan mumbled an expletive, angry at losing control of his men, but also feeling the benefit of the longest continuous sleep in almost a week. He walked to the front of the house and found Laurent standing by the front window smoking yet another cigarette.

"Good morning sergeant. Today is an important day. Something is happening in Carentan. The *boche* are hurrying everywhere. Some are leaving, but some are going to the town. There are many tanks to the south. I think they are trying to push them back."

"How do you know this?"

Laurent shrugged. "We have runners and lookouts. Many boys, they see, then they spread the word. Your radio man listened early this morning as well."

"What about Graignes? Can we get there?"

"We will try to find a way. The roads between here and there are very difficult. Many, many *boche*. For now, we must wait."

"What do you hear?" Sloan stood over Kellam, working his radio set, headphones on.

He shook his head, and kept working the knobs. After a few minutes, he took them off. "Something's definitely on. A lot of talk from our guys – they're moving, for sure, but I don't recognize the landmarks. Lots of talk from the beach. Sounds like we've got a lot of people ashore. The krauts are talking up a storm, too."

"This is delicious." Sloan slurped up the remains of the second bowl of soup.

Laurent smiled. "The *boche* have taken much from us, but we have learned to hide things well. The farmers are clever and give us what we need to stay strong for the fight."

The arrival of the Maquisards improved their lot considerably. The two older nuns bustled constantly, trying to keep the children out of the way. Juliette no longer seemed interested in the pretense of caring for the children. She spent most of her time hanging around the troops, listening and chiming in when she could. She sat near Laurent and Sloan, her empty bowl beside her.

Laurent continued. "This is the end. *Les boches ils sont finis.* We will take these weapons and kill every German in France, and then we'll purify the country of all the collaborators and anyone else who stands in the way of the New France."

"All the collaborators must die!" spat Juliette.

The maquisard smiled. "A purification. A great purification. Anyone who ever touched a German and didn't kill them. Shhhhhtttttt!" He drew is finger across his throat and smiled broadly.

Juliette's smile faltered. "Yes, of course."

Sister Ruth Marie waddled around the room and collected bowls. She looked over at Juliette with a knowing look and an arched eyebrow.

"Are you sure they won't come for you?"

Juliette glared at her. "I would worry about my own problems if I were you, Sister. The Church has many collaborators, too, you know."

Sister Thérèse scolded her. "Juliette! Shame on you! It's infamy!" She shook her head sadly, while Sister Ruth Marie continued her disapproving glare.

Juliette ignored them both.

"You have more weapons?" Sloan asked Laurent.

"*Oui*. We will bring you more. We have many of the bags dropped from the planes, as well as the supplies we have been given."

Willem finished his soup, listening to the banter between the paratroopers. The reunion with the others raised spirits and their enthusiasm was infectious. Juliette moved around the room, serving bowls, collecting dishes, directing the older girls. Willem watched the young men in the room watching her, all of them pretending not to notice the attentions of the others. One of the paratroopers in particular managed to keep finding reasons to interact with her – one of the new ones from last night, small and skinny, with a boyish face and dark, serious eyes. He offered to help Juliette, and she shyly accepted. Willem saw one of the other paratroopers nudge another, nodding toward the girl and the other paratrooper.

"That Green don't waste much time, does he?" Marino observed with a chuckle to no one in particular.

Willem smiled and continued his people-watching.

The loud voices drew the attention of the children, who approached warily. Willem spied one of the older girls watching them, two younger girls peeking out from the folds of her skirt. The face of the smallest girl was disfigured by a wrinkled pink scar around her eye, crossing her cheek to the corner of her mouth, lifting it slightly in a hideous suggestion of a Mona Lisa smile.

Marino noticed as well. "Hey, what happened to her?" he asked Juliette, standing in the doorway.

Juliette walked to the little girl and put a protective hand on her head.

"Hey, Marino, lay off. She's just a little kid," Jones reprimanded from the other wall, glaring.

Marino threw up his hands. "I'm just askin'. The little squirt don't speak English anyway, she doesn't understand me."

Juliette stroked the little girl's hair as she burrowed into her thigh, arms encircling the young woman's leg. "It is alright. She was burned, by a Nazi. They came to her house, demanding a place to sleep. Her mother was making dinner, fried potatoes. She offered some to the officer, and he knocked the skillet off the stove. The grease fell on the little girl. Her father went into a rage, attacked the officer, and they killed him. Later they killed the mother too, and her brothers. We rescued her, and now she hides here with the others."

Willem's heart broke, looking at the ruined face of the beautiful little girl, who bore more than a passing resemblance to his little nieces. Something in him hardened at the same time, the resolve that this was why he was here. Here was the real reason for going to war, to stop this kind of cruel inhumanity.

Time Bomber

The paratroopers swapped positions, and a new group entered the cellar to sit and eat. Doolan, McDonald, and Turturro adjusted themselves with their bowls, slurping the stew.

Willem recalled the events of the night before last with the wounded German boy. "Gentlemen, do you mind if I ask you a question?"

The three looked up, attentive.

"Why did you bring the wounded boy back here? I'm curious."

Turturro gestured with his spoon at MacDonald. "It was his idea. Ask him."

MacDonald shrugged.

Doolan chimed in. "It's what the Geneva Conventions says we should do. You take care of wounded. Doesn't matter whose. It's the right thing to do."

Turturro snorted. "That's bullshit, kid. Wake up. You think some crummy kraut's going to give you a shot a morphine and a pillow under your head? You saw. They'll shoot you for target practice and laugh while they're doing it. Just shoot the dumb bastard, that's what I said."

"It's not Christian. That's not how I was raised," Doolan replied.

Turturro laughed with savage glee. "Christian? I got news for you kid, old Jesus ain't got much to say about being a paratrooper, or this whole mess. You want to get home alive, you better forget about Sunday school for a while. What a waste of time."

MacDonald looked up from his bowl. "No, a waste of time is your crappy aim. You should have killed him the first time."

Turturro glared at him. "Shut your trap."

"You ever worked on a farm?" MacDonald pressed.

"Do I look like some kind of hayseed?"

"You ever slaughtered a pig?"

Turturro furrowed his brow, confused.

MacDonald continued. "You do it wrong, miss your spot, you turn a two-second job into an hour of chasing around, a squealing mess. That's a waste of time. Just do it right, get it over with."

Willem was appalled and fascinated with this turn of logic. Doolan gaped in horror.

Juliette listened from the other side of the room. "Yes, slaughter them like pigs. That's what they are. They don't deserve any mercy."

MacDonald turned to her. "Then why were you making bandages for him all night?"

She opened her mouth to reply, then turned away. Willem watched in silence as they finished their meal.

Later in the afternoon another cart approached the chateau, this time piled high with hay. The maquisards greeted the farmer, the same one who had brought the food two days ago. Sloan and MacDonald exchanged knowing looks. The farmer drove the cart around to the back of the building.

Underneath the hay were three of the canvas supply bags that had been dropped with the paratroopers. They lifted them out of the cart and brought them inside. The paratroopers crowded around and opened them like presents on Christmas morning. One contained ammunition and rations, the other a .30 caliber machine gun and a BAR. And, most surprising, two whole cartons of Lucky Strikes, wrapped in several issues of Stars and Stripes.

"Dibs the thirty!" Marino called out.

Green grinned. "I'm a heavy weapons squad guy too."

"Alright, me and you on the thirty. Hey, why's he call you Speedy?"

Green grinned and shrugged.

Sloan heard and chimed in. "Because he was the fastest guy at Toccoa. Best time up and down Currahee, no one else even close."

"Maybe in Second Battalion. We had some pretty fast guys in First." Marino replied.

Sloan shook his head and slapped Green on the shoulder. "No one faster than Speedy. No one."

They took the weapons downstairs to strip and clean them. Sloan put all the men not on guard duty to work, restocking ammunition, loading clips, performing maintenance on all the weapons. They spread out on the floor of the basement, bantering as they worked and Willem watched and listened, sitting against the wall.

"How's things going with your girlfriend?" Marino asked Green, eliciting a deep blush. Marino chuckled at the response. Green shook his head while Marino continued. "She's a looker. Know who she reminds me of? Judy Garland."

Green beamed.

"Yeah, right. Maybe if you cut off Judy's hair," Lezynski observed while he cleaned his M1.

"Forget about her hair. Look at her eyes, her lips. She could be her little sister." Marino leered at Green, expecting a response, but received none, as Green bent to his weapon-cleaning.

Sister Ruth Marie stood in the doorway in the basement, five bottles clutched to her bosom. "These are for you. We don't drink them. You can have them."

"Oh, ho, what do we have here?" Marino stood up and took a bottle, uncorked it and sniffed. "Apples?"

"It is *calvados*. It is very good for health." Sister Ruth Marie had a bland look on her face.

Lezynski stood up and took the bottle from Marino, then gathered the rest from the nun. He gave Marino a dirty look. "Thank you, sister. We'll take care of this."

Marino opened his mouth to protest.

Lezynski turned to him. "If you think I'm going to let you drink this stuff right now, Marino, you're crazy. If Sloan saw you slugging this back, he'd shoot you himself."

"I swear to God, the guy's got a horseshoe up his ass. I never seen anyone so lucky," Marino said, reassembling the Thompson, parts spread in front of him.

"Who?" Green asked, pushing the swatch of cloth down the barrel of his M1.

"Top. He gets captured by krauts, and the officer turns out to be from Evanston. We were dead meat. It's crazy. What kind of luck is that?"

Green considered it. "Why do you think it's Sgt. Sloan? Why not you?"

Marino shook his head. "I got luck, kid, but not that kind of luck. I make my luck. Check out the odds, make my bet. Always know the odds. No sucker bets."

"You think you can figure the odds on that kind of thing?" Green asked.

Marino laughed and shook his head. "No way. I just try to find the guys that know what they're doing, and the ones that seem lucky, and I stick with them. Sloan's lucky, I can tell. They ain't made the bullet yet with his name on it."

"The bullet?" Willem asked.

"We all got one. Somewhere out there, there's a bullet with your name on it, with my name on it. Stay lucky, it don't find you for a while. Me, I'm going home. That bullet is going to have to look a long, long time for Donnie Marino."

Willem smiled at the image of a bullet roaming around the planet, chasing after Donnie Marino, peering through windows, traveling across the countryside, hovering over city streets, tracking its intended target. His mathematical mind took the image and began applying more rigor, creating chains of causality, following the bullet back to the gun that fired it, the hammer lifting back and unstriking the firing pin, the round moving back into the magazine, the magazine unloading, the bullet returning to its shipping case, back onto the truck, back to the factory, the metal melted, the powder unmixed, the constituent elements whirling away back to their origins. He walked it forward again, looking at all the contingencies, how that course could be altered, sending that bullet flying off in some different direction, its violent intersection with Donnie Marino's brain altered, perhaps irrevocably.

Once again he was back in Dublin, lounging in Harrie and Billy's library at Clondarf with Spike last winter, wrapped in smoking jackets, bellies full, sipping brandy and smoking cigars, listening to Harrie on the piano and relaxing. Harrie doted on them as if they were her own sons. Though her marriage to Billy Kirkwood was childless, she had no shortage of maternal energy for them. Billy Kirkwood, retired from British military intelligence and the Bengal Lancers, was still well connected and alternately regaled them with tales of polo exploits and the shadowy maneuverings of the Allies and the Axis. He and Spike often compared notes in hushed whispers after meals while Willem read or sat with Harrie.

Willem and Spike spent long days hiking, eating, sleeping, and laughing.

"Really, Willem, you can't have it both ways. Either your math explains it all, or it doesn't. You can't claim rigor and then say it denies determinism," Spike challenged him in the drawing room one night after dinner.

Willem chuckled, at ease. The long walks around Dublin with Spike over the last several days had finally lifted him out of his dark funk, and the horrors of the squadron were temporarily forgotten on his leave.

"It's not an either or proposition, Spike. You can have two models that both work, but remain incomplete. Then the task is to find a synthesis to resolve the contradictions."

"Ah, the contradictions. How Hegelian. The mathematical dialectic?" They swirled brandy in bulbous snifters and puffed on their cigars.

"I know you don't believe in absolute determinism, because then where would your Free Will be, your sin and redemption? If you can't choose to be good, how can you sin?"

Spike laughed. "True, true. I am only challenging the primacy of your mathematics. How can you claim to explain nature's laws but still assert that they are unknowable at some level?"

"But there's the distinction: at some level. As long as you are clear about your level, you can claim what you will, using the proper models for your level. Quantum mechanics is about very small things. It works! But for you and I, Newtonian physics is a much better approximation."

"Yes, the approximation. So much for certainty."

Willem laughed again, reveling in the warmth and stimulation of his friend's clever mind and comfortable companionship. A few brandies later, the fire was dying, and they returned to the subject of the war, and Willem's experiences with the squadron.

"It is a mystery to me how some of the men keep going. The terror of the missions absolutely destroys some. Drives them barking mad. Just in training, we've had people just snap from stress, and turn into weeping, blithering lunatics."

The most recent event, the one that haunted Willem still, was that of the crews on a purportedly easy training mission dropping leaflets over France. The pilot had to be carried out of the plane after landing, having flown all the way home with the decapitated body of his engineer seated next to him. The engineer had been discussing oil pressure one moment and was slumped and silent the next, neatly beheaded by an errant piece of flak. The rest of the crew initially had no idea, but discovered the gory situation when the pilot would not answer. They moved the body to the back for the rest of the flight, but the damage was done.

Spike nodded, watching Willem over the rim of his glass, silent.

"And then there are the others, the ones who seem unfazed. They just get up and do it again and again, no matter how awful things get. Is it the training? Is it something inside them? And why do it at all?" Willem stared into the fire. Spike remained quiet.

"Talk about uncertainty," Willem concluded, tossing back the rest of his brandy.

Later Spike went up to bed, and Willem lay on the couch reading Joyce's *The Dubliners* from Billie's library. He fell asleep, the book open on his chest. At some point in the night, Harrie crept in and covered him with a blanket and turned down the lights. Once again he had the dream: he was sitting on Oisin's horse over the waves, looking up at the cliffs, keeping the horse from riding into the West.

He woke in the darkness, warm under the blanket, the fire having burned down to a faintly glowing bed of coals. The house was quiet, the ticking of the old German clock in the foyer soft in the distance, the coals tinkling as they crumbled into ash. Unbidden, it just came to him, a moment of intuition, unconscious inspiration, his inner mind reaching out to deliver the product of long rumination. The cliffs were the well, turned inside out. The hyperbola describing his survival odds could be represented another way, flipped around, then rotated. Instead of a pit, it became a mountain, a summit to be scaled. Instead of falling, he had to climb. That realization brought instant peace, a settling calm that pervaded his soul.

A new metaphor, Dr. Einstein's words echoed. The dream suddenly made some sense to him, his challenge clearer.

He woke the next morning in Dublin refreshed and tranquil, and that serenity followed him back to the unit. His calm was infectious, and the crew responded.

Back in the chateau basement, he returned to the image of the bullet, the one with Marino's name on it, but, this time, he imagined it as a function, a vector, the other contingencies as constituent vectors, moving and changing in space and time, multidimensional surfaces contorting and intersecting, giving rise to new contingencies, unfolding, bending, curving….

"Hey, doc, you okay?"

Willem's reverie came to an abrupt halt. He looked at the paratroopers, who were all staring at him. He furrowed his brow in response to the question.

Marino repeated it. "You okay? You looked like you were off in la-la land there."

Willem smiled and shook his head. "Just thinking about something, that's all."

Green smiled back at him, and they returned to their chore, the talk transitioning from baseball to women.

Willem listened to them a while longer, then gathered himself to stand. The soup he had for breakfast invigorated him, and with his new splint and now a matching crutch, he wanted to stretch his legs. He struggled to his feet, then tested the crutches. His head was clearer, and the throbbing in his leg much improved. If he avoided putting weight on the injury, he could maneuver comfortably. He traversed the room, passing in front of the other two prisoners tied to their chairs. Both had finished their meals and were tied up again.

Willem turned to the door and started out into the main room of the basement.

"Hey, doc, where you going?" Marino called out.

Willem looked back over his shoulder. "Just getting some exercise."

Marino looked at Green and jerked his head sideways toward Willem. "You know what Top said."

Green got up and followed Willem.

He circled the main room in the basement, passing by the doorway where the children stayed. The nuns spoke to small groups leading a lesson, but all the children looked up and watched Willem and Green walk by. Green held his M1 in front of him pointed at the floor.

"So where are you from?" Willem asked.

"New York. Up near Buffalo."

"You know where Geneseo is?"

"Sure, that's not too far from me."

"My uncle has a farm up there. We visit him sometimes. Nice country."

"Yeah, it's nice. Haven't been there in a while. Almost three years. Since before I enlisted."

They walked in silence, Willem breathing a little heavier with the effort.

Green watched him, interested. "Hey, don't strain yourself, Doc."

Willem smiled. "I've got to do something to kill the time. I also want to be ready when it's time to move. I heard the conversation before. I don't want to be a burden."

"You're no burden."

Willem looked over at him. "You don't have to walk with me, you know. I can manage this."

Green blushed. "Well, it's not that …. We're just … I mean …."

Willem waited patiently.

"Sergeant Sloan says we're supposed to stay with you all the time."

Willem cocked an eyebrow. "Why?"

Green gestured back toward the side room with his rifle. "Those guys."

"Sloan thinks I'm involved with them somehow?"

Green shrugged.

Willem continued his circling, mulling this new twist, trailed politely by his new bodyguard.

"Jesus Christ! What the hell happened to him?" Jones blurted.

The paratroopers stood in the foyer of the chateau, preparing to switch assignments. A knot of children milled in the entry to the kitchen, just come in from the yard in back. Two older boys held one of the younger ones between them, crying and clutching his hand, blood dripping on the floor. Juliette rushed over and a rush of animated French flowed back and forth.

Juliette turned to the paratroopers. "One of the boys took a knife from a soldier. They were playing with it and he cut his hand."

One of the older boys pulled the injured one close and spoke to him in low tones, urgently. The younger one stifled his crying and sniffled.

"Hey, that's my goddam knife!" Marino yelled, stepping forward.

One of the boys sheepishly held out the trench knife, the one Marino had taken from the dead German the first day in the mansion. Green glanced at Gardner, watching from the side. Gardner swayed unsteadily, his face pale.

Lezynski knelt down and pressed a rag into the boy's hand to stop the bleeding. "Let me see this. We'll get it fixed up. Tell him not to worry, we'll help him."

Juliette held the boy's shoulders and put her face next to his, speaking to him calmly. The boy bit his lip, sniffled, then slowly nodded his head. Juliette straightened. "I told him that he needs to be brave, and show the American soldiers that a French boy can be strong and brave."

"Hey, pal, you better go check on your buddy. He's acting a little weird."

Green looked at Marino. "What do you mean?"

"Jumpy. Nervous in the service. Something's wrong with him. I don't think the apple stuff is helping."

"Where is he?"

Marino gestured upwards.

Green climbed the stairs, searching each room and hoping to find him before someone else did. In the attic, he found Gardner slumped against the wall, staring out the dormer window at the sky, left hand on a bottle of calvados between his legs, his forty-five on the floor next to him in his right hand. He did not stir at Green's approach.

"Hey. Gardner. What's going on?"

Gardner turned his head slowly, face vacant. His red-rimmed eyes glistened atop dark sagging lids. He lifted the bottle and took a long draw. Some of the liquid spilled down his chin, and he drew the back of his hand across his mouth, the forty-five brushing past his nose.

He drew a heavy sigh. "We killed them."

"Who?" Gardner looked at him, face working.

"We killed them. I know we did. I saw it."

"Killed who? Tell me." Green eased down next to him, a careful eye on the forty-five.

"Me and Stevens. They said clear the street, so we did. Near Vittoria."

"In Sicily?"

"Vittoria."

"So what happened?"

"We threw grenades. Grenade in, wait for the bang, clear the room, next house. Down the street." He fell silent, then took another swallow from the bottle.

Green waited patiently.

"Sicily was like this. Jump all screwed up. I was by myself for the first day." Another silence.

"I found one of our guys, the Italians got him before he could get out of his harness. They stabbed him to death, butchered him, cut him open. When I got to him, the pigs were on him, eating him."

He stared at the floor, voice in a flat monotone. "I walked the next day, looking for someone from my unit. The bombers and the artillery had blasted the countryside. Dead animals and civilians everywhere. The smell."

Green watched him staring at the floor, transfixed by visions trapped in his head. His lips moved wordlessly, head shaking slightly from side to side.

"I found a cart turned over. The horse was dead, all swollen. Next to the cart, on the ground was the family. A mother and father and some children, all dead, in pieces. The mother had no legs, but there was still a baby in her arm next to her. There were flies all over the baby, in the eyes, crawling out of the mouth, the nose."

Gardner looked up for the first time, right at Green. "It surprised me. I walked around the side of the cart, and it scared me. I wasn't expecting it. I threw up, then I ran. The smell, and the flies. Later I met the other guys." He took another swig of calvados. He looked at Green and offered the bottle.

Time Bomber

Green took it and pretended to take a sip, then handed it back. He could see Gardner struggling again, face crumpling.

"We had to clear the street. They said clear the street. So we did." His voice started breaking and a shuddering sob convulsed his body.

Green sat down next to him and put an arm around him. "Hey. It's okay. It's okay."

Gardner broke down and wept. Green pulled him close and pressed his head into his chest, patting him on the back. They sat there for several minutes. Green reached down and gently removed the forty-five from Gardner's unresisting right hand.

The shuddering movements subsided, and Gardner sat up, rubbing his face with the palms of his hands, sniffing and coughing. "They called for a medic. We ran back. In one of the houses, there was a family, dead, blood all over the place. The lieutenant chewed me and Stevens out, why didn't we check. We said it wasn't our street, but I wasn't sure. I was so tired. They made us take the bodies out. Two little girls and an old lady. Now, I can't get them out of my head, or the cart. It gets all jumbled together. And I can't remember who threw the grenades."[2]

They sat quietly for another few minutes, Gardner now more calm.

Green broke the silence. "Listen, why don't we go back downstairs and you get some sleep. If Sgt. Sloan sees you drinking, he's gonna be pissed. I'll cover for you, sleep this off." Green stood up, holding the forty-five. He extended a hand to Gardner and hoisted him up, leaning forward with the effort of lifting the larger man, unsteady with alcohol.

Gardner tipped the bottle up one last time, draining the remainder. He tossed the empty into the corner, then reached down for his helmet and Thompson. He turned to Green and saw the forty-five, and their eyes met.

Green hesitated, then held it out. "Why don't you put this away?"

Gardner stared at him, then his eyes fell, and he reached for the gun. "Yeah." He holstered it and they went back downstairs.

"Sergeant, tell your men out by the road to be careful. The Germans are moving. The Americans are in Carentan. More *boche* are coming. There will be a big battle tomorrow."

Sloan watched through the field glasses out the second floor window. Laurent stood behind him. Through the budding trees, he could see groups of German troops hurrying down the dusty lane three fields over. In another week, the fully leafed trees would completely conceal the view, enveloping the chateau in foliage.

He turned back to the resistance leader. "Our radioman hears a lot of talk. Something is going on, so that makes sense. Can we make our move?"

Laurent shook his head. "Still too dangerous. We are staying concealed until the *boche* are in position, then we may move against their rear. But we don't want to get too close, or your friends may shoot us." Laurent grinned.

Sloan returned a grim smile. He knew all about friendly fire.

"Have you decided what you will do with the prisoners?"

Sloan shook his head. "I'm going to talk to them. We'll make a decision today."

Marino and Green lounged against the wall in the central room of the basement. Some of the children worked upstairs cleaning, others played in the back room supervised by one of the older girls. Sgt. Lezynski was back on sentry duty in the other side room, watching over the pilot and the two prisoners.

"Hey, Green, check that out." Marino nudged Green and nodded toward the opposite wall where Gardner slumped, deep in sleep. Two of the little girls, one with the scarred face, squatted next to the sleeping paratrooper, clutching paper dolls. They pointed to him and conferred between themselves in sing-song French.

"*He's a demon, but a friendly one.*"

"*A friendly demon? You mean an angel.*"

"*An angel? Does he look like an angel?*"

The smaller girl shrugged.

"*The chocolate was good.*"

"*Even demons like chocolate. He is a servant of the queen. Of course he would bring us gifts.*" The older girl sat down next to the sleeping figure and held two dolls, moving them in a pantomime.

Green and Marino watched, smiling.

"What are they doing?" Green whispered.

Marino shrugged. "Beats me, but it's pretty funny."

The smaller girl with the scar sat back on her heels in a tiny ball, studying Gardner's sleeping face. Tentatively, she reached out and gently touched the spiky fuzz of his Mohawk, rubbing her hand back and forth along the bristles.

"*All the children must obey! If you disobey, you will die!*" the older girl said in a stern voice, holding the one doll over the other.

The smaller girl looked over her shoulder and watched the older girl's make-believe.

"*Yes, your highness, we will obey.*"

The little girl turned back and reached again to touch Gardner's cheek, wiping a remnant of the grease paint from his dirty skin. She looked at her finger.

"*You must obey, or I will send my demons from the sky to destroy you!*"

The little girl rubbed her fingers together and studied Gardner's face, leaning close. His breathing was deep and even, his sleep undisturbed by the noise from the children. She turned back to the older girl.

"*He is a dirty angel.*"

The older girl ignored her and continued her game.

The younger one sat back and pulled out her doll, leaning with her back against Gardner's body, and began her part of the pretend game.

Marino slapped his thigh. "Hey, I know where I've seen you guys! At Bragg! Down at The Pump! That was you guys, wasn't it?"

Green smiled sheepishly. "The big fight?"

"Yeah, about the juke box. That was Sloan, wasn't it?"

Green nodded.

"I knew I knew him from somewhere. Now that's funny. Boy, what a donnybrook that was. All over a stupid song."

"Actually, that was all my fault. Me and my buddy kept putting dimes in before anyone else and playing the songs we wanted, and we started getting heat. They pushed my buddy, I jumped in, and we were getting beat pretty bad. Sgt. Sloan piled in and held off about ten guys until the MPs came, and he was the one that got busted for it. Second time, for him. He'd probably be an officer by now if it weren't for that."

"Filles! Evadez-vous du soldat! Ne le dérangez pas!" hissed Juliette from the stairs, shooing them away from the sleeping Gardner.

Sloan and MacDonald followed her down the stairs.

"Green, go out to the road. MacDonald, relieve Lezynski in there. Get the pilot out here."

Green slowly gathered his equipment, watching over Gardner to make sure he wasn't disturbed.

Sloan ignored him. "Marino, what are you doing?"

"I was just upstairs, Top."

Sloan made no response.

MacDonald ducked into the room where the three strangers sat, and soon Lezynski appeared, helping the wounded pilot. He was moving better on his crutches, and leaned against the wall near the sleeping figure of Gardner. The two little girls hovered nearby, watching.

Sloan pulled up an old wooden chair. "Doc, why don't you sit down?"

Willem shook his head. "I need to stretch my legs. I'm fine."

Sloan shrugged, spun the chair around and sat on it backward, leaning over the back. Juliette squatted on the floor, watching the girls, but listening to the conversation.

"Sir, I hope you can understand the position I'm in here, but I've got to ask you some more questions. Our new Resistance friends have some concerns about whether or not you might be a spy, and frankly, some of my guys are thinking the same thing. I'm not an intelligence guy, I don't do interrogations, but I'm just going to have to make do, because it's my responsibility and my decision. This whole thing is pretty fishy, with these two guys in there calling each other spies and both claiming to be Americans and both claiming to know you. The guy in the American uniform I don't trust, and the kraut, even though he sounds like an American, is obviously trying to kill the guy who is dressed as an American. And then there's you."

Willem followed this intently, immediately recognizing the seriousness of the tone and the potential ramifications of how the discussion could end. Marino watched from his seat against the opposite wall, shuffling his cards, his Thompson on the ground next to him.

"So tell me again why you think they are so interested in you."

Willem shrugged. "As I said before, I honestly don't know. I've never seen them before, and I have no idea what this is about."

"Have you ever been involved in secret stuff? Work for the government?"

Willem shook his head. "No. I've spoken to various people about joining some projects, but nothing ever came of it. I wanted to finish my commitment to the bomber group. I was waiting for the transfer to England when the offer came, and I turned it down."

"What offer?"

"Uh, to join a research group. It was – I mean, is – secret. But I declined, so it can't be about that."

"When was that?"

"Last fall. I arrived in England at the beginning of the year. I haven't been in contact with anyone from that group since then."

"Who have you been in contact with?"

Willem shrugged again. "My family, colleagues back home, a potential employer for after the war, nothing secret."

"You've got a job lined up for after the war? With who?"

Willem smiled. "Princeton University. At the research institute there."

Sloan's interest heightened. "Research?"

"The Institute for Advanced Studies."

Sloan shook his head. "Never heard of it."

Willem reached into his pocket and withdrew the letter. "I received this a few days before we left on this mission. It's a letter from Professor Einstein at Princeton offering me a research position after I finish my military service."

Sloan took the letter, unfolded it, and scanned the spidery script. He turned it over and examined the signature. "Hmmm. You think these guys have anything to do with this?"

"I can't imagine how. I'm not a spy, I don't have any secret formulas, I have no plans for secret weapons. I'm very proficient at the mathematics of certain theoretical problems in physics. That's what I've been talking with Professor Einstein about."[3]

Sloan handed the letter back and stood up. "I'll be honest with you sir, I don't know what to make of your story. I think I believe you, because you don't seem like a liar to me, but I've got no way to be sure. Meantime, I've got all these other people that are very suspicious and eager to make this problem just go away, if you know what I mean."

Willem lost some of his color and swallowed. He nodded slowly.

"But I'm not going to let that happen. I'm in charge here, and as far as I'm concerned, we've still got a mission, and you and these other two are just another load we've got to carry. As long as that doesn't interfere with our mission, I'm okay with waiting to see what else develops. But in the meantime, I hope you don't mind that these folks are going to be keeping an eye on you. There won't be any wandering around, and especially don't go near the radio. If the Maquis see you near the radio, they will shoot you. So just stay down here anyway, okay?"

Willem nodded again.

Sloan went back upstairs, and shortly afterward, MacDonald joined them in the basement. Juliette remained on the floor, watching the soldiers distractedly. The little girls crept back to Gardner, still asleep on the floor. Marino sat against the wall near Willem.

MacDonald sat down against the adjacent wall and stretched his legs out. "What're those little girls doing? Does he know they're playing dollies on him?"

"Y'know, old One Eye ain't so bad once you get to talking to him. I don't know why that Anders guy gets after him so much."

"Who's One Eye?" MacDonald asked.

"The kraut. Like One Eye Connolly."

"Who?"

"One Eye Connolly. You never heard of him? He's a guy back in Chicago, sneaks into everything. You have a big event, One Eye will show up, no matter what. Can't keep him out. A big fight, convention, big party, One Eye always gets in. Just like that kraut keeps showing up. Lezynski thinks he's the same guy he killed a coupla days ago. I think he's right. Guy just keeps coming back."

"Except I bet they don't shoot One Eye in the head, and he comes back again." MacDonald drawled.

Marino chuckled. "That's true. Andy Frain's guys just toss him out, but he does come back. One time he got a carton a peanuts and starting selling them at a White Sox game, and he walked up to Andy Frain and asked him if he wanted to buy some peanuts."

"Who's Andy Frain?"

"You dope. He's the guy does security at all the big games, everything. For crissakes, you know anything?"

Gardner opened up his bleary eyes and sat up, rubbing his face, sending the little girls scurrying away. He looked around, and saw the others watching him. He unscrewed the cap of his canteen and took a long drink, draining it. For having just slept he still looked exhausted, eyes red and puffy. He stood up and went to the other room where he loudly relieved himself into the bucket.

"Hey, that thing need emptying?" Marino asked when Gardner returned.

Gardner shrugged.

"Well, it's your turn when it does. I did mine, so it's someone else's turn, and you're it. Hoo boy, you look like you could use some Bromo Seltzer," Marino continued.

Gardner took it in without reply.

Sister Ruth Marie appeared and scolded the children, then Juliette for not keeping a closer eye on them.

Juliette laughed at the sight of Sister Ruth Marie chasing the little girls back into the children's room.

"What's so funny?"

"The sister. She is angry with the girls playing their games, but she is the one who encourages it. She reads them the scientific fantasy stories, then she is surprised when the girls take their pretend games too far."

"The what?" Willem asked.

"Scientific fantasy. Jules Verne. He is one of the greatest French writers. He writes fantastic stories about the moon, special machines, things like that."

Gardner was wide-awake and listening closely.

"Oh. The children love these stories?" Willem continued.

"Yes, they are wonderful. Not to my taste, but the children do enjoy them."

Gardner cleared his throat and chimed in. "Wells is a better writer."

Juliette looked at him in surprise. "Better than Verne? Bah. That is nonsense. Verne, and Voltaire, Rousseau, Dumas, Hugo, these are the best. Wells is no one."

"Wells? He the guy who did the *War of the Worlds*?" Marino inquired.

Gardner nodded. He reached into his pocket and took out the paperback, then tossed it to Marino.

"Yeah, that was him. Great story."

"Where'd you get this?" Marino asked.

"Morale tent at Aldbourne. They were giving them away."

Marino thumbed through the book and tossed it back, shaking his head. "Scared the crap out of my mom. She thought it was real. Worst Halloween ever. My old man made us all come in, she said we needed to hide in the basement. She was a wreck for weeks. Boy, was he pissed at Wells. He hit the roof when I went and saw *Citizen Kane*."

Gardner shook his head. "That's Orson Welles, different guy. He did the radio show. H.G. Wells wrote the book."

"Wait, Orson Welles didn't make that up? Same name, different guy, same story? What're the odds a that?" Marino queried the group.

"H.G. Wells writes a lot of scientific stories, good stuff. He predicts a lot of things that come true." Gardner looked at Willem. "Bombing cities from airplanes, he predicted that."

"I didn't know that." Willem replied.

"In '33, he wrote about it, in *The Shape of Things to Come*. Also rocket bombs, like the buzz bombs. A bunch of other stuff." Gardner's sudden volubility had everyone's attention.

"My father designed a rocket bomb, on a boat. He was an inventor," Willem shared. "My mother made him destroy the plans. She said it was immoral."

Gardner nodded. "Wells writes a lot about how technology changes morality."

"This is the book guy?" Marino asked.

"Yeah, the book guy."

"Man, I hope his other stuff ain't true. Martians ain't my cuppa tea. That son of a bitch on the radio sure made them seem real."

"That's Orson."

Willem chuckled, shaking his head.

Marino narrowed his eyes. "What, you know him or something?"

"Actually, he's a friend of mine."

"Orson Welles? The actor? No way."

Willem nodded, smiling at Marino's incredulity.

"How's that?" Marino challenged.

"When I was a student in Dublin, he was there starting his acting career. We became friends, we've stayed in touch since.

In fact, I just had lunch with him last summer, before I came over here. In New York. I met his wife."

"His wife? You met Rita Hayworth? Now I know you're lying."

"It's true, I did. She's a very nice lady."

"She's nice all right. Hoo boy, oh, what I would give."

"So you saw Citizen Kane?" Willem asked.

Marino nodded.

"What did you think?"

Marino pushed out his lower lip and furrowed his brow. "I thought it was kinda weird, but after I saw it the second time, I started to kinda like it. I think I get what he was trying to do, jumping around with the camera and all that. My buddies all hated it, but the papers loved it. Did you see it?"

Willem shook his head. "No, I never had the chance. That was a busy summer for me. By the time I had some leave and was back in a big town, it was already out of the theaters."

Gardner spoke up. "I saw it. Fantastic movie. One of the best I've ever seen."

Willem chuckled and looked around the room. "I must confess, gentlemen, I never expected to be spending any time during the war sitting in France discussing film and literature with some paratroopers."

Marino laughed. "Yeah, life is funny like that, ain't it?"

Willem became thoughtful again. "Last summer when I was in Chicago, a man I met with mentioned Wells, his predictions. Just like you mentioned. I had forgotten it until just now. Something else he had written." Willem was lost in thought.

Gardner stared at him. "This is about atomic bombs, isn't it?"

Willem's eyes went wide. "How did you know that's what I was thinking of?"

Gardner shrugged. "Physicist, secret agents, weapons. It had to be." He reached into his pocket and pulled out a magazine. "It's all in here."

"What is?"

"The atomic bomb program. My cousin sent me this and said federal agents are taking them all from the newsstands because it contains secret weapon stuff. He sent this to me to keep for him. I just finished reading it." Gardner held out the March issue of *Astounding Science Fiction*.[4]

Willem flipped through the pages, and then read intently. He gave a long whistle then looked up.

"This is amazing."

Gardner smiled. "You mean astounding."

Willem looked up with a question on his face, then flipped over the magazine to the cover and broke into a big grin. He tossed the magazine back to Gardner, who stashed it in his pocket. "Would one of you gentlemen mind accompanying me upstairs? I'd like to get some sun and fresh air, if that's possible."

"Dr. van Stockum, I'd prefer you stayed inside. For safety," Anders broke his long silence.

Stimmel made no comment.

"I'll be careful. Besides, one of the men will be with me. Who wants to go?"

Marino, MacDonald, and Gardner looked at each other.

"Didn't Sarge just say for you to stay down here?" MacDonald ventured.

Willem shook his head. "He said he preferred it. I need exercise, and I need some fresh air. Please, bring your rifle. I won't make trouble, I assure you." He wasn't backing down.

"I'll go," Gardner volunteered. He stood up and shouldered his rifle, then put on his helmet.

Willem used his crutches to push himself up and briskly swung himself forward and through the door.

"Boy, you really got the hang of that, Doc," Marino observed. Willem grinned. "As I said, I'm eminently trainable."

Marino looked at MacDonald after they left and lifted his chin. "He ain't no spy. These two clowns? Maybe. But he ain't no spy."

Willem and Gardner stood at the back door in the kitchen.

"May I go outside?" Willem asked.

Gardner shrugged. "Suits me."

They opened the door, and Willem noted the dried blood smears on the floor. He leaned on his crutches with one hand, grasped the railing with the other, and hopped down the three steps to the dirt courtyard behind the chateau, surrounded by outbuildings and a small barn. Gardner watched him closely, assessing his disability.

The land behind the chateau rose gradually to dense forest just beyond the small fields. More forest wrapped around the left, where the land rose again, and on the right, the sprawling apple orchard, now in full bloom, concealed the house in a wooded bowl. It was the first time Willem had seen the house from the outside, and he relished the fresh air and the late afternoon sun on his face. The soft breeze carried the scents of the blossoms, the freshly turned earth, the silage, the animals.

The weather had cleared again, and it was a warm day, with a clear blue sky. Perfect flying weather. Off to the north and east, the incessant booming and clattering of automatic weapons in the far distance. The sounds were now very clear. Gardner cocked his head and listened as well. They looked at each other.

"Sounds like things are heating up. Let's hope it's going well," Willem said.

Gardner made no response.

Willem swung across the courtyard, happy to move in the open air. Gardner ambled behind him, his rifle slung on his back, looking up into the blue sky and squinting against the bright light. They approached the barn, and Willem noticed the boots of the young German soldier from the other night protruding from behind the corner, still unburied from when he'd been dragged out of the basement.

Gardner noticed his gaze and gestured to the boots. "Who's that?"

"A German boy. One of the others shot him and he died inside the house. Looks like they haven't gotten around to burying him yet."

Gardner nodded, and they continued their stroll, their enjoyment of the afternoon untroubled by the corpse. They made one circuit of the courtyard, then Willem turned the corner and headed toward the side of the house. Gardner followed. As they neared the edge of the wooded area surrounding the house, a maquisard emerged from behind a tree and wordlessly pointed a submachine gun at them. Gardner locked eyes with him, but made no move with his own weapon. Willem looked between them nervously. The maquisard lifted his chin back toward the courtyard, and after a moment's hesitation, Gardner turned.

"Looks like we better go back this way."

Willem pivoted on his crutches, and they headed back the way they came. Gardner walked by his side now, staring straight ahead. They reached their starting point, and Willem stopped to raise his face into the sun, drinking in the cloudless blue sky.

Gardner watched him. "The French guys think you're a spy."

Willem couldn't tell if it was a question or a statement. "I certainly hope not. I'm counting on Sgt. Sloan to convince them of that."

"The other guys said you're a mathematics professor."

Willem smiled and nodded.

"What's your area of interest?"

"Well, that's evolving. I've worked a lot on special problems in algebraic geometry, but lately I've been dabbling in some other things. In fact, here's an example." Willem stopped to lean on the crutches while he reached inside his flight suit and pulled out the Dirac monograph he'd forgotten about. He handed it to Gardner.

"Some light reading for your collection."

Gardner flipped through the pages, stopping to scan a few paragraphs, then flipped some more. "You worked with Albert Einstein."

"Not yet. I'm hoping to."

"How'd you meet him?"

"I was at Princeton for six months before the war and met him there. My dissertation was on a topic of interest to him, and we spoke several times about it. When I left for flight training, we exchanged letters."

"Your dissertation?"

"My doctoral thesis. It was a special problem in relativity. He admired my approach."

"You know much about relativity?"

Willem smiled and shrugged. "Some. You have an interest in science?"

Gardner shrugged in return. "I'm an English teacher but I read a lot of science fiction. The science teacher at our school was a friend of mine. We talked a lot."

Willem nodded with a grin. "I'm guessing you don't get a lot of that kind of discussion with your fellow paratroopers."

Gardner looked up at the chateau and considered the question. "I don't really know these guys. Green's the only one I've spent time with. I switched units, so I didn't know the guys I jumped with here. My old unit took a lot of casualties, I was injured." Gardner paused, and became distant. "I switched."

Willem noticed that the small flicker of animation that had been in Gardner's face while they talked science was now gone, replaced again by the stony reserve he usually displayed. They stood in silence for a few moments, and the wind picked up, carrying a blizzard of apple blossom petals in swirling cloud, momentarily engulfing the two soldiers. Willem enjoyed the tickling sensation of the petals lightly touching his face, and the perfume of the flowers. He turned to make a remark to Gardner, but was startled to see him gone, completely obscured by the storm. Just as quickly, he emerged from the swirl, as if stepping into the world. He cocked his head, puzzled by Willem's expression of surprise and amusement. Willem laughed, and Gardner returned a smile.

Turturro stuck his head out the back door. "Hey, Top says to get inside. He doesn't want you guys spotted."

Willem and Gardner went back into the kitchen, then back down into the basement.

After a dinner of more soup, supplemented with rations, Sloan came back down to the basement and separated Willem from the others, leading him back upstairs. They sat in the dining room outside the kitchen, where Anders had been attacked the first time. Sloan gave him a wooden chair, which Willem this time accepted. He then picked up another and sat on it backward, leaning over the back facing Willem.

"So this is about some secret weapon?" Sloan asked.

Willem shook his head. "No, no. I told you before, I don't do anything like that."

"Gardner told me about a secret weapon, some kind of atom bomb? This has something to do with you?"

"It's all a fantastic coincidence, but no, I don't think it does. I guess I must tell you some more details."

Sloan scowled. "I hate to put it this way, but if you want me to keep those French guys from blowing your brains out, you better."

Willem pondered Sloan's admonition, then continued. "Last August, on my way to New York from Canada, I stopped in Chicago for a meeting with a prominent physicist working with the government. He wanted me to join him on a secret project, but he wouldn't tell me what, but I think I know what it was about."

"Who was that?"

"Dr. Szilard, at the University of Chicago."

"And what was the project?"

"Ah, he didn't tell me. He was very vague."

"What do you think it was?"

"What Gardner says, probably an atomic weapon. He never spoke directly about it, and I didn't ask. However, during our conversation, he mentioned H.G. Wells, and how he inspired him to think differently about a particular subject. At the time, I didn't pick up on it, but it was a hint for me. Regardless, I wasn't interested in anything other than following through on my determination to become a bomber pilot, so I turned him down. At the end of the conversation, he mentioned to me that Professor Einstein had recommended me to him, and that he had said he hoped I would refuse. I asked him what he meant, and he only said that Professor Einstein would be pleased with my answer."

"Your answer about what?"

"Whether to join the project. I guess he hoped I wouldn't. Maybe it was a test and I passed. It was after that he started to ask me questions about plans after the war, and then he offered me the job."

"So you haven't ever done any secret work, nothing for the government, nothing that would attract the attention of your friends downstairs?"

Willem shook his head, irritated. "They aren't my friends. I'm just as baffled as you. Those two say they know me, but I've never seen them before in my life. It's very odd."

Sloan let out an exasperated sigh. "You don't say." He leaned forward and put his head into his hands. He looked up. "How do we verify who you are? The French don't believe your documents. They say they could be forged."

Willem thought. "The man with the radio. Couldn't he make contact with London? If you can't reach my unit or the RAF, my brother-in-law works for the U.S. government in London. He could vouch for me."

"Hmm, that's a thought. They don't want us transmitting. They think it will give our position away. They especially don't want you near that radio. Maybe we take a chance. I don't know. I'll have to think about it."

In a room on the second floor, away from the children and the rest of the soldiers, Laurent and another maquisard stood behind Sloan. Anders sat in a wooden chair, hands bound behind him to the chair. Sloan crossed his arms and leaned forward.

"Okay, we're going to get some answers from you, and they better make sense."

Anders nodded. "I'll give you whatever cooperation I can."

"What are you doing here?"

Anders took a deep breath. "As I said before, my mission is to make sure Dr. van Stockum gets back to London alive and well. That is it."

"Why? Why him?"

"He has expertise that is critical to the success of the war effort."

"He says that isn't true."

"He's being modest."

Time Bomber

Sloan shook his head. "Who do you work for? Are you military?"

"I am an American soldier and I work for a special group that focuses on these missions. Rescuing key personnel from the battlefield. It's very secret."

"What's the name of the group? How do we verify your story?"

Anders shook his head. "I can't tell you that. I'm afraid you can't verify what I'm saying because you can't contact my superiors. It's impossible."

Sloan glanced over at Laurent. The Resistance leader took out a cigarette and put it in his mouth. He offered the pack to Anders with raised eyebrows, but Anders declined, shaking his head.

Laurent shrugged, put the pack away, and lit the cigarette. "I think, Sgt. Sloan, that maybe we should ask some questions. Perhaps we can get some different answers." Laurent glanced at the other maquisard, and they both stepped forward.

Sloan turned away.

Willem looked up at the sound of heavy footsteps coming down the stairs to the basement. He put the Dirac monograph down and watched the doorway. Private Green was sitting against the wall by the door, and Stimmel remained bound to the chair on the opposite wall, next to Anders' empty chair. The two Frenchmen came in carrying Anders between them, his head lolling. Willem could see bruises on his face, one eye puffy. Small black circles peppered his cheek. As they retied him to the chair, Willem saw more damage on the inside of one wrist. Stimmel watched impassively. Willem and Green exchanged glances, and Willem saw his horror mirrored in the other's face.

The two Frenchmen turned to Stimmel. "You will come with us."

Stimmel nodded, no expression.

They untied him and escorted him upstairs. Willem watched Anders staring fixedly at the floor in front of his chair, silent. He looked back at Green, who gave a small shake of his head. Willem picked up the Dirac monograph and tried to resume his reading, but concentration eluded him. The silence of the room was broken only by Anders heavy breathing, and the occasional sniff or cough.

Back upstairs, Sloan felt sick. Laurent seemed totally unaffected by the rigors of the interrogation. The other Frenchman massaged his hand, his leather gloves removed for the moment.

Stimmel took it all in with a bland expression.

"Let's be clear here, pal. You don't give us answers that make sense, these guys are going to make things very unpleasant for you. Anders said a lot of crazy things and it didn't go well. You want to just tell us straight up what's going on so we can get this over with?" Sloan struggled to keep the note of pleading out of his voice, but he cared less and less as the sessions wore on what the Resistance men thought about his nerve. This wasn't war anymore, it was something else, something worse.

Stimmel looked at the three of them and nodded. "Very well. I will tell you what I can, and hopefully that will satisfy you. I am a special agent sent here to stop Mr. Anders. That is all. My organization tracks his movements and we do our best to thwart his plans. I bear you no ill will, I'm not here to harm or betray any of you, and I will gladly stay out of your way as long as I can fulfill my mission of stopping Mr. Anders."

"Stop him? You mean kill him."

Stimmel shook his head. "Actually, no. Often, I have to kill him, but by merely slowing him down or diverting him, I can still achieve my objective. His mission is very time- and situation-sensitive. My job is very easy compared to his."

Sloan paused, mouth open.

Laurent stepped forward. "The other man said many things about Hitler and the end of the war. What do you know of this?"

Stimmel turned to him. "What he says is true. Hitler will be visiting near the front lines next week. He may die, and if he does, the war will end very quickly. That is part of Mr. Anders mission. He is telling the truth about that."

"Then why do you try to stop him?"

Stimmel smiled. "My objectives are much larger in scope than his."

"Do you work for the Nazis?" Laurent asked.

Stimmel shook his head. "No. The people I work for are from many countries. We hate the Nazis. This is just a convenient disguise."

"A dangerous one." Laurent observed.

Sloan raised his hand. "Wait a second. Just a minute ago you said 'often I have to kill him.' What does that mean? How do you kill a person 'often'?"

Laurent wore a puzzled look, the linguistic nuances eluding him.

Stimmel gave a short laugh. "Ah, yes, I did say that. It seems odd, doesn't it? A peculiar quirk of how I talk about my work, I guess." Stimmel smiled and did not elaborate further.

Sloan scowled and cocked his head.

Laurent looked between the two of them. "What does this mean?"

Sloan shook his head. "Nothing. Perhaps we misunderstand each other."

Laurent continued his questions. "You are American?"

Stimmel shook his head. "My ancestors were, but I am not."

Sloan looked up. "Your ancestors? Not German, not American, and you don't sound British. What are you?"

"A citizen of the world."

Laurent and Sloan looked at each other, then Laurent turned and nodded to the other maquisard. He stood up and pulled on his leather gloves.

Sloan looked back to Stimmel. "You aren't making any sense either, buddy. I'm trying to make this easy for you, and you aren't helping."

Stimmel shrugged. "I'm sorry. There's only so much I can tell you, and I'm prepared to deal with the consequences. It's part of the hazards of the job. Do what you must."

Sloan shook his head and sighed. "One more question. What do you have to do to stop Anders? Will you try to kill him again? Will you kill the pilot?"

Stimmel shrugged again. "Dr. van Stockum need not fear me. Whatever Anders says, I am not interested in Dr. van Stockum. His fate is his own business. Killing Anders, it depends. I think his window of opportunity is closing fast. It may be that I don't have to do anything more at this point. I think this is a new situation for all of us, which makes his mission very difficult to complete."

Sloan pondered this.

Laurent and the other man stepped forward. "We will ask questions now."

Later, Sgt. Sloan laid on the floor in the other bedroom on the second floor, away from the interrogation room, which had gone silent. He needed time to think, to be away from the questions, the contradictions, the demands of the others. He had successfully delayed the French in their insistence on killing both the strangers, as well as removing the pilot. The brutal questioning gave them no new information, and only raised more questions, none of which made sense. But at least they were consistent. Anders was here to protect the pilot, Stimmel here to stop Anders. But Stimmel has no interest in the pilot.

If Anders mission is to rescue the pilot, and Stimmel's is to stop Anders, how can Stimmel have no interest in the pilot? Despite all the pain inflicted, neither man contributed any further clarification to this conundrum.

The French were very interested in Anders' knowledge of the German dispositions and plans, and how he knew those things. They confirmed that much of what he said was true, which only reinforced their suspicions. For Sloan, it meant that the French insistence that they stay hunkered down and not push toward the Allied lines was sound advice, somewhat assuaging his sense of urgency. Now he could rest and collect his thoughts without feeling the pressure of needing to move.

He could not get the image of Stimmel's face out of his mind. Despite the brutal ministrations of the Resistance men, he remained impassive, almost at peace. In contrast, Anders never stopped struggling, arguing, pleading, cursing them. On the face of it, Anders' information and mission seemed to be perfectly aligned with their own. The other Americans grumbled and muttered about the French mistreating him, especially in light of the help Anders provided and how badly they all wanted to get home. The men badgered Sloan with questions about why they didn't help Anders get the pilot home and get this over with. He didn't have any good answers.

Neither did the pilot. Sloan could tell from the look on his face after seeing the two strangers after the interrogation that this was beyond his experience. He was in over his head as much as Sloan, it was clear. He was the key, though.

Willem lay on the floor with his eyes closed, vainly courting sleep. The other fresh-faced paratrooper, Doolan, sat by the door keeping vigil while Green slept. The rest of the Americans were out at their posts or scattered in other areas of the house. Anders and Stimmel sat in silence, avoiding eye contact. Stimmel's injuries did not appear as extensive as

Anders', despite similar mistreatment. Willem felt sick that he was somehow responsible for this, no matter how confused he was at the causes and reasons.

The sounds of the nuns putting the children to bed subsided, and the darkness grew deeper as the late sunset finally concluded the day. It must be near midnight, Willem estimated, but he still felt no inclination to sleep. He propped himself up on one elbow and looked around. The single oil lantern in the middle of the room cast a yellow light. A thin stream of black smoke writhed upward from it into the darkness. The hunched and motionless figures of Stimmel and Anders appeared lifeless in the half-light, save for the occasional faint movements of breathing.

Doolan caught his eye and acknowledged him with a faint lift of his chin. "Excuse me, sir, the other guys were saying you teach college?"

Willem smiled and nodded. "At the University of Maryland, before the war," he replied softly.

Doolan smiled shyly. "My dad wants me to go there when I get out. He played football for Curley. Did you get to see many games?" The paratrooper's boyish innocence struck Willem as strange, considering the rifle cradled in his lap.

He shook his head in response to the question. "No, but I met President Byrd several times. He's a very nice man." He chuckled at the memory of Dr. Dantzig's fulminations about the impossibility of building academic excellence while being led by a football coach.

"Back home, all my friends are graduating tonight, then they'll be off to college. I guess I'll catch up when I get home."

"From high school? Your graduation is tonight? Congratulations."

"Thanks. I wonder if I'll get a diploma?"

"Wait, how old are you?" The implications of the graduation were starting to sink in.

Doolan looked guilty. "Almost eighteen. Soon."

"Seventeen? But that means…. How did you enlist? How old were you then?"

Doolan smiled. "I used my brother's birth certificate, changed the name once I was in. They never figured it out. Passed all the physicals and everything."

"So you were what, sixteen?"

Doolan nodded, grinning.

An awkward pause followed, then Doolan cleared his throat. "Sir, can I ask you a question?"

"Sure."

"Why'd you do it?"

"What?"

"Join up. Chuck it all. I mean, you were a college professor. You must have been a big deal."

Willem smiled at this boy's perspective. All that time struggling to secure the next academic appointment, sitting quietly in the presence of the titans of math and physics, steering clear through the shoals of department politics and the ego battles, none of it ever made him feel like a big deal. He had big hopes and dreams, but how petty it all seemed compared to the war. Now, knowing better the insanity of warfare, his doubts took on new dimensions.

He laughed to himself. "I don't know about that. What about you? Why'd you join up?"

Doolan broke into another big grin. "That's easy. The uniform. When I saw those pictures in Life magazine of the paratroopers at Ft. Benning, I knew that was what I had to do. Plus, the girls love it."

"Oh, really? Did it work?"

"What?"

"The uniform, with girls."

Even in the dim light, Willem could see the deep blush on the boy's face, split from ear to ear with a smile.

Willem shook his head with a chuckle, then laid back down and stared at the ceiling. He tried to empty his mind, to no avail. It was then he noticed the vibration.

He pushed himself up again and looked at Doolan, now serious and attent, head cocked to the side. "What's that?" Willem asked.

Off in the distance, the droning of far off planes gradually grew louder, emerging from the ever-present grumble of artillery and explosions from the beaches. Then they heard the first crump, crump of the bombs.

"Uh-oh." Green said, now awake.

Everyone looked up, straining to discern what direction the planes were moving and how the bombs fell. There was a clattering down the stairs. MacDonald stood in the doorway breathless, still clutching his helmet to his head. Gardner and Turturro followed close behind, and then Sloan.

"Grab some dirt! They're headed this way! The guys on the road are hauling ass back here!"

The thumping was soon accompanied by the faint, high-pitched whistles of ordnance slicing through the air. Explosions ripped louder and nearer, and the vibrations of the detonations rumbled through the house. Small bits of dirt and dust drifted down from the rafters. The small lantern bounced and shimmied in a nervous dance in the center of the room.

A series of blasts rocked the building, popping ears from the overpressure and momentarily squeezing the air from their lungs. There was a crash of masonry and cracking timbers, followed by the screams of the children cutting through the din.

Green snatched up the light and ran to the other room, followed closely by Gardner. Willem struggled to his feet, fumbling for his crutches. He winced with each blast and watched the ceiling. The rest of the paratroopers huddled on the floor, hands covering their heads. Sloan watched the events, face slack and eyes glassy.

Willem limped to the doorway, and was met by Green leading a group of the children. The nuns followed, herding the rest, counting and recounting in the dim light, fussing and consoling the weeping little ones. The boys looked around wide-eyed. Gardner followed behind, carrying two of the littlest ones. They clung to him, faces buried in his shoulders.

The explosions moved off, slackening in fury and frequency.

Green turned to the nuns. "Is that all of them?"

The nuns frantically counted again, then turned to him nodding.

"Is anyone hurt?"

The two paratroopers bent over the children, examined each one quickly in the weak light, then shunted to the side for the next one. Miraculously, they had all emerged unscathed, despite the near miss. They settled down along the wall and crowded around, trying to avoid the two prisoners. Willem welcomed several children to his sleeping spot, spreading the paratrooper's rain poncho on the dirt floor for two children to lay on. The nuns went back to the ruined room with another lantern to retrieve as much bedding as possible.

Sloan snapped out of his daze. "Green and MacDonald, go upstairs and see if the others made it, and then make sure nothing is burning. Gardner, check out the rest of the basement and see which parts are usable. Doolan, give me a hand moving these guys."

Sloan and Doolan dragged the two prisoners back to the far corner, one on each wall, giving more room for the children to spread out. Anders and Stimmel took it all in without comment.

In the soft light of the lanterns, the children's sniffling and weeping continued unabated. The nuns soothed and shushed, to no avail.

Marino came down the stairs. "Everything's okay upstairs, Top. No one hurt, no fire. MacDonald and Lezynski are going back out to the road. Kellam's upstairs. The Resistance guys are scattered, seem to be okay."

Sloan nodded, then sat back down against the wall. The nuns put out their lantern, leaving only the small one in the center of the room. The room fell quiet except for the children crying.

Green cleared his throat and looked around the room, then started singing. All eyes turned to him. His smooth tenor filled the room:

> *"It seems to me I've heard that song before,*
> *It's from an old familiar score*
> *I know it well, that melody*

He took a breath, and all the children stopped crying to listen. He continued solo.

> *It's funny how a theme*
> *Recalls a favorite dream*
> *A dream that brought you so close to me*

Green continued, and the children watched, rapt. Even his fellow troopers looked on, affected by his unadorned singing. He finished the song and the sounds of the airplanes and the bombs could still be heard in the distance so he started right in with another song.

> *"I'll be with you in apple blossom time,*
> *I'll be with you to change your name to mine.*

Time Bomber

One day in May
I'll come and say:
"Happy the bride that the sun shines on today!"

What a wonderful wedding there will be,
What a wonderful day for you and me!
Church bells will chime
You will be mine
In apple blossom time."

"Kinda appropriate," Marino chuckled.

Willem thought of Dennie and the men back at the station, and their motivations for pursuing the near suicidal bomber life. As a Londoner, Dennie shared stories of the Blitz, the population huddled in basements and shelters or herded deep into the tunnels of the Underground stations while the Junkers and Heinkel bombers rained destruction from above. Huddled in the darkness, they would sing to keep spirits up and comfort their ragged nerves.

Willem cleared his throat and started off on the next song.

"Drink to me only with thine eyes,
And I will pledge with mine;
Or leave a kiss within the cup
And I'll not ask for wine."

The singing had the intended effect. The older children still stared, occasionally glancing upward, listening carefully and watching. The younger ones curled up, nestling against each other and the older children. Willem looked over. Gardner had the two children he carried in nestled under each arm, both sleeping. His head was back, and he snored softly, face completely relaxed. Willem caught Green looking at him as well, and their eyes met. They smiled at one another.

Willem sat back, making himself comfortable. As he drifted off, he noticed Stimmel blinking. In the soft flickering light of the lantern, he thought he could see the glinting reflection of wetness on his cheeks. Stimmel saw him staring, gave a small smile and looked away. Willem glanced at Anders, who only gazed at the floor, avoiding eye contact.

CHAPTER THIRTY-THREE

0630 June 11th, 1944
Near St. Jores, Normandy

"We must wash the children before Mass." The nuns moved quietly among the sleepy children, still tangled in bedding, curled around each other in small piles like puppies. The troopers cleared a path upstairs and shuttled back and forth, rearranging wreckage and scavenging supplies. Lezynski sat in a chair in the main room and looked at the abrasions and bruises of the handful of children injured the night before. He cleaned wounds and applied small dressings where needed. The children watched the proceedings in awe. Two stood next him while he worked, one of them resting an arm across his shoulder.

Trying his best to stay out of the way, Willem made his way up the stairs on his crutches, shadowed by a solicitous Private Green. At the top of the stairs, nothing seemed amiss, but then he turned to the front of the house and saw how close catastrophe came last night.

The front of the house was missing, a gaping hole next to the foundation abutting the children's sleeping room. Holes in the floor near the front wall revealed the basement below.

They walked to the front door and looked out, following the bomb craters out into the surrounding fields, searching the countryside for some target, some terrain feature that might excuse such sloppy delivery of the payload.

Willem took in the devastation and fought to control his anger. *"God verdome!"* he muttered.

He turned to Green. "Were there Germans encamped near here last night?"

The paratrooper shook his head. "I was out on the road. There was a lot of traffic heading east toward Carentan, but nobody was hanging around here. No way was anyone in those fields. We would have seen them."

Willem shook his head in disgust and cursed again.

"What?" Green asked.

Willem gestured abruptly out the door. "This. It's inexcusable."

Green looked out the door. "It's war."

They stood in silence looking out over the fields. Willem saw a convoy in the far distance, moving southwest, away from the thump and mutter of the battle to the east, which had grown louder than yesterday.

Back in the basement, the nuns set up a large copper tub in one of the other undamaged rooms, and the older boys shuttled pails of water, slowly filling it. The youngest children were already bathing, shivering as the older girls scrubbed them and washed their hair. The nuns hovered and scolded, fussing over dirty clothes, repackaging each child as neatly as possible, giving ample admonitions to stay clean. Every few minutes a child would attempt to sneak back in the ruined room to gawk at the destruction, only to be shooed away by a nun or a paratrooper.

The older boys went next, then the door was closed, and the older girls bathed the little girls, finally followed by the older girls. The nuns moved the children upstairs into one of the classrooms and began a lesson from Scripture.

"If it is safe, the priest will come from St. Jores and say Mass for us today. We do not know when, but if he comes, your men are welcome to join us." The older nun smiled at Sgt. Sloan.

He nodded in return. "Thank you, sister. I will tell the men. I'm sure some of them will want to."

"Today we eat well," Juliette announced from the doorway.
Willem and the other paratroopers looked up hopefully.
Anders ignored her, but Stimmel smiled.
"The bombers destroyed the barn of the farmer near here. Several cows were killed. He is a clever man and he contacted the butcher and they saved what they could. He is sharing the meat so the *boche* will not get it. We will have *bœuf* for dinner today."

Sgt. Sloan made his way through the trees back to the house. Their outpost overlooking the road had a perfect vantage for watching the movements east to Carentan. There was quite a bit of traffic in both directions, more away than toward. It was heartening to see, and gave him hope for the possibility of making a move back to their lines soon.

As he neared the house, three maquisards approached, Laurent and two others.

Laurent's face was serious. "Sgt. Sloan, I have bad news."
Sloan swallowed. "What is it?"
"Graignes. That way is now closed."
"Why?"
"The boche have attacked and it is not going well for your friends. There are many tanks coming from the south to reinforce Carentan. The result is not certain, but the reports we have are not good. I'm afraid we must look in another direction for your escape."

"What are the other options?"

Laurent shook his head. "There are not many. Your comrades are pushing the Germans across the Douve and that is concentrating them, pushing them together. That makes it more risky for us to move in that direction. We must go back to the south. I am taking my men back to the forest, but that is not in the direction you want to go."

"Wait a minute, you are leaving?"

Laurent nodded. "Yes, I must bring weapons and ammunition to the south to the fighters in Brittany. We are blocking the reinforcements moving from there to here. You are welcome to come and help us."

Sloan shook his head. "No, that's not our mission. We've got to get back to our units, back toward the beaches."

"*Mon ami*, I would say your objective is to stay alive. If you stay here, that will become more difficult. We are leaving today. I suggest you and your men come with us, without your prisoners. That is the only condition."

Kellam approached. "I'm going with them, Top."

"No, you can't. I need your radio."

Kellam shook his head. "Sorry, Top, but I've got to stay with these guys. Until London tells me otherwise, I'm helping them. Once I get away from here, I can transmit and hopefully get some new instructions. I'll pass on your info and get a message back to your unit. That's the best I can do."

"Do not mention this location." Laurent interjected.

Kellam looked at Sloan, who shook his head.

Laurent stepped forward and grabbed Sloan's arm. "I must tell you, sergeant, these men are spies. You must kill them, all three. The one who spoke of Margival, Hitler's death. That is a secret place, known only to the Nazis until recently.[5] They call it the Wolf Pit. How could he know this? You must be very careful with them."

Sloan nodded, and Laurent stepped away, pointing to the bags.

"Take what weapons you need. We will be leaving soon."

"You're getting pretty good at getting up and down those stairs, doc," Gardner observed.

Willem turned from the window to his current escort and took another drag on his cigarette. "I want to be ready when it's time to move. I'm determined not to slow you men down." He blew out a stream of smoke. "Thank you again for the cigarettes."

Gardner shrugged. "I don't know why, but I think I've lost my taste for them. I've got more where that came from. They gave us cartons and cartons before we jumped."

Willem stared out the window. "There go the French. Sgt. Sloan seemed pretty upset before."

"Yeah, there's something going on. They were arguing pretty loud."

"I can't say I'm disappointed to see them go."

"Yeah, but … the extra bodies sure were nice."

Willem shook his head. "I did not get a good feeling from that Laurent. I think I'm better off with my fate in Sloan's hands."

Gardner smiled. "I think you're right about that. Those two in the basement didn't have much more time, if the French guy had his way. They weren't so sure about you, either."

Willem took a drag on the cigarette and blew out a cloud of smoke. "Hmm. Well, let's hope we can better clarify that before a decision has to be made. It's an odd situation, where every effort to confirm my identity becomes further proof that I'm not who I am."

"Kinda like your own little Uncertainty Principle."

Willem turned to Gardner and broke into a broad grin. "Why yes, it is isn't it? Can't confirm a measurement without disturbing the system."

Gardner returned a shy smile. Willem noted how different it made him look, like a new person. They shared the moment in silence. Outside, raised voices drew their attention. They looked down at the front yard. Juliette shouted at the departing Resistance men, two of them restraining her. They watched Laurent raise a hand and wave dismissively without turning. She gestured at him and poured out a torrent of angry abuse, struggling against the two men holding her. Finally, they pushed her back roughly and she sat down hard. They joined the departing file of men.

"What do you think that's about?" Willem wondered.

Gardner shrugged, then looked up at Willem. "So exactly what was your research? You mentioned relativity yesterday."

Willem stubbed out the cigarette.

Gardner took out a pack of Luckys and offered him another, then just gave him the pack. "Keep it."

"Thank you. So, it's a problem in geometry regarding spacetime. Have you heard of spacetime being described as a surface that can be deformed?"

Gardner nodded slowly. Willem took out another cigarette and gestured for a light. Gardner flipped out a zippo and Willem leaned forward.

"Thanks. Gravity is that deformation. Well, I looked at the mathematics of what happens when those deformations are taken to extremes. What happens when a very large mass moves, or rotates? It turns out that spacetime can fold back on itself, creating closed loops."

"Closed loops?"

Willem nodded. "If a beam of light follows a path on one of those closed loops, it can travel in a circle and arrive back at the same spot before it left."

Gardner pondered this and looked up at Willem. "Time travel?"

Willem smiled and shrugged. "Theoretically. It's just what the math says. Not many people believe it, but Dr. Einstein agrees with my logic and technique. It's one of the many implications of his theory that trouble him, but it's those very problems that motivate him to look for deeper theories, like with quantum mechanics."

"What's the matter with quantum mechanics?"

"It feels incomplete. The troubling implications of the mathematics of quantum mechanics are that events at the atomic level are fundamentally random and unpredictable. It also allows for information to travel between two particles in ways that seem to violate the other rules of physics. Yet the math of quantum mechanics seems complete and makes startling and accurate predictions. It's a real puzzle. Relativity and quantum mechanics each work extremely well, but they make predictions that are incompatible. Dr. Einstein wants to figure out a way to bring them together in a unified theory, and he wants me to help. It's quite an interesting challenge."[6]

"It's funny to hear you describe feelings about math. I've always thought about math as something without emotion. Two plus two equals four, no matter how you feel about it."

Willem smiled. "Oh no, there are plenty of feelings in math, love even. The beauty of a well thought out proof is like art. It's spiritual. In a way, it's like talking with God about the mysteries of the universe."

Gardner smiled again. "Speaking of God, are you going to go to Mass? I think they're starting soon."

Willem shook his head. "No, that's why I'm up here. I didn't want to be in the way."

"No church for you?"

"Sometimes. My mother and sister are very religious, and I respect them for that. I appreciate the need for religion, and I see the good in it, but I have trouble sitting still for the details."

"Sounds like you believe in God. Is mathematics your religion?"

"Hmmm, no. Mathematics is my language, it's my art. It's a way of expressing myself, of seeing things about the world that are not obvious. There's no faith involved. Well, there is some, but things start with faith – intuition, really – and hopefully end with certainty. That's the difference. You have a feeling about an idea, then you prove it with logic and technique."

"Does it work for everything?"

Willem laughed. "What do you mean?"

"All your questions, your…doubts."

Willem shook his head. "Not even close. In fact, in some ways it makes it worse. The questions that torment me the worst are the ones least amenable to mathematics. Questions of the soul, the heart. The calculus for that hasn't been discovered yet. How about you, do you believe in God?"

"No. Yes. I don't know." Gardner became distant. "It's hard to believe after…." Gardner shook his head and stared off. "That randomness? It's out there. What kind of God allows all …." He waved toward the window, face troubled. "That?" He shook his head. "I don't get it."

They stared out the window together in silence, each lost in his own thoughts.

Willem finished his cigarette and stubbed it out on the windowsill. "I think I will go down and listen to some Mass." He turned toward the stairs and swung himself adroitly on the crutches. Gardner followed.

"I can manage." Willem called back over his shoulder.

"Still gotta stay with you, doc. Orders."

Willem scowled.

Rows of chairs filled the largest room on the first floor. They were occupied by squirming children, who turned to look at the olive drab strangers in back. Marino, Turturro, Lezynski, and Green stood in back, helmets off. Sheets and blankets were draped over the windows, muting the light. The priest stood at the front of the room, a small table with an ornate gold crucifix and two candles on a small table. The colorful embroidery on the priest's vestments glowed in the candlelight. One of the older boys served as an altar boy, a thin white surplice over his clothes. A faint whiff of incense tickled Willem's nose. Green caught his eye and gestured to a chair but Willem waved him off. He stood with the paratroopers in the back of the room – leaning on his crutches, listening to the Latin, watching the restless children.

His mind wandered back to Washington D.C., to Mass at Blessed Sacrament on Chevy Chase Circle, with his sister Hilda, Spike, and his mother, and all the Marlin children alongside them fidgeting and whispering in the pews. Uncle Willem was always a source of excitement when he attended Mass, and the children could never quite settle down. On the rare occasion he agreed to go, his mother and sister were happy for his company, but the benefit of his soul's salvation was usually outweighed by the toll it took on the children's attention and behavior. They would tug his sleeve and murmur in his ear: questions, observations, important facts that just couldn't wait until Mass was over. His sister Hilda would scowl and silently shake her head, but her children's adoration of their uncle made it difficult to stay annoyed.

That time with them and his teaching at the University of Maryland were the beginning of his real career. Dr. Dantzig had such big plans. They would stroll around campus, smoking cigarettes, Dr. Dantzig talking out his theories and his books, his plans for reorganizing the department and building a world-renowned institute, and how Willem would be there, with his connections to Princeton and Dr. Veblen, recruiting the best minds and taking Maryland to a new level of excellence. Dr.

Dantzig's son, George, had already made a name for himself out west at Berkeley, and it was his dream that George would return and join the department. When George joined the Army Air Force as a statistician in early 1941, Dr. Dantzig hid his disappointment in a burst of patriotic zeal and paternal pride.

Maybe that is why that summer became so intolerable – sitting still while the rest of the world prepared for war. The students at Maryland were typical American kids: friendly, energetic, optimistic, but painfully naïve about the outside world and maddening in their obsession with the trivia of their social activities. In the evenings, Willem's mother would read the letters from Holland, of relatives missing, homeless, or murdered by the occupying Nazis, and then the next day he would sit in the classroom listening to his students prattle about dances and football games. Then the draft board began inquiring about the skills of faculty members, and George started his job at the Pentagon. On that day in May, when he saw the military demonstration on campus, it all seemed to click. Willem would learn to fly and drop bombs on Nazis. It was the most logical solution, at least at the time.

What seemed so obvious became more complicated. How to drop bombs only on the enemy? It was a problem. And how to accomplish one's mission without squandering lives? The carnage during training alone almost broke his spirit. The winter of 1943, he came so close to tossing it all – until Spike rescued him during his leave and the trip to Dublin. Those weeks over Christmas with Harrie and Billy at Clondarf gave him the respite he needed to come to terms with his situation and achieve the spiritual balance necessary to endure the beginning of his missions. Each night friends and colleagues would die, and it took everything to get out of bed and keep going the next day. The responsibility for his men also kept him going, kept him distracted from his own peril. Just get the men home.

He was so lucky to have family relatively close by, people to confide in, to derive strength from. Toward the end of the stay with Harrie and Billy, Willem had done some reading, picking up a copy of Joyce's "Dubliners". He had spent a few rainy afternoons by the fire, relaxing with the book while Spike and Billy plied their spy trade in hushed conversations. The final story, "The Dead", stuck with him. It gave him an odd measure of peace at the end of that restorative visit. Joyce's lines about the snow falling on the living and the dead, after the turmoil the main character felt, confused and tormented by his passion for his wife, and his discovery of his wife's unresolved feelings for a boy from her youth, long dead – it resonated with him in a comforting way, as good literature often did, providing him food for thought on many later occasions.

Jock. Nate. Johnny. Colin. Young Declan, so new to the crew. Could all of them be dead? Colin and Toby were always quick to jump if there was a problem. Colin had survived two prior crashes. Willem's was his third crew. Could he be somewhere in the French countryside? And what happened to Johnny and Jock? He had a vague memory of a conversation after the crash. Wasn't Johnny alive? But they said he was the only one. Those first days were a blur of headaches and nausea.

The priest chanted the consecration prayers, then served communion. Willem stayed in back with Green as the others went up to receive. The Mass concluded, and the nuns glanced at the soldiers loitering in the back while they ushered the children back down to the basement. The older nun stopped in front of Leszynski.

"We will need help carrying food. The farmer is bringing us a very nice meal this afternoon." The paratroopers exchanged smiles.

"No problem, sister. We'll give you a hand."

Sloan looked up from his plate. Around him the soldiers spoke in loud voices, enjoying the hot food and company. Juliette sat off to the side, a plate untouched in front of her. She wore a vacant expression. Even the children seemed to keep their distance.

Earlier, the farmer of previous visits had rolled up to the house with his cart. On the back sat a large heavy pot full of stewed meat. Marino and Green carried it around back to a small fire. They placed the pot on bricks over the fire, then took turns stirring. The nuns appeared periodically and scolded them about something: the fire is too big, too small, stir, stop stirring. The paratroopers bickered over cooking technique, and stole tastes. Sloan had to break them up and make sure the assignments rotated at the right times. He fretted about the smoke from the fire, and warned them to be extra vigilant on the road and from the windows.

Despite all the activity, they remained unmolested. In the distance the German troops streamed along the roads, but they continued to fix their attention on rushing to the encroaching front, or retreating to the rear as fast as possible. In either case, the stand of trees in the small depression off the road remained uninteresting to the passing enemy.

Sloan put his plate down and stood up.

Juliette looked up as he approached but did not acknowledge him.

"I heard you also had a disagreement with Laurent."

She stared at her hands, slowly twisting a corner of her shirt. "He does not think I belong with the men. He says I must stay here."

"You want to go to the woods?"

She looked up, eyes blazing. "It is where I belong. I am a soldier!"

Sloan suppressed a smile at her determination. Were it not for her demonstrated courage when she saved him from Anders, he would have scoffed, but now, he could only admire her spunk.

"I'm sure he only wants the best for you, to keep you safe."

She waved dismissively. "I can take care of myself. I have killed more *boches* than some of those pretenders, those fakers."

Marino looked up at this remark. He gestured with his spoon. "You killed krauts? You're just a kid."

She scowled at him. "I am not a kid. I am nineteen years old. You know how many Germans I have killed?"

Marino laughed. "How many?"

Juliette held up four fingers. "With my own hands. Two I shot, two I stabbed. The last one was an officer in Rennes. He thought I was going to bed with him. That is why they made me hide here."

Sloan watched the exchange. This young girl! Back home she'd be hanging out and flirting at the hamburger stand, watching a rodeo, surrounded by boys eager for a date or a kiss. And here she is bragging about the men she killed. He shook his head.

Sister Ruth Marie spoke up, pointing a finger at Juliette. "Your comrades will betray you. You have spent too much time with the Germans. The communists have no faith or principles. They do not trust you because you lived with the enemy. You are expendable."

Juliette struggled to respond, her face working, mute with anger. She shook her head and looked down, biting her lip.

Sloan turned away. Marino watched the girl, his smile gone, his teasing quieted by her distress.

Sloan knew his mission was much simpler in comparison to the consequences of this war's toll on these people. Kill the

Germans and go home, get his life in order, move on. The present situation was just an obstacle for him. For them, it was their life, a mess that would linger long after the shooting stopped.

After the feast, spirits lifted. Unfazed by the destruction of the bombing, the children swept, shoveled and carried debris outside, directed by the soldiers under the watchful eye of the nuns. The soldiers hauled rubble and debris away from the living areas. The children's former sleeping room was ruined, closed off behind a heavy wooden door. After conferring with Sloan, it was agreed to move the two prisoners into the central area, and let the children and the nuns have the room. Anders and Stimmel now sat in their chairs to the right of the stairs, next to the door to the makeshift privy.

As the light waned, the nuns called the children back downstairs to the basement to prepare for bedtime. Willem watched with a smile.

"Listen up, you guys. I'm going back out tonight, and I need two guys to go with me. Don't worry, we won't be doing anything crazy, just another trip around to see where the krauts are. Without the resistance guys here, we need to know what's going on around that town, and figure out when we can make our break. Kellam listened before he left, and it sounds like we've got Carentan, or at least part of it. Anybody want to volunteer before I start picking?" Sloan looked around the room.

Marino shuffled his feet and looked at the floor. Jones raised his hand, and then Lezynski.

"Jones, you went last time."

"That's okay, Top, I don't mind."

Sloan nodded. "Okay, MacDonald's in charge. Sit tight and continue the rotations: road, window, and guarding these guys. We'll be back by midnight or so. We're not going far."

"Sergeant Sloan." Anders spoke his first words since the interrogation.

Sloan looked at him.

"I suggest you bring me. I can provide you valuable information about how the Germans are moving, but I need to see what's happening. I will not interfere with your men, and I will not make any aggressive moves. You have my word."

Sloan looked at him in disbelief, then shook his head with smile. "You've got some nerve, pal, I have to hand it to you. All is forgotten, huh? No way. You're staying here. You'll get up when we make our decision to move out."

"But Sergeant…."

"Pipe down. I've heard enough out of you."

Anders became agitated. "We don't have time! You need my help. The opening back to your lines may be very small, and open only a brief time. I can help you. Bring me with you."

Sloan stared at him then raised a finger pointing at him.

Marino interrupted. "Top, he did give us a lot of great scoop on the weapons and supplies. I'll go too and keep a gun in his back. Maybe he can get us out of here."

Sloan turned to Marino. "Keep your mouth shut, Marino. He's not going anywhere, and that's it. Jones, Lezynski, let's go." Sloan pounded up the stairs.

MacDonald organized them and rotated the watches. He and Turturro went out to the road, and Green went upstairs to watch at the windows. Gardner, Doolan, and Marino sat down in the basement with Willem and the prisoners. Juliette remained, sitting against the wall, disconsolate.

The nuns put the children to bed, then closed the door to the side room, admonishing the soldiers to be quiet. Marino was at it again, shuffling his cards, pestering everyone with his chatter and questions. Gardner and Doolan watched.

Marino and Willem exchanged smiles, and Marino gestured at Gardner.

"Hey doc, he says you discovered time travel. Is that true?"

"Well, I didn't discover it. I just showed how the rules of relativity could allow for it. Whether it's really true or not, I don't know."

"Okay, I'm game. How does it work? You got a machine like old Wells?"

Willem laughed. "No, no, nothing like that. It's because of relativity, and the connection between space and time. That was the amazing thing about Einstein's discovery, that connection. He was able to prove that time and space can change under the influence of mass and gravity."

Marino grinned, enjoying himself. He shuffled the cards and nodded. "Oh yeah, sure, that makes sense. Go on, doc. You getting this, kid?" He nodded to Doolan, who watched awestruck.

Gardner looked up from his book. Stimmel and Anders listened from their chairs.

"Time can be affected two ways. The first is if you travel very fast, near the speed of light. The other is if you are near a very, very heavy object. The mass itself changes time – rather it changes the shape of spacetime, and causes interesting effects. Time slows down."

The troopers around him gave blanks stares, except for Marino, who was nodding and grinning.

"I know exactly what you mean, Professor."

"You do?"

"Oh yeah. I spent the longest night of my life with this big fat broad."

The room erupted in laughter, and Willem grinned.

"I ain't kiddin'. She looked like Kate Smith, and she wouldn't let go of me. The sun couldn't come up soon enough. It was like the clock stopped. Now I know why."

The older nun shushed them from the door, and the laughter subsided. Willem noticed Gardner staring at him. He raised his eyebrows, inviting an inquiry.

Gardner paused for a moment, then spoke. "You mentioned loops earlier. How can that be? Isn't that impossible?"

Willem nodded. "Dr. Einstein and I spoke about that several times. It's called the grandfather paradox. If you go back in time and kill your grandfather, doesn't that make your existence impossible?"

Gardner nodded. "So? Is there a solution?" he asked.

Willem shrugged. "Maybe. Something must explain it. Either my reasoning and technique are incorrect, or there is something else that would explain that conclusion. Personally, I think my calculations are correct, so my money is on another explanation."

"Like what?"

"Oh, I don't know. Maybe there is a way for time to branch, like a stream, with different paths. If you go back, you go back to a different stream, or maybe by going back you make the stream branch. That way your actions don't violate what we call causality."

Doolan gaped. Marino grinned.

Gardner continued. "Wouldn't that mean then that there are multiple streams, multiple times? Different worlds?"

Willem rubbed his chin. "I suppose it would. Seems hard to believe, but that is where the theory takes us."

Marino was nodding again. "So that means anything is possible. Other lives where I'm a movie star, the President, the owner of the White Sox?" Marino said, leaning forward with a grin.

Willem chuckled. "Well, theoretically I guess."

"Hey, then tell me this: is there a world where I get to bang Rita Hayworth?"

More laughter, and Willem shook his head. "Absolutely, but you'll have to get her away from Orson."

"Then count me in."

Juliette looked up at Willem. "You are lucky. You have something to go home to, something important that has meaning."

Willem blushed. "Well, thank you. I… I hope it is a useful contribution."

She shook her head. "This war, it is such a waste. All this time, I thought I was fighting for a noble cause, fighting for freedom and equality, and it's all a lie."

"It's not all a lie. The Nazis are evil, that is real. They must be stopped. Everything we do to that end is a positive good."

Juliette shook her head. "But at what cost? How much evil must we do? If we sink to their level, what have we achieved?"

Willem fell silent, thinking about his bombs, the indiscriminate destruction delivered by his comrades in Bomber Command on the cities of Germany. The deliberate killing of civilians in particular was hard to rationalize, except with the most cold-blooded logic, which itself started to sound like Nazi thinking. Talking to survivors of the Blitz back in London and the horrors of the fires and destruction during in the winter of 1940, their thirst for vengeance was understandable. More than once his concerns about bombing accuracy had been met by his fellow fliers with a shrug, and a remark along the lines of, "Jerry's got his, and I'm going home. Civilians? That's their problem. They started it."

Marino chimed in.

"Just get home alive, that's the first step. All that other stuff will get sorted out."

Juliette glared at him. "I am home. Everything, everyone I love is destroyed, and now I am dead inside. What can happen now?"

"Aw, c'mon now, it can't be that bad. You're a good-looking girl, you'll do fine."

Juliette spat on the floor. "Yes, that's all men think about. 'She has a pretty face, she'll get what she wants.' Well, it doesn't work that way."

Marino pushed back. "Look, what do you want?"

She looked up at him, furious. "What I want? To be a soldier! I want to fight alongside the other soldiers, to defend my country, to avenge my family and my friends. To do the same as you. Why can't I have that?"

"You were doing stuff. You said you killed Germans."

"Yes, sneaking around, sleeping with those pigs, always hiding and running. Do this Dardette, do that, be a good girl. I want to fight in a battle, crush them, destroy their armies."

"Joan of Arc?" Gardner observed quietly.

Juliette turned to him. "*Jeanne D'Arc?* Yes, I suppose so. That would be an honorable thing, better than this." She heaved a big sigh.

Willem interjected. "But this is honorable. Taking care of the children, giving them love and comfort. You're good at it, you're like a mother to them. That has value, the highest value."

Juliette turned to him with bright eyes. "When I ran from Paris to hide, the first time, I joined a group of young communists, hid with them. After a massacre in a village, we went to help. People were lined up in a barn and shot because an officer was shot, and no one would inform. We helped remove the bodies and bury them. There was a young mother with bullet holes all through her back, through her arms. Underneath her were two small children, she was trying to shield them, for nothing. Even though she put her body between them and the Nazis, they still died. The bullets went right through her and killed them too."

The room fell silent.

"Before the war, I wanted to be a singer. My mother, she worked in the theater in Paris, and I always went to the music halls. Do you know The Little Sparrow? She was my idol, I would sneak in to listen to her. When the boche invaded and took over Paris, people said bad things about her, said she is collaborator, but I know she worked for the Resistance. That is why I joined. The Nazis took my family, they shot my father in the street, and my mother disappeared when she kept going to the adjutant to find out where my father was buried. My brother disappeared, and my friend was murdered by a Nazi officer in a brothel. What else could I do? I must fight them, with knives and bullets, to keep these children safe. It is not enough to wash faces and sing them songs. Someone must kill, to stop the evil. I must fight them, and now my own countrymen will not let me. It is all for nothing."

"It doesn't have to be."

Everyone turned to look at Anders.

"What do you mean?" asked Juliette.

"That this is for nothing. You can help me. We have the chance to make the most important contribution to the war. Complete victory. But only if you help me complete my mission. All of you." He looked around the room. "Home. Alive. No more war. It is possible. Help me."

Stimmel watched but made no comment.

"Listen, pal, we're all for it, but you kinda screwed it up by trying to pop Sloan. What was up with that anyway?" Marino asked.

Anders shook his head. "A miscalculation."

"One of many." Stimmel added.

Anders turned on him with a snarl. "Shut up!"

Stimmel shrugged and did not reply.

"It would not take many of you to help me achieve success. I know where the Germans are, and your lines are very close, a few kilometers down the road. With a vehicle, we could be there very shortly. The Germans will find this place."

"You know this? That the Germans are coming?" Juliette asked.

Anders nodded. "Soon. We must leave now."

"And take the children?" she insisted.

Anders paused, then shook his head. "Only Dr. van Stockum. His safety is my mission. The children will be taken care of."

Willem shook his head. "We all go, if the children are in danger."

"That's not possible, Dr. van Stockum. The nuns will take care of them. Your work is a much higher priority." Willem's face flushed.

"You keep talking about my work. What work? I haven't done any writing in years, or any significant research for that matter. What are you talking about?"

Anders shook his head.

"I can't discuss specifics, but it's more than just your work. You must return to London, and then the States. Your family, the Marlins, Dr. Veblen, it all awaits. Even Pic."

"How do you know about her?" Willem shouted, struggling to his feet and stumbling, his face crimson.

"She's waiting for you, Dr. van Stockum. To become your wife. It will all be clear when we …."

Willem lurched forward on his crutches, shouting. "Stop! Enough! You don't know what you are talking about!"

"I do, and you…."

"I said enough!" Willem swung himself toward the stairs and struggled upward, banging his injured leg in his angry haste. Sister Thérèse opened the door of the children's room and shushed them again with a finger to her lips, then closed the door. Gardner and Marino looked at each other, then Gardner stood up and followed Willem.

Marino turned to Anders. "Boy, you sure know how to make friends."

Gardner followed Willem into the front room. The ruined wall opened up into the night air. Willem fumbled for a cigarette, and, unasked, Gardner bent close with a zippo to light it. Willem accepted the proffered flame and blew out a big cloud of smoke. A soft rain fell again, the clouds having closed in for another wet night. They stood silently together in the dark. The anger Willem felt took him back to the day he stood in the Provost's office at Trinity, Pic's father lecturing him, humiliating him, destroying his future with his petty prejudice.

"You will not marry. Is that understood, Mr. van Stockum? I forbid it."

"But, sir…."

Edward John Gwynn, Senior Lecturer, Regius Professor of Divinity and Provost of Trinity College raised his hand, and Willem fell silent. The older man's dark bushy brow remained unmoved, his face stony. He stared at Willem, who stood flushed and nervous before him in his office, while he remained seated behind the expansive mahogany desk. He withdrew his arm, then leaned back in his leather chair with a soft squeak, folding his hands on his stomach and staring down the young man. Slowly, he gestured to the large work table off to the side, piled with manuscripts, one ancient piece of unrolled parchment, weighed down with two pieces of polished Irish limestone. A piece of glass lay on top for protection and a large magnifying glass with an ornate handle sat to the side.

"That manuscript there, it is over six hundred years old, a copy of another that was written another five hundred years before that."

Willem looked back and forth between the table and the man behind the desk, confused.

"Do you see that over there?" He pointed to the wall near his desk, to a framed letter. Willem looked at it, then shook his head.

"What is it?"

"It is a copy of the letter from Parliament granting the College independence, from before the Troubles. I fought very hard to ensure that the College would stand separate from the political turmoil we've been through, and we succeeded. That's over one thousand years of Irish history, our history. This is a special time for Ireland, for this college, for my family. Another important chapter in a very, very long history. Nothing can jeopardize that. Nothing."

Willem knew that Pic's Uncle Steven, a former Connaught Ranger, was active in Irish Nationalist politics and was now a politician in Galway. Both Gwynn brothers were ardent Nationalists, deeply involved in the struggle for independence from British servitude, and now struggling against the rogue elements of the Republican Army in the aftermath of the Civil War, a flame that was still smoldering almost a decade later.

"Sir, if you are concerned that I will somehow dishonor your family, I assure you…."

Gwynn waved his hand again, and Willem fell silent. "You are a student of some talent, I grant you that. You've proven yourself an able mathematician, and your gold medal is proof of that. The College has not had one for several years. Well done. I'm sure you will have a long and successful career. But I'm afraid that's not enough."

"Professor Gwynn, I love your daughter." The older man answered with only a slight shake of his head.

"Our family is part of the old history of Ireland, and now the new history. There are things happening right now that will determine the fate of this country for generations. Nothing can interfere."

"You keep mentioning family. May I ask why?" Willem's confusion began congealing into a cold anger as he sensed the direction this was heading. Professor Gwynn returned an icy stare.

"You are Dutch, Mr. van Stockum. Though I appreciate you have some Irish roots...."

"My mother's MacDonnell relatives are an old and respected family here in Dublin. My great-great grandfather sat in your chair. My family –" The older man waved his hand again, but Willem had trouble controlling himself.

"It's not your Irish connections I'm concerned about, Mr. van Stockum, at least not the respectable ones." Willem's eyes went wide.

"What does that mean, may I ask?"

"Please, Mr. van Stockum, your associations with the whiskey trade are hardly a secret. The generosity of the Jamesons is admirable, but it doesn't mitigate the disreputable origins of their wealth. That's not something I want my daughter tainted with. But that is not my main concern. The manner of your arrival here in Dublin, and the underlying cause, is what I will never consent for my daughter to become entangled with. I will not allow it."

"What are you talking about?"

The Provost colored at Willem's interruption. He was now dangerously close to insolence.

"Please Mr. van Stockum, let's not be crude. Your father, his illness. I will not allow it. Good day, sir."

Willem's face went crimson with rage, and his mouth opened and closed, soundless. Professor Gwynn ignored him, bent his head over his desk and started reading a document.

Speechless with anger, Willem stalked out, countless retorts swirling in his head, cutting, bludgeoning words to avenge the insults to the Jameson family, his father's honor, the disdain for their poverty and hardships, the charity from their friends and family.[7]

Willem took deep breaths to calm himself, then he turned to Gardner. "Do you want to go with him?"

"Who?"

Willem nodded back toward the basement. "Anders."

Gardner hesitated, then shook his head, a movement so small Willem wasn't sure he saw it.

"No. I'm in no hurry to go home."

"Do you have family?"

Gardner hesitated again, then turned away to face the opening in the wall. He spoke so softly, Willem had to take a step closer to hear him.

"Yes, but... things have changed. I'm not sure they'll take me back. There's too much......" Gardner looked over his shoulder back at Willem. "Nobody understands what happens over here. We do all this, see these things, and back home, they have no clue. Like it's two different worlds. And once you leave that one, you can't go back. You carry all *this*" – he waved his hand out into the darkness – "with you, and no one back home can understand it, nor do they want to understand it."

Willem could see he wasn't alone with his doubts and fears about what he was doing, why he was doing it, and what it meant for this future, if he was lucky enough to have one. He stared out into the night, visualizing the lines of craters, hearing again the screams of the children, and then thinking back to the creeping red tentacles of the fires snaking through the suburbs of Duisberg as they flew over....

"Is it real?" Gardner asked.

Willem looked at him.

"What?"

"The atom bomb."

Willem shrugged, avoiding his gaze. "I don't know...."

Gardner stared at him, unflinching.

Willem shifted his weight, leaning on the crutch, uncomfortable under the unwavering attention.

"...I suppose so."

Gardner sighed and shook his head.

"Do you think it's true, how powerful they'll be?"

Willem remembered Bohr's talk at Princeton, the calculations. Such energies! "The equations seem to indicate they will."

Gardner leaned on the wall, staring off into the night. "So much power. How will they use it?"

Willem shrugged and took another drag from the cigarette. Gardner shook his head.

"It won't be good."

Later, downstairs, Willem looked across the room at the slumped figure of Anders, who was snoring softly. Against the opposite wall, Doolan leaned against a pack, sound asleep with his mouth open. Marino and Gardner went out to relieve the other men at their posts. Stimmel watched him, alert and pale.

"No sleep?" Willem whispered.

"Not until the guards are awake. I don't ever take my eyes off him." He nodded toward Anders.

"You aren't German." Willem asked and stated simultaneously. Stimmel shook his head.

"Neither are you."

They shared a smile.

"So, what is your interest in me? I've racked my brain, and I'm sure we've never met. What is this all about?"

Stimmel smiled and lifted his chin to encourage him to continue.

"This doesn't have anything to do with the atom bomb, does it?" Willem added. Stimmel shook his head.

"But my work?" Willem frowned, struggling with Stimmel's lack of response.

Stimmel cleared his throat softly and nodded at Anders. "That's his interest. Really, I am only here to prevent him from interfering."

"Interfering? With what?"

Stimmel smiled. "The course of events. He's trying to exert, ahh, unnatural influence."

Willem shook his head, still confused. Stimmel maintained his Cheshire cat smile, silent.

"How does he know so much about me?" Willem nodded at Anders.

"He knows everything about your life. So do I. You are our common interest, but for different reasons."

"What does that mean? Stop speaking in riddles."

Stimmel smiled and shook his head.

"I'm sorry, Dr. van Stockum, I truly am. I am forbidden to give you any information. I know it is frustrating, but those are my orders. He doesn't have such strict procedures, but then again, he must be careful what he reveals as well – or he won't succeed, either."

Willem scowled and shook his head in frustration.

"What happened last night? After the bombing. You were crying."

Stimmel looked down, embarrassed. "Yes, that was… emotional. I was reminded of someone, a loss. That's all. It's a risk of the job."

CHAPTER THIRTY-FOUR

0130 June 12th, 1944
Near St. Jores, Normandy

The paratroopers moved both careful and sure through the misty darkness, confident in their improved knowledge of the local terrain. After final instructions to MacDonald and Turturro at the road, they struck out, working their way around St. Jores, avoiding the obvious dangers, working parallel to the main roads, following cart tracks and paths when convenient. After all the activity they witnessed during the day, the countryside was remarkably quiet, and they saw no significant concentrations of troops, at least in the immediate vicinity. To the north and west, the battle continued, lighting up the sky on the horizon with flashes and the glow of fires.

They came to the main road running between St. Jores and Carentan, and watched as several convoys passed. More were headed west than east. During a break, they hurried across the road, and continued their patrol. In the open country they made good time crossing the fields. It was wet, but not too muddy, and the darkness concealed them. The few lights in St. Jores allowed them to navigate by keeping the village to their left as they circled around.

On the north side, more empty fields and quiet.

Lezynski tugged on Sloan's sleeve and leaned close. "It looks wide open, Top."

Sloan grunted.

Jones edged over. "You seeing what I'm seeing?"

They turned to him.

"The krauts are gone! Let's get the other guys and head out," said Lezynski.

Sloan shook his head. "Not yet."

Tomorrow would be the day they could make their move. Except for the prisoners. The pilot's crutches would be a problem in these muddy fields. Leave him with the nuns and the resistance girl? They mentioned safe houses. And then the other two. He put it out of his mind for later.

Two hours later, they approached Turturro and MacDonald from the opposite direction and called out the password. All was quiet at the house, and they walked back, relieved to return to the safety of the chateau. Sloan's mind worked through the possibilities of a plan to reunite them with their units.

Sloan unloaded his gear, then supervised the rotation. They woke up Marino and Doolan and sent them out to the road. MacDonald went downstairs to watch the prisoners, and Turturro laid down to sleep. Lezynski took the post upstairs, and Sloan continued planning.

CHAPTER THIRTY-FIVE

0600 June 12th, 1944
Near St. Jores, Normandy

"Doolan's dead."

Sloan rubbed his face and sat up quickly, trying to process the news while clawing his way out of a deep sleep. "What?"

Lezynski stood in front of him, face creased with worry. "Doolan's dead. Throat's cut. And that Anders guy is gone. The other guy is still in the basement with the pilot. They say they never heard anything."

"Who was watching in the room?"

"MacDonald. He didn't see anything either."

"He was asleep."

"Musta been."

"Goddammit!"

"Where'd he get Doolan?"

"On the first floor. I think he was coming down to relieve MacDonald. That's probably when MacDonald was asleep."

"Did Marino see anything out on the road?" Lezynski shook his head.

Sloan stood up and hoisted his gear on, mind churning.

"Where's the French girl?"

Lezysnki shook his head. "Haven't seen her yet."

"Well, find her. We're getting out of here today."

They went downstairs and moved Doolan's body out back, away from where the children and nuns would soon be about. Lezynski scrubbed the pool of blood with a piece of torn curtain, with only limited success. The crimson smear on the wood floor remained obvious.

Juliette appeared at the top of the stairs, hair mussed.

"What happened?"

"One of the prisoners escaped and killed one of my men. We're going to leave today, and we're taking the pilot." She nodded gravely, eyes wide.

"And what of the other……?"

Sloan stared grimly back at her. "We're not taking him. Do you have a suggestion?"

She bit her lip and looked down at the floor. She took a deep breath, stood straight and lifted her chin. "I will make a plan. I will also help you with your escape, sergeant." She turned and went back downstairs. She returned shortly, leading two of the older boys. In a burst of fast French she gave them instructions, to which they nodded, donned frayed caps, and rushed out of the building.

"They are carrying messages to others to find out the latest news. They will also help me find a place for the prisoner."

Sloan sent Lezynski to the basement, and he went out to the road. He worked his way through the trees to the sentry post that overlooked the approaches to the long drive toward the house. As he quietly approached, he saw Green kick Marino, who sat up suddenly, clutching at his helmet. Sloan ignored the obvious signs of sleep in Marino's face.

"Hey Speedy, what do you see?"

Green turned toward the road. "A lot of movement for the last few hours. Started around four, just after we got out here. Mostly heading west, but all going through the village."

"Can you tell if they're staying on the road?"

"Looks that way."

Sloan lifted the field glasses and scanned the village and roads leading in. Clumps of infantry moved along, the occasional truck or car pushing through. The pace was brisk. He turned to the two paratroopers.

"We're moving out today. I'll send someone out to relieve you soon. Get your gear together. Not sure when we push off, but it may be very soon."

The other two nodded and Sloan left.

"It's about time. I was getting sick of this place," Marino observed.

Green nodded, non-committal.

"The boys from the village say your army is close. They have taken Carentan, and some are on the roads between here and Carentan. They are not far away," Juliette said in a rush.

The two older nuns interrupted and a conversation in French ensued. Juliette became agitated, and turned to Sloan.

"They want to move the children. They say it is no longer safe here." Sloan looked back and forth between them. More arguing in French followed. The two nuns went out and walked down the drive. Juliette turned to Sloan, exasperated. "They are going to see the priest. They would not listen to me."

Sloan sensed her desperation and felt a twinge of guilt having to add to it. "We're going to get ready to leave. We have to bury our friend, and then we leave."

Sloan turned to Turturro and Marino, standing nearby. "You two, take Doolan out back and find a good spot to bury him. Not near the kraut. Get me his dog tags. Make sure you mark it well."

Turturro grumbled, but Marino pulled him along outside.

"Shut up, before he figures out we never buried the kraut. You want twice as much work?"

Time Bomber

Down in the basement, Willem and Stimmel sat near each other, Gardner by the steps. The children fussed in the back room, the older girls having been left in charge by the nuns. They were having difficulty keeping the little ones under control, and the boys kept sneaking out. The older girls raised their voices at the younger children, but the men ignored them.

"Sir, try this on." Gardner approached, holding out a boot-like contraption with dangling laces. Willem took it and turned the straps and canvas over in his hands.

"What is it?"

"A brace I was wearing. I don't need it anymore, and I think it might help you walk better." He squatted down in front of Willem.

"Slip it over your shoe, and wrap this around, then lace it up." Willem followed the instructions, wincing as he eased it over the broken bones in his ankle, then snugged up the laces. It fit surprisingly well. Gardner gave him a hand up, and, leaning on one crutch, Willem tested it. To his surprise, the braced enabled him to place much more weight on the bad leg.

Sloan called down the stairs, and Gardner climbed halfway up to answer. Willem sat back down, and Stimmel turned to him.

"Dr. van Stockum, Anders will be back. He may be misguided, but he's very persistent. However, I think now it won't matter. Things are irredeemably altered, no matter what he does. My work is done."

Willem fought back anger. "What are you talking about? Altered? What is altered?"

Stimmel gave him that infuriating smile. "I think you know, Dr. van Stockum."

Willem stared at him, his mind racing. He swallowed, a knot forming in his chest.

"My work...?"

Stimmel raised his eyebrows.

Willem felt lightheaded and confused and scared to continue, but he was compelled to follow the line of reasoning to its conclusion.

All the hints and suggestions over the last several days fell into place. H.G. Wells and his machine, Dr. Szilard and his inspiration, these two strangers and their connections to his life. Stimmel nodded, watching the emotions passing over Willem's face.

"Closed loops," Stimmel said.

Willem swallowed, wiped sweat from his forehead, and shook his head. "You're from…?" Willem gestured forward, eyebrows arched expectantly.

Stimmel nodded. "But not yours."

Willem furrowed his brow.

Stimmel continued. "A different one. Similar, but not exactly the same, especially not now."

Willem shook his head, confused. "And him?" He gestured over his shoulder, meaning the departed Anders.

"A different one. Very different from yours and mine."

"A different one? How?"

Stimmel shrugged. "He comes from a world where events unfold in a particular way, and, due to decisions he made, end in a horrible catastrophe. He's been trying to undo that ever since, at any price, no matter what the consequences. I work with people who are determined to stop him, prevent him from making matters worse."

Willem fought vertigo.

"You're mad. What does this have to do with me?"

"He needs you to go home and continue your work. Your work, or rather, the work you did in his world, will set the stage for him to try and fix things."

Willem swallowed again. "But in your world… it's different?"

"It's always different. Each timeline is unique, but there are common threads – statistical clumping, if you will. Usually events play out a certain way, according to certain causality. However, there are always outliers. Sometimes a series of low probability events drive things in a fundamentally different direction, resulting in a very different timeline. His world is one such low probability sequence of events."

"Why is that a problem?"

"It's the cost of him trying to replicate that sequence. His difficulty is that the catastrophe is the necessary consequence of his timeline. He believes he can change that, but he hasn't succeeded yet, and in the meantime the same disaster occurs again and again. If each event occurred in isolation, it might not be a problem, but it doesn't. There are deeper connections, and his meddling attracts outside attention. Unwanted attention. We have to stop him and clean up the mess, before other parties intervene and take care of it."

"Other parties?"

Stimmel paused and took a deep breath, reaching a decision. "In your paper, remember the quantities of mass necessary to cause the spacetime deformations to produce closed loops?"

"Fantastic amounts, almost infinite."

Stimmel nodded. "Mass is energy. When your work, your future work that is, pointed the way toward quantum gravity, it opened the door to manipulating spacetime on a small enough scale to enable time travel, but the energies involved were enormous, and difficult to control. Anders' father, and he, attempted this before they fully understood it."

"The catastrophe?"

"Their experiments became more reckless, eventually attracting the attention of powerful forces, and they stepped in and put an end to it."

"How?"

"They destroyed the Earth. Rather than risk the reckless use of that power, they exterminated the planet."

"Then how can he be here, now?"

"He and his father escaped with their equipment. We don't know where, or when they are, but they've been trying to undo their mistake since, to no avail."

Right then. Willem knew this man was completely insane. That realization came as a great relief, suddenly lifting a great burden off him, and he laughed out loud. This was not his problem – just a chance encounter with a lunatic, or perhaps two. It did nothing to change his life, his plans. Now enjoying the intricacy of the delusion, Willem smiled and continued the game.

"How do you get home?"

Stimmel shook his head with a sad smile. "I don't, not the way you think, not strictly speaking. When I go back, it's to someplace similar, but not the same time and place I left. That's impossible. There really is no going home. I owe Sgt. Lezynski a big debt of gratitude. Because of him, I'm finished."

"What do you mean?"

"Retired. I cannot be subdued. It's not allowed. Kill or be killed, but we cannot be captured alive. I've been compromised, and because of that, I'll be retired."

"I'm sorry to hear that."

"Oh, no, it's good news. The best. Now I can live my life, in my own time. Or at least, one closer to my own."

CHAPTER THIRTY-SIX

1300, June 12th
outside St. Jores, Normandy

Willem and Juliette stood together at the front of the chateau. The older girls distracted the little ones in back, running them in the afternoon sun as a break from the darkness of the basement.

"Juliette! The little ones found a dead man behind the barn!" one of the girls called out.

"Merde," Juliette muttered as she hurried around back. Willem followed as best he could on his crutches. As he turned the corner, he saw a small knot of children gathered near the back barn, restrained by one of the older girls. Juliette pushed them away, shooing them back into the house. Then she came back to Willem.

"It is the boy from the other night. Uh, the smell. They never buried him."

"Should we…?"

She shook her head. "We are not staying here. I will move the children and the prisoner. We are finished with this place."

Sgt. Sloan approached. "Sir, are you ready? We'll be leaving soon." He turned to Juliette. "What do you hear from the boys?"

"There is fighting in the village. Someone shot at the *boche* and now they are shooting the people. And the sisters are still there." Juliette struggled to maintain her composure.

Sloan cursed. "Green, go out to the road and see what's going on."

The traffic through the village increased all morning, delaying their departure. On impulse, Sloan followed Green out to the road.

He joined Gardner, who was already out there, and Green. They took turns looking through the glasses. Smoke rose over the village, and the convoys continued through.

"We're going."

"Top, what about the pilot? And the kids?" Green asked.

Sloan shook his head.

"The pilot's coming with us. My first job is you guys, and getting you back to your units. I would love to help these others, but I can't, and now we've got to go. She's got options and other people to help her."

"What about the other guy?"

Sloan shook his head again. "Her problem. The Resistance guys will do something with him. Dumb bastard."

Green and Gardner looked at each other. Sloan handed back the field glasses and turned back toward the house.

"Get your gear together. We're moving out in fifteen minutes."

As he approached the house, the pilot stood in the doorway, leaning on his crutches. Sloan stood in front of him. Willem looked down from the doorway.

"We're leaving as soon as everyone is ready. We're taking you with us. If you can't keep up, my guys will take turns carrying you, but I've got to tell you, it's not going to be fun, because we'll be moving as fast as we can. Are you up for it?"

Willem stood up straight and took a few faltering steps, putting weight on Gardner's brace and leaning on his crutch as a walking stick, demonstrating his ability to walk unassisted. He kept his face bland, ignoring the shooting pain. Sloan nodded.

"Okay, looks like that works. Stay around here, we'll be moving out soon."

Sloan entered the house and stood at the top of the basement steps. Marino looked up from the basement.

"Get everyone together, we're moving out."

Marino nodded and turned away. Sloan climbed the stairs to the second floor and collected his gear from the side room he'd been sleeping in between watches. As he buckled his straps, Juliette rushed in.

"You can't leave yet. It is too dangerous."

Sloan scowled. "I'm sorry, but we're going. The krauts are pulling out, and based on what I saw last night, we've got a shot. Besides, they're getting too trigger happy in that village."

"But that is why you must stay. If they come here, these children are doomed."

"I'm sorry, but I've got to get my men back. This is our chance. You have other contacts, use them."

She shook her head. "No one will come out now, not with shooting in the village. We have nowhere to go."

"I'm sorry, I can't help you."

"What about the prisoner? What do I do with him?"

"That's your problem. I can't take him with me. He's not German. I don't know what he is. But I'm done with him."

They assembled in the courtyard, piling gear and weapons.

"Top, you want us to bring all this stuff?" Lezynski inquired. They had two of the .30 caliber machine guns, a BAR, and multiple canisters of ammunition. Sloan looked over the pile of ordnance.

"Take one of the thirties, two cans of belts, and leave the rest. Stow it in the house. We've got to move fast, and we're not going to be picking any fights if we don't have to. Everyone stuff their pockets with whatever you need for what you're carrying. And grenades."

"Hey, Green, you want to take first turn carrying?" Marino asked with a grin.

"Sure, no problem." Green slung the thirty over his small shoulder without hesitation or complaint. Marino nodded.

"Okay. I've got one can. Turturro, you take this one."

"Why don't you shove that up your ass, Marino. I ain't carrying your ammo. I've got enough of my own." MacDonald bent down and picked up the metal box with a scowl and turned away. Willem looked back as the line moved out, but the girl and the children were nowhere to be seen.

They pushed through the fields eastward, skirting St. Jores. They crossed the road that went south from the town without incident and continued parallel to the road heading eastward toward Carentan. Willem did his best to keep up, resting often, hobbling in bursts, then creeping with the others. The creeping was easiest, the open field walking difficult, walking slowly in a crouch almost impossible. He would wait until the sign was given to move ahead, then move as quickly as possible to the new position.

After a short while, he was drenched with sweat, breathing hard, his limbs on fire. But he remained determined to keep up.

They crossed an open field and assembled in a cluster of trees between two pastures. Sloan surveyed the way ahead, then looked to the sides to spot the flankers. Jones was supposed to be on the left and Lezynski on the right. He spotted Jones kneeling down under cover, waiting for the signal to proceed, but he couldn't find Lezynski. He swung the glasses back and forth, then saw him hurrying to them in a crouch.

"Problem, Top. Whole bunch of krauts up ahead. Looks like they're setting up, about thirty. They're all oriented to the north and east, looking away from us. If we go around, we'll have to go way north or south to avoid crossing in front of them. Probably setting up a defensive position for our guys coming this way."

Sloan considered this information.

"Take me up there. You guys sit tight, we'll be right back."

Willem heaved a huge sigh and sat down, wiping his face. His leg throbbed, and the respite was a mercy. MacDonald and Gardner kept a watch while the others sat down and drank some water.

"How you holding up, sir?" Green asked Willem.

"Good. I'm okay."

Green uncapped his canteen and took a long swig, then handed it to Willem. He drank and handed it back. Without a word, Green tapped Gardner on the shoulder, and he reached back and took the canteen. Marino and Turturro watched the exchange without comment.

Sloan and Lezynski returned, out of breath and sweaty.

"Looks like we've got a fight on our hands, but I think we can get the jump on them. If we hit them fast and then push through, we can pull it off. There are three emplacements with machine guns overlooking the road. I guess they're waiting for our guys to push this way. Marino, I want you on the thirty right up here, looking down on all three. Gardner, Turturro and Jones, I want you on the left, pushing in at forty-five. Lezynski and I will be on the right. MacDonald, you stay here and shoot. Speedy, I got a job for you. Remember Ramsbury?"

Green nodded and grinned.

"Think you can do it here?"

Green looked through the brush toward the German placements and nodded. He stripped off his gear and emptied his pockets. Willem watched, fascinated. Gardner turned to watch as well. Green put down his helmet and selected three grenades and put them in his pockets. He turned to Sloan.

"Ready, Sarge."

Sloan put a hand on his shoulder and pointed through the foliage. "Start from the right and go left. Marino, hold your fire until the grenades go off and Speedy is clear. Gardner, you and your guys, wait until Marino starts drawing return fire, then you start. Marino, concentrate on the middle. You see those guys getting close, watch your aim. We'll do the same on our side. Lezynski, let's go." Sloan moved off to the left.

"What's he talking about?" Marino asked Green.

"A little stunt we pulled during training, a problem like this. Worked like a charm. Just don't start shooting until I get out of there."

"You are fucking crazy."

"Yeah, that's why it works." Green crept away into the brush off to the right. Marino turned to Willem.

"Hey, doc, can you give me a hand with this?" Marino was setting up the machine gun behind a log, positioning the ammo canisters to his side.

"I just need you to hold this belt, make sure it feeds smoothly. If we need to change it, I'll handle that. Just keep your head down when they start shooting back at us." Willem crept up next to him.

"Happy to help."

MacDonald took a position behind another log to their right, with his M1 up, sighting on the Germans in the distance, making measurements, adjusting his sights. Willem sat up, peering forward to see what was happening.

"There he goes," MacDonald whispered. Willem glimpsed a small figure racing across the field toward the three emplacements. He ran clutching the grenades and, in a flash, they were gone, pitched into the middle of the three groups of Germans. The first group called out just as he passed the last one, but none had the presence of mind to raise a weapon before the first grenade went off. In rapid succession, three explosions ripped the German positions.

"He's clear," MacDonald said. He sighted through the rifle and fired, and Willem saw a German soldier spin and drop. Marino opened up with the machine gun, firing short bursts, traversing the muzzle back and forth between the three positions. MacDonald kept up a steady fire, drilling krauts every time they showed themselves. Still no return fire. The Germans were overwhelmed by the unexpected attack from the rear.

Finally, a few bursts of counter fire tore through the leaves around them, and Willem ducked behind the log, one hand held up under the belt as Marino continued firing. On cue, the two flanking groups opened fire, plunging the Germans into panic once again. The intersecting lines of fire tore through them, and several broke and ran. MacDonald calmly raised his M1 and tracked them, picking the stragglers off one by one. Willem raised his head again and watched the final minutes of the furious attack. It was over as quickly as it began.

"Hold up," MacDonald ordered. They watched the two groups converge on the machine gun nests and clear them out.

Sloan stood up and waved them forward.

"Let's go." Marino quickly stripped the thirty, slung the remaining ammo belt around his neck and tossed the can into the bushes. He put the gun over his shoulder and picked up the other canister. MacDonald trotted down the hill. Willem stood up and hobbled after him, Marino right behind him.

"Let's get to those trees over there by the road. Double time," Sloan ordered.

They moved out quickly, the fresh carnage immediately behind them. After fifteen minutes of marching, they rested under cover again. Willem was soaked in sweat, out of breath, leg throbbing again, but thoroughly energized with adrenaline after the attack.

Green rejoined them after having sprinted back to collect his things.

Marino slapped him on the back. "You had the pins out, didn't you?"

Green grinned and nodded. "I just hold the spoons until I toss them."

"While you're running? You're nutso, kid." Marino grinned and pushed him.

Willem sat down and reached a decision. He rubbed a hand across his forehead and looked around at the men quietly joking and conferring. Sloan looked ahead, plotting their next move with Lezynski. Only Gardner was quiet, watching vigilantly through the brush.

"Okay, let's move out," Sloan ordered.

"Sergeant, I'm not going," Willem stated.

Sloan turned to him. "What?"

"I'm going back to the house, to help the girl with the children. I think I can be of more use there. It's obvious I'm slowing you down, and your mission is a far higher priority than helping a wounded bomber pilot. I see that very clearly."

"By yourself?" Sloan scowled.

Willem stood up and leaned on his stick. "I made it this far, I can easily get back. I'll be careful. Besides, you and your men have cleared the way for me pretty thoroughly."

Sloan shook his head and looked around at the watching circle of men, then back at Willem.

"Whatever you say, sir. I don't think it's a good idea, but I can't stop you. Just be careful." He stepped forward and extended his hand.

Green interrupted. "Sergeant Sloan, maybe some of us should go with him?"

Sloan shook his head. "No, Speedy, we stay together. Our mission first."

Green and Gardner exchanged a glance, but stayed silent. Sloan turned back to Willem and shook his hand.

"Thank you, Sergeant Sloan. I appreciate everything you and your men have done for me. Can you do me one favor? Get a message to my brother-in-law in London. His name is Spike Marlin. You can reach him through the American Embassy. Let him know my whereabouts."

Sloan nodded and stepped back. One by one, the others stepped forward and shook Willem's hand.

"Take care, doc."

"Keep your head down."

"See ya, doc."

Willem nodded and smiled, touched by the spontaneous demonstration of concern. Turturro shook his hand with a silent nod and stepped away. Gardner gave him a thoughtful look, then a small smile as he held his hand. Green handed him his second canteen.

"Take it, you'll need it. Be careful."

"I will, thank you."

He turned to go, but stopped at a word from Sloan.

"Hold up, Sir." Sloan walked over, unstrapping the holster for the Colt Peacemaker, and holding it out to Willem.

"Take it. You need something to protect yourself." Willem looked from the gun to Sloan, unsure.

"Sergeant, I...."

"Sir, I can't let you walk unarmed back through enemy territory. I shouldn't even be letting you go, but you're a big boy. Let me show you how to work it."

Sloan withdrew the revolver and demonstrated the hammer mechanism, how it needed to be cocked back for the trigger to work.

"Pull it back, pull the trigger. Each time you fire. Careful, it kicks." Willem nodded, then strapped the gun on. Sloan nodded, then turned away, leading the group forward.

Willem watched the paratroopers head off across the field to the next line of trees, to the east and towards the advancing American lines. He turned back toward the chateau and set off, walking as fast he could, using his stick and clutching the canteen in his other hand, the big gun rubbing against his thigh.

CHAPTER THIRTY-SEVEN

1730, June 12th
between St. Jores and Baupt, Normandy.

Sloan and the paratroopers huddled in the ditch as the German convoy streamed by. Then they heard the airplanes.

Three P-47 Thunderbolts roared overhead, spraying the road with .50 caliber machine gun bullets, scattering the Germans. The planes banked around and zeroed in on the heavy trucks, releasing a scattering of bombs, detonating amongst the machinery with great effect. They circled again and again, weaving to avoid ground fire, cutting up the troops on the ground and rendering the road a burning hell of flaming machinery and dead Germans.

"Hold your fire. If they see us, we'll be surrounded. Let them scatter first and we'll get the hell out of here."

One of the Thunderbolts circled around and began bearing down on a line toward the ditch where the paratroopers huddled. Geysers of dirt sprayed up in two lines, stitching the ground toward their location. The plane roared overhead, the Americans miraculously unharmed.

"Orange panel! Orange panel! Who's got one?" Sloan screamed. The men fumbled furiously in their packs and pockets, as the plane circled again.

"I've got one!" Jones called out.

"Me too!" Lezynski added.

"Wave 'em! Go!" Sloan ordered.

"What about the krauts?" Turturro yelled.

"They won't matter if that plane gets us."

The P-47 lined up again for another pass, and Lezynski and Jones stood up holding the orange panels. The machine guns opened up again, the pilot unheeding of the frantic signals. The bullets ripped through the ground. Lezynski dove to the side, Jones spun around, blood flying.

Turturro screamed. "Goddammit! Fucking Christ! I'm hit! Those lousy fucking bastards!"

Lezynski and Gardner pulled out medic kits and started cutting apart Turturro's pants, while Green and Marino held him down. Turturro thrashed and cursed. MacDonald picked up the orange panel and waved frantically. The planes circled and shot up the retreating Germans but made no more passes over the troopers. Sloan crouched and watched for krauts. None noticed them or, if they had, none seemed interested.

Lezynski sprinkled sulfa powder on Turturro's wounds, then he and Gardner stuffed gauze in the bleeding holes while Turturro screamed.

"Shut up Turturro, you're going to live," Lezynski muttered.

"Fuck you, pal! Where's my morphine? Goddam it!"

Lezynski looked around. Green let go of Turturro's arm and fished in his kit and gave Lezynski a syrette. He pulled open the packaging and jammed it into Turturro's thigh.

"Happy?"

"Fuck you, Lezynski."

"You're welcome."

"Okay, quit the grab-ass, we've got to get under cover. What about Jones?"

Lezynski turned away from Turturro and crawled over to Jones' prone body and put a hand to his throat. He knew from the vacant pallor of his face what the answer was. He turned to Sloan and shook his head.

Sloan looked them over, then resumed his vigil of the surrounding fields. The column of burning vehicles crackled and popped, the Germans vanished in panicked retreat.

"Go after the krauts?" MacDonald wondered.

Sloan shook his head. "Let's just keep moving down the road toward the next town. They were running from something." He gestured at Turturro. "Get him up and let's go."

CHAPTER THIRTY-EIGHT

2110, June 12th
Outside St. Jores, Normandy

Willem leaned on his walking stick, panting, and looked off through the trees. The spire of the lone church in St. Jores peaked above the far treeline. Clouds scudded in and the light faded fast. In front lay a wide field, freshly plowed. The most direct route was across the field, but it would be slow going. He set out, trying to maintain a rhythm of stepping from the peak of one furrow to the next, looking up to keep the spire in front of him, but concentrating on maintaining his footing. He settled into a steady pace, pleased with himself, until his foot slipped on loose dirt and he tumbled to the ground, protecting his bad leg. He let loose a torrent of expletives in multiple languages, then rested. Overhead, the clouds thickened, and a light mist fell. He rolled over and pushed himself up. He wiped his muddy hands on his pants, grasped his staff, then resumed his hobbling.

By the time he reached the raised mound of the surrounding bocage, it was full dark, the rain heavier. His landmark was gone, and fatigue overwhelmed him. He slumped against the earthen ridge, exposed to the rain. In a final burst of energy, he scrambled up the bank and through the hedge, tumbling down the other side into another small apple orchard. He hobbled to the nearest large tree and lowered himself to the ground underneath, where it was drier than anywhere else. He listened to the light rain. In the far distance, the thump and rumble of the battles to the east and north continued unabated.

He settled against the tree, maneuvering into a comfortable position away from the dripping. Beneath him, the crackling layers of countless seasons of accumulated detritus wafted their fragrance, redolent of living matter in transition. He drew a contented sigh, and pondered his situation.

Watching the paratroopers methodically destroy the German machine gun nests, and the efficient brutality they applied to the much larger force, convinced him that the war was going to end, and it would be the ground troops who would finally win it. Rushing back to the squadron to get back in the air to drop bombs wasn't going to change anything, especially with his broken leg. How many weeks recuperating? The war would be over by then at this rate. If he were going to be of use to the innocent victims of this calamity, his place was here and now. Of that he was sure.

He thought of his crew: Johnny and Nate, Colin and his dark humor, quiet Jock, nervous Toby and his meticulous targeting efforts, and young Declan, who had so recently joined the team and was already possibly dead. They're all dead, I suppose, Willem thought. Maybe not Colin, famous for his quick egress from troubled aircraft. Vague memories of the crash hovered on the edge of recollection, but he couldn't be sure of what was real. Had he spoken with Johnny? What happened to him? He wouldn't know until he got back to the squadron, and even then perhaps never, several more lives having disappeared in the maelstrom of war. And Dennie, had he made it back? What stories they would share the next time they huddled over their cups in the Officer's mess. Dennie with his fatalism, would he believe the crazy turn of events? Willem surviving the crash, the rescue, and the two strangers and their mad tales?

Willem chuckled to himself, thinking of Dennie and his crew speculating with each other whether Willem had gone for a Burton. Would that make Dennie smile? Willem hoped so, whether or not he survived. If there is a heaven, and if Willem was headed there, he certainly hoped a pint of ale was on the menu, with good company, stories, and singing.

Why didn't he go with the one saying he was here to rescue him? No matter how ardently he professed his good intentions toward Willem, Anders' behavior toward the others marked him as a ruthless killer, and Willem wasn't going with him, no matter how dire the circumstances.

What of the other, Stimmel? Though he seemed kind, his ramblings seemed no less insane, with his talk of alternate futures and time travel. Yet he was so calm and sure, without a hint of madness. His lack of personal interest in Willem in some ways made his story more compelling. Clearly, he was delusional, yet there was something about him, his demeanor, that gave Willem pause.

And what of Pic? It hit Willem in that moment, the real reason he had stayed. Although the letter from Spike held out the prospect of some kind of reunion, and then the bizarre assertion from Anders that she was waiting for him, he knew it couldn't be. The Pic waiting back in London wasn't the same woman he loved at Trinity. Though she may harbor some of the same feelings, she was different, irrevocably so, and so was he. Ten years of separation, of growing, of pain and healing, the accumulated experiences of all that living. They lived in separate worlds now, divided by a series of choices and circumstances pushing them apart. Would it be too much to overcome, to renew their love? Perhaps, perhaps not, but regardless, it wouldn't be the same. The reason for going back to London wouldn't be what happened before, but what could happen in the future, and all the uncertainty that that would entail. And weighed against that, the urgency of the situation at hand won out, now without any doubt.

If he made it back, if he saw Pic again, if he ended up back at Princeton... perhaps if he returned to his research, Stimmel's ideas would be something to explore further – in the company of Dr. Veblen and Dr. Einstein, back in Princeton or at Maryland, wherever circumstances took him. But for now, he must fulfill his commitment to be of use during this great conflict, and the most pressing problem before him was the safety of those children. Nothing was clearer to him. Though he'd spent the last four years training for one kind of mission, this was the one presented to him at this moment, and he would not fail. The hoof beats of Oisin's enchanted horse thundered over the sea and echoed across the years: the hero on his quest. Willem smiled to himself at the image.

The rain let up, and a gentle breeze stirred. He stared up at the sky, looking for stars in the ragged openings in the clouds above. The faint glow of apple blossom petals on the ground around him reminded him again of snow, taking him back to Joyce's story again, the snow falling on the living and the dead, and it all made sense. He had some distance now from his passion, his love for Pic, and saw now how it fit into the rest of his life, what was connected, how it moved him, and its relative insignificance when compared to the vast sweep of events around him. Pic moved on one path, he another, perhaps intersecting, perhaps not, but there was here and now, and he knew what to do.

He took a deep breath and closed his eyes, trying to relax enough to sleep. Stimmel's ideas still nagged at him, and he toyed with higher dimensional geometries, manipulating some tentative equations, experimenting. The day's exertions took their toll, and Willem's breathing slowed and his mind wandered. He curled up at the base of the tree, cushioning his head with his arm, rolling to his side to protect his leg. The hard edges of the Colt dug into his thigh, but he fell immediately into a deep sleep.

CHAPTER THIRTY-NINE

0215, June 13th
near Baupt, Normandy

Sloan stopped and raised his fist, and the line of paratroopers came to a halt. Ahead was a small building, with no sign of guard or sentry. The road had been so quiet, they had left the cover of the woods and hurried along in the darkness and so made better time. The others took turns carrying the quietly cursing Turturro.

Sloan turned back and bent close, whispering orders.

"Let's check that place out. If it's empty, we'll hole up there until first light. How are you doing, Turturro?"

Turturro grunted a sullen response, which Sloan ignored. Lezynski and Gardner crept up to the house, searched around it, then went inside. Lezynski hurried back after a few minutes.

"It's clear, Top. Nothing inside."

They moved forward and settled in, sharing water and rations. Sloan set a watch, and the rest fell quickly asleep.

CHAPTER FORTY

0605, June 13th
near St. Jores, Normandy

Willem awoke, sore and stiff. The eastern sky was bright and the clouds were breaking up. For the first time in quite a while, he had the dream, but this time it was different. He was on the beach again at Sligo, but walking with his sister Hilda. There was no horse. They climbed on the slippery green rocks as they did in childhood, but they were adults in the dream. Willem was in his uniform, Hilda was in a dress and her apron, as if she had just walked out of the kitchen in Chevy Chase. She was telling him about her writing, about the children, about mother's paintings and news from Spike. I know about Spike, he thought in the dream, I was just with him.

Hilda reached down to give him her hand, but Willem turned toward the sea. There was Pic, sitting on the horse in a long white gown, her hair long and flowing, longer than she had ever worn it in his memory. She stared at him expressionless over the waves, holding the reins in one hand. She's not Neave, he thought to himself. He turned back to Hilda, but she was further up the cliff, laughing. When he looked back to the ocean, the horse and Pic were gone, but he wasn't sad.

Time Bomber

He sat up, and easily saw the village in the distance. He picked up his walking stick, and set out with renewed energy and purpose, the fitful night of cold and restless dozing now behind him.

CHAPTER FORTY-ONE

0730, June 13th
Baupt, Normandy

"Top, someone's coming!" Sloan struggled awake and sat up. In the distance, he heard an approaching vehicle. The others scrambled for weapons, taking up places at doorways and windows. Sloan listened carefully, fighting to contain the rising elation inside him as he recognized the sound.

Marino said it first. "That's a jeep."

Sloan smiled. "Everyone hold your fire. Let's see what's going on." He crept up to the door and peered out.

Down the road toward the village, the sound of the vehicle grew louder, finally appearing around a corner. Three paratroopers drove toward them, weapons ready, scanning the surrounding buildings.

"Careful guys, they look pretty twitchy. Give me a panel."

Lezynski pulled out the orange panel and handed it to Sloan. He stepped forward and waved it as the jeep approached. The soldiers in the jeep, who were looking the other way, did not see him at first. Then they looked left as they pulled abreast of the building. Sloan waved his arms, and one of the soldiers startled and swung his rifle around, squeezing off a shot. Sloan dove to the ground and screamed out.

"Hold your fire! We're Americans! Hold your fire!"

"You dumbfucks! Open your eyes!" Marino shouted from the window. The jeep scraped to a halt in the dirt road, and all three soldiers brought their weapons up.

"Flash!" One of the soldiers called out.

"Thunder. Man, are we glad to see you bozos," Marino replied. Sloan sat up and started laughing, joined in by the others from the house. The three soldiers in the jeep stared back, bewildered.

One by one the others came out, and the soldiers in the jeep debarked and walked over.

"What the hell are you guys doing here? Where are the krauts?" one of them asked.

Sloan stood up and brushed himself off.

"They moved off to the south and west yesterday. We ran into some. We've got a wounded man who needs a medic right away. Where are you guys from?"

"508th. We came down from Beuzville la Bastille last night. The krauts had us bottled up at those bridges, but they finally pulled back. There are a bunch of guys coming in right behind us. Load your guy in here, and we'll get him to our medics." The other paratrooper glanced at the spade on Sloan's helmet. "You all 506th?"

Sloan shook his head. "A couple of 82nd guys from the 507th, a couple from the 501st. We all got scattered in the drop, hooked up west of here, been trying to stay alive since. It's good to see you guys."

CHAPTER FORTY-TWO

0930, June 13th
outside of St. Jores, Normandy

Willem hobbled up the dirt road to the chateau, filled with eager anticipation to see the children and Juliette. Since waking at dawn, he'd made good progress, unobserved and unmolested despite his direct and unconcealed approach. He skirted the village to the south, but made no effort at stealth, crossing the road heading south. A few trucks passed in the distance, but they took no notice of the lone man hobbling with a walking stick across the fields.

As he approached the chateau, a figure left the house carrying two pails. Willem froze at the sight of a German uniform. Every hair on his body tingled, his muscles twitched with adrenalin. It hardly seemed fair to be captured so close to his return.

The person looked up and broke into a wide smile.

"Welcome back, Dr. van Stockum," Stimmel said.

Willem's knees buckled slightly with relief, and he sagged against his walking stick. His laughter was spontaneous and loud. "I didn't expect to see you. Hello there."

Stimmel set the buckets down and walked forward, reaching out with a smile. They shook hands, grinning at each other.

"What about your mission?" Willem asked.

"I think it's nearly complete. It's not strictly according to our regulations, but I want to make sure this young lady gets her charges to safety. As I mentioned before, this is a unique situation for me, and I don't see any harm in helping her now that your status is no longer in question."

Willem nodded. "I think I've come to the same conclusion. My idea of duty is evolving, it seems."

"As is mine." Stimmel turned back to the pump, then looked over his shoulder. "Can you help me at the well?" Willem nodded, and Stimmel bent down and picked up the buckets.

Willem followed him to the pump. "You know, I've been thinking about what you told me before, about you and Anders," Willem began, tentatively.

Stimmel nodded. "I knew you would."

Willem worked the pump handle while Stimmel held the bucket, water splashing both of them.

"There are so many paradoxes in what you say. If there are parallel worlds and alternate pasts and futures, what matter is it to him, or to you, what happens in our world?"

Stimmel nodded. "I apologize for being less candid before, but I wasn't sure how all this would end. Now that it's fairly certain Anders can't complete his mission, I think I can be more direct. Let me also say that I am a soldier – a field operative, not a scientist – so my explanations may be unsatisfactory to you from a technical perspective. I can only tell you what I know from my experience and training, but, as you can imagine, for subjects so complicated, and because of the nature of my missions, I'm not an expert by any means."

Willem nodded, encouraging him to continue.

"The quantum nature of spacetime was discovered in my world when the mathematics of higher dimensional physics were finally mastered, a synthesis of work done by many, many scientists over hundreds of years, in what would be your distant future. As you can imagine, it required the manipulation and very precise control of fantastic energies. Moving matter and information between worlds is really just an exercise in balancing energies, governed by the laws of thermodynamics. Granted, there is a lot more to it, but that's what it boils down to.

"Once we began those explorations, we soon discovered that others had already made these same discoveries, races and civilizations far more advanced than ours. We stayed out of their way, keeping a very low profile, afraid to invite their attention or scrutiny, given the powers they clearly had mastered that we were only beginning to learn about. Then we ran into Anders."

They switched buckets, and Willem continued pumping, riveted by Stimmel's tale.

"From the beginning, we were very careful in our explorations to disturb as little as possible. Our scientists discovered that how history unfolds in parallel worlds is connected at deeper levels, and even with the myriad fluctuations caused by the infinite contingencies of existence, most worlds follow a general path, sort of the average outcome. Think about the behavior of millions of molecules in a container, how they sum to produce an average temperature, or a pressure. Same kind of thing. Small fluctuations smooth out over larger distributions. But like with all processes subject to random fluctuations, there are unusual low probability events that can occur. Anders' world was one such fluke."

Willem stopped pumping and Stimmel put the second full bucket down and leaned against the pump. Willem continued holding onto the handle.

"In Anders' world, the war ends with Hitler's death at Margival, and you survive the war. Your subsequent work at

Princeton, along with others, moves the mathematics of theoretical physics forward by several generations, leapfrogging the long, slow progression that occurred in my world. The discovery of quantum spacetime happens far earlier, led by Anders' father. Together, they create the first machines to manipulate spacetime, which they use recklessly. Their activities result in the destruction of the earth by outsiders who want to put an end to the threat."

"What threat?" Willem asked.

"As long as our activities remained confined to our small part of the cosmos, centered around our planet, in our little solar system, no one in the wider multiverse cared. But Anders and his father had bigger plans, far beyond the confines of our planet and sun. Their early explorations were too aggressive, the energies mishandled, and they caused disturbances – big disturbances. Exploding suns, singularities at inconvenient times and places, meddling in the histories of other civilizations. They had to be stopped."

"So what is he doing now?"

"Trying to undo his mistakes. He keeps trying to recreate his world by meddling in events like here and now, in the hopes of returning to his lost world, but with a different ending. He hasn't succeeded yet, and in the meantime, he causes immense suffering and destruction each time he fails. Our concern is that unless we keep him under control, the outside attention may be turned toward more than just his world, his Earth. So we follow him and try to stop him, or at least slow him down."

Stimmel bent down and picked up the two buckets and started back toward the chateau. Willem followed slowly, lost in thought, rapidly digesting the ideas of quantum spacetime, the multiverse, and parallel worlds. Stimmel walked slowly, keeping pace with Willem, waiting for the next question.

Willem shook his head, then looked up with a smile. "You are a fabulous storyteller, Mr. Stimmel, I'll grant you that. I keep catching myself falling into your spell, believing your strange tale. But there's one problem you haven't explained. You mentioned before that you've done this before, stopped him, he's stopped you, that this is an ongoing battle. If he's killed you before, and you him, how do you continue? How many of you are there, or of him?" Willem smiled again, enjoying the game.

Stimmel returned the smile. "You are right, it's a strange problem. I honestly don't know how he does it, and I only understand in principle how we do it. When I am deployed from our operations locus, the machines track me, monitor my experiences, and the instant my mission is completed, I am recalled."

"So your mission isn't complete yet?"

"I'm still here."

"And if you are killed?"

"This part I don't completely understand. The machines redirect me before I leave on that trip."

Willem stopped. "Wait. You are saying the machine sends information back in time to keep you from leaving on that trip?"

Stimmel nodded. "Why is that so farfetched? They send my body back and forth, why couldn't they send information back and then act on it?"

"How?"

Stimmel put the buckets on the ground and lifted his shirt to show the silvery undergarment underneath.

"I have no idea how it works, but this is what we wear to maintain the connection back to the operations locus. If I am killed, they brief me on the events of that trip, and we take measures to avoid that situation, then try again. They tell me there is no way I can remember these things, because this body in this world didn't experience them. But I'm sure I have. I seem to know things not contained in my briefings. If the machines can share data across dimensions and times, why can't I share memories, feelings, impressions? At least that's what I think."

Willem burst out laughing, guffawing so hard he bent over, one hand on his knee, the other leaning on his walking staff.

Stimmel laughed with him.

Willem straightened up, wiping his eyes, chuckling softly.

"I must say, if we ever get the opportunity, I will buy you dinner and evening of drinks just to hear you spin yarns. My sister is a writer, and my family is fond of stories, but nothing comes close to your abilities. Bravo, my friend, bravo."

They resumed their walk to the house, and once again, Willem couldn't completely let go of Stimmel's story.

"Does it bother you that I don't believe you, that I keep laughing at your stories?" Willem asked.

Stimmel shook his head. "Not at all. It doesn't matter to me. Whether you believe me or not doesn't change anything."

"But your mission…."

"My role is very small. Once I've completed my assignments, it's out of my hands. I find all that matters at that point is the little things that keep any person sane and happy: integrity, compassion, honor, duty. All I can do is stay true to those. The rest is out of my hands."

Of all the things Willem heard, this unsettled him the most.

They walked to the back of the house, where they saw Juliette encircled by the children. She was bent over distributing pieces of bread, admonishing them in French. At the sound of their approach, she looked up, and Willem was struck by the dark circles under her eyes. Her face lit up when she saw the two men.

"They came back?"

Willem immediately grasped her meaning and shook his head.

"Just me. I thought you might need some extra help, and I was slowing them down."

She took this in, and her smile gradually disappeared, and she turned back to the children.

"Ah, that is good. More help is good. Thank you."

"What is the situation in town? Did the sisters return?"

Juliette looked up, all the same worry, and more, back in her face. She shook her head. "No, they are not here. The Germans are taking revenge. No one has been in town since yesterday afternoon. One of my boys is missing, so I am afraid to send the others out."

"What should we do with the children?"

"I want to take them away to a safer hiding place, but I can't move them until I am sure where that is. We can't just walk around, but we are running out of food here, and I don't know when someone might bring more."

Willem considered the situation. The first priority must be keeping the children safe, and the second must be food and water. With his limited mobility, he couldn't help much with the second, but he could supervise them, freeing the other two for foraging.

"After they eat, why don't we put the children back in the basement, and I'll stay with them while you two go out and find food, and perhaps a new place to hide?"

Juliette looked back and forth between Willem to Stimmel, thinking. "Yes, I could take some of the older boys. You must be careful, with that uniform." She pointed at Stimmel.

"Perhaps it is time to dispense with it. Do you have other clothes I could use?"

Juliette shook her head, then caught herself. "Maybe one of the older boys has something that might fit? You are not a large man." She turned to one of the boys and gave some brief orders in French and he hurried away.

Stimmel unbuttoned the German field jacket. In the process of removing it, the shirt underneath lifted up, briefly revealing again the silvery undergarment beneath.

The boy returned with a rough peasant shirt. Stimmel pulled it on, covering the uniform, the sleeves not quite reaching up to his wrists. He stretched his arms out, grinning. Willem thought he looked quite ridiculous, but he certainly didn't look like a German soldier, despite the pants and boots he still wore.

Juliette finished feeding the children, then herded them inside and down to the basement. Willem and Stimmel stayed upstairs, planning. Willem sat down against the wall to rest, his leg throbbing from his morning exertion.

"Do you want another weapon, in case the Germans appear?" Stimmel asked.

Willem shook his head.

"What good would it do? I am only one person, and it will only put the children in danger. I think the best I can do is keep them concealed and quiet until you return."

Stimmel nodded. "I will let the girl decide where we will go. I think I will be of use to her as protection and with carrying whatever we find. It's funny how our roles have changed, isn't it?"

Willem chuckled at the thought: first a mathematician, then a bomber pilot, now a nanny for French orphans.

Juliette returned. "They are quiet, but not for long. They are very restless and afraid. They know that the sisters being gone is a bad thing."

"I will go with you, and Dr. van Stockum will stay here with the children," Stimmel said. Juliette nodded.

"That is good. We can go to the neighbor farm first, and then...."

She was interrupted by the metallic click of a cocking weapon. They turned to the doorway to see Anders pointing a German MP40 at them.

"Don't move. Dr. van Stockum, you are coming with me. You, hands up."

Juliette complied, nervously glancing between the men.

Willem looked from Anders to the others, panicked.

Anders stepped forward and pushed Juliette in front of him, watching Stimmel the whole time. Stimmel remained calm and alert.

"I'm impressed, Timothy. You really don't give up."

"Shut up. Dr. van Stockum, we must leave right now. The Germans will be here shortly."

"*Bâtard!*" Juliette spat. "You led them here!"

Anders shrugged.

"No, they followed me. I needed transportation, and they objected. Come, we don't have time." He gestured to Willem, but he made no response.

"You know this one is finished, Timothy. Why make things worse?" Stimmel observed calmly.

"I told you to shut up. Please, Dr. van Stockum, come with me. I have a motorcycle we can ride to the Allied lines." Willem looked back and forth between the two men.

"Timothy, why not leave these people to their lives? There are infinite chances for another try. Let them go."

"I told you to shut up!" Anders screamed, pointing the machine gun at Stimmel's face. "You know what's at stake! My world, my people! There is only one chance, and I will not miss it, not again."

"But Timothy...." The machine gun exploded into action, spattering the wall with Stimmel's blood, and he fell backward, his face a crimson ruin. Willem dove sideways to the floor away from the gunfire.

Juliette stood to the side of Anders, her hands raised, the machine gun pointed away from her. Anders stepped forward and extended a hand to help Willem stand. Willem looked at Stimmel's body and felt clammy and sick.

In a blur, Juliette reached back, then stepped to Anders side and plunged a knife into his right side. Her eyes went wide as the blade was turned aside. He brought the gun around, but she quickly pulled back and slashed the knife against his right hand, partially severing his index finger. Anders howled and tried to bring the machine gun to bear, but she slashed him again, stabbing at his arm as she wrenched the gun from his hands. He stumbled forward and in one smooth motion she brought the gun around and smashed the stock over his head. Anders crumpled to the floor with a low moan.

Juliette flipped the submachine gun around and held it ready, visibly trembling.

"He is a spy, I know that." She pointed at Anders. Anders rolled to his back, clutching his bloody hand to the back of his head, grimacing.

"I'm an American! I have to finish my mission!"

"You are a liar!"

Juliette fired into his chest, knocking him backward. He squirmed on the floor trying to avoid her, but she stepped sideways, tracking him with the gun, firing in short bursts. Willem pulled his legs up and covered his head, rolling sideways to avoid the ricocheting rounds clattering around the room. The slugs from the MP40 knocked Anders back, but he made it to one knee, pushing himself toward Juliette, who was still firing frantically.

She drew a bead on his face and pulled the trigger again, finally knocking him to the floor in a gory welter. Juliette kept pulling the trigger with no effect, the magazine exhausted, Anders clearly dead in front of her. She looked at Willem calmly.

"Are you hurt?"

Willem uncurled from the fetal position, and looked up at her, placidly holding the machine gun trailing a wisp of smoke, the two bleeding bodies at her feet. He sat up slowly, heart hammering from the unexpected burst of violence.

Juliette opened her mouth to speak, and Willem saw her turn toward a soft crackling noise coming from the direction of Stimmel's body. The sound rose quickly to a sharp hiss. Juliette's eyes went wide, and then there was a quiet, sharp pop. Willem followed her gaze, and Stimmel was gone. Juliette froze in shock.

"*Qu'est-ce que c'est? Qu'est-ce que c'est?*" she screamed. Willem sat stunned, all his doubts swept away and suspicions confirmed by the evidence before his eyes. Juliette stared around the room wide-eyed and hysterical. Willem struggled to speak, then the crackling resumed, and Anders body disappeared.

Juliette let out another scream, followed by ragged sobs. The older children were at the top of the stairs, drawn by the noise and commotion, looking around, fear on their faces. Juliette continued screaming. Willem struggled to his feet, leaning on the stick, trying to regain control of the situation.

"You, children, back downstairs!" he gestured at them, and despite the language barrier, they complied. He hobbled to Juliette and put an arm around her, fumbling to comfort her while he tried to comprehend the last few minutes.

"Hey, what's going on?" He whipped around at the familiar voice to see Green and Gardner standing in the doorway, panting and soaked in sweat, weapons ready. Green strode forward and slung his rifle. He took Juliette in his arms and held her close. She buried her head in his shoulder and sobbed while he shushed her.

"We came back to get you. What's up, doc?" Gardner asked quietly. Willem shook his head, and gestured at the bloodstains.

"We... we had some shooting."

"Yeah we heard it. What happened?"

"The two prisoners had it out, and they're... gone."

"Gone?"

Willem opened his mouth to reply, then merely gestured at the bloodstains again, his mouth open, brow furrowed. Frowning, he let his hand drop, shaking his head. Gardner pushed on.

"Well, we've got to get out of here. We're taking you back to the other guys. It's only a couple of miles to our lines."

Willem looked back and forth between the bloodstains on the floor where Anders and Stimmel had lain, and the waiting paratroopers, shifting their feet, restless. The moment dragged on. The only sounds in the room were those of Juliette's distress and Green's whispered comforts.

"Doc, we..." Gardner started.

Willem straightened and turned to him. "There are Germans coming. We have to prepare. Did you see anything coming in?"

Gardner shook his head.

"We circled around and came through the woods in back. The town is crawling with krauts, lot of activity. We hauled ass back here to get you, and then we heard the shots."

"The children. We have to keep them safe." Willem leaned on the crutch and rubbed his forehead, looking around the room desperately. Gardner watched him with concern, then walked to the front of the house and looked out. He turned back to the others.

"I'm going upstairs to get a better look." He bounded up the stairs. Green continued calming Juliette, and her sobbing abated to sniffling.

"Are you okay?"

She nodded in response.

"What happened?" he asked.

She looked at Willem, searching for a way to explain. Willem shook his head. "The one in the German uniform was still here, helping her, then he came back, and there was shooting. They're both gone."

"Gone? Where? I see the gun, and the blood, but where...." Green was interrupted by Gardner bounding down the stairs into the room.

"We have to shake a leg. Krauts heading south out of town this way. Looks like they may be bugging out. If we get out to the road, we can draw them away if we need to, keep them away from the house. Get those kids hidden. Green, give me a hand with the stuff we left here."

Willem took a step forward. "I can help."

Juliette took a big breath and pushed away from Green's embrace. "I will hide the children."

She went to the basement, and the men went to the pile of weapons in the back room that had been left earlier by the paratroopers. Gardner picked up the BAR, and Green hefted the .30 caliber machine gun.

"Doc, can you carry some of these canisters?"

Willem stepped forward and lifted one. He tried carrying one in each hand, but found it difficult to walk without the stick. The thigh holster for the Colt caught the canisters, clanging and working loose. Willem remembered Sloan's warning. He hobbled to the top of the stairs and called Juliette. She climbed up the steps, a question on her face. He unbuckled the holster and handed the weapon to her.

"Do you remember what he said about how to fire it?"

She nodded.

"Remember, the first chamber is empty." She accepted the revolver and wrapped the thigh holster around her slender waist, just able to cinch it together.

Willem turned back to the smiling paratroopers. "I'll make several trips."

Green nodded, and picked up a canister with his free hand, balancing the machine gun over his shoulder with the other. Gardner did the same, and they headed out to the road, Willem hobbling behind.

CHAPTER FORTY-THREE

1715, June 13th
Carentan, Normandy

Sgt. Thomas Sloan ambled through the ruined streets of Carentan, oblivious to the bustle around him. The ride back to their lines this morning was a distant memory, the sudden dislocation surreal in its suddenness and totality. After the brief jeep ride from Baupt to Carentan, passing the destruction of the recent battles and the checkpoints, they were surrounded once again by olive drab and American accents. The 508th guys took Turturro to an aid station and he was whisked away in an ambulance. Lezynski and MacDonald took off to find the 507th, already aware of the depressing news about the massacre of some of their comrades at Graignes.[8] Marino found a clerk from 1st Battalion running an errand and followed him back to headquarters. The possibility of hot food, showers, and clean clothing was now the first priority, and the men separated without even a goodbye.

Sloan spent the afternoon looking for some way to give Jones' and Doolan's dogtags to someone from the 501st, until finally he found a graves registration tent set up next to a ruined building. The clerk there took his information, and finally he was free to find his way back to the rest of 2nd Battalion.

Wending his way through the milling crowds of troops, Sloan struggled to adjust to the casual atmosphere, which was oddly disconcerting. Now that the mortal danger of less than twenty four hours earlier was over and the mission was complete, no one recognized him. No one seemed to care that they were back. And what had they accomplished, beyond just staying alive?

The decision to let Gardner and Green go back still bothered him. Letting the pilot go, even though he was a British officer, was one thing, but Green was one of his men, one of the guys he was entrusted to lead back to their unit. Green's insistence on going back for the pilot was yet another conflicting mission priority. Sloan got most of them back, but he knew that wasn't good enough.

He saw a black enlisted man leaning against a deuce-and-a-half idling by a cluster of hastily erected supply tents. Sloan was seized with a sudden idea.

"Hey buddy, I need your truck."

The driver looked him over and shrugged. "So does everyone else. Can't help you, Sarge. I got to head back to the beach as soon as I find out where."

Sloan unslung his M1 and pointed it at the ground in front of the man.

"I'm not asking." He looked the man in the eye. The driver's eyes flicked to the rifle, and he shook his head with a big sigh. He stubbed out his cigarette and climbed into the cab.

"Where to, Sarge?"

Sloan hurried around to the passenger side and climbed in.

"Just start driving, and don't slow down for anything."

They barreled down the road west out of Carentan, barely slowing for the checkpoint despite the waves and shouts of the soldiers manning the barricade. Sloan waved and shouted back about picking up wounded, then urged the driver onward. They did the same as they passed through Baupt and headed toward St. Jores, the truck bumping and swerving to avoid dead Germans, damaged vehicles, and abandoned equipment.

In the space of less than an hour Sloan retraced the distance it had taken them a week to negotiate in the fits and starts of their wanderings. Only twenty hours ago this was enemy territory, the path of their deadly journey now an easy drive.

They pulled into St. Jores and drove to the church. It was empty. They asked someone in the village where the hostages were, and after several failed attempts using broken English and French, they were lead to a farmhouse on the edge of town. Three grim village men sorted through a jumble of bodies piled against a wall, accompanied by a clump of softly weeping women. Sloan saw the black and white fabric of the nun's cassocks in the pile, and his heart sank.

Sloan directed the driver to the chateau, and they drove along the dirt track. Sloan's spirits fell further when he spotted smoke rising above the trees toward the house. As they approached the woods, bodies of dead krauts littered the road, and by the turn-off there were two wrecked trucks. The smoke came from a smoldering fire in one of the trucks. He got out and instructed the driver to wait. M1 held ready, he approached the battle scene in a wary crouch. He found Green slumped over the thirty, the pilot next to him, sprawled between ammo canisters. Across the road he found Gardner, also dead, next to the spent BAR, surrounded by dead krauts, bloody trench knife still in his hand.

He carefully surveyed the surrounding woods, listening for any activity, trying to screen out the idling truck behind him.

He motioned for the driver to follow him up the drive, and he complied, easing the truck forward up the dirt lane toward the chateau.

Sloan approached the house and circled around, then went inside once he was assured there were no Germans in the vicinity. He found the children huddled in the basement, no sign of the Resistance girl. Using gestures and smiling reassurance, he led them out to the truck. With the driver's help, they lifted them into the back, eyes saucers of fear, but trusting the smiling American they recognized. They lifted the last one in, and together he and the driver raised the gate and bolted it into place.

"Stop up there on the way out." Sloan said, gesturing toward the carnage back by the road. The driver nodded and climbed into the cab. Sloan hung on the back as he rolled back down the lane.

Sloan jumped off and walked back to the bodies of the Americans. Gently, he removed the dog tags from the two paratroopers, as well as the identification papers of the pilot. He started back toward the truck, then stopped and turned back. He bent over the body of the pilot and turned him over, looking for the thigh holster and the Colt Peacemaker. He stood up and paced around the area for a few moments, then looked off toward the chateau, lost in thought.

In death, none of the three men really resembled how he remembered them. They lay in various attitudes, faces obscured, clothes bloody, no different from the dead Germans around them save for the colored fabric of their clothes, fading into the background destruction all around. For the first time since his brother's death, Sloan felt the stirrings of grief.

"Hey, Sarge, we got to get out of here," the driver called.

Back toward the mansion, the apple orchard blazed in pink and white, transfixed in a slanting shaft of light that connected the earth to a rent in the cloud-filled sky. A gust swirled and enfolded Sloan, tugging at his uniform and animating the trees to a shimmering dance, releasing a shower of petals fluttering in the wind, blurring the individual trees, smearing the scene against the green landscape. For a moment, the arresting beauty replaced the ugliness of the death around him, and before the spell could be broken, Sloan turned and walked to the back of the truck.

He put his hands on the metal rungs and pulled himself up, greeted by the muffled voices of the older children singing in French to quiet the little ones.

Endnotes

Chapter 1
Willem's correspondence with Albert Einstein is fictional, although the sentiments expressed can be readily found in Einstein's published letters.

Chapter 4
Correspondence between Willem and Dr. Oswald Veblen before and after his time at Princeton is located in the Oswald Veblen files in the Library of Congress. Events on campus, landmarks, and campus life are based on materials found in the University Yearbooks, *The Terrapin*, especially the 1939, 1940, and 1941 editions.

Willem's experiences at the University of Maryland are based on documents from the University Archives, particularly correspondence between Dr. Talliafero, Dr. Dantzig, and Dr. Byrd in the Department of Mathematics files.

Chapter 10
Although there is a large extant body of correspondence between the members of Willem's family during this time frame, this particular letter is fictional. Willem's brother-in-law and best friend Spike Marlin was posted in London, and they did see each other while Willem was assigned to Squadron No. 10.

Chapter 13
Willem's time at Trinity College in Dublin is based on recollections of family members, correspondence, and materials from the Archives of Trinity College

Chapter 16
The rigors of Bomber Command training are based substantially on Hastings, as well as Willem's letters to his family. The letter from Willem to his mother is real, written after his first missions in support of D-Day. The note from Dr. Veblen is real, located in the Library of Congress, but is associated with a different piece of correspondence. The letter to Willem from Spike is fictional.

Chapter 18
The books that Green and Gardner exchange are all real, the first paperbacks produced by the publishing industry for U.S. military personnel as leisure activities. They were stocked in the ubiquitous morale tents, given away free. They were smaller than a current standard paperback, slightly more rectangular, and printed along the long axis. The soldiers read them voraciously, carried them into the field, and traded them along with everything else of value.

Chapter 25
Quoted material is from H.G. Wells, *War of the Worlds*.

Chapter 32
Although Willem and Albert Einstein were at the Institute for Advanced Studies at Princeton at the same time, there is no evidence they collaborated. The conversations and correspondence between Willem and Einstein are entirely fictional.

H.G. Wells, in *The Shape of Things to Come*, does describe many aspects of WWII military technology a full decade before widespread deployment. Orson Welles was a friend of Willem's and Spike's during his days in Trinity, and Willem mentions meeting him in New York in family correspondence.

The description of the secret atom bomb project in *Astounding Science Fiction* is real, and caused a significant security controversy when it came out. The FBI actually confiscated as many copies as they could to prevent further dissemination and discussion.

Lyrics from *I've Heard That Song Before*. Music by Jules Style, lyrics by and Sammy Cahn (1942);

I'll be with you in Apple Blossom Time. Music by Albert von Tilzer, lyrics by Neville Fleeson (1920); *Drink to me Only with Thine Eyes* (According to Wikipedia, the lyrics are from *To Celia*, a poem by Ben Johnson written in 1616.

Further Reading

TIME TRAVEL AND PHYSICS

Clegg, Brian, *How to Build a Time Machine: The Real Science of Time Travel,* Duckworth Overlook, 2011.

Feynman, Richard. *Six Easy Pieces.* Basic Books, 1995.

Feynman, Richard. *Six Not So Easy Pieces.* Basic Books, 1997.

Feynman, Richard. *QED: the strange theory of light and matter.* Princeton University Press, 1985.

Greene, Brian. *The Hidden Reality: Parallel Universes and the Deep laws of the Cosmos.* Vintage, 2011.

Greene, Brian. *The Fabric of the Cosmos: Space, Time, and the Texture of Reality.* Vintage, 2005.

Nahin, Paul. *Time machines: Time travel in physics, metaphysics, and science fiction.* AIP, 1993.

Susskind, Leonard. *The Black Hole War.* Little Brown and Co., 2008.

NORMANDY INVASION AND PARATROOPERS

Ambrose, Stephen. *D-day.* Simon & Schuster, 1994.

Ambrose, Stephen. *Band of Brothers.* Simon & Schuster, 2001.

Beavan, Colin. *Operation Jedburgh*. Viking, 2006.

Burgett, Donald. *Currahee! A Screaming Eagle at Normandy*. Dell, 1967.

Center of Military History. *Utah Beach to Cherbourg*. CMH Pub100-12, USGPO, 1947.

Malarkey, Donald (with Bob Welch). *Easy Company Soldier*. St. Martin's Press, 2008.

Messenger, Charles. *The D-Day Atlas*. Thames & Hudson, 2004.

Morgan, Martin K.A. *Down to Earth: The 507th Parachute Infantry Regiment in Normandy*. Schiffer Military History, 2004.

Rottman, Gordon. *FUBAR: Soldier Slang in World War II*. Osprey Publishing, 2007.

Ruggero, Ed. *The First Men In*. Harper, 2006.

Ruggero, Ed. *Combat Jump*. Harper Collins, 2003.

Webster, David. *Parachute Infantry*. Delta Publishing, 2002.

Welch, Bob. *American Nightingale*. Atria Books, 2004.

Wilson, George. *If You Survive*. Presidio Press, 1985.

RAF BOMBER LIFE

Hastings, Max. *Bomber Command*. Michael Joseph, London, 1987.

Lake, Jon. *Halifax Squadrons of World War 2*. Osprey, 1999.

Pitchfork, Graham. *Shot Down and On the Run*. The National Archives, UK, 2007

RESISTANCE

Aubrack, Lucie. *Outwitting the Gestapo*. Bison Books, 1993.

Crowdy, Terry. *French Resistance Fighter: France's Secret Army*. Osprey, 2007.

Eisner, Peter. *The Freedom Line: The Brave Men and Women Who Rescued Allied Airmen from the Nazis During World War II*. Harper Perennial, 2005.

van Stockum, Hilda. *The Borrowed House*. Bethlehem Books, 2000.

van Stockum, Hilda. *The Winged Watchman*. Bethlehem Books, 1995.

A Soldier's Creed
By A Bomber Pilot

(Willem J. van Stockum)
Published (posthumously) in Horn Book, Christmas 1944.

I didn't join the war to improve the Universe; in fact, I am sick and tired of the eternal sermons on the better world we are going to build when this war is over. I hate the disloyalty to the past twenty years. Apparently people think that life in those twenty years, which cover most of my conscious existence, was so terrible that no-one can be expected to fight for it. We must attempt to dazzle people with some brilliant schemes leading, probably, to some horrible Utopia, before we can ask them to fight.

I detest that point of view. I hate the idea of people throwing their lives away for slum-clearance projects or forty-hour weeks or security and exchange commissions. It is a grotesque and horrible thought. There are so many better ways of achieving this than diving into enemy guns. Lives are precious things and are of a different order and entail a different scale of values than social systems, political theories, or art.

"Why are we not given a cause?" some people ask. I do not understand this question. It seems so plain to me. There are millions and millions of people who are shot, persecuted and tortured daily in Europe. The assault on so many of our fellow human beings makes some of us tingle with anger and gives us an urge to do something about it. That, and that alone, makes some of us feel strongly about the war. All the rest is vapid rationalization. All this talk about philosophy, the degeneration of art and literature, the poisoning of Nazi youth, which the Nazi system entails, and which we all rightly condemn, is still not the reason why we fight and why we are willing to risk our lives.

Here, let us say, is a soldier. He asks himself, "Why should I die?" You would tell him: "To preserve our civilization." When the soldier replies: "To Hell with your civilization; I never thought it so hot," you take him up wrongly when you sit down and say to yourself: "Well, after all, maybe it wasn't so hot," and then brightly tap him on the shoulder and say: "Well, I've thought of a better idea. I know this civilization wasn't so hot, but you go and die anyway and we'll fix up a really good one after the war." I say you take him up wrong because his remark: "To Hell with your civilization" doesn't really mean that he is not seriously concerned about our civilization. He is simply revolted by the idea of dying for ANY civilization. Civilization simply isn't the kind of thing you ever want to die for. It is something to enjoy and something to help build up because it's fun, and that is that, and that is all.

When a man jumps into the fire to save his wife he doesn't justify himself by saying that his wife was so civilized that it was worth the risk! There is only one reason why a man will throw himself into mortal combat and that is because there is nothing else to do and doing nothing is more intolerable than the fear of death. I could stand idly by and see every painting by Rembrandt, Leonardo da Vinci and Michelangelo thrown into a bonfire and feel no more than a deep regret, but throw one small, insignificant Polish urchin on the same bonfire and, by

God, I'd pull him out or else. I fight quite simply for that and I cannot see what other reasons there are. At least, I can see there are reasons, but they are not the reasons that motivate me.

During the first two years of the war when I was an instructor at an American University in close contact with American youth and in close contact with the vital isolationist question in the States, I often felt that there was much insincerity, conscious or unconscious, on our, the Interventionist, side of the argument. We had strong views on the danger of isolationism for the United States. We thought, rightly, that for the sake of self-interest and self-preservation the United States should take every step to ensure the defeat of the Nazi criminals. But however sound our arguments, our own motives and intensity of feeling did not spring from those arguments but from an intense passion for common righteousness and decency.

Suppose it could have been proved to us at that time that the participation of the United States in the stamping out of organized murder, rape and torture in Europe could only take place at great cost to the United States, while not doing so would in no way impair her security. Would we not still have prayed that our country might do something? And would we not have been proud to see her do something?

There is an appalling timidity and false shame among intellectuals. The common man in the last war went to fight quite simply as a crusader. I am not talking about politics now, I am not either asserting or denying that England declared war from purely generous and noble considerations, but I am asserting that the common man went and fought with the rape of Belgium foremost in his mind and saw himself as an avenger of wrong.

After the war the common man went quietly back to his home. The intellectuals, however, upon coming back, ashamed of their one lapse of finding themselves in agreement with every Tom, Dick and Harry, must turn around and deride the things they were ready to give their lives for. As they were the only vocal group, the opinion became firmly established that the last war was a grave mistake and that anyone who got killed in it was a sucker.

And now, in this war, these intellectuals are hoist with their own petard. They lack the nerve and honesty to represent the American doughboy to himself for what he is. They do not give him the one picture in his mind which would stimulate his imagination and which would make him see beyond the fatigues, the mud, the boredom and the fear. The picture is there for anyone to paint who has a gift for words. It is a simple picture and a true picture and no one who has ever sat as a small child and listened with awe to a fairy story can fail to understand. The intellectuals, however, have made fun of the picture and so they won t use It.

But some day an American doughboy in an American tank will come lurching into some small Polish, Czech or French village and it may fall to his lot to shoot the torturers and open the gates of the village jail. And then he will understand.

There is a lot of talk among our intellectuals about our youth. Our youth is supposed to want a change, a new order, a revolution or what not. But it is my conviction that that is emphatically NOT what our youth wants. Have you ever been in a picture house on a Saturday afternoon, when it is filled with children and some old Western movie is ending in a race of time between the hero and the villain? Have you seen the rapt attention, the glowing faces, the clenched fists? What our young men really want is to be able to give that same concentrated attention and emotional participation, this time to reality, and this time as heroes and not as spectators, that they were able to give to unsubstantial shadows, before long words and cliches had killed their imaginations. Killed them so dead that they can no longer see even reality itself imaginatively.

It is up to the intellectuals to rekindle the thing they have tried to destroy. It is as simple as St. George and the Dragon. Why not have the courage to point out that St. George fought the dragon because he wanted to liberate a captive and not because he wanted to lead a better life afterwards? Some day, sometime, my picture of an American doughboy in a Polish village will become true. Wouldn't it be better for him then to have the cross of St. George on his banner than a long rigmarole about a better world?

As long as our intellectuals and leaders do not have the courage to risk being thought sentimental and out-of-date and are not willing to stress that nations as well as individuals are entitled to their acts of heroism and chivalry, they will never be able to give our youth what it needs.

It is true that every fairy story ends with the words: "and they lived happily ever after." How irritating a child would be, though, if it interrupted its mother at every sentence to ask: "But, Mummy, will they live happily ever afterwards?" It simply isn't the point of the fairy story and it isn't the point of this war.

Presumably we won't live happily ever after this war. But just as a fairy story helps to increase a child's awareness and wonder at the world, so this war may make us more aware of one another. Perhaps we shall learn, and perhaps some things will be better organized. I hope so. I believe so. But only if we engage in this war with our hearts as well as our minds.

For goodness' sake let us stop this empty political theorizing according to which a man would have to have a University degree in social science before he could see what he was fighting for. It is all so simple, really, that a child can understand it.

Made in the USA
San Bernardino, CA
27 June 2014